Not!
Another Story About Princess Diana

Not!
Another Story About Princess Diana

S. E. Clarkson

iUniverse, Inc.
Bloomington

Not! Another Story About Princess Diana

iUniverse books may be ordered through booksellers or by contacting:

iUniverse
1663 Liberty Drive
Bloomington, IN 47403
www.iuniverse.com
1-800-Authors (1-800-288-4677)

Because of the dynamic nature of the Internet, any web addresses or links contained in this book may have changed since publication and may no longer be valid. The views expressed in this work are solely those of the author and do not necessarily reflect the views of the publisher, and the publisher hereby disclaims any responsibility for them.

Any people depicted in stock imagery provided by Thinkstock are models, and such images are being used for illustrative purposes only.

Certain stock imagery © Thinkstock.

ISBN: 978-1-4620-0271-9 (sc)
ISBN: 978-1-4620-0273-3 (ebook)
ISBN: 978-1-4620-0272-6 (dj)

Library of Congress Control Number: 2011903289

Printed in the United States of America

iUniverse rev. date: 4/28/2011

Contents

Introduction

THE DAY, THE WEEK, AND the month began like any other in the desert. The sun was up, it was already warm, and the birds were singing. The only difference was that Steven had risen uncharacteristically late—so late that his wife had already relieved the US mail of its charge. It was this charge that changed everything. By the end of the day, he had received a summons from the British consulate, which was only answered to assuage his wife's curiosity.

BY THE END OF THE week, he had learned of the reemergence in his life of a former love and had gained a daughter, a potential son-in-law, and some very distinguished in-laws.

By the end of the month, he was forced to reexamine his estrangement from his mother country.

1~*A Matter of Some Delicacy*

THE ONE IRRITATING HABIT PAM had left—or the one Steve had not yet come to terms with—was her habit of waiting for the mailman. Although he knew that Pam was no more attracted to the representative of the US mail than any other thirtyish, personable male who crossed her path, he was still rightly aggrieved that anything that came from the US mail sack could compare with being in the same house as himself, but at least she didn't spend half an hour making herself up beforehand as their neighbor did. To add to his sense of aggrievement, if something didn't keep her interest, she was likely to abandon it, only for it to be rescued by Steve when the effective date had long past.

Thus it was on this particular morning Pam had descended on the mailman before his white Jeep had rolled to a stop and returned to find Steven waxing lyrical on the pope's funeral.

"You wouldn't think there would be so many people with nothing better to do."

Pam pushed her long hair aside so she could regard him over a tanned shoulder. "Would you say the same if it was the Queen's funeral?"

"The sovereignty is necessary. The pope isn't."

Pam rightly ignored this and returned her attention to the mail. "Who do you know at the British Consulate?"

"Nobody, and well may it remain so."

"Well somebody's writing to you, look." Pam proffered the envelope with the British Consulate crest on the back.

"Anything else?"

"Just these." She turned the other letter over. "Frontier—the telephone bill and this catalog from the Smithsonian."

"That's going to be worth a giggle. Let me see." He held out his hand.

Pam surrendered the two envelopes before tearing open the third one and extracted the contents. "Twenty-eight dollars, not bad. Are you going to read the letter?"

"Ever hear of a comedian named Mort Sahl?"

"Yes, but I don't think he had anything to do with the British Embassy."

"I wouldn't be too sure of that. He was one of the first satirical comedians, made jokes about things like religion, sex, the Queen, even"—he lowered his voice dramatically—"the Kennedys. He was quite funny, not like these spiteful schoolgirls you get on the late night shows now. The thing is, he used to use a newspaper as a prop, and his attitude wasn't, 'Aren't I funny?' It was, 'Isn't this funny?' Like this." He turned his attention to the catalog. "You fancy this? A palmetto velvet robe, polyester spandex, tasseled zipper pockets, 'lounge with impunity' palmetto patterned stretch velvet, and get this, 'You can answer the door or entertain your weekend guests with gracious aplomb.'"

"We don't have any weekend guests."

"We'd have to if they're to be entertained with gracious aplomb, and another thing." He brandished a copy of the *British Weekly*, a newspaper that was geared to expatriates of the sceptered isle and Northern Ireland. "This tosser[1] Robin something or other, he's writing a review on *Inspector Lewis*, a crime series set in Oxford. Anyway, Lewis has a woman boss and so he calls her ma'am, but this ponce says, 'Chief Supt. Jean Innocent—a good name for a copper—who, in quaint British fashion, Lewis calls Mum.' Mum is short for mother. You'd hardly call your boss mother."

"And what does ma'am mean?" Pam asked, finally distracted from the demands of the British Consulate.

Depends whether you're after a knighthood or getting out of a parking ticket, although getting out of a parking ticket would be harder. It seems all you've got to do to get a knighthood is to whine on an American talk show. You usually use it for any woman in authority, from Her Majesty to a traffic warden. It's short for madam."

"That must come in handy. Why would you need to speak to the Queen or a traffic warden? Are you going to read your letter from the ambassador?"

"The Ambassador lives in the Embassy in Washington. The Consul lives in the Consulate and the Consul General lives in the Consulate. Do you know why Katie Couric reminds me of Liberace?"

"Are you going to read it?" Pam said in an "enough of this fol de rol" tone. "Or are you"—she tapped the envelope against his chest—"a little"—she tapped him again—"scared?"

"There's only one ambassador to a country, but there are as many consuls as there are cities large enough. There's a consul general in the major cities like Los Angeles, and I think if there is something going on that affects Britain or their interest, you can get a trade mission. And no, I'm not scared, it's just that there's nothing I need from them, and they've had all they're going to get from me, and right now my watering my Chilean Mesquite's more important. I'll read it when I have my coffee."

"It might be important."

"If it is important, it's important to them, not me. An unsolicited letter is sometimes important to the sender, never the recipient." Steve stood. "Did you see Brian?"

"No, why?"

"I just wanted to borrow his ladder. Better check the roof before the wind gets up."

An hour later, Steve, the future of his Chilean Mesquite secure and their neighbor's ladder still unborrowed, was sitting on the back porch when Pam came with a plate bearing the letter. "Your coffee, Milord, and the mail."

He noticed his hardwood letter opener lying on the plate. "You're determined that I open it, aren't you?"

"Isn't that what people usually do to their mail? Otherwise you can't read it, unless you have x-ray vision to add to your other superpowers."

"Tell you what, you open it. I give you permission."

"You *are* scared."

"I just don't want to give England another chance to disappoint me."

"That's too clever for me." Pam picked up the envelope and attacked it with the letter opener.

"You're opening a letter, not chopping firewood. I've had that paperknife thirty-three years I—"

"Bought it in Kenya in 1972. You watched an old man carve it by the wayside and asked him to carve another one. While you were waiting for him to finish the second one, you missed a bus that your buddies had caught to the hotel where Pan's People were playing. If this was the second knife, it's the one that caused you to marry me and saved one of Pan's People, was it Ruth you fancied? Anyway, they want to see you."

"Pan's People²?"

"You wish, no them"—Pam thrust the letter at him—"on a matter of some delicacy."

"Some delicacy?" Steve finally accepted the letter and glanced at it. "At my convenience. That's nice of them, no petrol money so—let's make it in three weeks. No, let's make it four. Then we can visit Eddie on his birthday, check on the British Club—the cricket season will be started by then—and we can

4

come back that way, visit Media Partners for lunch, and swing through LA. We'll spend an hour at the British consulate and spend the afternoon on the beach at Santa Monica—magic. I wish I could be married to me. What?"

Pam held up a hand, two fingers extended but with the wrist outward in the peace sign, not the soldier's farewell. "Two things. How do you know the consulate is on the way to Santa Monica?"

"Wilshire Boulevard is opposite the Ambassador Hotel where Clark Gable and Carole Lombard used to have an afternoon idyll after a hard day's filming."

"And how do you know they only want you for an hour?"

"They're only going to get me for an hour. I don't owe them any consideration, so after that it's Santa Monica. I suppose they've got grandkids by now."

"Carole Lombard and Clark Gable?"

"No, Pans People."

Pam sighed. "I'll phone Eddie."

2~Enter Chadders

"CHARLIE, THIS IS MY MOM, Pam, and my dad, Steve."
It was four weeks later, and they were in Eddie's
local bar, Captain Bombay. Eddie had taken time
off from playing pool to introduce them to the bartender while
the girl he was trying to impress was in the bathroom.

"So," Charlie said after he served a couple of customers,
"was Eddie born in England?" He eyed Pam. "You don't look
old enough to have a son that big."

"She had me when she was twelve," Eddie said with
practiced aplomb.

"No, Pam and I've only been together nineteen years." Steve
grinned. "I came here with an English wife, dumped her, and
married Pam. That's what most English guys come here for,
and the money."

"I thought Eddie favored you." Charlie used this as another
excuse to appraise Pam. "So it's nice he calls you Dad."

"Steve, you're up." Eddie had sunk the eight ball and turned
to anyone interested to explain how he did it, leaving Steve to
rack the balls.

"Have you met my dad, Steve? Steve, this is Liane."

"I'm pleased to meet you." This was hardly true. Whenever
they saw Eddie, they always were introduced to a different

6

girlfriend, whose only thought seemed to be that Eddie looked like Charlie Sheen, and one or two of his drinking partners, whose only interest seemed to be getting as close to Pam as the proprieties allowed. Steve turned his attention to Eddie. "Don't put the black down on the break. I need to get my fifty cents worth."

"Mom says the Ambassador wants to see you—shit." He had failed to sink a ball on the break.

"No, the Ambassador's in Washington. I'm going to the consulate in LA—orange top corner." Steve sank four balls in succession before he missed an easy blue and turned to find Eddie had disappeared. "Where's he gone?"

"Probably outside to have a smoke or something. I'm Jamie," the newcomer introduced himself and used the opportunity to sit next to Pam. "So you're Eddie's mom. Shouldn't he be visiting you on Mother's Day?"

"It's his birthday tomorrow, and we have business up here, so we—"

"What am I on—stripes?" Eddie took his time in surveying the table. "So you've got to see the Consul. Do you know what for? It's probably something to do with pissing in Princess Di's Memorial Fountain because the restroom had closed at Waterloo Railroad Station in London. What was it you said? 'All water and no loo'—they call a restroom a loo in England," he said to anyone within earshot.

"I don't think they'd ask me in for a chat about that."

"What else can they want you for?"

"Well, they've got all they're going to get from me. Are you going to use that stick or just lean on it? And whenever I know what they want, I'll let you know."

With a combination of luck and Eddie's lack of concentration, the game went Steve's way until it came down to the eight ball. To match Eddie's crassness, he put his wallet on the side pocket as in competition play and promptly sank the eight ball.

Eddie had already congratulated Steve and turned his attention to Liane when the white ball inexorably trickled in the corner pocket. The "next one up" had already racked the balls, and Eddie was on his way out with Liane to smoke or something when Steve tapped him on the shoulder, "You're on, sunshine—the table."

"You?"

"Scratched on the black."

Steve joined Pam at the bar. "That was the cleverest shot I've seen you make."

"What?"

"Going in off the black so you could sit with me." Pam squeezed his hand.

Steve looked for the bartender. "You are very complimentary. vodka tonic, Michelob Ultra, and I wonder what love's young dream is having."

As if on cue, an arm was draped around his shoulder. "Newcastle. Have you met my dad? He's got to see the British Consul tomorrow because he took a leak in Princess Di's Memorial Fountain."

The bartender's quizzical glance was not to do with Steve's personal habits.

"I know—I scratched on the black."

****

The traffic on Wilshire was as bad as Steve remembered it, but Pam managed to find a parking place while surviving Steve's lecture on the Ambassador Hotel.

"And Xavier Cadged used to play in the Coconut Grove—I've just thought of something."

"We're at the wrong place?"

"No—well, not exactly, but if we park in the same building as the Consulate, we could get our parking validated and it wouldn't cost us anything."

"But if, as you say, we'll only be there an hour, is it worth it?"

"Well it would be under cover, so it would keep the car cool."

"You just want to get a few dollars out of 'them,' while on the other hand, we could be parking in the same place as Carole Lombard and Clark Gable."

"I wonder if the Brown Derby's near here"

"The what?"

"The Brown Derby—shaped like a Bowler. Jack Benny and George Burns used to have breakfast there."

"Right." Pam edged out into the traffic. "You'd better direct me, and I hope this is important. We've spent twenty minutes looking for a parking space and ten minutes discussing it."

"The main thing is you get to Santa Monica in time to spend time on the beach, right? Here it is. Better start getting over now."

Twenty minutes later, they were in an anteroom of the British Consulate, after having made themselves known to the well -bred receptionists who, in deference to Openness in Government wore a badge that proclaimed her to be Joanne Mortimer and her function to be a consular aide.

"She seems nice," Pam ventured after they seated themselves.

"They breed them in Surrey, and when they're old enough, they either send them to places like this or to work for Richard Branson or an answering service. You remember when I phoned Dave and this bird answered sounded just like her. I thought Dave had gone straight."

Twenty minutes later, they were still there, and Steve decided to let his feelings be known. "Excuse me, but the appointment was for nine thirty, and as we have another appointment, we have to leave by ten thirty."

"Another appointment?" She raised a well-shaped eyebrow.

"Yes, we reckoned this would take an hour, which would give us time to get to our next appointment in Santa Monica."

"I ... see." Joanne took some time to absorb the fact that anyone would have an appointment after visiting the British Consulate. "I'll see if I can get someone to see you."

"Thank you, and if you could tell him he's only got forty minutes left?"

"She's just doing her job," Pam admonished him as Steve rejoined her. "If you want to give someone a hard time, wait until you see the schmuck who's late. She's just a—"

"Consulate aide," Steve supplied. "Sounds like a make of cigarette from the fifties."

"Mister Jackson?" Joanne approached them. "Mister Chaddersly-Corbett has—will see you now."

"Nice of him." Steve caught Pam's warning glare. "Sorry, it's the traffic it makes me nervous."

"If you'll follow me?"

"Don't you want to come?" Steve said to Pam as he was about to rise.

"No, you're bad enough when you are in contact with them on your own, and if I'm there, you'll be worse, doing the Tom Sawyer showing off in front of Becky Thatcher."

"Right, well said, well—" Steve stood and turned to Joanne, who had been watching this exchange. "Lead on."

He followed her through a door to the side of the reception area, which opened onto a corridor with doors along the right wall.

"I don't suppose you know what this is about?" Steve ventured.

"No—don't you?"

"Unless it's about my pension, I have no idea."

"Well it's not about your pension, but it is something important. I was hoping you'd tell me. You're sure? I mean, you came all this way without knowing?"

"We had other reasons, watching some cricket, seeing old friends, seeing Pam's son—"

"And Santa Monica."

"Yes, and Santa Monica."

"Your wife seems a very nice person. She's American?"

"Yes—well, you get a lot of Americans in Pasadena."

"She's beautiful."

"Yes, well, they're going to break your heart or drive you crazy, so you might as well get a good-looking one. Uncle Ben said choose one with good legs. It's as good a way as any."

"Yes, she's got dancer's legs. I suppose it was your sense of humor that attracted her to you."

"I thought it was my lost look."

"Really—well, being American—"

"Shouldn't you knock or something?" Steve realized that they had been standing in front of one of the doors that lined the corridor.

"We, er …" Joanne pointed to a discreet light above the door.

"Right," Steve took a deep breath, "I've driven three hundred miles to see this tosser. I've been kept waiting half an hour, and now I've got to wait outside his door like a—I think I'd better leave before I forget that you're a lady or that I'm a gentleman."

He hadn't noticed that the light had gone out and Joanne was actually holding his arm until she had given a brisk knock at the door and opened it. "Mister Chaddersley-Corbett, I have Mister Jackson for you." She stepped back and ushered Steve forward like she was producing a missing file from behind her back. "I'll look after your wife," she whispered.

Steve had the impression of a tall man with graying hair rising from behind the desk who was dressed in black jacket, striped trousers (they actually *were* pin-striped trousers), and some sort of club or military tie that was just subdued enough.

His main thought, however, was that a girl who had admired his wife's legs had just offered to look after her.

"Mister Jackson—may I call you Steven? Charles Chaddersley-Corbett." He smiled, showing teeth that matched his gleaming half-inch of cuff. His handshake was firm, without disguising the fact that he was a Freemason. "Do sit down. Can we get you something? Tea, coffee, water? I suppose it's a bit too early for"—he looked at his watch—"of course ten in the morning. I always get confused going west but never do going east. What about you?"

"The only time I've been confused is when I took Pam to see a concert at the Avi Casino and I thought we were late, as it started at seven and we didn't leave the house until six thirty, and when we got there the doors weren't open. Then I realized the AVI Casino was in Nevada, so as it was winter, they were an hour behind. We thought it was seven-fifteen, but it was only six-fifteen, which explained why the doors weren't open."

"I see—a different time zone," Charles consulted some papers in front of him and then apparently changed his mind. "Why—winter?"

"I'm glad you asked that. Arizona doesn't have daylight-saving time, so half the year it's the same time and half the year Arizona's an hour in front."

"When Nevada puts the clock back—I see."

"I worked at Hoover Dam once, and we were working on the Nevada side and had lunch on the Arizona side, and by the time we'd got to the lunch room, we were already five minutes late getting back."

"It must be very confusing for you."

"No, I just set my watch, when I wear one, on Arizona time, even when I go to England."

"Yes, England," Charles said, as though he had spotted a familiar landmark. "Do you mind if I ask you a few questions?"

"Not at all, as long as it takes no more than forty minutes. My wife wants two hours on the beach. We have to get to Santa Monica by eleven and so leave here at ten thirty."

"Splendid." Charles reclaimed the sheaf of papers before him. "Full name, Steven Edwin Jackson, mother and father both English—right?"

"Right."

"Born in Wolverhampton in 1942, which—yes?" Steve had raised an admonishing finger.

"No—Coseley."

"Which is now part of Wolverhampton."

"Part of it is now part of Wolverhampton, but the part I was born in is now I believe part of Dudley, but when I was born it was Coseley—Coat of Arms, Council House, everything—so I was born in Coseley. Unless somebody's moved the goal posts again. After all, they changed the area of the Black Country."

Charles steepled his fingers. "Would it be safe to assume you were born in England?"

"As houses, sir."

"Good. Please call me Charles. Now ..." Charles found his place on the paper and in the conversation. "Attended Tipton Green, St. Mary's, Manor Secondary Modern School"—he allowed himself a wintry smile—"Coseley, Dudley Tech, went to work for W. G. Griffiths as an apprentice toolmaker, and then suddenly left your apprenticeship to enlist in the army. Why was that? I mean, how were you released from your apprenticeship? Don't you sign papers and things?"

Steve was suddenly very wary. "Is that important?"

"Let's assume everything is ... necessary."

"But why is the reason I joined the army any business of some consulate wallah?"

"Actually I'm some embassy, er, wallah."

"From Washington?"

"From Washington."

13

Jesus, Steve thought. *That is the thing about traveling west. He's actually flown in from Washington to see me. It couldn't be about Northern Ireland, it's too long ago. Besides, fighting terrorism's become flavor of the month since 9/11. Sine Fein was actually advocating recycling lemonade bottles instead of armed insurrection. So what could it be to bring Charles, and he did look senior, halfway across America to see me?*

"I don't know who told you about me having a slash in Diana's fountain, but it was just a joke. Listen if you wanted to shed a tear for the old country at Waterloo and the toilets were closed, you wouldn't march halfway across London to do it in Di's fountain, would you? I mean, you could do it in the Thames, and those arches, they stink so much nobody would—"

"Steven, Steven" Charles flagged him down, "I don't know what on earth you're talking about. It doesn't matter whose fountain you've, er, relieved yourself in, and it's got nothing—directly—to do with Princess Diana. Now, tell you what, sure you wouldn't like some tea?"

Steve shook his head.

"I'll ask you a series of questions, which you either answer, truthfully or tell me you're not going to—no hard feelings. Then I tell you why we've asked you to come here. Then you go with the missus to the seaside. Fair enough?"

"Fair enough. Just one question, if I may. Talking about Pam—my missus, that bird Joanne."

Charles gave an old Scout's smile. "Miss Mortimer doesn't piss in anyone's fountains either. Right." He took a fountain pen from his pocket and ran it down the list. "Why did you leave W. G. Griffiths?"

"Mutual disenchantment. It was a terrible place, and they didn't like me much either."

"Which is why they released you from your indentures?"

"Yes."

"Right, you left W. G. Griffiths in '63 but didn't enlist until '64. What was the difference? Round-the-world tour, writing your first novel?"

"A hernia."

"A hernia?"

"When I left Griffiths, my dad got me a job at the steelworks, but that was as bad as Griffiths, so I declined. He couldn't understand this, so he said it was the steelworks or the army— no contest. Only, when I went for a medical, they discovered a hernia, and that had to be cleared up first. Doctor Pornan, he was Indian, our GP got me to get special treatment or it would have been two years. The Health Service was just about to be swamped, so he wrote to Mr. Benison, the surgeon who ran minor OPS at Wolverhampton Royal Hospital, and used his influence."

"Good—and you remembered the surgeon's name," Charles said, waylaying any subsequent failure of memory. "And the hernia, was that due to the wrench of leaving W. G. Griffiths, or ...?" Charles let his smile finish the question.

"Actually it was"—Steve searched the wall behind Charles' distinguished head, coming to rest on a photograph of a young Queen Elizabeth—"sex. I'm sorry." He wrenched his eyes away from the photograph.

"Was it, by God?"

"My first serious girlfriend and we'd discovered sex, and we were going at it. Well, you know how it is."

"Yes, I believe I do, or rather how it was." Charles encouraged him with a comradely smile. "And what happened to, er?"

"Chris?"

"Yes, Chris."

"She dumped me."

"Because you were enlisting?"

"I think it was the other way round."

"I see. Bad luck but still, ill wind, yes?" He turned the page. "Army record, first class, straight from basic training to parachute selection course, 16 Parachute Workshops - First Parachute Logistic Regiment," Steve noticed the slight squaring of the shoulders. "Irish Guards myself."

"You made your presence known in Iraq," Steve conceded, "as did One Para, the Armed Forces are the only thing this country's got worth a—anything, and these tossers you've got in now seem determined to run them down. Do you think Blair would have been let in the White House if we hadn't done such a good job in Iraq?"

"Quite, but as a civil servant, my politics begin and end with the ballot box so ..." His eyes dropped to the papers before him. "After nine years, you'd had enough. Nine years, about the time you start thinking of a career. What made you leave?"

"Northern Ireland. I did three tours and didn't want to give the IRA another chance, and when it was time to make a decision about reenlisting, we had the worst OC and the worst Sergeant Major we'd ever had. It rather tipped the balance in favor of civvy street."

"Can you remember who they were?"

"I'd rather not."

"Fair enough." Charles turned a page and quoted, "'Intensely loyal to people who earn his respect'—but we can't choose those set in authority over us, so you are loyal—intensely loyal—to people who earn your respect. I suppose you set high standards, and when people don't live up to them, that's when you have trouble with authority." Again he quoted, "'Officer Commanding: Corporal Jackson, why do you always come in front of me on these silly, petty little charges?' 'Corporal Jackson: 'I don't know, sir, why don't you have a word with the silly, petty little people who bring the charges?' I say, that's rather good."

"I'm glad you like it. It cost me ten quid[3]."

"What about women?"

"If you're offering me one, I'm married, but thanks anyway."

"Yes it mentioned your sense of humor here somewhere. I mean women as authority figures—I mean, you've made one or two references to your wife wanting to go to Santa Monica, which is influencing the length of this interview. Would you say that your wife or women in general wield a great influence on you?"

"Pam doesn't wield anything. I'd do anything for her as she'd do anything for me. If I do anything that makes her unhappy, I stop doing it. If I do anything that makes her happy, I do it again—if physically possible—and the same goes for her. As for women in general ..." he considered the question carefully. "The last boss I had was a woman, and I loved working for Lori. I'd just grown tired of working, and I think," he paused, "the best boss I worked for was a woman."

"Who was?"

"Queen Elizabeth." He nodded at the photograph. "Nine years."

"Yes, well said. Now during your army service ..." He didn't look at the papers before him, as though he was indulging a personal whim or he'd come to the purpose of the interview and didn't need to remind himself of it. "Six months in Aden and three tours in Northern Ireland. Ever shot anybody?"

Steve answered as though he was reading from a report. "During my tour of duty in Northern Ireland, on two occasions we came under fire from prepared positions. I, together with other members of my section, returned fire until the firing ceased."

"So you don't know if you—" Charles paused, uncharacteristically searching for a word until Steve uncharacteristically helped him.

"Killed somebody. No, I don't know. There was at least fifty yards of open ground to cover, and I didn't feel it worth the risk to check on the health of somebody who was trying to kill me. The firing stopped, and we moved on, although there was found to be—"

Oh my, heaven preserve us, thought Steve. *That's it, all this, "Can I get you some tea? Irish guards myself. Intensely loyal."*

"You want me to kill somebody—what's 'is name—Dodi Fayed's dad. I mean, I know he's a bit of a pain in the arse, hinting at conspiracy in Di's death, but what's it—a bit drastic. Couldn't you get the SAS to do it? I wouldn't mind, but I don't want to be one of the loose ends that have to be tied up—right?"

Charles allowed himself a smile. "What an imagination—you should be a writer. And no, we don't want you to kill anyone." He found his place in the papers before continuing. "Left the army in '73, got married '74, child in '77, emigrated to United States in '78, divorced in '84, now we're getting to the nub."

"I was wondering," Steve said, "when we would get to the nub that is."

"Quite. After your divorce, you had quite a time with the ladies—until, of course, you met Pamela."

"Right, in retrospect more than I should have done."

"Well no one could blame you—footloose and fancy free. There was one particular young lady ..."

"I would hope that they were all particular. I like to think one still has standards."

If Charles was shocked by Steve's change in tone, he didn't show it. "November 1984. Can you remember whose company you were enjoying then?"

"Yes," Steve answered, immediately prompting Charles to suspect that the question wasn't completely unexpected.

"How long did the relationship last?"

"I don't know."

"You prefer not to say, which is your right."

"My preferences don't come into it. I don't know."

"Forgive me, I'm a little confused," Charles said, who was anything but. "Would you care to explain?"

18

It was the first time Steve had hesitated to answer a question. "There are other people involved."

"Yes, I do see, and naturally the question is—would it be fair to say that you were intimate?"

"It would. It would also be true on my part."

"Well, it takes two to ..." For once, Charles seemed to lose his way, and he was honest enough to not seek refuge in his papers. "I was trying to be delicate, but this relationship, would it—Steven?"

Steve had moved his gaze to the far corner of the room, and when he spoke, it was obvious he was too concerned with the first question to consider the second.

"When I met Lydia, she had this ex-boyfriend, and she was representing his company—something to do with jewelry. She did three trips over, and on the third we had this blazing"—he suddenly smiled—"yes, blazing row about *Chariots of Fire*. Funny how we keep coming back to Dodi Fayed. He produced it."

Charles couldn't remember ever having been with Dodi Fayed to get back to but wisely stayed silent.

"Anyway, the following day she went to San Francisco on business, and when she came back, she told me that she'd slept with this baseball player."

"What?" Steve, as Charles suspected, had been speaking mainly to himself, and the interjection had reminded him that he was not alone.

"You said that the lady in question had slept with someone in San Francisco."

"No, I said *she said* she'd slept with someone else."

"Isn't that the same thing?"

"It doesn't really matter. It was just an excuse to end our relationship. Me saying that Abrahams shouldn't have had a professional coach made me a Nazi. Taking offence at her sleeping with a baseball player made me 'typically English.' Either it was a reason to put the kibosh on our affair or in reality, her ex was never really her ex. I had a letter from her shortly afterward. It seemed that she didn't know what she wanted from me but blamed me for not giving it to her. I think it's a Jewish thing."

"Yes, but I think it's rather a woman thing. But as to the baseball player, it doesn't really matter. Did you know she had a baby?"

"Yes." If Charles was looking for a reaction, he was disappointed. "There was a couple in Huntington Beach, Albert and Barbara Alejandro. Albert knew Lydia's mother when he was stationed in Europe, and they kept in touch, usually at Christmas. Barbara keeps me informed about the baby—baby? She must be—"

"Twenty-two," Charles supplied, earning him a sharp look from Steven.

"Yes, twenty-two, and quite a looker apparently. She's going to be an attorney," he finished in a tone that said nobody was perfect.

"You say 'quite a looker.' You've never seen her?"

"No, since the breakup I haven't heard from Lydia except that letter and a telephone call, but I was at work, and Pam answered it. She thought Pam was my answering service until Pam set her straight."

"And that was when?"

"Pam moved in with me July '86. It was shortly after that."

"So it could well have been to tell you about the child. Well, by that time ..."

"Among other things."

"You didn't return her call?"

"No."

"In case the baby was yours—I see."

"No." Steve's tone sharpened, and he focused his gaze on Charles to add definition to his words. "No to both. No, sir, you do not see, and no, it wasn't in case the baby was mine. Pam

20

can't have any more kids, and my son by my previous marriage, if he was mine biologically, was such a waste that ... So no, it was in case the baby *wasn't* mine. Got any kids, Charles?"

"Yes, two."

"Still with Mommy? I mean, if you don't mind me asking."

"No, unfortunately, and I don't mind you asking, but we're running short on time."

"Get to see them, the kids?"

"School speech days. It rather depends on my—the memsahib."

Steve's focus again moved to the corner, and what he said next Charles would remember for a long time, and a less honourable man would have claimed it as his. "I suppose that's the trouble with kids," he said softly. "If you love them, you can never quite get rid of the bag they came in. Sorry." He roused himself. "Next question."

"Yes, quite." Charles had seemed to share Steve's introspection or had visited a betrayal of his own. "Your wife didn't mind an ex-girlfriend calling you up?"

"No, although we were just living together at the time, but no, in fact when we went to England on a holiday, she expected to contend with a gaggle of jealous ex-girlfriends. I think she was a little disappointed."

"And you've had no—I'm sorry, I've already asked you that." Charles made a cross on the paper in front of him. "I think we got a little sidetracked. 'Never get rid of the bag they came in.' Now, the monarchy—the Royal Family. Could you give me your views, generally?"

"Which one?"

"Well, aren't they the same?"

"I'm a Wolves supporter. I support the institution of Wolverhampton Wanderers Football Club, but I admit they put some right tossers on the pitch sometimes."

"I see. So—both."

"I think the monarchy is something that is uniquely British. I am English. It's what makes us—different. Yes I'm a monarchist, but in the civil war, I would have fought on Oliver Cromwell's side."

"So you are a monarchist, but not blindly. You might disapprove of certain monarchs—fair comment?"

"Right."

"And the Royal Family?"

"You're not going to tell them, are you?"

Charles was not sure if this response should be taken seriously, so opted for, "You do have the right not to answer."

"Yes I do but ..." Steve took a deep breath. "I think the Queen is very gracious. I read somewhere that she wore gloves when shaking hands with people to avoid human contact. Practical really, the number of hands she has to shake. Barbara Strident doesn't like shaking hands, but nobody gets all bent out of shape about that. She seems a little strict with her kids but is more affectionate to her grandkids and she did support them when their mom died. She's the old-school duty and honour, and she can't understand the modern world where honour takes second place to convenience.

"I think Nick the Greek tries too hard to be English. Charles apparently survived a very unhappy childhood, so it has to make him tougher, and I hope he can find some peace with Camilla. He's para-trained, you know. His two kids, considering what they've been through, seem to be quite stable. Their mother seemed a nonevent. Somebody suggested to her that it would be good for her image to visit the victims of mines—she thought she was going to South Wales.

"Princess Anne? Anybody who tells the media where to get off has something to recommend her. The Queen Mother—I think when she went, it was the era that went with her. I believe that started England's demise. Sorry, not when the Queen Mother died. I was thinking of her brother killed in the First World War. All those junior officers, 'the flower of a generation' after the war. We had to field the second eleven." He brightened momentarily at the sporting metaphor, and then his face clouded as he shook his head sadly. "Not their fault. They just weren't up to it, were they?"

"Yes, well put—"

But Steve hadn't finished. "She could use hand sanitizer I suppose, but gloves are more elegant, don't you think?"

"I don't see—"

"Hygiene—the Queen, shaking hands."

"Quite, yes, now the monarchy, a sense of continuity even if we get the odd duff, fair enough?"

"Couldn't agree more. You see, Charles, unfortunately our thinking is too much controlled by the American media. I'm sorry," he waved down Charles's stillborn protest, "but there it is, and they don't like it because they haven't got one. 'Don't want one.' Did I hear 'an antithesis to all we hold dear'? Bollocks, saving your presence, m'dear." Charles wasn't sure if he was being addressed or if it was the photograph of the Queen. "Why is it then that they tried to infiltrate it with *Wallace Simpson* then tried to imitate it with *The Kennedys*? I mean a New Camelot, a bunch of drunkards, and a failed publisher? Do me a favor, and the big deal they made about Diana. If she hadn't married Charles. I mean, you can hardly conquer the world with one GCE in cooking and what aboutywhat about Madonna?"

"But he was Argentinian."

"Madonna, Charles, not Maradonna, tosser though he may be. Pay attention." Charles had hoped his interruption might slow Steve down, but he was in full spate. "Madonna, falls off her horse and says bollocks and she thinks she's the Queen Mum." Again Charles would have interrupted, but by now Steve was in full flow. "So now what have we got? *President Bush,* the next dynasty, the next Camelot—don't make me laugh. Who would you sooner have next to you in a foxhole, Prince Charles or Georgie Baby? He'd have probably scarpered by then anyway. Not that I've got anything against the Americans as a people. I

mean good and bad in any nation, right, Charles? And my good
lady wife is American, Pasadena, California, as was the mother
of Sir Winston Churchill, arguably the greatest Englishman in
living memory, and don't forget Angie Dickinson."

"Angie—?"

"Angie Dickinson—police woman. I—" He suddenly
stopped. "Oh my good Lord, that's probably where they got it
from, the Beatles—"

"The Beatles? Sorry, not quite with you." Charles reached
for a glass of water.

"Of course, *Sergeant Pepper's Lonely Hearts Club
Band*—Pepper Anderson. Anyway, I digress. So don't worry,
if there's another civil war, I would be a royalist. In fact, I would
personally kick Tony Blair's arse."

"Well," said Charles slowly when he was sure Steve had
finally run down, "we *don't* want you to assassinate the owner
of Harrod's, and we certainly don't want you to boot Mister
Blair in to touch. Do you want to know what we *do* want you
to do?"

"No idea, sunshine, but if you tell me I will, and if I think
there's a good enough reason, I'll do it."

"We want you to take a DNA test."

"You want a—why?"

"Well to—I didn't know about the baseball player so, it's to
discount him, also to discount her—the chap she was living with
in Belgium at the time, you see." Charles put his elbows on the
table and laced his fingers together and spoke over them. "After
finishing university—in fact acquitting himself quite well—
Prince William, after a well-deserved rest from his studies,
was taking a brief course in financing. During this study, he
was having lunch in a pub with either his fellow students or
his tutor when he met this young lady who was studying law.
Apparently she was on a short visit to the central criminal
court—the Old Baily. Also, I believe, to visit her maternal
grandmother. Anyway, William appears to have been smitten.

She was, after all, er, quite a looker. Telephone numbers were exchanged. With me so far?"

"I saw her once, you know."

"Who?" By now Charles had come to realize that Steve's deviations were just that, to slow the conversation down to what he was comfortable with, and being the diplomat that he was, he waited for him to return.

"Angie Dickinson. She was in a play at this theater in Beverley Hills called *Love Letters.* So William picks up a good-looking bird in a pub. Good luck to him." For one who had set a time limit on the interview, Steve seemed determined to postpone the inevitable end, but Charles, having successfully navigated the last fence, was determined not to be sidetracked on the run in.

"The young lady was the daughter of Lydia." Charles unlaced his fingers and closed the folder in front of him. "That's why we would like you to take a DNA test, because, Steven, you probably have a daughter, and she will probably one day be your queen."

Charles, having delivered the object of the interview, waited for Steve's reaction—and waited and waited.

"You say she's a looker." Steve nodded slowly. "She would be—her mother." He looked up sharply. "Is she married?"

"The mother?"

"Well if the daughter was married, we wouldn't be having this chat, would we? Stay with it, Charles."

"I really couldn't say."

"Is that civil service double talk for you know but you're not going to tell me but you want me to believe you don't know without actually lying? So tell me, Charles, because if you know enough that Ali is not the father you know whether he married Lydia or not."

"Would it make any difference?"

Steve stood. "Tell Joanne I'm sorry we can't stop for tea."

"But we've not finished yet!"

"Yes we have. Your hour is up, and I did tell you I had another appointment, taking the missus to the seaside. Tell you what, we'll call in on the way back. Don't worry about lunch. We'll get some fish and chips at the King's Head. In the meantime, you can find out if Lydia's married or you can find out if it's part of the official secrets act or if I can be entrusted with it, and if the answer to the second is yes, we can take it from there. We'd bring you some chips, but the King's Head don't do carry-outs."

He had reached the door when Charles voice stopped him. "Steven, it's curious you want to know if her mother's married but you've never asked her name."

"I know." Charles thought that was all the response he was getting and was deciding whether to enlighten him when Steve spoke again. "It's not Jackson, is it? Take care, Charles."

Charles looked at the closed door for a full five minutes before he pressed the intercom, "Joanne, Mr. and Mrs. Jackson are leaving or have left. They may be returning sometime this afternoon. If that is so, you will contact me and not let them out of your sight, even if it means—and where's the damn tea!"

"They did say they would be returning later this afternoon, Mister Chaddersly-Corbett, and I'm sorry about the tea, but you didn't order any, and as I didn't know how long they'd be staying—"

"Of course, I'm sorry. Could you get me a cup?" Charles was going to embellish his apology, but he didn't know if three time zones before breakfast and an hour with Steven Jackson would excuse his rudeness.

3~England vs. South Africa

EVEN PAMELA'S PATIENCE WAS STRETCHED to the limit when, with a cursory, "I'll tell you when we get there," Steve took the wheel and headed down Wilshire Boulevard. To her relief, he, with uncharacteristic recklessness, didn't spend a half hour looking for a place to park but chose the nearest lot to the beach for less than five dollars. Her forbearance was stretched dangerously thin, however, when a Japanese couple asked him to take their photograph and he insisted on taking three at different angles, "To get it right." But eventually they were on the beach, towels spread, lotion applied. To their right, the beach curved toward Malibu, and to the left, the pier hummed with the usual colorful activity. Pam checked the proximity of the nearest lifeguard, as she always did, although she was never likely to require their services, and draped herself carefully on her back before turning her brown eyes upon him. "Well?"

And Steven told her.

"Lydia had a baby that might be yours and she and William are—if she is and if they are, what would that make you?"

"A pain in the—"

"Only this time a royal pain."

Steven laughed for the first time that day. "Well said, 'By appointment Royal Pain in the Arse.'"

Pamela waited until his appreciated appreciation had subsided before she ventured, "I suppose they wanted you to take a DNA test."

"How did you work that out?

She frowned and lay back, covering her eyes in that characteristic way she had when she was marshaling her thoughts. "As I see it, there are two im—you know, not definites. Come on, help me out."

"Imponderables."

"Thank you." She uncovered one eye long enough to ensure that Steven was pondering her lotion shiny stomach.

"Whether the daughter—do we know her name?"

"No."

Pamela was going to uncover her eyes again but apparently decided against it. "Whether the daughter is indeed going to marry William—King Billy, the Irish will love that—which is out of your hands, and if you are the father of the fair—whoever. So they wanted you to take a DNA test because without that, everything is irrelevant, right?"

"Elementary, my dear Jackson."

"So when are we going to get the results?"

"I don't know."

This time the hand slowly came away from the eyes, causing the lifeguard to tend to his duties. "You didn't take the test."

"I told them I'd discuss it with you first and then we'd have lunch at the King's Head, and then, if it's all right with you, we'd call in on the way back."

Pam returned to her contemplative position. "Where's the harm? They can hardly expect you to pay for the wedding, and she's not likely to expect eighteen years back child support even if she did raise the kid herself, so take the test, and then—no wait, is there anything you want from *them?*"

"For instance?"

"I was thinking you might want to meet your daughter. Don't answer, you've wanted to ever since we've been together.

So have the test, if it's negative, wish the couple well, and get on with life with your gorgeous wife. If it's positive, you don't take a blood test or tell them anything about your family until you meet your daughter. Because that's all they'll be interested in. As soon as they're certain there are no hereditary diseases and not *too* much insanity, no Jack the Rippers on your side, they'll discard you and get someone safer to pass off as whoever's ..." She paused as another thought struck her. "That's why they haven't even told you her name. So that's my advice, DNA test yes, anything further, negotiable. Now go and check the bikinis, and if you get as far as Malibu, turn back, because I'll be getting a bit peckish by then. Wait!"

The last command caused Steven to freeze in the act of getting up.

"Why couldn't we have this discussion back at the Consulate? Then we wouldn't have to go back, or do you think I need the sea air to get my deductive faculties going?"

Steven grinned. "It certainly gets something going. No, I wanted to mentally prepare myself for the next surprise."

The next surprise, however, presented itself before he was prepared for it. After two hours of lying on the beach, or rather, Pam lying down and Steven getting up to walk either along the pier "in search of Jim Rockford" or northward along the beach where "the more you get toward Malibu the less the bikinis" and the allure of fish and chips overcame Pam's affinity to the sun, they packed their baggage. After Pam had personally thanked the lifeguard, they left the beach, dumped their luggage in the car, and made their way down Ocean Boulevard to the King's Head.

When they arrived at the King's Head, things improved even further, probably because of its British connections the Kings Head was showing a rugby match between England and South Africa as opposed to every other television station, which had another preoccupation, after the cardinals, in their wisdom had chosen an ex-Hitler Youth to be God's representative on earth. The Olympics had taken over, or rather, five repeats of every swimming race Brian Whelps won, to be followed by a portly woman, apparently his mother, jumping up and down as far as her girth would allow. It had even usurped the Republican convention, which had beaten Hurricane Gustav into third place.

"We'll probably have to wait ages for a table," Steven muttered, indulging in the favorite affectation of the Englishman abroad, the aversion to the Englishmen abroad. "All these yuppies reminding themselves they're English."

"That's what bars are for, sweetie," Pam murmured. "If you got a table in time, he wouldn't sell so much beer, would he? You did say that the owner was a Brummie. Now why don't you order us a table and I'll get us some drinks? Carling Black Label, right?"

"Right, and don't go near the gift shop or we'll have to take out a second mortgage." Having watched Pam to the bar, Steven made his way to the restaurant entrance. "Table for two please."

"Yes." The willowy hostess consulted her clipboard, and her eyes swept the room before returning to him. "About twenty minutes?"

"Fine." The glance at the clipboard and survey of the room were irrelevant, as they always said twenty minutes.

"Your name please?"

"Jackson, Mr. and Mrs."

"Would that be Steven and Pamela?"

To his annoyance, Steven actually felt his jaw drop. How could anyone know? He'd told Eddie the night before, but he was at work. No one else knew except—Charles, the bastard.

"Steven!" The bastard metamorphosed, having changed from his black and pinstripes to stone-colored slacks and a bush shirt. "I managed to take you up on your kind offer. Took the liberty of booking a table. Jill and I were getting quite concerned, weren't we?"

"Pam's getting drinks at the bar," Steven said to regain his balance while trying to remember making an offer, kind or otherwise.

"Splendid. I'll get my drink, and if Jill could hold our table—no, tell you what. Why don't you give our table to the next in line and we'll have the next one? Can do?"

The last question was directed at the hostess (obviously Jill) who made a show of consulting her clipboard, frowning slightly. "Yes, I think I can arrange that. I'll get a waiter to bring your drinks over." This earned her another "splendid" and a treasury bill, which disappeared faster than her frown.

"Right, lead on." Charles, drink in hand, smile hoisted, prepared to mix. "I take it the Missus enjoyed the seaside. Is that her at the bar? I say, she is a looker. Well done."

"She did, it is, thank you, and right here is good enough. I take it Joanne is holding the fort." Steven raised his hand to signal Pam. "Pulled rank on her, did you?"

Charles didn't appear to take offense. "Well, after twenty years service with HMG, a trip to Santa Monica is well earned. Actually, I said that I was going to track you down as you left rather abruptly, and the King's Head would be far more convenient than trolling the Santa Monica beach, although I always did want to see if the lifeguards were like those in Baywatch."

"They're better." Steven was still trying to attract Pam's attention. "Those birds in Baywatch all peroxide and silicone, while the real lifeguards." Steven winked. "What you see is what you get."

"You mean you've—"

"At my time of life? Still, there was once when we were living in Long Beach we were on Bay Shores and I was lying with my sunhat over my face, checking out this lifeguard through the air hole. She looked Filipino—you know, all tight and muscular. Anyway, I went for a dip, I can't stay in one place too long, and when I got back, I was rearranging my hat for the—you know—and there was this great big bloke there. They must have changed shifts while I was in the water. Then I heard this voice next to me saying, 'He doesn't cut such a figure, does he?' Pam knew what I was doing all along."

"You've certainly got an eye for the ladies, Steven, and the missus doesn't mind your wandering eye?"

"As long as that's the only thing that wanders, and just so we're on the same page. After consultation with the memsahib, I've decided to do the DNA test. I mean, it'd look bad, wouldn't it? 'consular'—no, sorry—'embassy official caught nicking silverware from the King's Head.' I mean, what would Her Majesty think?"

"Why would I, er, nick silverware?"

"Because it would have my DNA on it, sunshine."

"You have the natural distrust of government agencies of most ex-soldiers," Charles replied a tad huffily, "but I assure you there is no deceit intended. After all, you are English, er, British."

"Unless you've given Coseley away."

"Ah, the good lady." Charles turned his attention to Pam, who had arrived, drinks in hand, to warm the atmosphere, looking from Charles to Steven.

"Thanks, love." Steven took one of the glasses and indicated Charles with his head. "Charles from the Consulate. Apparently I invited him to lunch. Joanne couldn't make it. Charles, this is Pam, who I distinctly remember inviting to lunch."

"Delighted." Charles transferred his drink to his left hand and extended the right. "Sorry I didn't get to meet you back at the shop, but I trust Joanne took care of you."

"Oh yes, we had quite a chat." Pam looked around. "You didn't bring her with you?"

"No, someone has to mind the shop, and as I was just saying to Steven, rank has its privileges."

"By the way, I told Charles that we've decided a DNA test is in order, so you don't need to worry about him stealing the silverware."

"I'm sure Charles wouldn't stoop to anything so underhanded. I like your shirt." Pam fingered the lapel. "Do you know where I could get Steven one?"

"'Fraid not, m'dear. The old ball and chain got it for me."

"Actually, it's the ex ball and chain." Steven cut in, in an unexpected show of sympathy for Charles. "And I'm sure it takes all his time to get to see his kids, so we'll have to wait till we can visit Marks and Spencer's."

"Oh, I'm sorry. It must be hard."

"Not to worry." Charles's smile stayed valiantly in place. "Happens to the best of us, eh, Steven?" And suddenly he changed tack. "As you've already decided to oblige with the DNA test, you won't suspect my motives if I ask to buy you a drink?"

"Very civil of you, Charles." the remainder of the lager disappeared.

"And Pam? Oh I see." Pam's glass had suffered a similar fate. "Damned attractive and can take her pints. So it's two pints of Carling Black Label."

"Hang on," Steven demurred, "better not. Thing is, how long are you open?"

"We?" Charles said warily, thinking this wasn't going to be as easy as he thought. "You mean the Consulate? HMG? The sun never sets old son, we're here to serve. Problem?"

"The thing is," Steven said slowly, "England are playing South Africa at rugby, and it's being shown here, Wondered if I could see that before I shed a—whatever for the Old Country, and if so, I don't suppose it's in your bailiwick to get me out of the drunk tank if Santa Monica's finest take too close an interest in my," he made a shaking motion with his hand, "driving."

"England and the Springboks—bloody. Sorry, Pam. My bailiwick, nice word that," Steven inclined his head graciously, "is to deliver you, alive and breathing, to the nearest outpost of the empire before William kicks over the traces, even if I have to get you drunk, again saving your presence, Pamela, drugged, hogtied, or photographed in bed with a donkey, so this is what we'll do. We'll have a civilized lunch, and then we'll watch the match. Meanwhile I'll be pouring as much Carling Black Label down you as I can. Then I'll get a car from the Consulate to come down and pick us up take care of the DNA, and then we'll drive you back here to your hotel. Have you got a hotel? No? We can arrange one. Any preference?"

"I've always wanted to stay at the Georgian on Ocean Boulevard, and I promised Pam that someday we'd stay there."

"Right, the Georgian it is." A sudden thought seemed to strike him. "You won't be bored, will you, Pamela? I mean watching rugby for two hours."

"No, I like rugby, and besides, you can pour as much Black Label down me as you want as well."

"You're a lucky man, Steven. Right, three pints of Black Label and point me to the telephone."

"I thought you'd have a cell phone." Steven picked up the glasses. "I'll get these—least I can do."

"Sorry, figure of speech." Charles pulled a cell phone from underneath his safari shirt. "Bloody things. I meant, point me to better reception. And put the drinks on Mister Chaddesley-Corbett's tab, number three-three-one. Don't forget, it's all on HMG." Charles went outside to find better reception or more privacy.

"Seems all right for a civil service lackey." Steven put the glasses on the counter. "Three pints of Black Label please, on Chadder's tab."

"Chadder's?"

"Sorry, Mister Chaddersley-Corbett. Chadders is what we used to call him at school."

"Right, twelve dollars." She punched in the amount and number.

"And put in a two-dollar tip," Her Majesty's Government's newest representative added magnanimously.

"Ta, very much our kid[5], I'm from Smethwick[6]. Must have gone to school with his sister. Seriously, though," she put the drinks on the bar, "what are you doing with the smoothie? I mean, he talks like somebody from the BBC [4]and you— well ..."

"Don't get embarrassed. When my sister married and moved to Wolverhampton[7], she was moving up in class."

"So," she looked round to see if anyone required her service, "what is the score with you and him? I'm Sharon, by the way."

"Steven, if I told you, you wouldn't believe me."

"Well, tell me something I would believe. Which of you is with the bird?"

"Which do you think?"

"I don't know. I can't see her with either of you. Excuse me, duty calls."

Steven was joined at the bar by Charles. "All fixed up. I've even managed a room at the Georgian with an ocean view. Ah, splendid, I see Pam is joining us." He picked up his drink, and with his innate courtesy, picked up Pam's.

Steven had the feeling that, as he had agreed to furnish the DNA sample, Charles's day was done, so he could relax, and except for a passing reference to a lager-flavored DNA, business wasn't mentioned. They ate their fish and chips, Jill earned another "splendid," and then they retired to the bar to watch another epic battle between England and South Africa. As there weren't any South African supporters to discuss the finer points of the game with, Steven relaxed also, so much so that when Pam asked a question about the game, he was able to defer to Charles without embarrassment, citing his preference of Kipling's

They watched the "Gentlemen's Game Played by Ruffians" to the "Ruffians' Game Played by Gentlemen," and while Charles didn't "pour lager down them," their glasses were never empty long enough to stop the afternoon from being well lubricated, so much so that with a good-looking wife and a hotel room not half a mile away, the prospect of traveling up a rush hour Wilshire Boulevard, chauffeur driven or not, became less attractive to Steven.

"Listen, Chadders," he confided. "You don't mind if I call you Chadders?"

"Haven't been called Chadders since I was at school. What is it, old son?"

"Do you suppose I could just ..." Steven looked around as though seeking inspiration. "Tell you what, why couldn't I just chew on a toothpick, slip it back into the cellophane whatnot it came in, and you could take that back to school? Then your driver wouldn't have to come all the way back down here and we could, you know?" Steven inclined his head toward where he thought the Georgian was.

"I'm afraid not, old son." With the lager-fueled euphoria, added to England's narrow win over South Africa, the normally perceptive Steven missed the slightly embarrassed cloud that passed over Charles' handsome features. "I don't have to just deliver the saliva, I have to deliver it contained in one Steven Edwin Jackson—British subject of good standing, albeit resident of Arizona. I mean, I could have spent a pleasant lunch and got the toothpick from anywhere, and HMG want to be sure they've got their money's worth."

"What a suspicious lot you work for, Charles, almost as bad as the DWP. Well, it was just a thought." Steven stood a little unsteadily. "I'll go and take my leave of Sharon."

Unbeknownst to them, they were the subject of Sharon's whispered conference with her colleague, Susan. "Well, who do you reckon is with the long-haired bird then? I can't see her with either one of them. I mean, the older one's too smooth and the other one's too—"

"Rough?"

"Yes rough, I suppose. Not bad looking, though, but when he opens his mouth—yes, rough, I suppose."

"I shouldn't worry, love." Susan hoisted a tray of glasses. "I don't think it's either. When the smoothie came back from using the telephone, I heard him say he fixed up a hotel room for them. He probably fancies a bit of rough."

****

When they finally got back to the Consulate, they were conducted, no waiting this time, up to the third floor, where Pamela renewed her acquaintance with Joanne, Charles disappeared, and Steven was ushered into an upscale version of the previous office where behind the desk sat a younger, sharper edition of Charles. Standing to his right and slightly behind stood an older man in a suit that had been fashionable thirty years before. That was the only impression Steven had of him, which in the light of subsequent events was probably how he preferred it. He realized the younger man was talking to him.

"Mister Jackson?"

"None other."

"Good lunch? Charles look after you all right? This won't take a moment. Oh, I'm sorry." His glacier smile looked anything but. "This is Doctor Ferguson, who'll do the honors." Steven nodded at the old man, who was already rummaging in the doctor's bag. "Uh yes, this won't take a moment." He produced a cotton swab. "Open wide please. Under the tongue if we could." Steven felt a brief tickling sensation of the swab and it was returned to a plastic tube, which disappeared into the bag, but instead of closing it, he produced a syringe. "This won't hurt just a pinprick is all."

"I know it bloody well won't," Steven said with unintentional irony. "A DNA sample is what we agreed on, and that is what you got."

Doctor Ferguson stood undecided with the hypodermic in his hand and looked toward the figure behind the desk. Steven only realized later that he never introduced himself. "Well, we thought we could kill two birds with one stone and not waste any more time than necessary." The smile that dared Steven to be unreasonable was lost.

"I'm not wasting my time. You've had all you're going to get from me. I'm out of here," Steven turned on his heel and left, taking care not to slam the door. He had the satisfaction of seeing that the smarmy bastard behind the desk was so surprised, he'd forgotten to stop smiling. Steven's anger supported him through countless offices, and as many polite smiles, until he found Pamela, who was explaining to Joanne about her son Eddie. "Pam! We're leaving. Joanne, it's been—real. Got Eddie's telephone number? Good, let's go." Steven consciously had to loosen his grip on Pamela. "The bastards. They let Charles soften us up, and then they brought on the heavy mob—a sodding blood test to save time. Sorry." His apology embraced them both. "Let's go, we'll probably have to get a taxi. I think the ride back to Santa Monica has been taken off the table."

As they moved toward the stairs, Joanne reached for the phone to order the car to take the Jacksons back to Santa Monica, hoping to get Eddie's telephone number the next time, if there was a next time, and wondering if he'd got his looks from his mother or his father.

4~"The Rose Parade doesn't come down this far."

T HE NEXT STOP WAS A visit to the Leven Ash Hotel (the owner, Lisa, to her credit refused to call it an "assisted living facility"). The purpose was to visit one Richard Pottenger, Pamela's ninety-two-year-old grandfather. Dick was not happy about his situation. A tentative suggestion to join them in Arizona was rebuffed with mutterings of scorpions, rattlesnakes, and wet backs. They were fortunate to find him in the lobby, as usually they had to ask someone to find him, and that someone felt it their duty not only to escort him to them but to convince them, and him, what a fine time he was having. His current irritation was Maria, the activities director whose function seemed to be to irritate as many of the guests as possible in the shortest space of time by putting on her geriatric Chita Rivera act,

"She tried to get me exercising the other day, and I told her, what did I want the exercising for? She said something about discipline, and I told her I've got a son who's an ex-marine, a son-in-law who's an ex-paratrooper, and I was a combat engineer in the Pacific in WWII. What could she tell me about discipline?"

"And did she take the hint?" Steven felt Dick had accepted him enough to ask the question, although he never realized he knew about the ex-paratrooper bit. He realized he was guilty, like so many others, of talking in front of old people as though they weren't there.

"There she is." Dick nodded toward where a dark-haired woman was coaxing one of the patients across the lobby with aid of a walker while casting glances in their direction.

"Never mind about her for the moment," Pam said. "Is there anything that's bothering you? Anything we need to talk to your conservator about?"

"They never tell me anything. I don't know if my house has been sold yet and if they know about my account in Wells Fargo."

"Lisa said she'd spoken to the conservator, but I'll call her and ask her what's going on."

"Hi, Dick, you've got some visitors. That's nice." Maria had disposed of her charge and joined them, turning her beaming smile on Pam. "He's so cute. When he gets a little stronger, we're going to do exercises together, aren't we, Dick?"

"How can I do exercises when I can't walk?"

"But when your legs get stronger—"

"If my legs were stronger, I'd walk out of this place." He turned to Steven, dismissing Maria. "I'd come and live with you if you hadn't moved to Arizona. That's too far."

They'd been through this before, so Pam intervened. "Can you show us around? Why don't you show us the dining room? Take your time." Pam had already seen the dining room but wanted to talk to him away from the attentions of Maria, who mercifully took the hint, and with a, "Nice to have met you," she went to spread her sunshine on someone else who would probably have preferred a cloudy day.

"This is nice." Pam looked around. "Do you sit anywhere or do you have a special place?"

"She's too pushy. She gets right in your face, and we just don't get on." Dick was still fuming about Maria.

"Never mind about her. I'll get Lisa to tell her to leave you alone."

"Will you people being staying for dinner?"

"No thank you." Steven turned toward the new interruption, a stout, pleasant-looking woman with a definite Caribbean accent. "We had a late lunch. We'll catch you next time."

They had planned to leave Pasadena shortly after lunch (not at Leven Ash) and reach Mohave Valley by eight, when they planned to watch the Steelers/Chargers game with their neighbor. Unfortunately, due to Maria's attempted attention, it was some time before they were alone with Dick, and apart from his complaint about the food and Maria, he seemed reluctant for them to go, a reluctance that was as sharp, at least for Pam, and even Steven felt a certain empathy toward a life that was slowly draining away.

"We're not going to make it to Brian's in time, are we?" Pam asked after they had left the cloying atmosphere of Leven Ash and were walking toward the car. "And you knew, didn't you?"

"Well, you're all he's got left."

"I appreciate it." She linked her arm in his. "Why don't I buy some lunch."

"Cameron's?"

"So you know how to get there?"

"Follow Colorado Boulevard until the grandstands run out. Remember, 'The Rose Parade doesn't come down this far.'"

"Fine." She gave his arm a squeeze. "You get us out to the desert, and I'll take it from there."

Steven was never sure afterward if he had planned it or if he was "thinking on his feet," but after they had left the urban sprawl of Los Angeles, he made no mention of relinquishing the wheel until they were approaching Palm Springs.

"We can stop there and stretch your legs and use the powder room." Steven nodded to where the twenty storeys of the Morongo Casino pierced the horizon.

"Fine, I'll take over then. Are you hungry?"

"No but," Steven made a show of considering something, "I'm sure they've got a sports book there."

"So?"

"So we'll be able to watch the Steelers game there, have a couple of beers and a sandwich."

"That'll make us very late."

"So? Do you have a train to catch? We can pull over somewhere between Rice and Vidal Junction and have a nap."

So it was, after watching the Steelers beat the San Diego Chargers on one screen and the Angels beat another team on another, they drove on through the desert night, turning off the freeway at the Desert Center to pull up in the deserted glory of Rice. It always amazed Steven that there was a spot on the map representing Rice as big as those denoting Twenty-Nine Palms, Yucca Valley, or Parker, but where they were all large enough to warrant at least a filling station and restrooms, at Rice there was—nothing, or more exactly there was the remains of what might once have been a filling station and a dead tree, festooned, for some reason, with hundreds of tennis shoes.

"Shall we stop here or press on to Vidal Junction?"

"Press on. I think I may need to use the facilities."

"You know," Steven mused, "according to the map, Rice is as big as Vidal Junction, Twenty-Nine Palms, or even Parker, so if someone was relying on it, they may expect Rice to have facilities, even water."

"Why don't you have a word with the map makers?" Pamela lightly scratched his hair. "They might even rename Vidal Junction after you."

"Cartographers."

"Pardon?"

"People who make maps, they're called cartographers."

They drove on through the night, each enjoying the desert and the proximity of each other until, by the time they reached Vidal Junction, Pamela had slipped into a light doze. Steven made a series of maneuvers to face the way they had come, which had the effect of waking Pam. "Where are we?"

"Vidal Junction. Do you want to go now or finish your nap?"

"I can't see the—"

Steven jerked his head backward. "They're back there."

"So why ...?" Pamela slowly turned her head. "I suppose there is a good reason why we're facing the other way and after I've been mystified long enough you'll let me hear it."

"If we pulled in the other way, our headlights would shine directly into the motel rooms and disturb the guests' sleep or—whatever. It's all right." He forestalled her response. "You never learn if you don't ask. Now do you want to finish your nap or use the ..." But Pam had already snuggled down into the car's seat, mumbling something about putting the cartographer before the horse.

At the same time that Steven was mystifying his wife in the Mohave Desert, they were the subject of a conversation in London.

"Apparently this character was found and he had no objection to the DNA test but got a bit shirty[8] when the blood test was mentioned—something about having spilled enough blood for England. A bit dramatic, but he had just returned from lunch with Chaddersly-Corbett."

"Do we know what upset him?"

"No, as I say, Chaddersly-Corbett had just taken him to lunch at some place in Santa Monica. They'd watched England play the Springboks on the telly and arrived back here with quite a rosy glow. Perhaps it was the thought of the needle that set him off. I'll get Chaddersly-Corbett to have another word with him. Apparently they got on quite well. His wife's quite a looker."

"I thought they were getting divorced."

"The subject, you ass, what's his name, Jackson?"

"Well anyway, we've run into a bit of a bump in the road here. Miss Biderman insists on meeting with her father while she's in California visiting these friends of her mother's. Apparently demanded it as soon as we had ascertained it was he, so we can't just drop Jackson back into the desert, much as we might prefer to."

"And she's firm on this?"

"As the proverbial camel's arse in a sandstorm, old boy, so as Chaddersly-Corbett has some sort of rapport, you'd better keep him on stand-by."

"Yes I'd already thought of that. Apparently some of the Jackson genes—we could have saved the cost of a DNA test."

******

Two weeks had passed since their abrupt decampment of the British Consulate General in Santa Monica, and Steven had decided that "they" had lost interest in him or had gotten him mixed up with someone else. Pamela was pandering to her current obsession with keeping the swimming pool clean when the telephone rang. "I'll get it." Pam made her way to where Steven had rigged up the "pool" telephone.

"It'll be somebody worried about our mortgage, our cable facilities, or our credit," Steven said and tried to keep the "I told you so" expression off his face when his wife's face lit up as it did when she answered the telephone to someone other than those concerned with their cable facilities or their credit, "Well hi! I'm fine, just trying to keep the swimming pool clean. It's about a hundred, just about right, but it'll be too hot to do anything later on. Oh yes, still spoiling him rotten. Yes, he's about two yards away flat on his back. No, completely sober, he's just catching some rays." She finally turned to Steven. "It's Charles Chaddersley-Corbett from the Embassy."

Steven took the phone carefully. "Chadders, what can we do for you?" He squeezed Pam's shoulder in a gesture that asked her not to go too far away.

"Steven, old son, we rather hoped you'd have second thoughts about the old blood test."

"No, Chadders, old son, I'm quite satisfied with the first thought. If I'd been told about the blood test to start with—but I'm not going to be made a fool of."

"I'm sure there was no intention of—"

"Well the blood test's out, and if there's nothing else, call us again when you're near Santa Monica. Lunch is on us this time."

"Well that makes it a bit awkward, actually." Charles paused, hoping Steven would feel obliged to throw something into the silence, but all he got was, "As we say in the Colonies, it's your nickel, old son."

He could hear the fragile control as Charles answered, "Steven, I admit that we were rather presumptuous in assuming that you would take a blood test, but you can see that one is no good without the other. So, is there anything I—we—can do to prevail upon you to take the blood test? After all, it's confirmed that the lady is your daughter, and I'm sure you'd like to see her happily married."

"Well, that's a start."

"Sorry?"

"Seeing my daughter happily married. Therefore, if I can presume that I'm invited to the wedding, I think I'd better see my daughter first. I mean, frightfully bad form if I turn up at St. Paul's—it *is* St. Paul's by the way? Anyway, there I am, 'Pleased to meet you. Best wishes on your marriage to my future king, and by the way, I'm your dad.' Look, Chadders, I know the score. It wasn't you who arrogantly assumed---. Anyway, I want to see my daughter. Then I'm sure we can work something out."

"Of course. She'll be in Los Angeles in a couple of weeks. Can you make it to the Consulate by then? I'll phone you with the date."

"No! Not quite, Chadders."

"I beg your pardon?"

"I don't know if I want even my wife there when I meet my twenty-two-year-old daughter for the first time, even less a passel of Consulate, sorry, Embassy flunkies. No offense meant."

"None taken, but um, I don't know if HMG would be quite happy about that. After all, she is your future queen."

"But she was my daughter first, Chadders old lamb, so if she doesn't want to see me on my own, I'll respect her wishes, but she's going to tell me herself, and if she does, then much as I regret causing HMG any unhappiness, so be it, and they can be quite *unhappy* about it. What do you think, I'm going to steal her? "

"Well," said Charles carefully, "you did steal her mother's heart."

"Touché, Charles, but don't get romantic with me, I'm married."

"Yes quite, and the blood test?"

"Just get my daughter to phone me, Charles, and I'll look after you."

"Right, could you hang on a minute?"

"Yeah, okay."

"Will that be, all right?"

"I'm not going anywhere, Charles."

Steven hooked a chair toward him and sat down, "You heard all that?" He gestured toward the phone. "Probably checking with head office."

"Yes, so you're going to meet your daughter and you're going to give them a blood test for her sake. I thought you were a bit easy on Charles. Are you getting mellow, or is he getting to you?"

"Neither, it's because he didn't give me that guff about 'you're English the same as me.'"

"But you are English."

"Yeah, but not the same as him—public school, officer material, job in the civil service waiting for him when he left school."

"Your chip's showing."

"I hope that's plural."

"I know, Coseley," she recited. "That's what stops you from becoming unbalanced. You've got a chip on both shoulders. What?"

Someone had come on the line, and from Steven's expression, it wasn't Charles.

"Allo? Mr. Jackson?"

"Speaking."

"This is Judith. You are my father, I think?"

"Apparently." *Chadders, you bastard.*

****

"So you're going to meet your daughter, how do you feel?" Pamela asked. They were once again traversing the Mohave Desert on their way to "California," having arranged to meet Judith in the patio of Media Partners.

"You know, I really don't know. Intrigued, nervous, apprehensive. I really don't know, anything but—I really don't know." Assuming that this was specific enough, Steve looked out the window, once more letting the passing sagebrush and cactus brush irksome thoughts away, but apparently not all.

"So what's not fair, apart from the usual?"

"Pardon?"

"What particular inequity were you referring to?"

"What?"

"You said," Pam said slowly, "'That's not fair.' Are you going to tell me what isn't fair?"

"Sorry." Steven realized he'd been thinking out loud. "After all this harassment, and I don't think that's too strong a word, about the blood test to see if there's anything in my history that would throw a blight on the nuptials," his grammar was slipping with his indignation, "what about him?"

"Who, William?"

"Yes. You know Kathy's family?"

"Yes, for quite a long time, and it seems even longer," said Pam in that particularly level way she had when Steve's ex-wife was mentioned.

"Well, they had so many skeletons that Luke had to build another closet."

"And this has to do with what?"

"Well, his family, the Royal Family, would need a whole palace full of closets. I think I'll demand a blood test of him before he marries my daughter."

"'My daughter'? Aren't we being paternal? How long have you known about her, two weeks? Why don't you ask her when you meet her? I'm sure she'll have plenty to ask you. You can also ask her if her mother had any objection to the blood test. It just occurred to me, far be it for me to cast doubts on the ... history of Lydia, but she didn't come to you unsullied."

"You know, I never thought about that."

"You wouldn't. That's what you've got me for, my sweet." But apparently she'd had enough of Lydia's history. "Can we stop for breakfast when we get to Twenty-Nine Palms?"

"Sure, I can phone Wendy Mulligan from there."

"Why phone Wendy Mulligan? You'll be seeing her in a couple of hours."

He told her.

Three hours later, they were being given an uncertain welcome by Dan, the security guard in the foyer of Media Partners. "Steve, how are you? How's retirement?"

"Fine." Steven took the proffered hand. "And yourself? You're looking well."

"Yes well what can we—anything special?"

"I'm meeting someone on the patio, so if anyone asks for me, send them out there, would you? And if anyone gets nervous, especially the sacred cow," he raised his eyes toward the second floor, "you can tell them that Mr. Vaughan both knows and approves." Steve turned toward the double doors leading to the patio, and Dan thought he'd escaped when Steven said over his shoulder, "We've really sorted Iraq out, haven't we? That's why they killed Crazy Horse, you know, they thought he'd got weapons of mass destruction."

He had chosen midmorning so that the patio would be almost empty, and he still arrived half an hour before the appointed time so that he had time to peruse his newspaper while he waited and went over the telephone conversation with Judith. She had no objection to eschewing the attendance of an escort from the consulate, refusing even a chauffeur, but unbent enough to let them find her a hire car. He hadn't described himself to her and had even flirted with the idea of carrying a copy of the *Arizona Republic,* but with the help of Pam, he had decided it smacked too much of John le Carre.

However, he needn't have concerned himself, as he was the only one he had seen in the building whose face didn't reflect six hours in a cubicle with only a monitor for company, a corporate pallor, as it had been described. It was fortunate that he had arrived early, as the lunch truck had arrived by about 10:20 (like most offices, the lunch break was dictated by the arrival of the lunch truck), and people had started drifting out, some to light up cigarettes and others to pursue their addiction to the cell phone. One or two had cast speculative glances in his direction, but he had lifted his newspaper, hopefully preventing any closer attention.

He was still in this position minutes later when, without looking up, he felt something in the air. He couldn't name it (later he learned it was a *frisson*), but on raising his head, the reason became obvious. A young woman had just exited the building and was walking toward him. She was wearing a severely cut pinstripe business suit, which went with the small attaché case she carried but emphasized her striking figure. Her jet black hair cut straight across the forehead framed her china blue eyes. She looked, Steven realized, like her mother did when they first met. That must have prevented a lot of awkward questions. He stood as she approached, and they observed each other quietly.

"You must be Judith."

"You must be my father."

"I've got the DNA test to prove it."

"Really."

"Please," he indicated one of the chairs, "you obviously found it all right."

"Yes, I loved your directions: 'get off at Buena Vista and head toward the mountains and turn left at the Seven-Eleven.' What would you like me to call you?"

"Whatever you're comfortable with." He remembered he'd made the same response to Eddie years before prior to getting spectacularly drunk on tequila. "I am your father, although absent, through no fault of my own, for the first twenty-two years of your life." He noticed her eyes widened at this. "And my name is Steven Edwin Jackson, so that's anything from Dad to Mr. Jackson."

"What do Pam's sons call you?"

"Well, Robert calls me Pops, and Eddie? It depends, usually it's Stu or Dad. If I beat him at pool, it's stepfather, and if I beat him badly, it's less complimentary. I'm sorry about this. It's normally quiet this time of the day but ..." he indicated the lunch truck. "I'm sorry, I never thought. Perhaps you'd like something to eat?"

She wrinkled her nose at the smell of burning fat emanating from the lunch truck. "No thank you. I had a bagel for breakfast and that keeps me going all day. Like a camel, yes?" As if to contradict herself, she reached in her bag and placed a bottle of spring water on the table.

"Are we to embrace, or are you going to be very English?" He carefully moved the chair out of the way, and they held each other waist to waist face to face. She kissed him lightly on the cheek and then suddenly held his jaw in her hand while she studying his face. "Yes your eyes, dangerous. You look very English. Are you still English? Have you become an American?"

"No, I would have to renounce 'All previous faiths and fidelities,' which would be a lie. I can't stop being English, although it's a trial sometimes."

"You shouldn't. You really do look English."

"Thank you, if that's a compliment."

"Why wouldn't it be?"

"Well the last time your Mother called me that, it was just worse than being a Nazi. I'll tell you about it sometime."

"Oh no, now, I've waited too long already." She arranged herself in the chair. "But before that. What is this place?"

"Media Partners. It's a payroll company that works exclusively for the entertainment industry. This is where the checks for the overpaid stars get signed. I used to work here."

"And they don't mind us meeting here?"

"No, I told the security guard that Mr. Vaughan said it was all right."

"And is there a Mr. Vaughan?"

"There is, head of the accounts department, nice chap. He sings 'My Way' at the Christmas party."

"And he's a friend of yours?"

"Not exactly. He always finds time, or found time, to have a pleasant word, but I wouldn't call him a friend."

"Then why does he let you use ...?" She held her hands palm upward, fingers splayed, indicating the patio.

"Well, he doesn't exactly know." This time she said nothing but just looked at him until he continued. "On our way, here I

51

telephoned Wendy Mulligan, a girl I know who works here, and asked her which, if any, of the directors were out for the day, and George Vaughan was. So …" This time it was his turn to give an almost Gallic shrug.

"My mother didn't say that you were so devious."

"I probably wasn't then. It's happened with age."

Then she did something she must have copied from her Mother. She lowered her head and pulled her bottom lip in between her teeth and looked at him from beneath her eyebrows. "Poppi," she whispered, "is this where you bring your girlfriends?"

"You can ask your mother about that, as she was the last girlfriend I had."

"Apart from your wife."

"But she's not a girlfriend."

"But she was a girlfriend before she was your wife. Yes?"

"Yes, but when she was my girlfriend it was long before I worked here. That was when—"

"You left my mother."

"No."

"What happened between you and my mother?"

"Apart from you?"

"Including me." She laced her fingers together and put her hands flat on the table. "Tell me all about it, from the start."

"Are you going to take notes?"

"No, I won't need to."

"Yes." He had already had an indication that not far beneath her impish, almost flirtatious demeanor there was a mind that missed very little. She must be a formidable attorney. "Feel free to interrupt with any questions, right?" He leaned back and looked up at the sky or what was visible of it over the elevated Interstate 5. "I first met your mother in 1984, June I think, at the British Club in Garden Grove. It was a Saturday night. I can't remember who she was with, if anyone, or who I was with, if anyone. I was probably wasted."

"Wasted?"

"Juice of the grape. A little—" he made a tipping motion with his hand. "Anyway, she said something to me, and whatever I said must have impressed her, because the following day, which was Sunday, I went in there after playing football and she came in with ..."

"Barbara."

"Thank you, yes, Barbara. So we arranged to meet again, and we saw each other quite often until she went back to Belgium."

"And you were married then?"

"If you can call it that."

"What would you call it?"

He shook his head slowly. "You've got me on that."

"But you were actually living with your wife when you met my mother."

Steven took a deep breath. "I was living with my wife when I met your mother in late June 1984, but before she went back to Belgium, I was not living with my wife. I actually moved out on the Fourth of July. Most of my friends knew of the situation between us and at least two had offered me a place to stay if things got ...too much, and on the Fourth of July things got ... too much." His voice took on a reminiscent quality. "Everyone was having a good time and asking when I was coming over. I finally found somebody sober enough and left there and then. They'd left the key under the flower pot."

"So would you have left if you hadn't met my mother?"

He waited for quite a while as though he was again waiting for some help, but since none was forthcoming, he eventually conceded, "I really don't know. I called your mother my moonbeam. You can't lean on it, but until it lights up your cell, you don't realize that you're a prisoner. I was a bit poetic in those days. But if your Mother did have an influence, it's nothing to be ashamed of. She probably kept me from killing someone. Anyway."

He roused himself. "Your mother went back to Belgium about the end of August, and we continued the relationship by post and occasionally telephone. The next time we saw each other was toward the end of that year. She was selling jewelry for Ali. As far as I know, she was quite successful at it, and then she went back—it must have been about Thanksgiving—so it was back to letters and the occasional telephone call. We didn't have e-mail then. Then it was about March of the next year—yes it must have been March because she took me out for my birthday, but by this time things … I think she may have decided to go back to Ali, if she had ever left him, because I noticed whenever she referred to him it was as Ali, not 'my ex.'

"Once I was with her at Albert's house and Ali telephoned. I couldn't leave, so I heard her half of the conversation. It was like a mother calming an anxious child. I told her I couldn't compete with that. She told me that I could 'drive her back to Ali.' Things came to a head, for want of a better phrase, when we watched the movie *Chariots of Fire* and there was this particular scene where these two academics—one was played I remember by John Gielgud—were trying to convince him that having a professional coach was not quite sporting. She said it was racist. I said it wasn't. She said I was a Nazi. Anyway, I drove her home to Albert and Barbara's, and just before she went in, she told me she'd got this new boyfriend, a baseball player from San Francisco. As close as I can recall it was because I was 'too English,' so that was that. I went home."

"And you never saw her again?"

"Actually, I drove her to the airport, so I did drive her back to Ali. She left for Belgium, not San Francisco, so I don't know what happened to the baseball player, if he ever existed. I don't really know what happened it was all quite confusing. I did get a letter from her about two months later, very garbled with little diagrams and notes in the margins, but it didn't clarify anything. If anything, it showed she was just as confused as I was but did explain that it was all my fault and she was going to be devoted to Ali because she *knew* she couldn't rely on him. I kept it to read when I became sober. I was drinking quite a lot in those days. I used to take it out now and again to see if I could understand it. A friend once gave me a very old photograph, but when I took it to Arizona, it crumbled to dust within a couple of months and the same thing happened with Lydia's letter. You have to be very careful with papers because of the heat and the dryness. And I never did decipher it. Obviously I hadn't sobered up enough."

"So you are saying you don't know why my mother and you parted." When Steven continued, Judith wasn't sure whether he was answering her rare interruption or he was completing a thought.

"Either I *was* too English, or she was too Jewish or she'd never left Ali or—" He suddenly seemed to change tack. "She called me about a year, or maybe—yeah, it must have been, because I was living with Pam by then because she answered the phone. Your mother thought Pam was my answering service, which I suppose she is, among other things."

"Pam, your wife?"

"Pam who is now my wife," he corrected her gently.

"And where is Pam, who is now your wife, now?"

"She's waiting at the Hill Street Café on the corner."

"Does she mind?"

"No, she suggested it. She thought that we should spend some time alone."

"She must be very sympathetic. Will I meet her?"

"Yes she is. And I'm sure she would love that. We'd better be making a move soon anyway before someone recognizes me and joins us. I was at work when your mother called, which seemed to surprise her. She once told me that I was the only guy she knew who had a steady job. Pam told her to write and that I'd love to hear from her, which I would have. Anyway, that was the last time she made contact. I hear occasionally from Albert and Barbara. They told me about you and that's it."

"Until you heard from your Embassy."

"Until I heard from the Embassy."

"Did you ever think about, me, whether I was yours?"

"Yes, quite often."

"But you never tried to find out for sure?"

"Have you heard of Marilyn Monroe?"

"The movie star?"

"Yes, the movie star." Judith wisely kept silent. "She was married to a baseball player called Joe di Maggio, quite famous. He was supposed to be the true love of her life. In fact, there was a suggestion they were trying to get back together when … Anyway, I'd read that he put flowers on her grave every birthday, and it so happened that I was doing a job up near Westwood, where she was buried and I was reading the *LA Times* and it said somewhere that it was her birthday that day. She would be— I don't know how old she would be that day, but it was her birthday. I asked Steve Schwartz, the guy who was driving, if we could detour and check it out, but then I changed my mind. If he didn't, I didn't want to know. The same with if I wasn't your father. I wouldn't want to know. As you get older, you have fewer illusions, so you guard them jealously."

"Bravo, Poppi," she said softly.

"Now," he roused himself, "what about you? Have you …" He smiled suddenly. "I was about to ask you if you'd got a boyfriend but obviously that's what brought us together, so, you live in Belgium?"

"Yes, in Antwerp."

"With your mother?"

"No, I have an apartment, or how you say, a flat, near my job."

"Any brothers or sisters?"

"No."

"I suppose Ali didn't want anymore. If you'll pardon me for being a little indelicate, are he and your mother married? I wouldn't ask, but traditionally it's the father who gives the bride away and if there's a stepfather who might have thought he was the father it can get a little—pardon?" He realized that sometime during his arrangement of her wedding that she had spoken.

"Ali died."

When his emotions had subsided somewhat and his breathing had returned to normal, he managed one word, "When?"

"In, I think"—she squinted over his shoulder as she was apparently calculating—"1986. And no, they never married. My mother is still unmarried."

"So Lydia brought you up by herself?"

"She had some help from her mother, and Ali's parents helped a bit, but mostly, yes, she did it by herself."

"I never knew. I wonder why Barbara never told me." He looked at the glass facade of Media Partners as though he might find the answer there, and she wisely waited while he recovered his composure before continuing. "Your mother," he said finally, "she—I'm sure has told you her version of our affair, and it might differ from mine but, people, especially after so many years, can have different perceptions of the same event, but although they differ, they are both true to them."

"Are you lecturing me, Poppi?"

"Yes, I suppose I am, and I certainly don't have the right. I'm sorry."

"Not at all. You are most sympathetic." She arranged herself more decorously in the wrought-iron chair. "Now what else do you want to know about me?"

"What sort of a lawyer are you?"

"A very good one."

He smiled. *Oh yes,* she thought, *that's why my mother fell for you.* "What branch of the legal profession currently enjoys your talents?"

"I'm doing investigative work for the European Commission on financial matters. I catch the rich people who want to get richer by using their wealth to avoid the financial regulations."

"Like the Securities and Exchange Commission?"

"Exactly, but as I said, I am very good. I can't tell you anymore. I was planning to work for two, three years for the commission and then go in to practice for myself, but then I met William."

"Speaking of whom, what was your first impression of him?"

"I was attending a seminar in London, during the lunch break at a pub. That is correct, the pub?"

He nodded.

"He was there. I was with a group of people, and I think one of my group knew one of his group so we, how do you say," she interlocked her fingers together, "joined each other, and he was sitting next to me. He was charming and so good-looking, like most English men, but he asked me for my telephone number, which I thought was inappropriate, but he was very knowledgeable about finance." She suddenly laughed, throwing her head back, causing the people at one of the other tables to look over and the cell phone users interrupt their conversations long enough to give a quelling glare. "He said he was training to take over the family business. Do you know, Janine, one of the girls at the seminar, asked me if I'd like to see *La Boheme*. Of course, I love the opera, and *La Boheme* is my favorite—so tragic, so doomed." She suddenly looked at him questioningly. "I think it is your favorite too."

"Actually, yes it is," he conceded.

"Ah yes." She nodded sagely as though she'd remembered part of a poem. "A passion for lost causes"

"What I had forgotten is that I had told Janine that it was my favorite and William had asked Janine what I liked to do for relaxation, and he'd even found out my favorite opera. You English, you're more devious than the French, so we made a foursome, and he saw me every night, no evening," she corrected herself severely, "and when I went back, he would telephone me. He even spoke to my mother, very respectful, and, here we are."

"How is your mother?"

"She was sad when Ali died, but what can I tell you. All this time and you didn't ask about her. Did she break your heart?"

"She certainly bruised it."

"She would like to see you again if your wife wouldn't mind."

"She's my wife, not my jailer—her phrase, not mine—but as she, your mother, lives in Belgium and I live in Arizona, we'd have to arrange it for when she visits California, if she still does."

"But you should see her before the wedding. It would be better than meeting at the rehearsal lunch."

"If I'm invited."

She took his hands and held them tightly, looking directly into his eyes. "Will you come to my wedding, Poppi?"

"If I don't, it will be because I'm at a funeral—as guest of honor. Now let's go and meet Pam."

5~His English Fix

T HEY WERE DRIVING DOWN THE Santa Ana Freeway in the general direction of Orange County, each busy with their own thoughts, or rather Steven was, while Pam (hopefully) was giving her attention to navigating the midmorning traffic.

Steven having used the security guard's telephone to inform a Mr. Middleton-Scriven at the Consulate General (where *did* they get those names) when *he* would be available for a blood test, they'd gone to meet Pam. Although Judith was quite respectful, almost to the point of deference, there was a singular lack of affability emphasized by Pam's natural warmth. In fact, although Steven had taken pains to affirm that his relationship with her mother, if it was ever alive, was dead and buried by the time he'd come under Pam's sunny influence, Judith's very politeness was taken as a kind of rebuke.

He remembered something a child psychologist had told him about children of estranged parents. They never gave up on the hope of a reconciliation between their parents until one of them had a "significant other," no matter how long after the irrevocable rift. Steven asked why Adam had not objected to any of his mother's swains. Doctor Goldstein smiled his world-weary, six-hundred-dollar-an-hour smile, and said,

"Apparently they got bored with her before they'd got a chance to be significant." With something of a jolt, he realized that was why Kathy's family had turned so hostile. They must have really expected him to remain as a backup while Kathy was trying to keep some one's attention long enough to become "significant." If he hadn't been with Pam, he wouldn't have been warned off her father's funeral (he'd gone anyway).

"What are your plans?"

He dragged his mind back to the present. "We could go to the club tonight. I think there's a quiz on Friday night, and this morning we can book into a motel and then shop or spend some time on the beach and see Eddie tomorrow, and then Sunday—"

"I was thinking more about your plans regarding your daughter rather than when the best night is to go to the club."

"Well," he mused, "they're not totally unconnected."

"Of course, you got to know her mother there."

"And—yes."

"In the club?"

"Well, more exactly, in the parking lot."

"So," Pam said with uncharacteristic fury, "you conceived Judith in the parking lot of the British and Dominion Social Club and then you went home and slept with your wife?"

"No! I had moved out of the happy home before Judith was a proverbial twinkle in my eye."

"That's something, I suppose." Then another thought seemed to strike her. "Weren't you conceived on a train?"

"Oh yes." He hadn't realized she'd remembered the story he had told her. During the war, privacy was at a premium when, as a result of the bombing, three or four families could be living together in one house, which, if the plumbing was damaged, were hardly fit for human habitation anyway. If the husband was in the services, as an indulgence, he would take his wife with him to Wolverhampton railway station where, on the strength of a penny platform ticket, they could extend their tearful good-byes as far as Birmingham, where the wife would catch the train back to Wolverhampton. If the good-bye was particularly tender, she would travel as far as London and back on the strength of wartime passion and a penny railway ticket. It was common practice to pile all the luggage in the doorway at the back of the carriage, and it was here, in a bower constructed of kitbags belonging to the second battalion the South Staffordshire Regiment, Steven was conceived.

"There seems to be some sort of a pattern developing here. You were conceived on a train, your daughter was conceived in a parking lot—you've never heard of beds?"

"Adam was conceived in a bed, and look how he turned out. And besides, that was the only privacy my mother and father had. That was during the time they couldn't even kiss without a blanket separating them from Uncle Ben and his family, and if it wasn't there, it was in the air raid shelter, which was a glorified tin shed and even more crowded."

"I can see that, but"—Pam seemed reluctant to let go of her anger—"you had a perfectly good apartment, what was ... Why a parking lot?"

Steven dragged his mind forward forty-five years. "It was after a soccer dance. We were standing outside, and some people who were leaving the dance blew the horn and waved, and so we waved back. Then we waved at the car following them and they waved back, and so it went on. Lydia got all—she had a thing about families, and it just happened. It was seeing all those families going home, or it might have been something completely different." He paused as if he trying to remember something. "I was coming out of the club once just at this place where it—Lydia, well you know. Anyway, there were these two women I knew, married women with families. They were lying on the grass between the car park and the chain-link fence. They were really getting to know one another. I mean—"

"I think I get the picture, but moving on, when Judith was conceived?"

"Yes?"

"It wasn't in your pickup, was it, the Toyota?"

"No," he lied gallantly. "Do you know I was in the Airborne?"

"Well, you're in the Parachute Regimental Association. When we go to England, apart from your sisters and Dave, all the people we meet are ex-paratroopers—not that I'm complaining—and you walk with a limp from an injury sustained parachuting, so yes, even if you hadn't told me, I think I'm sharp enough to work it out by now."

"That was rather cutting, Pamela, but did you know that Judith calls me Poppi?"

"Yes."

"And she's Jewish?"

"Yes and the significance of this is?"

"Well after the war, when America, very generously, gave half the British protectorate of Palestine to the Jewish people and then the Americans supported the wholesale influx of Jews to the state of Israel, which was bursting at the seams, and then the Americans forced the British—"

"Is there something to this besides a political lecture?"

"Well there were the Arabs on one side the Jews on the other and the British in the shape of the 6th Airborne Division in the middle. And it ended up, as in most similar situations when you're trying to be fair to both sides, with both sides hating us. That's where the Airborne got their second nickname, *kalionets*. It's Hebrew for Poppy, a red flower with a black heart. What do you think?"

Pam concentrated on her driving.

****

As they had no definite appointment until the one he'd set up with Middleton-Scriven on Monday morning, Steven was able to throw himself into the role of considerate husband. This usually included maximum time at the beach and at least one visit to Eddie. By the time they'd reached Orange County, all the beaches were probably full, and so Pamela was content to exposing the maximum of her person to the sun by the motel swimming pool. Friday night they went to the quiz night at the British Club to improve Pamela's knowledge, but the only thing she learned from a bleary-eyed albeit well-spoken individual named Martin, was that there was a cricket match on Sunday. They spent all of Saturday morning, and well into the afternoon, at the beach, or rather Pam did while Steven followed his habit of getting up every twenty minutes to "have a look around" in the afternoon. The beach having filled up to past their comfort level, they went back to the motel, where Steven had a siesta and Pamela went down to the swimming pool to get more sun. Steven was sure that one of her ancestors was a desert lizard. Nevertheless, she returned to their bedroom in time to share a tender moment with him and another nap before getting ready to surprise Eddie at Captain Bombay's.

"I don't believe it. Are you two buying property up here?" Eddie was playing pool with a young lady of such personality that it caused Steven to rechristen the bar Captain Bimbo's. "This is Tammy. These are my parents. Well what brings you here?"

"If I told you, you wouldn't believe me."

"I don't believe you dated Angie Dickinson, but you told me. Angie Dickinson was a movie star," Eddie explained to Tammy, "and Stu always tries to make Mom jealous by saying he dated her." Eddie signaled the bartender to put their drinks on his tab. "Well are you going to tell me?"

"The same reason as before. I have to give a blood test to prove I've picked up no bad habits in America."

"You know, I'm really worried about you. I mean, bullshit is all right but this is not new bullshit. I think you're getting old."

"By the way, I met your stepsister yesterday, the one who's going to be Queen of England."

Like many good men before him, Eddie was not quite sure how serious Steven was, "So you met my stepsister. Is she hot?"

"I wouldn't know. She's my daughter." Steven turned to Pamela, who was talking to the bartender. "What's Judith like, I mean, to look at?"

"Oh yes, very beautiful."

"Now you've got my mother at it. Are you guys on that peyote? You should either get off that shit or bring me some."

As they were leaving, Eddie was explaining to Tammy how his stepsister was going to be Queen of England.

They made the beach on Sunday morning in time for Pamela to choose her favorite spot and spent, for Pamela, a brief time there (Steven only went for three walks) when it was time to leave. In the new spirit of consideration, however, before they drove to the cricket field, he called at a liquor store for a six-pack of Corona Light, Pamela's favorite tipple for watching cricket, sans Blackthorne cider. The six-pack outlasted the British club's innings, but Pamela was an experienced enough cricket wife/widow to join in the completely spurious discussion about where to go afterward. This time, as the club was in full sunlight, Steven was able to indicate the very spot on the grassed surround of the parking lot where the two Scottish housewives had returned to the Isle of Lesbos.

There was a Friday crowd, which was the boys night out, and there was the Saturday night crowd, where the age was significantly higher and what passed for a dress code was practiced, and then there was the Sunday afternoon crowd, where one "laid the dust" after the sporting endeavor, which merged into the Sunday evening crowd, where one took the wife, girlfriend, or whoever was acquired on the Friday night. There was the Thursday night crowd, where it was strictly after the soccer practice, and the Tuesday night where soccer players "shared" the club with the formidable presence of the lady's whist team. Steven had, during his time, garnered speaking acquaintances with all of these bodies, and Pamela realized that given their infrequent visits to the club, his first action was to renew contact with people he had not seen for a while. Pamela called this his English fix.

He was thus engaged this particular afternoon while Pamela was "getting them in" when Barbara leaned her well endowed chest against the bar, and after looking from side to side confided, " Pam, what's Steve's second name?"

"Jackson." She didn't add it was the same as hers.

"Only," Babs leaned further over, "there's a woman called here for him, said she'd call back in half an hour. She sounded French," she added in a gravedigger's whisper. "If she calls again, what should I do?"

"Just call him to the phone. It's probably his lawyer. Could I have two pints of cider?"

"Sure, Blackthorne or Strongbow? What would he want a French lawyer for?"

"What would you want any lawyer for? One of each please."

"Yeah right."

It was half an hour and two pints of cider later, while Mick Priestley was asking him why he followed the Wolves, when the telephone rang.

"It's for you, Steve." Babs took the telephone off the bar. "You just go through that door and use the store room," she said. "It'll be quieter."

Steven opened the door to a chorus of remarks.

"She's got some bottle[9] calling here. Doesn't she know his missus is here?"

"I didn't know he still had girlfriends up here."

"Well if he does, they're on medication. It must be his sister."

"How would he have a French sister? He's from Coseley."

"I think his dad had a bike."

Steven closed the door and picked up the telephone.

"Poppi?"

"Judith?"

"It is all right calling you at your club?"

"Of course, that's why we have a telephone." Steven nodded his thanks as Barbara passed his pint of cider through the bar door.

"And your wife, she is well?"

"Positively blooming, thank you." *On a pint of cider and the company of five Englishmen, I think she can manage.*

"Good. I have to go back to England."

"Yeah, well obviously, you couldn't expect William to come here to get married."

"Poppi, you're so funny. It is the English, yes? I wanted to see you before I went back, but there is so much, you would not believe, but I can phone you in Arizona. That is all right?"

"That's fine. I'll look forward to it."

"Now I want to ask you something—I want to ask something *of* you," she corrected herself gravely. "Is that the club where you met my mother?"

"It is, I thought you knew that. Is that what you wanted to ask of me?"

"No, it just happened, no, occurred, yes, occurred to me—not happened uh what is it, um." There was a gabble of excitable French. "You are thinking something and something else comes in your thoughts."

"Occurred, something occurred to you, my dear."

"That's it. It just occurred to me, you are very good with the English."

"Yes I've been told I speak it like a native, and what was it you wanted of me?"

"Will you promenade? Shisk, I'm sorry, I'm finding the word."

"I'm glad that wasn't it. Just take your time, I'm quite comfortable." Steven settled down on a beer keg. "Let me think, promenade. I take it you don't want me to take you to the promenade concerts or to the seaside, so you must want me to walk with you—a walk, is that it?"

"Yes, that's it, you accompany me, walk with me."

"Good. Where?"

"At the church, through the chairs through the gap."

"Now you've lost me."

"Have you been drinking, Poppi?"

"No, but it's a thought. Now do you want me to walk with you to the church?"

"No, silly, we ride to the church, in the horse and cart."

"I think you mean a carriage but let's press on." Any further conjecture was cut short by a squeal of delight from the telephone. "I have it all the time." He was about to think, *Lucky girl.* "Listen, *who gives this woman in holy matrimony—I do.* You understand? Please."

"You want," Steven said carefully, "me to walk you down the aisle to give you away. If that is indeed what you want, I would be honoured and privileged."

"Oh, thank you, Poppi, I am so happy, but you, twenty-one years without a daughter and then she's an imbecile."

"You are no sort of imbecile," Steven answered sternly, "and don't let me hear you say that again, please. Although you did sound a bit like Hercules Poirot on one of his better days."

"Ah Hercules Poirot. You like the Agatha Christie?"

"Can't get enough of her, my dear."

"Oh I nearly forgot—"

"Something else you want of me?"

"Not surely, but my mother will be with us in England, but she will be with a friend, so your wife doesn't have to worry. We can have dinner together with William."

"That will be very nice." It never occurred to him that Pam *should* worry.

"So I will tell the choreographer that you will walk me down the alley and give me in holy matrimony, yes?"

"You can tell whoever you want, my dear."

"And I will phone you in Arizona."

"Yes, you have the number?"

There was another tirade of French. "I could get it off the flunkies, but so much fuss. You give it to me?"

He recited their telephone number, including the international code, and had her read it back to him,

"I will like having a father. You will give my regards to your wife?"

"I will." He would have preferred something warmer, but he merely said, "Good night, Judith."

"Good night, Poppi."

He picked up the telephone and handed it through the doorway to Barbara and then retrieved his glass which, not surprisingly, was empty.

****

Eddie, as usual had volunteered the services of Tina, his house mate, as cook, and so they dined with them. After she had refused any offer of help, Steven insisted on taking them to Captain Bimbo's for a drink and some pool. Steven himself nursed one beer all evening, as he was driving, and surprised the company by announcing that they would have to take their leave just after Eddie had sunk the black.

"You leaving already?" Eddie was disappointed that none of his admirers had put in an appearance. "Let's have one more game."

"Right, one game and then we really must go."

By the time Eddie had returned from the bathroom and surreptitiously checked the parking lot, Steven had racked up the balls, an expression he always found slightly vulgar.

"So, why do you have to leave early?" Eddie broke the rack, sinking one of the stripes.

"We have a big day tomorrow."

"What have you got a lunch date with—shit!" He had just missed an easy shot and glared at his stick before replacing it.

"Right, red, corner pocket." Steven pocketed the named ball, followed by the blue, green, red, and yellow. When he missed the purple, Eddie had disappeared.

"He's outside talking to a girl," Pamela informed him from the bar.

"Well at least he's not smoking." Steven settled down on the bar stool to await Eddie's pleasure, which transpired to be Liane, who they had met before, so after Eddie had reintroduced them, he consented to take his shot, which he duly missed.

"I'm sorry." Steven relinquished the bar stool. "What am I on?"

"Solids."

"Am I?" He surveyed the table. "I'm doing rather well, aren't I?" he said to the amusement of most of those present.

"So, you were going to tell me who you're going to have lunch with tomorrow."

"Wendy Mulligan, are you any the wiser?" Steven tried for the purple and missed.

"She's that hot chick at Media Partners you got those British Jazz CDs copied for. So why do you have to leave early?"

"That's the one, but I don't think her husband would appreciate the hot chick bit. And we have to leave early because I, we, have to go to the British Consulate first."

"Sure Dad sure, red—top corner, blue—side. Steven's only his family name you know." This for the benefit of Liane. "His real name is James Bond."

"Without the hairpiece. Oh bad luck, did I put you off?"

Steven finally fell on his sword, or rather his pool stick, by scratching on the black, thus ending the game, and so after apologies to Liane for having to leave so soon and good-byes to Eddie, they left, but only after the admonishment, "The next time you come up either stay off that peyote or bring me some."

The following morning after telephoning Media Partners and confirming that Mrs. Mulligan would be available for lunch, they fought the early morning traffic, and after enlarging Pamela's vocabulary by one or two Anglo-Saxon expletives they finally made it to the British Consulate. This time, however, there was no scurrying with the masses to find a parking space. With a mention of "Middleton-Scriven's expecting us" and a flash of his Arizona driving license, they were ushered through. "Thank you, sir, would you see Miss Joanne, the seventh floor?"

"A hyphenated name *does* work with you guys," Pamela observed tartly.

"I think there's more to it than that, love," Steven corrected gently. "Did you see that badge on his collar? Royal Corps of Commissionaires. I could have been one if I'd behaved myself." He carefully backed the car into a parking spot while Pamela enjoyed her usual last word.

"I shudder to think what you could have been if you behaved yourself, my sweet. I mean, look where we are through your misbehaving yourself. It'll be nice to see Joanne again."

The feeling was apparently mutual, as Joanne's face lit up on their arrival. "Pamela, Mr. Jackson, how nice to see you again. I'll just take Mr. Jackson through and then we can have some tea. It is tea you take, isn't it? It's you"—she turned a look of censure on Steven—"who takes the coffee."

As on the last occasion, they didn't get either. Steven didn't think it was relevant, but he nevertheless allowed Joanne to escort him up a staircase to a room that seemed to be directly above the reception area. Whoever had briefed the commissionaire had apparently had a word with Joanne, or perhaps the commissionaire had informed them of their arrival because this time there was no waiting for the light to go off or

71

on. Joanne rapped the door smartly and opened it to announce, "Mr. Jackson, gentlemen." She held the door open for Steven, smiled him through, and hurried back to tell Pamela the rest of the good news.

The character behind the desk was the same one who had tried to hustle Steven into giving a blood sample, while the other occupant of the room was gazing out of the window at the demolition of the Ambassador Hotel across Wilshire Boulevard. All Steven could see of him was a trim silhouette and a chalk-striped back. As neither of them saw fit to favor him with their names, he christened them Desk and Window respectively. Of Doctor Ferguson there was no sign.

"Mister Jackson." The Desk even managed a wintry smile, so they must want something *else* from him. "Please." He indicated a chair in front of the desk. "How are you?"

"Keeping busy," said Steven pointedly as he leaned on the back of the chair. "Where's the Doctor?"

"He'll be with us shortly, but first a few questions."

"A few *more* questions? What else could you possibly need to know? Besides the fact that I prefer women, and given my reason for being here, I'd have thought that was obvious."

The smile stayed valiantly in place. "Yes of course, just a few details. Have you ever been incarcerated since you've been in the United States?"

Well, Lord cosset and preserve us, thought Steven, *they thought a light dance through Jackson's private life and then dump him back in the desert when the real father surfaced, but now after the DNA test and me seeing Judith* and *Judith accepting me as her father, we need to know what I've been getting up to now in the States.* He vaguely heard the Desk mumbling to do the right thing and embarrassing the crown when he suddenly said, "What's the matter, the Yanks wouldn't play?"

There was a silence in the room, which attested to the fact that his shot wasn't very wide of the mark. "Now I don't have much time."

"Are you taking your wife to the seaside again?" Without turning his head from a perusal of Wilshire Boulevard and the construction going on across the street, the Window decided to join the conversation. He made the word seaside sound particularly foul.

"What I do after I leave here, when I leave here, what I've done before I came here, and what I tell you while I'm here is only what I choose."

What happened next was so sudden and quiet that it surprised all of them and had a sense of unreality. Steven moved so quickly across the carpet that the first thing the Window knew of it was when he felt a slight breath on the back of his elegant neck, "They used to meet there after a hard day's filming."

"They who?" The Window was almost able to keep the slight tremor out of his voice.

"The Ambassador." Steven nodded his head at the scene of activity opposite. "Clark Gable and Carole Lombard, an afternoon tryst after a hard day's filming, and why not, they were married? Most people associate the Ambassador with RFK being shot in the kitchen or Xavier Cugat playing in the Cocoanut Grove, but I prefer the thought of old Carole stroking Gabie's fevered brow after a trying day on the set. They called him the king, you know. Of course, that was before Elvis Presley."

The next time Steven spoke, his voice sounded so distant that the Window was forced to unbend enough to display his aquiline profile to the room in order to hear him as Steven had resumed his former position, leaning on the back of the chair.

Steven had been winding himself up for this ever since he saw the manila folder on the desk, and he wasn't going to slow down now. "Right, I've had two prosecutions for DUI, that's driving under the influence of drugs or alcohol," he confided

73

to the Desk, "I've been fired for stealing, although they could never prove it or they would have prosecuted me, and what else? Oh yes, this side of the pond I'm a Pittsburgh Steelers fan and over there I'm a Wolves supporter. Now do you pair run to names?"

"I don't think that is necessary," said the Window in another display of verbosity.

"You want to know everything from my post office box number to the name of our bull terrier bitch, so," he gave a chilling smile, "humor me."

The Desk, without needing to consult the Window, said, "I am Gerald Craven, and my colleague at the window is Simon Bryant."

"We had a commanding officer called Bryant once. Nice chap, but he'd got this high-pitched voice, so everybody called him Flossie. A bit cruel really, but I suppose that's the best we could come up with on short notice. So," he took his jacket off, "you'd better call your geriatric Scottish vampire in so I can get on with my life."

Surprisingly, the Desk did just that. He lifted the telephone receiver in front of him and spoke. Steven noticed he didn't identify himself. "Could you ask Doctor Ferguson to step in?" After a brief interlude, there was a tentative knock on the door, which opened to admit the good doctor. Steven was sure he was wearing the same clothes as before and probably carrying the same instruments, hopefully sterilized.

"Help yourself, Doctor." Steven rolled up his sleeve. "Make sure you get enough, because that's the only chance you get."

"Yes, er, quite. If you'll just roll up your—oh, you have done. Well, could you clench your fist? That's fine. Just a little prick."

"That's quite all right, Doctor," said Steven, all sweetness and light. "Little pricks don't bother me."

With surprising dexterity, Doctor Ferguson extracted two vials of Jackson blood, and with a brief nod to the audience, quit the stage.

"Well, Mister Jackson." The Desk closed the manila folder. "I don't think we need trouble you further."

I wouldn't count on that, old darling, Steven thought, by now sure that they were not privy to Judith's decision to have him walk her down the aisle. "No trouble at all, gentlemen, I'm sure, anything I can do. Good day to you."

Steven had already collected Pamela from Joanne (they were actually showing family photographs to each other), took his leave of the commissionaire, and departed along Wilshire Boulevard en route to lunch with Wendy Mulligan before Simon Bryant left the demolition of the Ambassador Hotel to the professionals and was about to relinquish the window. "Quite a little shit, hm?"

"Quite, sir." Gerald Craven finished making a note and closed the folder. "But he does seem to have the ear of his daughter, and she seems quite a strong personality."

"Well, better that than too far the other way. If she wants her own way, it might not be the best, but at least it's hers and not the next half dozen people she speaks to like you-know-who. Has any thought been given to some sort of title or something? Not quite a K but enough to keep him quiet like that actor chap who was rambling on the telly about the SNP."

"Might be a bit of a problem actually, sir." Gerald Craven deftly deflected any blame from himself. He had actually done his homework, which included boning up on Steven Jackson's military history in far greater depth than Charles Chaddersly-Corbet had seen fit to (due to the fact that at the time of Chadders' involvement, Steven was not seriously considered as Judith's father, just someone who had enjoyed her mother's favors). He had also lunched with old Hardwick from Chancery who was a veritable hoard of information on soccer.

"Apparently," he said with affected nonchalance, "when Mr. Jackson was about to leave the army, he had the usual interview with the RO, sorry, resettlement officer, and the RO was supposed to make a token attempt at reenlistment. Obviously it was seldom, if ever, taken up once they got that far, but they had to go through the motions like when a divorce lawyer asks you if there's any chance of reconciliation after he's already banked your retainer."

"Brown jobs," supplied Simon Bryant helpfully, "and I take it Mister Jackson didn't see fit to serve the Queen any further?"

"Actually his words were, 'I've had nine years of you people ordering my life. I think I can take it from here.'"

"Yes, sounds a right bolshie bastard, and what was the response?"

"I quote, 'Reenlisting Corporal Jackson would be as ill advised as having to deal with Corporal Hitler or Corporal Bonaparte again.' Bit strong that?" There was no response, so he continued, "They seemed to have had a history, something to do with rugby, but his Officer Commanding really wanted to keep him, so he was offered a promotion to sergeant, but he refused on the grounds that they didn't offer Stan Cullis a knighthood."

"Stan Cullis?"

"I think that was his OCs response, sir, but he said that ignorance was no excuse, and he proceeded to give him a lecture on Stan Cullis. He was captain of England and Wolverhampton Wanderers before the war and then went on to manage them until the early sixties, quite successfully apparently, but there was a South African bit of nonsense. Besides, we didn't win the world cup until sixty-six. Until then soccer managers—well."

"You mean"—Simon Bryant regained the window and looked northward up Wilshire Boulevard, as if to reassure himself that Steven had indeed left—"he actually refused preferment because the manager of his local soccer team didn't get a knighthood?"

"Apparently so, sir."

"Yes, quite a shit. Well," he squared his shoulders as though a weight had been lifted from them, "it's their problem over the pond now. God help us and preserve us from a home posting, what?"

"And so say all of us, sir."

As Steven would have said, I wouldn't count on it, old darlings.

6~Flight from the Media

FTER GIVING WENDY MULLIGAN THE two jazz CDs and a lecture on the contribution of British jazz to American music over lunch, and having by mutual consent "had enough of California," they made their way back to Mohave Valley. This time Steven drove to give Pamela a chance to be calmed by the desert. Once back, they regained their usual balance with customary ease. They both watched the sunset play its usual tricks on the Boundary Cone, and they both worked on Steven's book. Steven studiously avoided the television, as the Olympics was still on, although he did, while trying to find if there was anything about Judith on the television, see Brian Whelps win again, but managed to switch the set off before Mrs. Whelps started jumping up and down.

They swam, they lay in the sun, they made love, and every Saturday night, they watched the British comedies on the Public Service Channel, and if it was provided by the BBC, to see how many double-barreled surnames they could spot in the credits. Judith called about every two weeks to keep them informed of the wedding preparations and also to reassure herself of her father's continued good health. It was on the last call she told them about the engagement. It was to be a very private affair, and he was not to feel slighted, as he and "Pamela," as his wife had belatedly become, had not been officially invited. It was shortly after this that an incident occurred that foretold that their lives would never be the same again.

It started seemingly innocuously enough with a telephone call from the *Arizona Republic*. Steven was in the midst of explaining that they already subscribed to the *Arizona Republic* when the caller explained that he was not a salesman but a reporter and asked if he could have a few brief comments on his daughter's engagement to the future King of England.

"What?" Steven subjected the ear piece to a piercing look until he seemed to grasp the situation. Then he replaced it, took a deep breath, and shouted, "Who gave you our telephone number?"

After a surprised pause, he was informed that if it wasn't common knowledge among the journalistic fraternity, then it soon would be, so Steven should really start making his plans. Now if he could have a few words. He got just that, Steven explained that the future Queen of England was Belgian, a lawyer, and he had met her mother at the British and Dominion Social Club after a dance to finance the soccer team, the proceeds of which (the dance not the meeting) were $451, and that was all he was getting, which was more than anyone else. Then he said, "Now if I could be excused, I have some plans to make."

The telephone receiver was barely back in the cradle when he yelled for Pam without realizing she was standing right behind him. "Anything wrong?"

"Nothing we can't handle. Could you get a suitcase packed, just the essentials? We'll buy anything else we need. We're going to visit Eddie, among others."

While Pamela was thus occupied, Steven made a call to his neighbor. "Glen, a bit of a family emergency. Could you look after the trees and keep an eye on the place? ----No, don't worry about the pool. We'll acid wash it when we come back." *If we come back*, he thought.

"Sure, are you expecting anybody?"

"Nobody at all, thanks," Steven replaced the receiver, wishing he could be there if anyone tried to violate the Jackson property.

He called Garry next and explained why they wouldn't be at church for a few weeks and not to worry, they'd be in touch. After speaking to Lorraine at the National Bank of Arizona and confirming that there would be two thousand dollars available in cash from their account, Steven finally called Eddie and remarkably, didn't have to speak to his answering service. "Eddie, Steve, got three questions for you: are you at home, sober, and have you got a credit card with at least two thousand dollars on it?"

"Yes, yes, and why?"

"Is Tina there?"

"Yes, and that's four questions."

"It'll be better if she uses hers then there's no direct connection through you to your mother. What I want you to do is book a motel room, a decent one, for three nights in your name, or as I say, Tina's would be better, and also get me a cell phone with unlimited minutes on it."

"What's happening, Steve, because you're really scaring the shit out of me? Have you killed somebody?"

"Not lately. The thing is, the story has got out about your stepsister and William and the press are about to descend on us, so I want to get your mother out of this. By the way, could you call Robert and tell him?"

"I—sure, but I never believed you. So you really do—"

"Yes."

"And she really is?"

"The engagement's about to be announced."

"Holy shit, I never believed you. I thought you were just bullshitting."

"Don't worry, I usually am. After all, I never dated Angie Dickinson or Sharon Laurence or Sybil Danning."

"Who's Sybil Danning?"

"Another blonde I didn't date. I'll see you in about four hours."

"Sure, Dad, sure. Be safe."

Uncharacteristically, Steven hung up without asking Eddie if he wanted a couple of words with his mother.

So after collecting two thousand dollars from the National Bank of Arizona, calling at Mohave Valley Post Office to hold their mail, and depositing their library books at the library next door, Steven and Pamela disappeared.

Glen looked after Steven's trees, and anyone who approached the house was told that there was nobody home, and no, although he'd been asked to keep an eye on the place, he didn't know where they were and didn't ask because he minded his own business and why didn't they do the same. Reporters who made their way to the Mohave Valley United Methodist Church fared no better. Yes, they were told by Becky, the church secretary, Steven and Pamela attended church regularly, a lovely couple. Always helpful with the rummage sale or the recycling for the foreign missions, but no, she didn't know where they were. They had told someone that they'd be away for a couple of weeks, but he had respected their privacy and hadn't asked where. "After all, that's what people come out to the desert for, isn't it, honey?"

Garry had also told Pastor Gene, and so he was forewarned when the congregation was enlarged by a number of smartly dressed strangers. He made a point of asking the good Lord to look after Pamela and Steven, wherever they were, and to protect them from undue interference in their lives.

The British and Dominion Social Club also did not escape scrutiny by the fourth estate but dealt with it in their own way. One journalist with an exaggerated idea of the power of the press, especially his contribution to it, expected the club to furnish him with liquid refreshment. The president that year was a feisty Glaswegian, Joe Donnelly. Some of his best friends were English, he informed the sharply dressed interloper, but he could never understand their habit of buying drinks for strangers, but nevertheless, he was welcome as a guest. Some of the stranger's more resourceful colleagues were already at the bar trying to turn the conversation round to the missing pair.

A few of the older hands said surely they remembered Steven with the good-looking dark-haired girl, but they couldn't remember anything about a daughter. Although he did put it about a bit, not as much as Barnsy, but then Barnsy was a legend. But Steven had his share—of course, that was before he met Pam. As the drinks flowed, some of it almost not paid for by the gentleman of the fourth estate, Steven's adventures became more lurid. There were even some who attested that they could show the very spot on the parking lot where the deed was done. No one was quite sure how they came by this information, and the suggestion that a Wedgewood Blue plaque was going to be erected there never got the attention it deserved.

No one who had been privy to these stories would associate the hero, and no one in Mojave Valley connected the missing retiree/unpublished writer with the stocky, slightly balding character who was at that moment less than a hundred miles away enjoying the swimming pool of Don's Turf Lodge Motel in the company of his statuesque wife or girlfriend, but then people who saw Pamela first very rarely noticed Steven, but it was afterward remarked that he was very polite to the staff.

They watched television, and the Republican party conference was by now overshadowed by the approach to the Louisiana shoreline by hurricane Gustav, which was good and bad for the Republican Party, George Bush did not attend the opening day, as he wanted to concentrate on Hurricane Gustav, but considering his reaction to Hurricane Katrina, it was doubtful whether the good people of the Gulf Coast were reassured. John McCain was still looking for a running mate, but Mrs. McCain did give a speech urging all Americans to give generously to the victims of Gustav in an outfit that would have kept the average family in New Orleans for six months. Brian Whelps was still winning, or the tape of him winning was still being run. They even had one of him winning underwater, and his mother was still trying to jump up and down, fortunately not underwater. Using his newly acquired cell phone, Steven contacted Glen and was assured that some suspicious characters had been summarily dismissed. To Glen all strangers were suspicious, but this time his fastidiousness had not been misplaced.

His study of the answering machine owner's manual was now bearing fruit, with a "just got to pop into the office for an hour," he would leave his wife anointing her body with sunscreen oil and drive the few miles to as near to Disneyland as he could find a parking place. He would then lock the car and become ostensibly one of the people he hated most, those wandering about muttering into cell phones. In reality, he was calling his answering machine and ruthlessly deleting all requests from the press to call him back and answering the remainder. If he didn't know them, it would be collect, as Eddie had warned him about the horrendous prices charged by the cell phone companies for outgoing calls, and Steven assumed that if they wanted to speak to him badly enough they would accept the call. If this procedure took more than a few minutes, he would wait until he'd walked a further block before he called again. These elaborate procedures were designed so that no one monitoring his calls could pinpoint his location. When Pamela had ventured the suggestion of a little paranoia, she had been met with the alternative that the captain of the *Titanic* could have been a little more paranoid about icebergs.

One of the collect calls that was accepted was from someone representing NBS, *The Gee Nelo Show,* and Steven listened politely (he was sitting in the shade of an enormous palm tree outside the Anaheim Convention Center at the time) to such phrases as, "Looking forward to working together," "interesting guests he can interact with," and "host sympathetic to his cause." Steven was too polite to ask what his cause was supposed to be, but after five minutes of listening to this vocal treacle oozing out of the phone, he just as politely asked why money had not been mentioned. After a shocked silence, he was told that *that* was not the way it worked, the value, prestige of appearing on the NBS—in fact, some people actually paid to "give their side of the story."

"I'm sorry, sir, I've forgotten your name," Steven inquired mildly.

"My name's Wayne."

"Well, Wayne, have you ever heard of a company called Media Partners?"

"I don't believe I have. Is this your agent?"

"No, Wayne, it's not my agent, but I suggest you read the top left-hand corner of your paycheck next time you to get one because Media Partners is the biggest, and to their mind the best, payroll company that services the entertainment industry, and one of their clients is the NBS. You may also be interested to know, Wayne, that I spent three happy years working for the said company, so I know exactly how much your boss, his minions, *and his guests* get. Do you know ...?" He mentioned a well-known attorney. "She's the one who made that statement about it not being a crime to be poor. Well I know, to the dollar, how much her appearance on your show distanced her from being indicted. Are you still with me, Wayne?"

Wayne rallied manfully. "Of course, some people get paid, but you're in the position where any publicity for your book would far outweigh any fee."

Why would he assume that Steven was writing a book?

"And just how many literary agents would be in this studio audience at five-fifty an hour? Not many, I suspect, and those watching the show at home are probably asleep by the time the first guests are introduced. That's why I watch it, and those who can get through the monologue probably can't read. It's not exactly University Challenge, is it? So, Wayne, lovely chatting to you but I've got to return someone's call from *The Letterman Show*. I would prefer Charlie Rose on PBS, but there you go. So see what you think I'd be worth, and have your people call my people. I've waited years to say that. Take care, Wayne."

On another occasion, Judith left three messages, each one rightfully more frantic than its predecessor. He had waited until he had taken Pam to the beach before he answered her, as he surmised that walking up and down Bay Shore Drive would be sufficient frustration for anyone who was trying to locate him.

"Poppi, where are you? I've been calling your house but you're not there. I'd thought I lost you already."

He assured her that he was not lost to her and explained briefly the situation regarding their flight from the media.

"That is very sensible," she announced gravely. "I can appreciate the problem. Fortunately, William takes care of all that for me. He's so good at it. You cannot imagine."

"I'm sure he is." Steven was, by this time, walking along Second Street. "Yes I'm sure he would be. Of course, he's had the training, you see, and he's also got the charm that I haven't got, but I'm glad he's taking care of you."

"No charm? Poppi, don't flirt with me, I'm your daughter, and yes, William takes care of me. I'm looking forward to you meeting him. So you are all right? And you and Pamela are still coming over? 'Over the pond,' yes?"

"'Though hell should bar the way,' my dear. In fact, I've got to call the flunkies and—"

"Can I interrupt you?"

He involuntarily shrugged before he realized she was six thousand miles away. "Yes, but it's not a good habit to get into, please—"

"'Though hell should bar the way.' That is from where?"

"It's from a poem called 'The Highwayman[10].' He's just about to go rob a stagecoach to get the housekeeping money, and he's taking leave of his girlfriend 'the landlord's red-lipped daughter,' and he's telling her that he'll be back. 'Look for me, my darling, watch for me, my darling, I'll come to thee, my darling—though hell should bar the way.'" (This last quote garnered a long, speculative look by two girls who had just exited from the Sportsman's Bar.)

"So romantic. And did he get back with the housekeeping money?"

"I'm afraid not." Steven involuntarily realized he'd left Pam long enough and did an about turn, almost colliding with the erstwhile patrons of the Sportsman's Bar. He apologized and received smiling assurances that there was "no harm done" before he returned to the conversation. "Sorry about that, where was I?"

"No housekeeping money."

"Yeah right, somebody grassed on him."

"Grassed on him?"

"Betrayed him. One of the servants at the Inn, an ostler, he looked after the horses, who nursed a dark passion for the landlord's daughter, betrayed him to the authorities, and they shot him."

"Shot him, dead?"

"Dead."

"And did she marry the ostler?" inquired the ever-practical Judith.

"I don't know. The poem ended when she was still waiting for her lover at her bedroom window."

"So sad. You have a thing about sad things I think, Poppi— 'The Highwayman' and La Boheme, I think if you were a woman you would be Madame Butterfly, waiting for Lieutenant Pinkerton, but Pamela makes you happy I think."

"Yes she brings out the best in me and if I was a woman we wouldn't be having this conversation."

"You are so funny. But I'm glad—and you have to call the flunkies?"

"Yes, but I wanted to speak to you first. They will probably want to arrange for me to come over the pond for the rehearsals and all that stuff, but I'm negotiating an appearance on a television talk show, if that's all right with you."

"You'll get paid for this talk show?"

"Believe it."

"Then by all means, you can buy me a drink when you get to London."

"There's this tradition that when a future queen has a drink with her father, she picks up the check."

"So many traditions. I've never heard of that one."

"I know, I just made it up."

"Poppi, you are crazy, but seriously, do the television show. It's a pity I am so involved with the wedding; I could be your agent. My mother would approve." He wondered why she thought he would need her mother's approval. Perhaps it was a Jewish thing. After he had said his good-byes to Judith and gave her his telephone number to be used in an emergency, and to be given to no one else, especially the flunkies, he returned to Pam and voiced his curiosity. For once, she was less than helpful. Turning to look at him over a well-oiled, shapely flank, she said, "Perhaps she never quite gave up on the child support."

7~Dennis, Lonny, and Cowboy

THE NEXT DAY, STEVEN AGAIN left Pamela ensconced at the swimming pool and made his way to "the office." This time it was Simon Bryant who had demanded rather huffily that Steven got in touch with him urgently. Steven couldn't remember if he was the Desk or the Window. Probably the only difference was the size of Her Majesty's photograph in their respective offices. There certainly wasn't much difference in Steven's estimation. In accordance with this, he chose to answer in the lee of a giant rubbish skip near Angel Stadium, to the concern of three winos who were about to use it as a bar, but with the assurance that Steven was not expecting to stay for lunch and five dollars for the inconvenience, he was accommodated.

"Bryant!"

"Steven Jackson here, Mister Bryant, returning your call. How are you? Sound a bit liverish."

"I've left three calls on your answering machine."

"So I'm answering all three at once. What can I do for you?"

But Simon was obviously not as easily mollified as Steven's newfound friends, "I would appreciate it if you would kindly make yourself more readily available, as there is a lot to discuss."

"Yes, someone earlier said that I would make a good Madame Butterfly."

"What?"

"You know—'One Fine Day'—waiting by the telephone if they had telephones then. Actually, Mister Bryant, we're taking a short sabbatical. Madam has taken a fancy to a little sea air, so as we have such a lot to discuss, what do you want?" said Steven in a voice that suggested that the small talk had run its course.

"Very well, first there is the question of the transept guests. You have been allocated five places."

"The what guests?"

"The transept guests," Simon Bryant explained with studied patience, "are the honoured guests, usually close personal friends or relatives, who occupy the transept near the altar where the actual ceremony takes place, and as they will be in the public eye, and naturally some people are more accustomed to being in the public eye than others—"

"In other words," suggested Steven helpfully, "you need five people who won't let the side down. Well, I think my two sisters and their respective husbands can be relied on not to steal the hymn books and yes, I think President Obama can be trusted to behave himself."

"Who?"

"President Barak Obama. You must have seen him. Been on the telly a lot lately, I would have liked Enoch Powell[11], but he's no longer with us, but I think President Obama will come. Unless, of course, McCain gets elected in spite of that waste of space he's saddled himself with."

"Actually," said Simon Bryant, "he's already invited as head of state, but I suppose you will be bringing your wife."

"Of course. Would you rather I brought yours?"

"Would you please be serious?"

"So how many are coming from Judith's mother's family?"

"I'm led to believe five, the same as yours."

"I've been to Saint Paul's. That transept is quite big. How many do you think it holds?"

"I have no idea."

"I think you do, but when I was last there, it was in the company of my nephew. He's a quantity surveyor, and he reckons about one hundred and fifty." (Steven did have a nephew who was a quantity surveyor, but the only time he had been to Saint Paul's was in the company of Pamela, who, for all her qualities, was not a quantity surveyor.)

"I really don't see—"

"That leaves one hundred and forty. I was thinking of this movie I saw with Elizabeth Ashley, her husband was suffering from amnesia and they'd thrown this big party, and he asked how many of the guests were friends and she said 'all of them,' and he said 'we must have real problems if we have this many personal friends.'" He turned and winked at the winos. "Makes you think, doesn't it?" He heard the clearing of the throat from six thousand miles away.

"I suppose you'd better tell me where you are."

"I'm sorry, Mister Bryant, I didn't catch that. I was still thinking of Elizabeth Ashley."

"I said we need to know where you are."

"You told me to be serious."

"Yes?"

"Well seriously, bollocks … I've been in touch with my daughter, and you can get in touch with me by the method already employed, but as for giving you my location, we are not going to have the press descending on us as happened last time. Now if you think for some reason that I'm not going to show up, have you ever had a daughter, Mister Bryant?"

"No." With his reaction to the mention of a wife, Steven had suspected, and now he was sure, that any relationship Simon Bryant had was not one that would garner children.

"My daughter has been kept from me for twenty-one years, and I have only known her a matter of weeks, but in that time she has become very dear to me, and I will be there to walk her down the aisle in front of the whole world, 'though hell should bar the way.' Now what else do you want to know?"

With Simon Bryant duly chastened, they proceeded to discuss the ticklish problem of accommodation, as the wedding had been provisionally set for May (Steven wondered if they had to book St, Paul's), the rehearsals of the "principals" would be in April. Then, of course, there would be the question of fitting for a morning suit, unless Mister Jackson had one. Of course Mister Jackson had one, he was informed. He wears it to clear the brush in 110 degrees. Of course he's not got a morning suit; now who's not being bloody serious?

"Quite, but HMG would be inclined to reimburse the cost of hiring one if, of course, it was returned undamaged."

"Right, I'll remember not to get into any fights in it, but then again, I think I can afford to hire a suit for my daughter's wedding."

"And accommodation, you can either fly over for the first rehearsal and stay here until the actual event or fly back to America and return in time for the dress rehearsals. Actually, we would prefer the former. I will estimate the cost and let you know how much HMG would be prepared under certain circumstances to reimburse you."

"I'll let you know, Mister Bryant, but I think we can let Gee Nelo sponsor both mine and my wife's expenses."

"Who is Gee Nelo?" was the cautious response.

"He runs a talk show in Los Angeles, and we're currently negotiating for an appearance."

"I don't think HMG would be happy about that."

"I'm not sure how happy Gee Nelo would be. Do you know a Mister Charles Chaddersly-Corbett, known to his intimates as Chadders?" Steven inquired mildly.

"I do, but I fail to see—"

"Well Chadders would tell you that I will be cooperative with you people, for my daughter's sake—who, by the way, I have been in touch with and got her approval. But the happiness, or otherwise, of HMG is of singular unconcern to me. In fact, if I can screw what I intend to out of this, I'll be happy enough for both of us, so let me know when you need me and I will make myself available. Now if there's nothing else, I need to get back and turn my wife over before she's done too much."

By now the three gentlemen of the skip had given up all pretense of ignoring him, and Lenny, who seemed to have elected himself spokesman, as he had worked for NBS, said, "You sure gave that mother some shit. I hope you get on the Nelo show and sting the sucker, he can afford it."

"Thank you." Steven reached into his jacket. "Would you do something for me?"

"Sure, but"—the spokesman of the trio indicated their situation—"what could *we* do for you?"

Steven extracted two twenty-dollar bills. "My daughter's getting married in May. It'll be in the papers. Her name's Judith, and his name's William. I'm Steven, by the way."

"I'm Lonny, this is Dennis, and the one who won't shut up is Cowboy. He used to own the Angels."

"Gentlemen, would you drink my daughter's health? Thank you, and thank you for your hospitality." Had he mentioned the fact that his daughter was an attorney the hospitality might not have been so readily offered, especially by Dennis, the second member of the trio? Dennis had suffered a life-altering injury while working on the 17th Street overpass, not enough to make him dangerous or unable to perform the basic functions but enough to ensure he would never work construction again and vulnerable enough to put his trust in a lazy attorney. By the time he had recovered enough to attend to his affairs, the token compensation had been devoured by the hospital and after "care" bills, and his attorney was not returning his calls. He was seriously debating whether to kill himself or his erstwhile litigator when he met Lonny. Met was perhaps the wrong word. Dennis had just been asked to remove his presence from a bar near the stadium called The Dugout when he saw Lonny, having just received the same rejection as Dennis, about to be relieved of his wallet by two muggers. It could just have easily been the bartender, or his ex-wife, or her boyfriend, who was at that moment taking his ease on the bed that was still on Dennis's credit card. It could even have been Lonny himself just because he was there. However, the sight of them brushing aside Lonny's feeble defense and helping themselves as though it was their right touched a long submerged nerve in Dennis. "Leave him alone."

The larger of the two looked at Dennis, and after noting a possible source of further booty, turned back to his work, ignoring him. That did it—the silent dismissal. With a primeval growl, Dennis launched himself onto the last person who was ever going to insult him. It was the surprise that did it. He threw three punches, of which only one connected, but his impetus carried him forward, and he had just enough presence of mind to lower his head before it came in to contact with the mugger's nose. His partner having remembered urgent business elsewhere, the would-be mugger was driven back, enough to make him sink to his knees where he put his hands over his head, whimpering softly. Dennis stood over him as though debating whether to hit him again. "Right," he said finally. "Get out of my sight before you piss me off."

Having seen him off, Dennis turned to Lonny, who was just struggling to his feet. "Have you got any money left?"

"About twenty dollars." Lonny was about to surrender his wallet when it was nearly struck from his hand, and for a moment, he thought he was going to suffer from the residue of his rescuer's anger.

"I don't want your money. I bet I've made more money than you've ever seen. I meant have you got enough money for a cab. There's a telephone at the end of the alley. Say that you're calling from the bar. They won't send anybody if they think you've been thrown out. Stand at the corner, and when it comes, go and meet it. They won't get out of the cab if they don't have to, lazy bastards. Now brush yourself down. You look like a bum, and you've got blood on your lip. Got a handkerchief? Yeah, you look the sort, now a bit to the right. That's it, I guess you'll do."

After following the staccato instructions and apparently passing muster, with a mumbled thanks, Lonny turned to go.

"Hey, I'm Dennis. I hang out 'round the Dugout if you need me. There's some strange characters 'round here."

After this dramatic start, Lonny and Dennis were drawn to each other as only two of life's victims are, both recognizing the frailty in each other, but Dennis wished sometimes that they could go a day without Lonny telling someone, usually him, that he used to have the anchor desk at NBS. But then, maybe he wasn't perfect.

The way they met Cowboy was less dramatic. In fact, anything less dramatic would be hard to imagine. They were sitting at the back of the Dugout, out of sight of the customers, to appease Tony's sensibilities, eating stale chips while discussing life's contrariness. To "take the edge off the day," Tony had supplied a quart of Michelob in appreciation of their consideration of his clientele, when Cowboy just—arrived. Without money, introduction, or food, he just arrived. Even his name was by courtesy of Lonny. He just walked round the corner of the Dugout, sat on an empty crate, and waited to see what life was going to do to him next.

"What the fuck do you want, sport?" said Dennis amicably enough, but not in a tone to invite intimacy.

"Nothing. I just want to sit here, if that's all right?"

Dennis looked at Lonny, and seeing no violent objection, said, "Go ahead. You eaten yet?"

"I don't know."

"You just can't shut him up, can you?" Dennis said to Lonny.

"Positive mine of information," came the reply. "You want some chips?"

"Sure, thanks."

"Better not give him any beer, though, he looks the sort that would turn ugly when he's got the drink in him," Dennis offered.

"A regular raging bull." Lonny was enjoying the joke. "What's your name? After all, you are eating our chips."

"I don't know."

"I'm Dennis, and this is Lonny, and before he tells you, he used to work for NBS. So you've not got a name. Where're you from? You got folks somewhere?"

Their visitor hung his head and shook it as though the hopelessness of his situation had been brought home to him. In fact, he seemed close to tears.

"It's all right, could be worse." Dennis' tone suddenly sharpened. "You ain't a lawyer, are you?"

This time the head shaking was more vigorous, "Hell no."

"Well that's all right, long as you ain't a lawyer. What shall we call you?"

"What about Gene after Gene Autry?" Lonny was inspired to suggest. "After all, our beach house is on his parking lot. Gene, all right?"

"No," the newcomer said, showing some muscle at last. "It sounds like a girl's name."

"Gene, short for Eugene."

"That sounds like a lawyer."

"Hell right it does. Whoever heard of a cowboy named Eugene? Sounds like a lawyer and a pansy one at that—what?"

Lonny held up an admonishing finger and then pointed it at the nameless one. "Cowboy! Came riding in from the prairie Cowboy."

"Hell yes, Cowboy," Dennis toasted their new arrival. "Maybe a little beer wouldn't hurt. What do you think about that, Cowboy? That Lonny's got brains. Did I tell you he worked for NBS?"

So Cowboy it was.

With the inclusion of Cowboy into their group, life took on an added dimension, while Dennis was the muscle and Lonny was the mouthpiece (always handy when they came in to contact with Anaheim's finest). What Cowboy added was something that neither of them would admit to. He filled the human need of having someone to take care of. Not that he was that much trouble; he was quite content to tag along after them, dreaming his innocent dreams and to do his share of the work. The only exception was when, mercifully infrequently, the name of the late President Reagan came up in the conversation, which would have the effect of producing in him an incoherent rage. When there were no tasks to be performed, they were quite content to adjourn to their "summer cottage," the Dumpster on the parking lot of Anaheim Stadium, and discuss the benevolence of Cowboy's namesake. They were occupied thus when they made the acquaintance of an Englishman who appeared to be using their patio to conduct some heated negotiations through his cell phone. They tolerated this intrusion because of the entertainment value of the conversation and he showed his appreciation by giving them forty dollars to drink his daughter's health.

8~Another Hard Day at the Office

TEVEN, FOR IT WAS NONE other, was meanwhile deleting the remainder of the entries on his answering machine while driving along Katella Boulevard when something Judith had said stopped him. He called the number of Luna Personal Representatives.

"Luna Personal Representatives, Darlene speaking. Can you hold?"

"No."

"How may I help you?" she said without missing a beat.

"Steven Jackson returning Mister Wernick's call."

"I'm sorry, Mister Wernick is in conference at the moment. Can I get him to call you back?"

"No." Steven's shortness was probably due to the fact that he was being one of the other characters he hated most, those who talk on the cell phones while driving. "I need to sell myself and Mister Wernick offered to do it for me, so I'll call *him* in half an hour, and if he's still too busy, I'll get another pimp, and you have a nice day, Darlene."

As he didn't envisage the call lasting long, he used Captain Bimbo's as an office and waited until the half hour was up before using one of the benches supplied for the benefit of the smokers to call Luna Personal Representatives.

"Luna Personal Representatives, this is Darlene, will you—"

"Steven Jackson, is Mister Wernick there?"

"Steven! Hi, Solly Wernick, glad to meet you."

"Mister Wernick?"

"Solly please."

"Solly." He sounded greasy enough to be a good agent. "You kindly offered to represent me, and under certain circumstances you may. The contract will be for two months, because after that I intend to disappear into grateful obscurity. By then I'll be forgotten anyway, and I'll want my fee up front, less your cut, of course."

"Well, Steven, it doesn't work exactly like that. You do the interview and you only get paid when it's shown."

"Well that's what we got you for, sunshine, to make it work that way. Did you ever see the movie *Ricochet?*"

"Sure, why?"

"Well I was in that movie as an extra, and my scene was cut due to an artistic difference with the director. I'll tell you about it sometime. The point is, Solly, I still got paid for it, so if I get a contract with the Nelo show, they'd pay me just so that I wouldn't appear on Letterman. *That's* how it works."

"I think you are rather overselling your appearance value here."

"As I said, that's what I've got you for, snowflake. If you can handle it, I'll call you about this time tomorrow and see what you've been able to come up with. Take care, Solly."

****

"Another hard day at the office, my dear?" Pamela greeted him as he got back to the motel.

"I know, it never stops, does it? We'll go down to the beach tomorrow. I need to phone Anne and Pat and tell them about the wedding of their niece and tell them to expect a call from Bryant or one of his lackies."

True to his word, Pamela was already oiled and sprawled elegantly on a beach towel, a straw hat covering her eyes, not too far from the water and the nearest lifeguard by eleven o'clock the following morning, which would be seven o'clock in the evening in England.

"When are you going to do your yuppie thing?" Pam said from beneath her hat. "You know, walking up and down Second Street with your cell phone in your ear, the last of the movers and shakers."

"Actually, my dear, I'm going to call them from here because pound to a penny they'll want to speak to you."

He phoned his elder sister first, "Anne, Steve, how are you?"

"Hello, love, I was just thinking of calling you."

"Well you wouldn't have got me. We're at the beach."

"You're—at—the beach. But I thought you lived in Arizona?"

"Well we had to move here rather sharpish."

"Oh, what have you done now?"

"It's nothing illegal and nothing dangerous. It's a matter of … convenience. The thing is, what are you doing in May?"

"Are you coming to visit us?"

"Not exactly. I want you to come to my daughter's wedding."

"Your daughter's? How did you get a daughter?"

"The usual way, more or less the same way as you got your three sons."

"Nothing about you is usual. So was this girl you had a fling with just before you met Pam—German or Dutch, wasn't she?"

"Belgian, and she had a fling with me."

"Right. Well we could get over to Belgium. I suppose they probably fly there from Manchester."

"Well you won't have to do that. She's getting married in London."

"Let me get this straight—this daughter who I've never heard of before is Belgian and is getting married in London. So that's where her husband comes from. She's marrying a Londoner."

"You could say that. It's Prince William. Hello! Are you still there?"

"Yes, I know where *I* am. It's you I'm worried about. Have you been drinking?"

"No, it's only ten o'clock in the morning."

Anne gave a weary sigh, "Is Pam there?"

"Yes, she's right next to me."

"Good, put her on."

Steven gently put the phone under the straw hat and flopped on to his back, listening to Pam's side of the conversation.

"Hi, honey—Yes, I know, we didn't know. The first we heard was a few weeks ago—Yes, we've had lunch with her. She's beautiful, but then again her mother was quite attractive. Your brother's got good taste in women—Yes, I know he must have been—I don't really know. Why don't you wear what you wore to Carl's wedding? You looked great.—Well I'm just going to get a simple suit, but his lordship is getting full morning suit. Well, honey, we've got to go. We'll be in touch. Bye, honey.— Yes, I'll tell him. Love to Sam. God bless."

Without moving the straw hat, Pam handed the cell phone to Steven. "She says she loves you, look after me, and keep away from those London tarts."

He next dialed his younger sister's number. "Pat, this is Steve. How is Clive?"

"He's married to me."

"But apart from that, all right?"

"You didn't have to call to remind me you're a cheeky sod."

"Are you enjoying your swimming pool?"

"Great, I don't know how we could manage without one. I suppose it's more so with you being in Arizona."

"Well, at the moment we're on the beach. Pam fancied some sea air, and we had to leave Arizona for a while."

Pat's response was so predictable, it almost came out as one word, "OhmyGodwhathaveyoudonenow?"

He repeated his earlier reassurances while reflecting that with all their differences, Pat and Anne had at least one similarity—always thinking the worst of him. "Actually, I called to invite you to my daughter's wedding."

"What daughter?"

"I've only got one."

"How did that happen?"

"Similar to the way your three kids happened, I would imagine. It was a Belgian girl I thought I was love with while I was in between wives."

"And you slept with her."

"More or less, I believe that is the conventional way." He decided not to elaborate on the exact circumstances of the conception.

"Well I've never heard of her."

"You will. The thing is, are you coming to the wedding?"

"Is the wedding in Belgium or America?"

"It's in England, London to be exact."

"It's a pity I'm not still working for the registrar's office. I could have officiated."

"I'm afraid not."

"So it's a church wedding."

Or a synagogue. "Actually, it's in Saint Paul's Cathedral."

There was a forbidding silence and then, "Is Pam there?"

Once again the cell phone disappeared under the straw hat, "Hello, Pat, how's Clive?"

From what Steven heard, the conversation ran along the same lines as to his other sibling.

"We didn't know until three weeks ago. -- Yes, Prince William. -- No, we've not met him yet. --I'll probably wear what I wore at Carl's wedding and Steven's first thing when he gets there is to be fitted for a morning suit. A Mister Bryant will be calling you with the details. He's very nice." She aimed a kick in Steven's direction. "Got to move now, hon. I'll see you when we get there. Love to Clive. Bye."

"What was that about, very nice?" Steven began to break camp.

"Well he probably is to anyone else. You rub him up the wrong way."

"Yes, well, with that third-rate public school accent, if anybody will rub him up the right way, it'll be Pat. She'll probably want his autograph."

Next morning Steven had returned from the office even before Pamela had made her way down to the swimming pool. "I've got to go to Studio City to see Solly, baby. Will you be all right for lunch? He'll probably want to take me to Spargo's to soften me up."

He kissed his wife good-bye, and an hour and half later, he was entering the parking lot of Luna Personal Representatives. As he was approaching the glass doors, a Filipino in a FedEx uniform was leaving and held the door open with his foot. Steven nodded his thanks, thus entering the lobby unbeknownst to the redhead speaking into a telephone and giving him the opportunity to study the best pair of legs he'd seen for one and a half hours. "Right, that'll be Tuesday afternoon definitely. No, that doesn't apply because if it's not here by Tuesday afternoon, you obviously don't want our business badly enough and we'll look elsewhere."

After a decent interval, Steven coughed discreetly, causing her to cover the mouthpiece and uncover her smile. "I'll be right with you," she mouthed silently before returning her attention to the telephone. "That's it, we'll see you Tuesday afternoon or not at all. Now if you excuse me, I have someone waiting. Good-bye."

She turned her considerable attention to Steven. "Now, how can I help you?"

Up close he saw that she was a real redhead, the ones with green eyes, and if she had passed forty, the years had danced gently with her.

"I have an appointment with Mister Wernick. Steven Jackson."

"Yes, Mister Jackson for ten thirty."

"Yes." He noticed that she didn't have to consult anything,

"I know I'm early. I overestimated the traffic, but that's what waiting rooms are for."

"Well you're here, that's the main thing. I think you'll be more comfortable in here."

She opened a door to admit him to a room that was definitely a cut above the lobby. A muted carpet covered most of the floor. There were deep sofas of naugahyde fronted with glass-topped coffee tables, and the walls were adorned with images of an earlier time: Jean Harlow, Laurel and Hardy, and W. C. Fields. There were potted palms in the corners.

"Can I get you coffee, or I suppose you prefer tea?"

"I actually prefer coffee to tea, but any caffeine after ten o'clock makes me go crazy."

"Now that would be something to see. Perhaps some water?"

"That's fine, thank you."

When the water came it was in a carafe complete with a bowl of ice cubes and some slices of lemon, "I'm sorry, I forgot if you wanted ice and lemon, so I thought you could help yourself." She smiled. "Now if you'll excuse me, I've got a couple of chores to attend to."

Steven poured some water and picking up a magazine, settled back on one of the couches. Darlene ensconced herself at a small computer and scrolled down, making adjustments, breaking off twice to answer the phone with identical messages that Mister Wernick would be committed all day but she'd tell him they'd called. All the time, Steven noticed she would glance over at him at short intervals and smile. It was as though she was checking to see if he was still there.

"Excuse me, are you afraid I'm going to escape?"

"Well, if you did, I could hardly tackle you in this skirt."

"Now *that* would be something to see."

She laughed at this, and Steven noticed that she abandoned the computer completely and gave her full attention to him. "So your daughter is to marry Prince William. You must be very excited."

"I haven't had time to think about it much. I've been too busy keeping away from the press."

"Really? I would think she's beautiful. Have you got a photograph of her?"

"Actually, no, I should have asked. You see, I've only met her once, but she is a looker, as was her mother. I've got a photograph of *her.*"

"Your wife lets you keep a photograph of an ex-girlfriend with you?"

"Not *with* me, they're in a shoebox somewhere together with the rest of my dusty memories. She's not *that* tolerant."

"But still she lets you come up here on your own, a good-looking guy like you."

Let's not lose all touch with reality. "Can I ask you a question?" Without waiting for her permission, he went on, "Are you Solly Wernick?"

She opened her green eyes wide. "Do I look like Solly Wernick?"

"No, you look like Rhonda Fleming, but—"

"Excuse me, hold that thought." She picked up a telephone, which apparently hadn't rung. "Yes, oh yes, I'll bring him in right away." She replaced the receiver. "Thanks for the compliment. I've seen photographs of Rhonda Fleming, and Mister Wernick will see you now. If you'll walk this way."

Steven resisted the impulse to make a bad joke and followed her swaying form into the inner sanctum of Solly Wernick of Luna Personal Representatives.

"Mister Wernick, Mister Jackson, --and Jack Draney and Bob Peterson called." Darlene put a piece of paper on the enormous desk and turned to leave.

"Mister Jackson, Steven, if I may. Welcome." Solly Wernick made the difficult journey round the desk, giving Steven the chance to study him, and if Hollywood wanted a caricature of a short, fat, balding, sleazy agent, they need have looked no further. "Has Darlene been looking after you?"

"Better than lunch at Spargo's, thanks." Solly finally made it to him, and when Steven took the proffered hand, it was surprisingly dry and firm.

"That's great. Well, sit, sit." Solly indicated the two client chairs and was about to wheeze his way back to his reclining throne when he apparently thought it was beyond him at the moment and leaned against the desk instead, "Right, as we're both busy, I'll cut to the chase, NBS are willing to offer you a contract for a month, four shows maximum. Is something bothering you Steven?"

"I *am* happily married," Steven murmured as he watched the retreating form of Darlene.

"Steven." Solly apparently decided he was sufficiently rested to circumnavigate his desk and regain his throne. "I will charge a considerable fee in the next month for looking after your interests, so I'll tell you now," he nodded toward the door that had just closed behind Darlene, "tread carefully."

"I'm sorry, no offense meant. Are you and her ...?"

"Me and her? Oh no." The idea seemed to amuse him. "I'm the Pole you wouldn't touch with a ten-foot barge."

Steven joined in the joke, "Very good, I like that. *I liked it better the first time I heard it.* Now, you were saying?"

"Right this is the way it works. NBS will offer you a month contract, four shows maximum, which may include the *Today in LA Show.*"

"So I might get to be interviewed by Anne Curtis. I'd do that for nothing."

"I hope you're joking." Solly's expression indicated that this would be considerably worse than lustful thoughts about Darlene. "There will be a retainer whether you appear or not and an appearance fee anytime an interview is aired, plus there will be residuals if the interview is used after the contract expires and if they want you after a month and if, you're satisfied with my handling of it, we renegotiate."

"So," Steven said carefully, "the retainer I get whether I appear or not? Just as long as I don't appear for anybody else."

"Right! All you have to do is attend a suitability assessment, like a job interview when you've already got the job, and tell anybody who asks, like the newspapers, that you're under contract to NBS." He did a rapid calculation on a sheet of paper and underlined two figures before turning it round and sliding it across to Steven, "The top figure is the appearance fee, per show, the bottom one's the retainer, and the figures are what you get after my fee, the bottom line, baby. All right?"

Steven literally licked his lips. "This would certainly cover the cost of a morning suit and a trip to England." He briefly outlined the conversation with Simon Bryant and the suggestion that the Nelo show would subsidize his participation at the wedding.

"Steven, Steven, listen." Solly leaned forward as far as his girth would allow. "They're going to make a bomb out of this, so get yourself a piece. Everybody else is." And with frightening perception, he asked, "What does your daughter think?"

"I called her just before I returned your call. She approves. In fact, she said that if she weren't so busy, she would be my agent. I think it was that that made me get in touch with you."

A beautiful smile lit up the unlovely features of Solly Wernick, and he leaned back in his chair. He spread his pudgy arms as wide as he could to let Steven know that God was in his heaven and Solly was looking after him, when a sudden thought struck him. "Maybe I should look after you over there, as your daughter will be too busy."

"I don't think that'll be necessary. I think she'll always find time to look out for her old dad, not that I've got any reservations about your performance." He hastened to add, "In fact, I think you've done very well."

"Listen, when you hire Solly Wernick, you're not getting some schmuck. Now Darlene's got the contracts. They are as I've explained them to you, so if that's agreeable, you sign them and you get at least the bottom line. I've got a couple of telephone calls to make, and then we'll have some lunch— here, not at Spargo's. The traffic, right?" Darlene had appeared. "Steven is going to work with us, so get him what he wants to eat, and we'll have some lunch on the patio. And he's going to tell us about his movie career in *Ricochet*."

"There's just one thing, if I may," Steven said as though he was fearful of destroying the carefully formed bonhomie.

"Anything you want, Steven."

"When do I get the check?"

"You sign the contract, Darlene witnesses it, she's a notary public, she dispatches it by special courier to their corporate offices, they're only a couple of blocks from here, and they cut you a cashier's check. I might add, your contract stipulates that your participation and exclusivity is contingent upon the money being in your account. In fact, I could make *three* telephone calls and the cashier's check for the retainer could be in your hands before you leave this office." The chubby arms again spread wide asking what more could Solly possibly do.

"I just have to call somebody in London to make sure I'm free."

"Any problem?"

"I don't anticipate any. You see," Steven winked, "I'm a very good friend of his boss's future wife."

****

"I was an extra in this movie called *Ricochet*, with Denzel Washington and John Lithgow, and this particular scene was set in a fairground, a carnival, right?"

Solly had dealt with Mr. Peterson and Mr. Draney and joined them in the glassed-in patio that was adorned with palm trees and waterfalls. The food had arrived within five minutes, just enough time for Darlene to set the rattan table with silverware, condiments, and glasses of iced water. Steven took another bite of his sandwich (pastrami on a French roll with everything but whipped cream) and chewed it thoroughly, swallowed it, and wiped his mouth before he continued. After all, there was a lady present.

"We were in a scene where John Lithgow had to run past us chased by Denzel Washington—excuse the name dropping. Anyway, this assistant director didn't get on and he kept messing up the scene. He was the worst director I ever worked with." He didn't mention that the only other one was Steven Spielberg. "So there it was, there was this bird and this tall guy on one side of the alley near the Ferris wheel, and there was me on the other side talking to these three women. You get the picture?"

He waited until they both nodded. Solly was chewing his usual skinless breast of chicken on sesame, no mayo. Then he continued, "We were supposed to be there as part of the crowd, looking happy, when John Lithgow came running out of the alley chased by Denzel Washington. One of the women said, 'There's supposed to be a big black guy come running out here with a gun and we're supposed look *happy?*' So there we were, and John Lithgow came running out all well and good, and then before Denzel Washington came out, something went wrong and we had to stand there in T- shirts, because it was supposed to be summer, although it was two o'clock in the morning and it was bloody freezing, and suddenly this tall guy who was on the other side of the alley talking to the bird disappeared—don't ask me where. He'd had enough.

"Anyway, it looked strange, her standing there on her own. I mean, she wouldn't be, would she? So I excused myself from the three ladies and went over and joined this bird. I asked her where this tall bloke had gone. and she just said he'd gabbled something in Spanish and left. Volatile lot these Latins—so I offered to stay with her and—I mentioned it was freezing, didn't I? So I happened to mention this thing I'd learned in the army about body heat, basically a healthy body next to you is the best way to maintain your body heat, and the next thing you know we were kissing. No tongue," he asserted virtuously for Darlene's benefit.

"So Denzel Washington came running out, supposedly chasing John Lithgow. He jostled one of the women opposite and made sure she was all right before he went back to his trailer. I remember I thought that was nice of him. So there were two things, one, how would it look on the movie when John Lithgow came running out and I was talking to these three women and this TLB—"

"TLB?"

"Tall Latin Bloke was chatting to this bird, and hot on his heels came Denzel, only this time I was wrapped up with the bird."

"Fast worker," murmured Darlene in a rare interjection. "And the TLB?"

"Gone like a barmaid's smile at closing time, my dear. Anyway, I was wondering how I could explain to my wife about the ..."

"Heat transference?"

"Exactly. We hired the video, must be about fourteen years later, and you know what? They'd cut the whole scene, nada—zilch ---nothing. But I still got paid for it. I've got the pay slip."

Steven had the feeling he had made a point, but he had forgotten what it was. At that moment, Darlene had to excuse herself, as a special courier had arrived from NBS.

9~"I hope we get to Wembley before that"

BRIAN WHELPS WAS AGAIN DECORATING the television screens. The only difference was, it must have been a recording, because he was commentating on it himself, *"How can you describe someone, even yourself, swimming fifty yards, turning around, and swimming another fifty yards?"*

When his efforts had exhausted him, he switched to a shapely young gymnast, and as it was BBC, Steven wasn't subjected to the vocal orgasms of the "experts."

They had flown from Las Vegas with no more than the usual terrors for Steven and the secret joy for Pamela of having him fully dependent on her and were now ensconced in the Victory Services Club within walking distance of Hyde Park and in close enough proximity to the earthier delights of Paddington.

"When you can tear yourself away, you are to meet your daughter in an hour. Shouldn't you be getting ready?" Pam advanced from the shower far enough into the room to see the nubile young figure on the balance beam. "Thank God for that. I thought you were getting a thing about Brian Whelps' mother."

Steven, with no great effort, dragged his eyes away from the screen to confront the dripping figure of his wife. "*I'm* going to see my daughter and *you're* having a shower?"

"They've got Pot Black on in the TV room, and we must be well turned out. I'm a Jackson now, as you never tire of telling me. Now move yourself. You don't want to keep your daughter waiting."

An hour later, Steven was enjoying his favorite view of London leaning on the parapet and looking across a hundred yards of the Thames to the Royal Festival Hall. A tripper pulled up at the embankment pier, discharging a gaggle of school children. One or two of them offered timid smiles. When he was younger, they would have averted their eyes fearfully. His aura must be gentler these days; must be old age. A line of barges plodded purposely past. It was a pity about the bend in the river or the Houses of Parliament could have been seen and Westminster Pier with Boadicea urging her bronze steeds forward.

To his right would have been the old Hungerford Footbridge. He'd wended his weary way back over that a few times after his less-than-successful forays in to Chelsea and Fulham. At the other end of the bridge there used to be a coffee stall outside Waterloo station where he would console himself with a steak and kidney pie as a substitute for love. That's why love was so important now: the digestion couldn't take the steak and kidney pies.

The new bridge didn't look too bad suspended on those flying supports. He wondered what they'd done with the old one.

"Poppi, you came."

Steven forsook his study of the Thames to turn and see his daughter skipping across the road from the direction of Charing Cross, her face alight in welcome.

"Why would I stay away? Although," he indicated the "London eye" on the opposite bank, "I could do without that."

She hugged his arm. "We'll see what we can do about it."

Pamela and Steven had barely got settled in the Victory Services Club when Judith had called. She wanted a little quality time, she had said, before the madness, just the two of them. Pam was pointedly not invited.

As they walked, he interspersed his conversation with remarks about the passing landmarks. "That footbridge is new. It used to be—the old one, I mean—up against the railway bridge. You don't seem to have any trouble with the paparazzi."

"I am staying in a small hotel in Kensington run by an old solider and his wife. It is quite handy for the palace."

"Yes, it would be. What regiment?"

"What?"

"The old soldier, what outfit was he with?"

"Outfit? What is outfit?" She removed one hand from his arm to make a fluttering movement.

"What military formation did he serve with when he was a young soldier?"

"I shall make a point of asking him." Her hand returned to his arm. "I hope you don't mind, but we're not quite alone." Steven turned his head enough to see two figures who had followed them from Charing Cross. "Do they not look discreet? I would like you to meet my mother. It is a problem, no?"

"Your mother, fiancée, future ma-in-law, Nick the Greek—"

"She's dead."

"Sorry, I meant the Queen. I forgot about Diana. Is there such a thing as grandmother-in-law?" By now they had reached the obelisk, and Steven stopped to consider it, forcing her, and her protectors to do the same. "I thought there were two. We nicked them off some Egyptian."

"Nicked? How is Nicked?"

"Misappropriated, poached, purloined, pilfered, filched, half-inched." He leaned to whisper in her ear. "Stole."

"Like you stole the Suez Canal."

"No we *bought* the Suez Canal. We borrowed the money off the Rothschilds and had to offer the whole of the British government as security. I wonder how much you'd get for this lot. I say 'we,'" he corrected himself, "I don't think anybody from Coseley had much to do with it."

"Perhaps he half-inched one back." She nodded toward the obelisk. "The Egyptian you nicked them off."

"But why would he take just one? Are you making fun of me, young lady?"

"Oh, Poppi." She laughed, a particularly musical sound, and leaned her head against him. "That is what daughters do, but I think we had better move on. We are making my escorts nervous. Your wife is all right?"

"She's fine. She's watching pot black on television in a well-stocked bar with about ten old soldiers for company."

"Pot Black is snooker, yes? William's father taught me."

"Correct—speaking of which, you don't quite hit it off with Pamela. Any reason in particular?"

"Well obviously she took my mother's place in your affection."

"No," he corrected firmly, "your mother had already rejected my affections together with everything else about me. It must have been"—uncharacteristically, his mathematics deserted him—"over a year before I met Pam. I'm sure there should be two."

"Do you want to look for it now? And if you're concerned, we'll drive through Trafalgar Square and see if that sailor is still there."

Despite Judith's sarcasm, he wasn't ready to return to the subject of Lydia. He turned, and with his back to the Thames, leaned against the parapet. "You know, when I was in the army, we were going through this thing when they wanted to disband the Paras, and so to justify our existence, we had to do twice as much as other units. I'm keeping this short."

"Oh please, Poppi," again that peculiar fluttering of her hand, "I'm sure it is ... relevant?"

"Yes, quite relevant, and thank you. Now they had to prove that we could do twice as much in any conditions as anybody else, and so while we were on exercise, we had to work twice as hard for twice as long and for this one particular exercise, I think we'd had two or three hours sleep in four days. When we were driving back from Salisbury Plain, that's when I first saw Stonehenge."

"Stonehenge?"

"That's another story. Anyway, sleep deprivation can do strange things to you, and for days afterward, I had the feeling I'd made a date to meet a girl by Nelson's Column at eleven thirty on March 21, my birthday. I didn't know if I'd actually made a date or it was a dream, but just in case, I took the train up to London and got to Trafalgar Square that night."

"And?"

"She didn't show up. Perhaps I got the night wrong or perhaps ..." He rubbed his forehead as though he was trying to reconnect with a time that was past. "That's it, the time I was thinking of, midnight, but she might have been confused, which midnight, the start of the day or the end, so I decided on eleven thirty, but I don't think I specified a.m. or p.m. I mean, what can you do at eleven thirty at night?"

"I'm sure you would have thought of something," she said with great patience. "This was what year?"

"About '72."

"Well, we didn't see a girl who'd been waiting there for thirty-five years, but I could send one of them," she inclined her head toward her guardians, "to have another look. 'Sorry, Mister Jackson will be a little late—two wives and a daughter late, in fact.' Now about my mother."

"Sorry, I stand chastened and rebuked. Now about your mother, you must realize that, for whatever reasons, she left *me*."

"What *you* must realize," she said as though she was chanting a well-practiced mantra, "when a man and woman split up, the children never—"

"Children? You have brothers, sisters?"

"I'm speaking generally. The children of a failed relationship always feel ... incomplete while there is a chance of a reconciliation, and if one of the parents meets another, regardless if they were so-called 'innocent party,' then that partner is seen as the impediment to the parents getting back together."

"I see, are you sure you're not a divorce lawyer?"

She laughed, and he saw what had obviously captivated William, but then the smile died. "My mother missed you."

"Your mother always saw herself as a victim. Perhaps it's a Jewish thing."

"You know much about Jews?" she said slowly.

"As much as I know about women," he said with another unexpected capitulation. "That's the Savoy, underneath that big clock. Noel Coward had a suite there."

"I'm quite happy where I am. You were going to say something else?"

"I suppose it was the same thing with Ali. I think your mother went back to Ali, if she ever left him, before I met Pam."

"Ali is irrelevant."

"But the letter she sent made it clear she had gone back to Ali."

"I assure you, Ali was never a part of our lives."

"It seems so unfair."

"Life, Poppi," she said with all the sagacity of her twenty-two years, "is often unfair."

"I never thought we could have gone the other way. That's a nice walk. We could have gone as far as Boadicea."

"Boadicea?"

"Yes, Boadicea, a queen of the Iceni tribe. She fought the Romans to a standstill. Never quite conquered them, but she got their attention."

"So," she said slowly, "it's a *statue* of Boadicea, not one of your girlfriends."

"No, but I wouldn't have minded meeting her. I think I would have served her well. In fact, if I'd been one of her commanders, she would probably have prevailed."

"Served." She seized on the word. "I am sure you would. You English have a thing about strong women."

"Oh yes," he agreed, "the last job I had, a woman took over the department and asked me if I minded working for a woman. I told her the three best bosses I had were women, Queen Elizabeth the Second, Margaret Thatcher, and Pamela Jackson. Did your mother ever mention a baseball player from San Francisco?"

"No, never."

"So when she telephoned—oh my." He suddenly turned from her and leaned over the rail. She was going to make a remark about him looking for the lost Obelisk, and then she noticed the tension in his back as though he was about to retch.

"Poppi, are you all right?"

He nodded silently, gripping the embankment rail. Whatever had caused his emotion had obviously exhausted him, for when he turned to her, he seemed reluctant to continue. "Do you mind if we sit down?"

"Of course." She shepherded him gently to a bench in the embankment gardens.

"I'm sorry, it's just life. When you're your age, it's one long laugh, but one day it will make you bloody cry. I think that's from a film somewhere." He seemed to rouse himself. "When am I going to meet this young man of yours? I've got an interview with one of your flunkies on Monday, some details about a preliminary rehearsal, and I fly to LA on Tuesday to meet another tosser from NBS."

"I think I should have a talk with Pamela first. After all, she may be overawed meeting someone famous, do you think?"

"I think you underestimate Pam. After all, you know me and strong women. From what she knows of your fiancée, she thinks he's a very nice young man, and she's looking forward to meeting him, but as for being over-awed, no, I think Pam is too … balanced to be overawed. She wouldn't be overawed meeting Mick Jagger."

****

They met in a wood-paneled pub somewhere behind Knightsbridge Barracks. The only other occupants were a pair of characters who were playing dominos at a table against the back wall. They never moved the pegging board and bore a striking resemblance to the two who had followed Judith out of Charing Cross underground.

It was a strange arrangement. Steven was to meet William unannounced, while Judith and Pam had spent the afternoon together and were to join them for dinner.

"Mister Jackson." He didn't look old enough to drink, but the handshake was firm enough, and he looked you in the eye. "I'm pleased to meet you. I'm in the chair. What will you have?"

"Do they run to Carling Black label?"

"I'm sure they do. Lager? I took you to be a beer man."

"You can't get Carling in the States, so I make up for it while I'm here."

"Will that be a pint or a half, sir?" The bartender asked in a voice that sounded more used to announcing the hymns in church.

"A pint," Steven said shortly. "They don't sell halves where I come from." *Why did he say that? "Get that chip off your shoulder, Jackson."*

"So do you miss Banks'?"

"Never got the taste for it. That was my father's second disappointment in me."

"What was the first?"

"I didn't want to work in the steelworks. He'd got a job for me all fixed up. I only had to go for the medical examination. It was his joke. They had these special X-ray machines to see if they could find any work in you. It took a long time for us to be reconciled, but being in the army helped, especially the paras. What about you?"

"I'll finish university, do my stint in the army, and then join the family firm."

"Yes, of course." Steven was not sure how to proceed, so he characteristically dove in. "What do you expect me to call you?"

"William! No titles in the bar."

"Good, you can call me Steven. Mr. Jackson sounds as though I'm talking to a lawyer, and Corporal Jackson would be too much of a mouthful. Speaking of which, cheers." He took the pint glass off the pewter tray and raised it to his lips.

"Yes cheers. Before I forget, shall we?" William motioned to one of the tables against the wall. "Do either of your sons want to come? It could be arranged."

"I'm sure they'd jump at the chance. It's a question of getting time off work."

"Yes, I see, but if they can, it can be arranged. A place can be found for them."

"That's very kind of you, really, but moving along, did I hear somewhere that you're an Aston Villa fan?"

"Indeed I am, and who do you follow, West Bromwich Albion?"

"Hush your mouth," Steven told his future king as he looked round in mock alarm, causing the domino players to look up nervously before he continued. "Although my father's three brothers and his parents were Albion supporters, he was the only Wolves supporter in the family. Sheer cussedness, I suppose. And speaking of which, I must mention that your father has been notably absent from Wembley on Cup Final day. But then again," he reflected somberly, "so has Abide with Me and so have the Wolves, for forty-five bloody years."

"Perhaps your daughter will one day present the cup to the Wolves."

"That will mean your grandmother *and* your father passing on. I hope we can get to Wembley before that. They might not even be holding it at Wembley then."

"If I may," began William, as though he was asking permission to talk about something other than the Wolves, "apparently you have had to endure quite a bit of intrusion in to your private life, which is to be regretted, but it had to be known what your feelings were about the monarchy—how you would react to all this. But nevertheless, it must have been unpleasant. I'm sorry."

Steven's reaction was delivered with such leaden dispassion, it sounded as though he was reading from a script specially written for this opening. "I have not been the best of fathers. In fact, had it not been for you and Judith meeting, I wouldn't have been a father at all, and having said that, I would not do anything to embarrass my daughter. Besides that, most of the more vociferous detractors of the monarchy just want to cover up their own shortcomings with the shortcomings of the monarchy, even if they have to be invented for them by the Yellow Press."

"And in America are we seen as something of a soap opera?"

"As I told someone the other day, I forget who, if they're not decrying the monarchy, they're trying to imitate it. Actually, although they wouldn't admit it, most are curious about the monarchy, especially you and Princess Anne. They're almost as fascinated about you as they are about Mick Jagger."

"Are they?" William laughed, but he obviously wasn't finished with the previous topic. "So all the rootling around in your past was a waste of time."

"And money." Steven drained his glass. "One of the flunkies could have just bought me a beer and asked me or just asked my daughter. After five minutes in my company, she could have set their minds at rest. I'm sure I don't have to tell you how sharp your future wife is."

"Indeed not, and speaking of which ..." As if on cue, there was a delighted peal of laughter from the corridor, and the door was opened to admit Judith and Pamela.

"Are we too soon? Are you still having the boy talk?"

"No, we are finished. I'm satisfied about his intentions toward my daughter and that he can keep her in the style to which she deserves to be accustomed."

"And that is all? Good, I expected you to be analyzing how Wolves lost the nineteen thirty-nine Cup Final. Oh no," Pamela caught William's startled look, "you *were* talking about the Wolves."

"William," said Steven with uncharacteristic urbanity, "I don't believe you've met my very perceptive wife."

"Mrs. Jackson, a pleasure." William took Pamela's hand and bowed over it. "I trust you had a pleasant afternoon."

10~"I might even kiss them better."

S TEVEN WAS INDULGING ONE OF his favorite phobias, his fear and hatred of flying. As Pam was not there for solace, he had to make do with two large vodkas and some sinus medication. This had the effect of numbing him into a fitful dream where he was the best man, but instead of Judith and William, it appeared that a baseball player was marrying his ex-wife. *How the heck did she get there?* The dream was so disturbing that he was actually relieved to wake up at thirty thousand feet to be the subject of a concerned gaze from the girl in the next seat.

"That was some dream."

"Dream?"

"Yes something to do with a baseball player and St. Paul's Cathedral."

Steven rubbed his eyes as though he was trying to get his brain working. "Where are we?"

"Somewhere above western Canada."

"Good! Are we going to Los Angeles?"

"It's a bit late to ask about your destination when you're thirty thousand feet in the air."

"Don't remind me. I know we're either going to Los Angeles or Heathrow. I live in Arizona. I've flown to London then back to Los Angeles then back to London and then back to Los Angeles, so I know it's either one or the other."

She smiled. "It's Los Angeles."

"So we're nearly there?"

"About two and a half hours."

Two and a half hours—one hundred and fifty minutes—that's nine thousand seconds. That took thirty seconds, so that's eight thousand nine hundred and seventy seconds of terror. Who could be terrified for that long? Should check with the *Guinness Book of Records*.

"Jackie."

"Sorry?"

She proffered her hand. "Jackie."

"Oh sorry, Steven."

Again the smile. "I'm pleased to meet you, Steven. Can I borrow your shoulder?"

"You're not going to cry on it, are you?"

"No, I just need a nap."

"Well, give me a minute, make it two, to visit the powder room, and then my shoulder's yours."

He made his way to the bathroom. There was no line, so that would be two minutes plus thirty seconds to circumnavigate Jackie and a hundred and fifty seconds, so that's eight thousand eight hundred and twenty seconds to go. It was uncannily within a second or two of his estimate when he settled himself in his seat. Jackie's face rested on his shoulder, and she was asleep.

The worst thing was, if anything happened, Pam would be alone when she got the news probably on the TV. He had spoken to Don, so there would be no worries about the financial arrangements, and she'd still have Eddie and Robert. The trouble was they'd had twenty years together but he'd barely known his daughter twenty days, and what about the wedding?

His mind went back to the interview with one of the flunkies. Apart from Chadders, they'd all looked alike.

To be fair, there had been no problem about them springing for the tickets to LA and back after they'd made sure that Pam wasn't going with him, and they had offered to pay for the room at the Victory Services Club. The first rehearsal had been set for twenty days' time. If that went well, there would be a dress rehearsal, after which there would be a rehearsal lunch with the Queen in attendance. Pam would like that. But then there had been a certain straightening of papers and the clearing of the throat. The bridal party, which was him and Judith, would be accompanied by an escort of the Blues and Royals.

"Harry's regiment, right?"

"Er, yes."

"Good show, him doing his bit in Iraq, don't you think?"

"Yes quite." Obviously Harry's military exploits notwithstanding, the interruption was unwelcome. "The Blues and Royals, the escort, that is, are all over six feet plus their ceremonial helmets, and the bride is quite tall and—obviously HMG would be responsible for the cost—"

"Are we talking about an adjustment to my wardrobe, sunshine?"

"Slightly elevated shoes to make it more symmetrical. After all, it will be televised."

"Why don't you get the Parachute Regiment to do it?"

"Do uh, do what?"

"Be the escort. After all, the groom's father is Colonel Commandant of the Parachute Regiment and proud to be so— done his jumps and all—and you don't have to be six feet or any height as long as you can do the job."

"You obviously have no idea of tradition."

"Listen, snowflake." He said softly, "I didn't give a knighthood to a wife beater, and, love my daughter as I may, and love Her Majesty as I may, from a respectful distance of course, if you think I'm going to go poncing up the aisle of St. Paul's wearing high heels, then I think that's why you tossers play rugby. You don't have to tell the goalkeeper when you move the goalposts."

****

"-----Fold up the drink trays and return your seats to the upright position. We will be landing at Los Angeles International in approximately twenty minutes."

"Jesus Christ!" He was so distracted, he didn't bother converting it to seconds.

"Well hello, sleeping beauty, do you need ..." Jackie indicated the bathroom.

Steven straightened up, rubbing his eyes. "How long have you been awake?"

"About five minutes. I've just been making myself presentable for my boyfriend." She settled herself in her seat. "Thanks for the shoulder."

"Thanks for the company."

They finally landed after Steven had politely declined Jackie's offer to hold his hand. He must have told her about Pam getting the feeling back in her hand after takeoff. When they had finally rolled to a stop, Steven, apart from helping Jackie retrieve her overnight bag from the overhead racks, had characteristically refused to join the usual scuffle to get in line to deplane.

"It doesn't go any further," Jackie indicated the slowly moving phalanx in the aisle. "We have to get off here."

"Help yourself." Steven moved his knees sideways to allow Jackie to leave. "I don't leave with everybody else. It's not worth the hassle. Besides," he added with a singular lack of foresight, "there's no one waiting for me."

He eschewed the usual scrum around the luggage carousel. He used the time to review his itinerary. Get a shuttle to Burbank it would probably be best to get a motel near to NBS, but he didn't know where their corporate offices were. He could phone

Solly but, he smiled to himself, if he just asked for downtown Burbank and directed the shuttle driver to one of the really good hotels—after all, NBS were paying. Then he'd phone Pam. No, it was still too early. Pam wasn't a morning person. By now the melee round the carousel had thinned out, and he recognized his suitcase and claimed it before he continued the revision of his evening. Get a motel, something to eat, a couple of drinks at the Burbank Bar and Grill, and leave before the teeny boppers arrived. Then it would be time to phone Pam.

"Mr. Jackson?" He was being addressed by a light-skinned Amazon with almond eyes.

"Yes, unless ..." he looked around for another Jackson more worthy of her attention.

"Steven Jackson?" She held out her hand. "Naomi from NBS."

"None other." Her hand was cool and firm.

"I'll take care of this." She actually took his suitcase from him and signaled to a skycap. "Welcome to LA, or should I say welcome back?" She linked her arm through his. "No, this way." They passed the line, and Steven had the presence of mind to wave to Jackie, who was, after the first flush of reconciliation, explaining to her boyfriend about the dream of a baseball player wearing high heels in St. Paul's Cathedral. They went through a corridor that Steven had never seen before, and for a moment he actually thought that the girl Naomi had mistaken him for someone else and he was actually being kidnapped, but worse had happened to him in Los Angeles.

"I love your accent."

"Glad you like it. I put it on especially for you.-" He was used to people confusing his accent with anything but English and was aware that he sounded like, in his sister's words, "a scruff from Coseley trying to sound like Noel Coward." "-Do you mind telling me where we're going?"

"To the hotel, where else?"

"Where else indeed."

By now they had come out onto the concourse, and the heat of Los Angeles enfolded him like an embrace. The skycap was loading his suitcase into the back of a limousine.

"Are we going in that?"

"Well, it's a long way to walk, honey, especially in these heels." Naomi opened the back door. "Make yourself comfortable." Nothing further was said until Naomi had successfully navigated the chaos of Century Boulevard and was in the northbound express lane of the San Diego freeway when she unclipped her cell phone. Steven heard the words "inbound" and "package," which he assumed referred to him, before she clicked it off and handed it over her shoulder. "Do you want to call your wife and let her know you're keeping out of trouble? Just dial 873 and then the country code—I think it's 44—and then your wife's number."

"Thank you, I think she'll still be asleep."

She gave a honeyed chuckle. "She must have a clear conscience, or she must assume you've got one."

"At my age, she's not got much option, dear."

****

"Just the one bag, sir?"

"Damn." Steven hated to be woken up by someone else. He felt it put him at a disadvantage.

"It's all right, sir, the lady's got your shoulder bag."

Looking past him, Steven saw that Naomi had indeed got his bag draped over her right shoulder while she was speaking into her cell phone, probably telling someone that the package had arrived safely. She sent the bellhop on his way sharply before turning her attention to Steven. "You look so cute when you're asleep, I hated to wake you. We're already checked in. I'll collect the key and see you by the elevators. Don't get lost."

"I think I can find my way to the elevators."

Naomi unlocked her snappish smile. "You'll probably want to take a nap, and then we'll decide about the evening."

We? Nevertheless, Steven made his way to the elevators, and as he was waiting there, he became aware of his opulent surroundings. He expected someone to ask if they could help him, meaning, "What's a scruff like you doing here?" when Naomi came to rescue him. "It's always best to send the bellhop to the room first."

"Yes, I'll remember that."

"We'll get you settled in, and then I'll go take a shower and we'll decide what you want to do." *Again the we?* "You seem uncertain about something. Any questions?"

"Just one, where are we?"

"The Beverly Wilshire. I hope you like it. They filmed *Pretty Woman* here."

"I didn't like it much."

"The movie?"

"Yes, I thought the song was great. In fact, I don't think Roy Orbison's done anything I don't like, although some of them came a bit too close to home. But the movie, I think it's because I got fired once by somebody who thought he looked like Richard Gere."

"Did he?"

"Well if you can imagine a fat Richard Gere with glasses, I suppose he did. I thought the offices were in Burbank?"

"That's the corporate office. We're not expected there until Thursday. Here we are, room 311," she unlocked the door and dumped his suitcase on the bed, "You can't see the Hollywood sign from here, but you don't like anything over the third floor, right?"

Again the "we," and how did they know about the third floor? "I'm sure I'll be safe. What are you doing?"

"I'm unpacking."

"Don't you think I can do that?"

"Of course it's just—is there something you don't want me to see?"

Steven shrugged and turned away. "Knock yourself out. I'm going to take a shower unless you want to do that for me." Without waiting for a reply, he retired to the bathroom, and the warm jets had just begun to loosen his shoulder muscles when there was a knock on the door. *I was only joking.* "Yes?"

"I've left some clothing out on the bed. Feel free to change it if it's not suitable." *Thanks very much.* "And you'll find a robe on the door. Please wear it before you come in because beneath this urban veneer, I'm just a simple country girl and you wouldn't want to get me all hot and bothered."

"Sure, anything else?"

"Yes, where did you get those cute knickers?"

Five minutes later, having showered off the ravages of an eleven-hour flight, Steven knocked on the door. "Marks and Spencer's[12]—and you needn't avert your maidenly eyes, I am suitably robed."

Naomi, for once sans cell phone, was sitting on the bed facing the bathroom door. "I took the liberty of putting your stuff away and laid something out, but I didn't want to be too intrusive." She indicated a silver-framed photograph lying face downward on the bed. "Your wife?"

Steven picked up the photograph. "I picked up the frame in Searchlight—that's between Vegas and somewhere else—Needles. I got the best picture I had to do it justice, and naturally it was one of Pam."

"May I?" She accepted the photograph from Steven and looked at it, pursing her lips, "She *is* a looker. Is that a tattoo on her cheek?"

"Actually, it's part of an American eagle. I took it from an old passport. Don't tell anyone. It's probably a federal offense."

"She really is beautiful."

Steven accepted the photograph back and studied it briefly before placing it on the bedside table. "Yes, I am lucky. Speaking of which, I had better phone her."

"I'll give you some privacy then. I'll be back in about two hours. Will you be all right?"

"I think I can cope."

"Well," Naomi pointedly looked at the photograph, "that answers a rather delicate question. Obviously I won't have to arrange some company for you."

Steven hadn't bothered with the clothes that Naomi had selected. After all, if they were going out, he would have to change again, so he watched the television news and assured himself that the newscaster's smile was still in place and everything was right with the world. John McCain had apparently found a running mate. There were pictures of her trying out the podium at the Republican convention. He half expected it to be Mrs. Whelps. Hurricane Gustav had largely spent itself, but George Bush had spent so much time being photographed with the victims that he was apparently too tired to attend the convention, although his mother, father, and wife were there. Brian Whelps had picked up another endorsement, and his mother and one of the gymnasts were going to share the honor of being on the Wheaties package. She and Brian weren't going to be on *Dancing with the Stars*, thankfully. Five o'clock in the afternoon. That must be nine in the morning in England. What was it? Eight hours in time and a thousand years of civilization. His hand stopped midway to the telephone—*ahead, you tosser, ahead.* Eight hours *ahead.* That would make it four in the morning, and she surely wouldn't wake up singing. So nine in the morning would be one in the morning here. He'd fix a reminder to her photograph and call when he got in. Rolling off the bed, he rummaged through the promotional items on the desk—writing paper, ballpoint pen, envelopes, "what's on at the Hollywood bowl," what's off at the Hollywood a-Go-Go, but no sticky tape. He made it all the way to the telephone this time and punched in 00.

"Front desk, this is Janine. How may I help you?"

"This is Mister Jackson in room—on the third floor. Could I get some Sellatape—Scotch tape?"

"I don't exactly know, Mister Jackson, have you had an accident?"

"No."

"Then, if you don't mind me asking, what exactly is the scotch tape for?"

"I'm going out for the evening and I want to tape a reminder to call my wife when I get in."

"Of course, Mister Jackson. I'll get some tape sent up to you, but we can telephone a reminder when you come in."

"I'd rather have the tape—humor me."

"Certainly, Mister Jackson. Is there anything else I can do for you today?"

"I don't suppose you can get Wolves in to the premiership?"

"Pardon me?"

"Never mind, what about a vodka tonic?"

"I'll put you through to room service. If there is anything else I can do for you, please let me know, and have a nice evening." Janine was already scribbling, "Wolves, premiership, English," on her to-do pad.

****

Unseen by Steven languishing on the third floor, the sun had set behind (or probably in front of) the Hollywood sign, and after eschewing the promise on television to get rich in real estate, or to buy enough cutlery to equip a battalion of Ghurkas, he had, out of morbid curiosity, flicked through Tony Blair doing his village idiot on the Letterman show and Michael Cain apologizing for the empire on something else before slipping into an uneasy doze when the telephone woke him. As was his habit since his service days, he became aware of his surroundings before he opened his eyes, so it wasn't a surprise when he heard Naomi's voice, "I'll be there in about twenty minutes. Can you be ready by then?"

Ready for what?

"Yes I think I can throw a few things on by then. Shall I meet you in the lobby by the front entrance?"

"Are you sure you don't need me to come to your room to collect you?"

"I think I can find the parking lot. How shall I dress? I didn't pack my dinner jacket[13], so it'll have to be on the informal side."

"I'm sure you'll look fine, and it will be informal. You won't need your old school tie."

"Right, twenty minutes."

As he had not donned the clothes Naomi had set out for him and he being a fast dresser, Steven was outside the front entrance before the prescribed twenty minutes—in fact, just in time to meet Naomi entering.

"Ah, there you are." *Where else would I be?* "And on time." She linked her arm in his but not before giving him a swift appraisal, as though she was debating whether to send him upstairs to change his shirt.

"I remembered to forget the old school tie."

"You look fine, will I do?" She did a graceful pirouette displaying her outfit, a black leather miniskirt and a severely cut jacket. It was as though she'd started to dress like Tina Turner and changed her mind halfway through. The effect was not unbecoming. Apparently the conveyance had changed with the ensemble, for in response to a whistle that wouldn't have discredited a New York porter, a valet appeared from the parking garage driving a low-slung sports convertible.

"Thanks, Miguel." She slid behind the wheel. "Let's go, Steven, LA awaits us."

They had already merged into the stream of traffic on Wilshire before she spoke again. "Any thoughts on where you'd like to eat?"

"Yes." He had decided before he went to sleep. "There's a deli in Sherman Oaks on Ventura Boulevard on the"—he closed his eyes in concentration—"north side of the street, opposite a news stand. I was there with a girl once. Think you can find it?"

"Sure." She changed down a gear and did a right turn on to Robertson that had Steven pressing himself back into the seat.

By dint of her driving and seeming disregard for the traffic laws, they reached the deli in just under twenty minutes. Or rather they reached where the deli should have been, for there was Ventura Boulevard and there was the news stand, but opposite it, if the garish notice was to be believed, was a newly opened video store. "Rent two and the third one's free."

Naomi was already speaking to some mysterious correspondent on her cell phone. "A good deli close to Woodman and Ventura. Get back to me as quick as you can, he's got that lost look. Right." She turned to Steven. "Do you know how many guys would love to be in your place with a woman like me with all expenses paid?"

"I should imagine quite a few." Steven continued to stare at the plastic bunting, which was already curling in the heat, like dead flowers on a forgotten grave.

"Right and do you? How long have you been married?"

"Nineteen years. I'm surprised you didn't know."

"I just wanted to—when was the last time you ate here?"

"When I still had my illusions."

"And when would that be?"

"Is it important?"

"Humor me."

Steven surprisingly complied, "My birthday, March 21."

"And your wife didn't mind?" Naomi seemed to lose track, but then she rallied. "Which March 21? What year?"

"Nineteen eighty-five."

"And you expect." Her cell phone trilled. "Hang on." She flipped it open violently. "Yes, right. Got it. Thanks, bye." She was reluctant to let go of her anger. "You really expect a business to be the same twenty years later? The family who owned it, the Solomons, moved in '87, and we can be at their new place in twenty minutes, unless you'd like to stare at some plastic flags for a little longer?"

"March on," Steven said meekly.

"I presume this was Judith's mother." Naomi performed that terrifying tactic of simultaneously conversing and navigating LA traffic. "So it wasn't just a one-night stand."

"Bunting." Apparently Steven had grown bored with his disillusionment.

"What?"

"Bunting. Flags fly from a staff. What hangs down from a string is called bunting. I was actually staring at plastic bunting. You're actually not supposed to hang flags down, only bunting. Not many Americans know that."

"We live and learn." Naomi didn't feel so sorry about lying to him about the Solomons now.

****

"So, you're Australian?" They were in a pseudo-Irish pub (are there any others?) where the question was put to him by a girl with interesting circles under her eyes who, Steven had the feeling, had been deliberately sorted out by Naomi.

"No, English."

"Oh, I'm sorry."

"Sorry that I'm English or that you thought that I was Australian?" He waited until she had opened her mouth to reply before continuing, "Whatever you're sorry for, dear, I shouldn't be. Life's too short."

It was the fifth or sixth bar they had been in since leaving the Riverside Deli and Bakery, where he was complimentary enough for Naomi to apparently forgive him for the bunting. He had not remarked on the absence of the Solomons, and after asking where the river was, had been happy enough to surrender to Naomi's guidance, for after all, she was a good sort just doing her job. As long as he knew what it was, because he noticed that every bar that they visited there was always someone to needle him, and Naomi was seldom out of earshot.

Fortunately, it was one of the few advantages of his service in Northern Ireland where, with some questions, it wasn't what the answers sounded like, it was what the answers could be *made* to sound like. He remembered when Mrs. Thatcher, no longer the leader of the Conservative party, was making a speech in the House of Commons about a single European currency. She had paused, as though suddenly realizing that she didn't have to weigh every word, and suddenly proclaimed, "You know, I'm rather enjoying this." So he let Naomi do her job and give the girl her money's worth. There was always Pam's photograph to keep him on the straight and narrow, but if he wasn't happily married … He became aware that the girl was speaking to him again. "You're not offended that I thought you sounded Australian?"

"No, my dear, and if they are, we won't tell them." he used a ploy that he had seen employed by Noel Coward while he was being interviewed by some velveteened twit[14] from the BBC. He would give answer designed to throw them off their stride and wait while they spluttered, and just as they had recovered their composure, he would continue, apparently unaware of their discomfort. "Of course, as you know, Australia was a penal colony, so all of the first Australians, apart from the Aborigines, were prisoners who came from working-class areas. The rich didn't need to steal; all the stealing had been done for them. So quite a few of them would speak like me. Obvious, really, isn't it, m'dear?"

And so it went on. Always there was someone who Naomi knew well enough to introduce to Steven who was always curious about something English. "You've got David Beckham and the London Bridge and we got Madonna. Although that bridge has never seen the River Thames. The River Thames, dear, the river that flows through London."

And then there was, "Mel Gibson makes two comments about the Jews and true or false, he can't apologize enough. He makes a movie slagging the English, none of which is true, and he gets an Oscar," and on the strength of another vodka tonic thoughtfully supplied by Naomi, when the subject had moved to a well-known game show host, "He said, 'I'd rather believe the movie.' I saw him do one show when one of the contestants was actually his tailor. Well, I think the tape's been up his inside leg once too often."

It was all great fun and taken in the best of spirits. The only slight hiccup was when the subject got around to Prince Charles. "Do *you* think Camilla's attractive?" The question was put to him by a dark-skinned girl who's pinpoint pupils made it clear that she didn't need a vodka tonic to bring her up to par.

"I don't know. I don't attach too much importance to outward appearances." Steven affected his world-weary voice. "A bit shallow, don't you think?"

Disregarding her boyfriend's embarrassed changing of his position, she blundered on, "But you don't think she's attractive, do you?"

"I don't think *you're* attractive, dear," Steven smiled thinly, "but I'm too polite to mention it."

"I think our problem with Prince Charles is that he represents the feudal system," her boyfriend intoned in the measured cadence of one who's trying to keep his temper. "I mean, he wouldn't have a job if it wasn't for his father, would he?"

"Actually, it's his mother. His father isn't the sovereign, he's just a duke," answered Steven, disregarding Naomi's warning glance. "Do you think George Bush would have got the job if it hadn't been for Daddy's influence? And Leila Ali"—by now Naomi was really alarmed—"would anyone have heard of her if her father hadn't have made his living beating other people senseless—usually black people?"

By now, all subtlety abandoned, Naomi actually dragged him out to the parking lot, and once inside her sports car, made no move to start the engine.

"Would you like to have someone else?"

"If you mean have in the biblical sense, my dear, I'm sure that I can keep my passions within due bounds until I see my wife again, but if you mean generally, you're more than adequate. In fact, I thought we were having fun."

"What have you got against Muhammad Ali?"

"Nothing, I've never met the man. I was just making a comment about a public figure, one of the freedoms we all cherish, although he's not the fighter Rocky Marciano was. Rocky never got beaten, but I think you're mad at the wrong person, Naomi."

"Right, and who should I be mad at?"

Steven told her, and also why.

They sat for quite a while as Naomi digested his revelation. Finally she switched on the ignition and put the car in gear, and if this wasn't enough distraction from her thoughts, she added, "Do you really think Grace is unattractive?"

"Was that her name? How singularly inappropriate. I think what I said was that I found her unattractive. I've always found bad manners less than engaging. Actually, I think she's a bigot, don't you?"

"Oh Steven," Naomi said softly, "they are going to love you."

Steven had no more idea of who the "they" were than who "we" were, and while he was pondering this, he became aware that Naomi was speaking again. "I think it's time we checked out this pub called the Maid Marion, near Vineland. Right?"

"That's it, but I think it's only fair to tell you that we might not get in."

"Do tell, and why would that be?"

"I got fired from there."

"That's the second best way I know to round off the evening, right sweet stuff. If they refuse to serve us, just say, 'Why not?' Nothing else, okay?"

"Sure, but they'll probably say, 'You know why.'"

"I hope they do."

"I notice you didn't ask me why I was fired."

"I don't have to. You're that honest, you are"—they had stopped at a red light before she found a suitable adjective— "beautiful. Your wife's named Pamela, right?"

"Pam, yes."

"Sorry, Pam, just this once," and holding his head on either side, she forced it back against the backrest and gave him a long, moist, open-mouth kiss before waving to the impatient driver behind and accelerating away. "Right, the Maid Marion."

Steven had almost recovered from Naomi's libidinous assault when they reached the Maid Marion, rather the site of the Maid Marion, for the hostelry had appeared to suffer a similar fate to the delicatessen on Ventura boulevard, or Larry had become a tarot card reader.

In variance to his dismay at the fate of the delicatessen, his attitude to the demise of the Maid Marion had a restrained smugness. He sank back into his seat, muttering softly, "Larry, Larry, Larry—not the smartest man in the world but smarter than some who think they are. Never too old to learn, just sometimes too stupid, and arrogance makes fools of us all. The acceptance of your weakness is the beginning of strength." He roused himself. "Well, that's put the kibosh on that. Where shall we go now?"

"Oh I think we can find somewhere. So why were your services terminated at the Maid Marion?"

"A reason is singular but excuses come in groups, as in this case because he said the business hadn't picked up enough, and he also said I wasn't fast enough."

"So he actually contradicted himself."

Steven nodded slowly, forgetting that Naomi's attention was on the road. "Exactly, well done."

"And the real reason?"

"It's a long story."

"We've got all night."

"Which I don't intend to use talking about Larry."

"Have you ever been beaten up by a woman?"

"No, but I don't imagine it's very pleasant." And after a pause, he added, "Unless you're into that sort of thing," and after a shorter pause, "which I'm not."

"So you're not going to tell me."

"I don't think so."

"Please," she murmured, and when there was no response, she did something that not only shocked Steven it, in his own words, "Scared me shitless." Without taking her eyes off the road, she dropped her right hand into his lap and did something that caused him to gasp in pain. "Pretty"—she squeezed a little harder—"please."

"Right," he said hoarsely, "if you insist, and you obviously do, I'll tell you." He was relieved to feel the pressure of her grip relaxing, but her hand didn't move. "Larry was a bit homophobic, and like most of them, he was never quite sure which side his toast was buttered, if you follow me." Her hand gave an encouraging twitch. "So he tried to compensate by insulting the staff, just the blokes, of course. Trouble was, he could dish it out but he couldn't take it. One time I went in to work and I'd had my hair cut the night before, and he said, 'Have you had your hair cut? You look like somebody who's just come out of that gay bar up the road,' and I said thanks for the tip and not to worry I wouldn't tell his wife that he hangs about outside gay bars. Then there was his wife, Renee. She used to come in on a Saturday to do the books, and she used to bring her sister's kid in, sort of repressed maternal instinct. That should have said something, good Catholic girl, married seven years and no kids. Anyway, Craig, one of the customers who used to work for Texaco, asked me who the kid was, and I told him it was Renee's nephew. When Larry came in, somebody mentioned what a good-looking kid he was. 'Yes,' said Larry, puffing out his chest. 'Takes after his dad, doesn't he?' So there he was, passing off his nephew as his own kid."

"This Larry," said Naomi thoughtfully, "would he look like a fat Richard Gere with glasses?"

"You're never off duty, are you?"

"You forgot what happened at the traffic light, sweet stuff? Are you all right?" Steven had been assailed by a violent coughing fit, which had doubled him over, causing Naomi to be so concerned that she actually replaced her right hand on the steering wheel to pull into the parking lot of a liquor store.

"It's all right," Steven managed finally. "This doesn't happen very often, just the excitement I'm sure." In fact, he had been so concerned with the circumstances that he had actually forgotten to inhale.

All concerned now, Naomi would not drive further until she had obtained a bottle of mineral water from the liquor store and his breathing had returned to normal.

"We still friends, sweet stuff?"

"Of course, if you still respect me in the morning."

"Good! Enough of business. Let's go and relax. I might even kiss them better."

11~Breakfast at the Claredon and Slow Dancing in LA

U NLIKE STEVEN, PAM WAS NEVER aware of her surroundings before she opened her eyes, and so she reacquainted herself with her new surroundings when the telephone woke her in North Audley Street. In compensation for Steven's enforced absence, Pamela, in a surprising show of assertiveness, had insisted that her accommodation be upgraded from the spartan delights of the Victory Services Club to somewhere with a telephone and a garden, or at least a balcony. Steven had just as surprisingly agreed to arrange it with "them" on the condition that he furnish her with two telephone numbers "just in case," Peter, who she had met, and Winkie Price, who she had definitely not. She was duly ensconced in a discreet little hotel on the borders of Mayfair and Marylebone. It was not the Beverly Wilshire, but she did have the use of the garden where she could read, enjoying the spring sunshine, and Hyde Park was within walking distance. It was also homey, as was the couple who ran it, a Mrs. Murdoch, and a character (presumably her husband) who was referred to only as The Captain. To add to the military flavor, as well as footing the bill for the added luxury, "they" also provided the telephone number of a Major Ashford-Bowdler, "to keep an eye on you," which Pamela perceived as ensuring she didn't take it into her head to join her husband in Los Angeles, thus guaranteeing his return to the land of his birth. In any event, with Peter and the previously unknown Mr. Winkie Price on hand, she didn't anticipate troubling the worthy major, and the Victory Services Club was within walking distance for a bit of light relief.

The second thing she noticed was that Steven was not lying beside her. He was presently waiting behind the velvet rope of the Club LA while Naomi worked her magic on the doorman.

"'Allo, Pamela, this is Judith. Did I wake you?"

"I was getting up anyway." Pamela gave a rueful glance at the empty space beside her.

"Are you bored terribly without Poppi?"

"I manage, thank you."

"I'm sorry I've been neglecting you." Pam didn't realize she was supposed to be entertained, and if the need arose there was Major Ashford-Bowdler (although she would have preferred Chadders), not to mention Peter and the shadowy Mr. Price or the old soldiers at the Victory Services Club. "Would you like to come to breakfast with me, er, and my mother?"

"Thank you, that would be nice."

"It is not a problem?"

"No, give me the address and I'll get a taxi."

"Oh no, we'll pick you up. I mean would it be a problem, you with my mother, I mean her and Steven?"

"Judith, honey," Pamela was fully awake now, "it wasn't a problem dealing with his old wife, his old comrades, and at least one old boyfriend, so your mother won't be a problem, especially as she's in London and Steven's in Los Angeles. What time can you get here?"

"Oh, we could be there in half an hour."

"I'll need at least an hour. If you get here before, then you can wait in the lobby and I'll get down as soon as I can. Tell your mother I'm looking forward to meeting her. Bye for now." Pamela gently replaced the receiver and addressed it thoughtfully. "I may be a country girl at heart, but I've been off the farm for quite a while, honey."

An hour later Pam, showered and dressed, was reading the newspaper, having explained to Mrs. Murdoch that she was going out to breakfast and reassuring her that it was no reflection on the cuisine of the hotel, when Judith arrived.

"Pamela, how nice you look." She kissed Pamela, continental style, right cheek to left cheek, left cheek to right cheek. "We're meeting my mother at the Claredon. Have you been there?"

"I don't think I've heard of it." Less charitable people than Pam would have suspected that Judith already knew this, "But if you chose it, I'm sure it will be fine. Let's go."

"So she's lumbered with entertaining his daughter and her mother while he swans off to Los Angeles, well," Mrs. Murdoch sniffed virtuously as she watched them depart. "I hope he's worth it."

Worth it or not, Steven was by then being introduced by Naomi to the relaxing delights of slow dancing at the Club LA.

****

"Miss Biderman's party?" The maître d' of the Claredon gave an approving smile, "Certainly. If you would follow me, your other party's already here." Lydia stood as they approached, and Judith introduced them, "Pamela this is my mother, Lydia. Mama, this is Pamela."

"I'm pleased to meet you." Pamela was relieved to find that the hand was warm and dry. She hated clammy handshakes. "I've ordered mimosas, is that all right?"

"Never have breakfast without it," Pamela replied lightly as they seated themselves. She assessed Lydia. She was certainly still attractive, an older version of Judith. They had the same light blue eyes and strong jaw line, but there was a tightness about the mouth that bespoke of some tension. But that apart, she was still very attractive. She must have been something when she and Steven were together *And what were you, girl, chopped liver?*

"Is this your first time in London?"

"No, I was here with my father on business, and Steven and I have been here many times."

"Ah, Steven," she said, as though Pamela had reminded her of a distant memory. "He is well?"

"Oh yes, thriving, and looking forward to seeing you again."

"And he is still beautiful?" said Lydia gaily, which earned her a warning glance from Judith, but Pamela was up to it.

"I think his years sit well on him."

"As yours do on you, yes?"

"Besides you'll see him at the rehearsal lunch. You can make your own mind up."

"I hope to see him before then, as soon as he gets back from Los Angeles." She pronounced it attractively in the Spanish style. "How long will he be there?"

"Until they get tired of him, which shouldn't be too long."

"Really, how strange. I found Steven very entertaining."

"He still is, but he can be very abrasive when it suits him, and I don't think LA will keep his interest long without me."

"I see, and you have been together how long?"

"Nineteen years. We had just moved in together the last time you telephoned, don't you remember?"

For the first time, Lydia looked a little discomfited. "And you've been together all this time?"

"Day -- and night."

"And he has had no adventures? With women?"

"Mama!" Judith was moved to protest.

"But I'm sure Pam doesn't mind?" She looked inquiringly at Pam.

"Actually I do."

"Oh, but you mustn't mind me, my dear. We continentals are very—open about affairs *de la coeur*. I thought Americans were."

"We are and I don't, but the waiter is too polite to interrupt us. so I suggest we postpone our discussion until after we order. Deprivation always gives me an appetite." Pamela may have been mistaken, but the look Judith gave her mother appeared to say, "Serves you right."

****

Steven awoke as usual. Whatever debauchery he had become involved in, whether real or imagined, as long as he stuck to vodka had no physical ill effects. He was aware that it was the usual BCM (Beautiful California Morning), and he was fit to do battle with the media moguls, or wannabe moguls. He did, however, have certain misgivings about something and he knew he wouldn't be in balance until he remembered what, however disconcerting. Rather like balancing a checkbook when you *know* your fiscal deficiencies.

When he finally recalled it, however, it was not totally irreversible. When they had finally reached the Beverley Wilshire, instead of dropping him at the main entrance, Naomi had summoned the parking valet. "Just a night cap, sweet stuff, before I tuck you in." As politely as possible, he had explained that he had not called his wife yet. "No problem." *She actually said, "No problem."* "You can use my cell phone in the doorway here, the reception's great. I'm going to have a brandy. I suppose you want to stick to vodka."

It was as though she didn't want him out of her sight. He remembered a printed joke that had done the rounds at Media Partners. It had a picture of a beautiful woman and underneath the caption, "However good she looks, there's some guy somewhere who's really tired of her shit." Well, gorgeous as she was—good luck to him. He seated himself on a concrete bench and dialed the number of North Audley Street. He had been looking forward to talking to Pam and indulging in delicious silences where they could just listen to each other breathe. What he'd got, however, was a Mrs. Murdoch who declared that the *lady* in question was entertaining *his* friends at breakfast, but she would tell her that he had called, not-at-all, she was sure.

He almost dropped his cell phone on the table as he arrived at the same time as the drinks before handing it to her with a careful politeness. He noticed that she didn't pay (probably a corporate account) and her drink was quite large (probably a treble).

"That wasn't long." She had arranged herself on a small sofa called a love seat.

"She wasn't in." And not knowing if he was supposed to join her or sit opposite, he perversely chose the latter.

"She's probably gone out for breakfast. We'll try again later." *Again the we.*

"Will we?"

"Something bothering you, sweet stuff?"

"Actually, yes."

"It wasn't our bit of harmless fun at the traffic lights, was it?"

"No, it's you."

"And what could be bothering you about me?"

"Naomi." he laced his fingers together on the table in front of him and stared at them. "I never try to change anyone's mind. If I want to buy a car, I offer what I think it's worth and I either buy it at that price or I don't. It's their decision whether to sell or not. If I want to sell a house, I ask a fair price, and anyone can decide whether to buy it or not. If I ask $200,000, that's what I'd sell it for. If someone offers me $199,000, I don't return their call because if I wanted to sell it at $199,000, that's what I'd ask for. If I want to sleep with a woman—well at least wanted to—when I was younger, I'd ask her as nicely as possible and left it up to her. Just because you look like you do." At this point, he made the mistake of looking up and catching her eyes regarding him thoughtfully, which caused him to lose his way. "You shouldn't—I mean, well, it's an insult to Pam, isn't it?"

"Ah yes," she said gravely. "I do tend to manipulate. Comes with the territory, darlin'. I'm backing you into a corner so I can force my attentions on you. How devious, you bein' a happily married man an' all."

"Do I really sound like that? How pompous. I stand suitably chastened. It's just that when I get tempted to go off the rails, it's always with a beautiful woman, so if I do I picture them naked and then picture me naked, and it sort of gets it into perspective, but it didn't work this time because I pictured you naked and forgot what I was doing."

"Now you're being charming."

"Oh God, that's worse than being pompous."

"I'll take it." She patted the couch beside her. "Talk to me and we'll have a night cap before I tuck you in. I won't keep you up too long." She signaled the waiter, and Steven noticed with a shock that her glass was empty.

"It's all right, I never have more than four hours sleep, ever since I was in the army, but am I keeping you from anyone?"

"Nobody important enough to go home to. So what do you do in Arizona?"

"Well, I drink vodka and occasionally tequila, watch sunsets. Actually, I find it more interesting looking in the opposite direction. There's a rock to the east of us that, when the setting sun picks out the different textures, it actually looks like it's moving, I look after my wife, work on the house and the yard, and write."

"You write? You never told me."

"It never came up."

"With most writers, it's the first thing out of their mouths."

"I'm not most writers."

"But you must realize that the opportunity—have you got anything finished?"

"Yes, one finished and three I'm working on."

"How do you expect to get published if you don't tell anyone?"

"It doesn't matter so much if it's published."

"Then what's the point in writing?" She looked around as if she was appealing for a witness. "I mean, how can you sell it?"

"The important thing is that it's written, not that it's read. Some of the most beautiful flowers in the desert bloom where no one sees them but they're still beautiful and they still bloom and when you—when someone makes love, does someone have to see it or *pay* for it? No, but it's still making love."

"So," she said carefully, "you don't want anyone to read what you've written."

"I didn't say that, I said it's not the most important thing. It would be nice to be published, but if I can write something that I think is meaningful then if nobody reads it or if they read it and they think it's rubbish, it's still meaningful, isn't it? 'So in love with the footlights he doesn't know if there's an audience there, and probably doesn't care,' someone said that about me, a hundred years ago."

In answer, she just leaned back as though exhausted. "Wow."

"Here endeth the lesson." He carefully replaced his glass on the edge of the table and pushed it forward with his forefinger. "And what do *you* do for fun?"

"I'm still making my way, sweet stuff. Not much time for fun, except having a late drink with writers who don't want to be published."

"You are very kind." He went to reach for his glass and stopped. "And what do you do *not* for fun?"

"Who don't *care* if they're published," she corrected herself pedantically, "I'm sorry, what did you say?"

"I said that you were very kind and asked what you did without having fun."

"I'm a screener. I entertain people to see if there's any mileage in them on a talk show and *what* talk show."

"Is that why you're trying to get me drunk?"

"Among other—you noticed."

"It would be hard to miss." As if to illustrate the point, he lifted his glass and drank. "But it wouldn't work, the getting me drunk, I mean."

"So you are impervious to my cunning ways."

"Not at all, it's just that when I get drunk I *know* I'm drunk, so I talk rubbish as a defense, because a man's never as dumb as when he thinks he's being smart and all drunks think they're being smart. Speaking of which, and I'm not suggesting you're drunk, but"—he looked pointedly at her glass—"according to LA's finest, you shouldn't be driving tonight. I'll gladly share my room with you. I can sleep on the couch."

"I'll sleep in *my* room, sweetheart, and no one sleeps on the couch. There's nothing to be scared about. I just need to feel the warmth of human contact." She smiled at his confused look. "Yes, the room you're sleeping in, the room that I'm charging the drinks to, if you inquire at the desk, you'll find it's registered to Miss Naomi Letts. No smart remarks, so let's have the last one in *our* room. Then I can tuck you in."

So, half an hour later they were having a night cap in *their* room and talking, almost as friends, or rather he was talking because Naomi, although having formed her assessment of him, was by nature a listener. So he talked about Northern Ireland, about Wolverhampton Wanderers, about the Black Country, and she listened, occasionally asking a question that reminded him that she absorbed everything rather like his elder sister. How long he would have continued to talk and how long she would have listened was curtailed by jet lag sneaking up on him (when he was in the middle of discussing the delights of Coseley Tunnel). She gently took the glass from his hand. "All right, sweet stuff, it's sleepy time down south. Can you undress in the dark?"

"Yes uh—yes." He didn't ask her why.

"Right. I switch the light off, you get undressed, and I collect your clothes and hang them in the closet. Did I mention I can see in the dark?"

"No," he replied sleepily, "but it doesn't surprise me."

She smiled. "Then you get between the sheets and I get between the comforter and the top sheet. Will that play for you?"

"Play is not the word I would have, used but ..." When she switched the light off, he complied, and her claims to night vision were borne out by the fact that, as he lay in bed and heard her moving about the room, she was talking to him and never once stumbled or knocked against the furniture. "The reason we're doing it this way is that I don't really want to see Pamela's photograph, and if you saw me undressing, in spite of yourself, you'd want me, and I'm sure you'd ask nicely and I—I'm sure it would be beautiful, but I'm not sure I could stand your pain in the morning." He felt the bed move slightly as she got in.

Notwithstanding the drink, his exertions on the dance floor, and jet lag, Steven, especially in a strange bed, found it hard to get to sleep, and he thought that Naomi had already succumbed when he felt her move and realized she was awake. "I shouldn't tell Pamela about this. She might not understand," she whispered. "In fact, I have a hard time understanding it myself. G'night, sweet stuff."

Now with the smog-filtered sun streaming in through the windows, he was trying to decide if her presence was real, as there was no sign of her in the room. The scent could be her perfume, or it could be the usual hotel deodorant. Could he have dreamed it? He looked at Pam's photograph and saw that there was a piece of paper twisted in the frame, and with a sense of misgiving, he saw that she had used the adhesive tape supplied by Janine to attach the room key to it.

Forgive me for using Pam's picture, but I wanted to be sure you saw this. I will call for you at 8:30. Try to be ready by then. Thanks for last night "It is better to die on your feet than live on your knees." Try to phone Pamela. XXXX, N

He was showered and dressed and was actually pacing up and down, having once more unsuccessfully tried to call Pam, this time not even reaching the formidable Mrs. Murdoch, when Naomi arrived.

"Don't you look spiffy? Well, are you ready?"

"Thank you, I am ready to engage the enemy."

"You make it sound like war. Is that what you think?"

"It's certainly a conflict, and you think so too or you wouldn't have tried to dampen my powder last night."

"Au contraire, sweet stuff, I told you business was finished and there's nothing like some friendly pyrotechnics to round off the evening. You shouldn't be so modest," she added thoughtfully as she pulled out into the traffic. They were well on their way before she spoke again. "So you see this as a verbal brawl."

"Either that or, as I said to my wife, they want to ridicule Prince Charles and have me as a captive audience. If that's so, they'll be disappointed. I'll send the T-shirt back. I've already banked the check." The last thought seemed to cheer him, and then he added more soberly, "Speaking of Pam, thank you, but I couldn't reach her. I would like to try again before the meeting."

"Sure, you can use my cell in the lobby." They had apparently arrived, as Naomi parked in front of a smoked glass building. "The cell phone's clipped to the dashboard. After you've called, Pamela wait in the lobby till I come for you. Hang on." She held his arm to restrain him, and then, holding his head, she pulled it forward until their faces were inches apart, and for a moment he thought she was going to kiss him good-bye. "Whatever they do or say, don't sign anything. You've got an agent, right?" He nodded as much as he was able to in her grip. "Whatever they say, 'My agent deals with that.' You promise?"

"Yes, I promise."

This time she did kiss him, chastely, on the lips. "Stay well, sweet stuff," and they walked into the building, apart from Steven opening the door for her, as though they had never been closer than the width of the LA River.

"Hello." The double syllable on the final letter was uniquely Pam, so for once the gods were with him.

"Hello, I'm glad I don't have to go through Mrs. Murdoch."

"Hello, love, she arranged for anything that comes from 213 area code to come directly to my room. She says no one else would be calling from Los Angeles."

"I didn't telephone you yesterday. It would have been about three o'clock in the morning there, and I just missed you this morning, as Mrs. Murdoch said you'd gone out."

"I know, I'm sorry I missed you. I've been to breakfast with Judith and Lydia."

"How was it?"

"Judith was charming. I really think she's warming to me."

"And?"

"Lydia was somewhat less, but I'm seeing Judith later on. She seems to have adopted me since Willie has been busy seeing to things. Are you all right?"

"Yes I'm quite ready for them, especially now that we have spoken. Why?"

"I've just called your future king Willie."

"I'm sorry, I'm a bit preoccupied with this thing."

"Never mind, it'll soon be over and the check's in the bank. Then you can get yourself back here and have a holiday at their expense. We'll actually go home with more money than we came with. That should make you feel better. Are they looking after you?"

"Yes, I've got this chaperone called Naomi, and she's taking care of everything. In fact, I'm speaking on her cell phone."

"And she ...?"

"She's seeing if they're ready for me."

****

At that exact moment, Naomi was actually speaking about him. "Drop him down a hole. Cut him loose. He's a liability."

"He's got nothing at all?" Carl Gressier was head of network procurement, a position as odious as it sounded and was, as Naomi referred to him, "My immediate inferior."

"He's got plenty, but we can offer him nothing he wants. He's got no ego, so he doesn't want his bit of fame. He's got enough money for what he needs, and he's cashed the check. So," she drew the word out, "cut him loose."

"And the time and money we've spent on him?"

"Mark it down to experience, we've done it before, send him." A thought seemed to strike her. "Do you know the story of the Trojan horse?"

"Something to do with USC?"

"No, I'm thinking of a leak."

"You want to go to the can?"

Carl wore his crassness like a banner. After all, no one could be that ignorant. Could they? Naomi took a deep breath. "We have his contract for a month." She breathed a silent prayer that Steven hadn't signed anything, "So we leak the information that—leave that to me, the important thing is we get our friends across the street to chase him and leave a clear field for us on your favorite agenda."

"And all this in less than twenty-four hours?"

"I'm the best screener in the business, Carl, that's why you hired me, but see for yourself."

"I wouldn't miss this." He lifted the internal telephone. "Get Glazer and Roberts in here. When?" He looked at Naomi. "Where is he?"

"He's outside at the moment talking to his wife on my cell phone. I'll send him in."

"No, wait 'til Roberts and Glazer get here."

"Do you want me in on this, or perhaps I might be a distraction—that is if you still want to see him?"

"See him? You bet your sweet ass I want to see him after what we've laid out, and yes, we don't want him showing off, so you'd better leave us, I'll get Judy to send him in when we're ready."

*****

Steven had a feeling of abandonment after Naomi had left, in spite of being asked at least three times if he wanted a drink by the artificial-looking girl behind the receptionist desk. He had declined at least three times and was told he was welcome three times and had also referred her to his agent once or twice, when, in response to a telephone call, he was told that Mr. Gressier was looking forward to seeing him. After leaving her in charge of Naomi's cell phone and being ushered into the office, he was introduced to Mr. Gressier—"Call me Carl"—and two of his associates. Although one of them welcomed him aboard and the other was looking forward to working with him, he couldn't remember their names and neither of them was Naomi, which increased his sense of abandonment. After the usual questions about warm beer and the Queen, he was asked if England had a black history month.

"No but we sometimes have a test series against the West Indies. I suppose that's the nearest we get, and there is a series against India and Pakistan, but I suppose they would be brown history months. Do you have brown history months? Or do the Mexicans have to make do with Caesar Chavez day?"

"I don't see—" Carl began, startled by Steven's lack of innocence.

"Caesar Chavez, as in Chavez Ravine where you threw all those Mexicans out of their homes to build Dodger Stadium. Not you personally, Carl," Steven added magnanimously. Carl looked for support from either side, and while one of his lieutenants was trying to find inspiration in the ceiling, tiles the other reluctantly came to his boss's aid.

"The reason we ask this," he said, drawing a line on his notepad as though he was cutting a steak, "it is black history month and should you be invited to appear on our show," he obviously didn't know that Steven had already cashed the check, "one of the other guests will be Congresswoman Edwina Walters, the Reverend Al Jackson, or the Doctor Jesse Sharpe and Ms. Yippee Goldstein. Would you have any problem with this?"

"The more the merrier, sunshine." He stopped suddenly and didn't continue until he was sure he had their full attention. "I suppose that's why Naomi isn't here. Funny, she didn't strike me as the overly sensitive type. Now where were we?"

"Do you know the significance of Rosa Parks in the civil rights movement?" the same voice continued doggedly (it was actually Roberts).

"The bus lady? She refused to give up her seat for a white person. I've often wondered how far she had to go."

This caused Glazer to interrupt his study of the ceiling. "What has that got to do with anything?"

"I'm glad you could join us. My point is that my father walked four miles home after work. I've often wondered how far Mrs. Parks would have had to walk if she didn't have the bus fare. Not"—he held up his hand to forestall any protests—"that I'm disputing her right to have a seat. In fact, I would have offered her mine, her being a lady, of whatever color, but that's just the way I was brought up by the very man who walked home after doing an eight-hour shift at the steelworks. There is also another thing I've just realized. She did more for Civil Rights with her bottom, that's ass to you," his smile embraced them all, and uninvited, he took a sip of water as though to get rid of a disagreeable taste, "than each of the other four ever did with their mouths."

After that the atmosphere definitely cooled. What did Mr. Jackson (as he had belatedly become) think of Gloria Ladler, a well-known show business lawyer?

"My first impression was that her nose was crooked, but in the light of subsequent events, I realized that was the only part of her that was straight."

12~"Is she pregnant?"

THERE WERE HANDSHAKES ALL AROUND. He was thanked for his input, and the term food for thought was bandied about. Before he knew it, he was being driven back to the Beverly Wilshire by an anemic individual who had obviously been dragged off another assignment and seemed to disguise his lack of presence by firing a series of inane questions, most of which Steven couldn't be bothered to answer.

Had he seen the Queen?

What did he think of Posh Spice?

What do crumpets taste like?

Did he play cricket?

All in all, he was a poor substitute for Naomi.

Although he reckoned he had given at least as good as he'd got, the interview had made him feel slightly nauseous, so much so that he had forgotten to ask his driver's name and only just remembered to thank him before he hurried out of the car and made his way to his room.

If before he had felt abandoned, now he felt positively deserted but decided to make the most of it and just wait the bastards out. He had disciplined himself to only telephone Pam every other day, because although their relationship meant at least as much to her, she could stand their temporary separation

157

better than he. His mood was lightened somewhat when he checked at the desk for any messages to be told by Janine that she couldn't guarantee Wolves Premiership but she would try to download a television channel that showed the latest football results (she pronounced it soccurr).

After thanking her politely, he told her, as a matter of fact, there was something else she could do for him. Did she know the nearest store that sold western gear? She did and even offered to accompany him, which he politely declined out of a perverse loyalty to Naomi. On returning from his errand and telling Janine that she wouldn't believe him if he told her what his purpose in visiting the store was, he was informed that she had been successful in her efforts just click on "in-house services" and follow the instructions. It even had some old games on. He was forestalled by using this extra diversion, however, for as he was admiring his purchases, the telephone rang. "Hello, sweet prince, how did it go?"

He kicked his shoes off and lay on the bed before answering, "What a nice surprise. I gave them their money's worth and they couldn't get rid of me fast enough. Now it's just a question of waiting here till they send me back over the pond. It could be two or three weeks, but there is a swimming pool and you can get football on the television. Are you all right, I mean, stuck on your own?"

"I almost wish I was, what with Major Ashton-something, calling me every five minutes and Mrs. Murdoch clucking round like a mother hen. I don't even have time to miss you." Then she added with uncanny perception, "I know they mean well, but it's as though they're afraid I'm going to fly the coop and get the next plane to LA in time to drag Naomi off you. I've not even had time to phone Pete yet, and I don't think I'll get around to Winkie Price. I *am* seeing a lot of Judith, and she's sweet but nobody's fool. Speaking of which, I've had an idea. Do you want to hear it?"

"I don't know, it depends on how much it will cost me and if it's to do with sex."

"It won't cost you a penny, and it may have something to do with sex, but not us."

"Go on," he said guardedly.

"Lydia is … unaccompanied, and I thought, with the help of Judith's future husband, we could get Chadders included in the wedding party and then …" He could feel her shrug over the telephone. "What do you think?"

"I don't know, it seems a bit obvious. After all, she has her pride, but if it can be done—"

"Steven, he is a member of the diplomatic service."

"I suppose so, but what about Chadders? Would he go for it?"

"As it is being arranged by his future king, I'm sure he'd be delighted, and on a personal level, I don't know if I mentioned this, Lydia is still a looker. Not wishing to burst your bubble, sweetheart, but I think she *is* over you. But looking on the bright side, I'm not, so hurry back."

Steven's estimate of two to three weeks for their separation was to prove joyously generous, as he was just deciding whether to avail himself of the swimming pool or try to navigate the television menu when there was a knock on the door. With a sigh, he climbed to his feet and opened it, to be greeted by the figure of Naomi. "Well, are you going to invite me in?"

"Sorry I thought it was someone to change the towels," he said foolishly.

"Going to change your life, sweet child." She brushed past him. "You want to stay here for almost a month or get back to your ever lovin'? Tell me the truth, I can take it."

"I've still got almost a month."

"Listen, I'm about to do the most unselfish thing I've done in my life, so, assuming that the answer is in the affirmative, when you get round to closing your mouth, how long will it take you to pack?"

"Ten minutes."

"I'll help you, let's go."

This time his estimate was much closer, because twelve minutes later he was thanking Janine for her attempts to provide entertainment and regretting he wouldn't be able to use it before being almost dragged by Naomi through the lobby doors.

In variance to her previous verbosity, Naomi was strangely quiet on the drive south on the 405 Freeway, and although he was aware that she was protecting him from something, she seemed almost angry. It wasn't until they pulled into the preferred parking that he ventured to break the silence. "Something bothering you Naomi?"

"Why?" She reached for her cell phone.

"You seem a little ... taciturn."

"You and those five-dollar words. I was just a bit miffed that there were no red lights so I could take advantage of you." She held up her hand, forestalling further conversation, and turned her attention to her cell phone. "Limited liability—yes, got it, and joint guest appearances for which we claim residuals." Then she said yes three times in quick succession while waving a sky cap over. "If another network calls you, tell them you're free to talk to them but any details—just the two cases in the trunk, honey." The last was to the sky cap, who, after a long look at Naomi's legs, loaded Steven's luggage on to a dolly, "Smoking gun, believe it. Eight o'clock tomorrow." She one-handedly closed the cell phone. "Right, let's go." She locked the car, and they were already at the check-in before she spoke again. "Here's your ticket, first class. There will be someone to meet you at Heathrow to take you to your wife. Sounds too good to be true?"

"*You* seem too good to be true, Naomi."

She smiled. "Right, sweet stuff, you won."

"I certainly didn't lose, did I."

She held both of his hands in hers. "I'm going to leave you now. I don't do airport good-byes. Tell Pamela to look after

you, hear? I'm not going to look back. Stay well, sweet stuff."
He was under no restrictions as he watched the departing form
of Naomi, but apparently not all her anger had left her, as she
actually snarled at some yuppie type who sought to importune
her.

Due in no small part to Naomi's attentions on the dance
floor and the alcohol she had poured down him, Steven slept
most of the flight. He didn't try to work out the complexities
of the in-flight entertainment but did eat, as the attendant had
woken him and he felt it churlish not to. Also, with his terror of
flying, he needed all the good karma he could get. It seemed to
work, as he arrived at Heathrow in a pleasant daze, and this air
of post-somnolent euphoria lasted until he got to the baggage
claim area. "Mr. Jackson? Neil Burrington, Lord Chancelor's
Office." He didn't look old enough to have a driving license,
and why couldn't he have a card with "Jackson" on it? Then
he'd have a fair chance of getting away. His demeanor wasn't
helped any by the fact that when he was away from Pam for a
time, he had an almost voyeuristic pleasure in seeing her from
a distance first. He hoped at least this character would make
himself scarce before he met Pam.

"You thought I might get lost?"

"Just thought with jet lag, might be able to help with customs
and whatnot. We've got your bags, this way."

To his credit, Neil was mercifully quiet on the way back,
leaving Steven to think of Pam and recognize familiar landmarks
and reading the advertisements of what the celebrities were
doing on and off the screen. Something in one of them seemed
to strike a chord, as he roused himself from his lethargy to ask
Neil, "Wherever we're going, could we go through Trafalgar
Square?"

"I thought you'd be in a hurry to see your wife."

"I'm sure we can manage a few minutes longer apart, if it's
not too much trouble?"

"Well it is a teeny bit out of the way, and with the traffic—"

Steven smiled as though he'd just listened to a boring joke. "Is that a no, Neil?"

"Not at all, certainly only too happy." The rest of the placating bromide was lost, as Steven had resumed his weary contemplation of the West London scenery.

They finally arrived, via Trafalgar Square, at North Audley Street, at a pretty, albeit nondescript, building with '20s-style white-framed windows.

"This it? Thanks." Without waiting for an answer, Steven was across the pavement through the glass-fronted door and lobby beyond and halfway up the stairs before his momentum seemed to run out.

He didn't know which room she was in.

Retracing his steps at a more sedate pace, he reached the bottom of the stairs. Neil would know; at least he could do something useful. At the side of the lobby there was a small counter with a bell marked "Inquiries" he hadn't noticed before. He rang the bell, and since there was no immediate response, hit it with more enthusiasm. This had the effect of the door behind the counter marked "Private" opening to reveal a trim-figured woman with tight grey hair and steel grey eyes, which regarded Steven curiously. "Can I help you?" She moved the bell out of his reach, as though fearing a further assault on it.

"I was hoping to see my wife, Mrs. Jackson."

"And you are?"

"Mr. —Steven."

"Oh, so you finally returned."

"Apparently."

"The lady *is* in. I'll see if it's convenient." She picked up a white phone and dialed a number. "After all, you don't want to go barging in." Her tone said, "Even you."

"Pamela, my dear, I've got something for you in the lobby. The wanderer has returned." The grey eyes favored Steven with a glance. "Apparently I have a person who claims to be Steven. Description? Blue eyes, short blond hair going grey. Well, passable looking, a little rough around the edges. Excuse me, just leave them there, Neil, thank you." Neil dealt with, she returned her attention to Pam. "Right, we'll take a chance and send him up. Not at all, my dear." She replaced the receiver gently. "You may go up. It's room three at the back, our best room. Leave the luggage, The Captain will take care of it, and tell Pamela I'll send up a cup of tea in fifteen minutes."

Knowing she was watching him and feeling slightly ridiculous, he ascended the stairs for a second time, this time getting all the way up, and having located number three and feeling even more ridiculous, he knocked on the door.

She must have been waiting for him because the door immediately opened and he was dragged inside and pushed against the door, slamming it shut. "Don't say anything." She pulled him to her, crushing him, punishing him for their separation.

"Well," she said as she eventually relaxed her grip on him, "finally, I thought you'd never get back."

"Getting back wasn't so bad. It was getting past your guardian downstairs. By the way, she said she'd be sending up a cup of tea up in fifteen, no maybe now thirteen minutes."

"We'd better keep our clothes on then." She stepped away from him, still holding his hands. "Shall we go for a walk in the park, or have you still got jet lag?"

"I don't know if I'm included in the tea, but a walk in the park sounds great, and let the jet lag take care of itself." A thought suddenly struck him. "I didn't get you a present. It was a bit rushed at the end, but I could have found time—"

"But you got back to me. That's the main thing."

"But I bought myself something that's—although I suppose they'll be paying for it."

"I'm curious. Can I see it when The Captain brings your luggage up?"

Half an hour later, having had tea (there *were* two cups) and having taken their leave of an anxious Mrs. Murdoch, they were walking along Rotten Row enjoying the earthy smell of the horses, the late afternoon sunshine, and each other. Steven appeared to be watching two Dobermans in the care of a larger version of Mrs. Murdoch. "Did you speak to William about Chadders?"

"Judy did all the arranging. He will be at the rehearsal and later at the rehearsal lunch, where he will make himself known, but not as a friend of yours. After all," she gently nudged him with her hip, "we want to give him a fighting chance."

"I suppose it will be all right," Steven begrudged.

"I told you, my love, he's a trained diplomat."

"Yes, there is that. It'll be nice to see Chadders again. Do you know the barmaid at the Old Kings Head in Santa Monica thought he and I—"

"If you'd gone to the same school, you might have been."

They walked on in silence for a while, pondering the inequities of the British school system before Pam spoke again.

"Speaking of—"

"What, me and Chadders?"

"No, I mean the opposite, moving right along. Tell me about LA."

"I can't remember how much I told you."

"Tell me all of it."

"Well," Steven left the Dobermans to their business and transferred his attention to the trees bordering Park Lane, "I was met at the airport by Naomi."

"What was she like?" She squeezed his arm. "Don't forget the details."

"She was tall, blackish, quite attractive in an Amazon sort of way, very self confident, and very amusing. We did the rounds of Hollywood, Burbank, and Studio City. By the way, the Maid Marion has gone to the knacker's yard."

"That's no surprise. Larry was a twerp. It's a shame for Irene, though. I wonder what happened to Jamie."

"He's a qualified chef, too good for that place, so I'm sure he'll find something else when he's ready. Where was I?"

"Apparently tripping the light fantastic with some nubile— what was her name?"

"Naomi. Then we talked and talked, or rather I talked and she listened. She's a screener."

"And how did you know that, I wonder?"

"Obviously she's not the sort who would be satisfied by just ferrying people from the airport, so I asked her what her main function was and she told me she was a screener. She screens people to see if they'd be suitable."

Pam threw her head back and gave a delighted peal of laughter. "I thought you said screamer. I wonder where my mind was. So was she, not nice, what's the word I'm looking for?"

"Very striking and good company. That's her job, but never mind.

"Then she took me to the corporate headquarters. That's when I was finally able to phone you while I was waiting to be interviewed. Then I went into the interview room, where I was asked a lot of stupid questions, to which I gave some uncomfortable answers—uncomfortable for them, that is. I just danced them around a bit. No wonder the media is like a ... I can't understand why Naomi would work for dingalings like that. And finally I was driven back to the hotel by someone who wasn't Naomi."

"She was probably screening someone else," Pam said with an edge to her voice.

"On the way back, I was asked more asinine questions, which I didn't bother to answer. I'd barely got back to the hotel and phoned you when Naomi arrived, and it was, 'Break camp, load up, move out, PUFO.'"

"PUFO?"

He smiled shyly. "An old army expression, 'PUFO—pack up and something off,' the something beginning with F."

"We live and learn. So?"

"So twenty minutes after she arrived, we were tearing down the 405 Freeway heading toward LAX. I'm sorry I didn't have time to buy you a present."

"You already said that. I told you, I wasn't expecting one."

"Probably not, but I should have brought you one, especially as I bought myself one, sort of."

"Not a motorbike?"

He smiled in spite of himself. "No, not a motorbike."

"That's all right, then, when do I get to see it?"

"As soon as we get back."

She hugged his arm in encouragement. "Good—so what happened then?"

"She saw me through the preliminaries, first class, and a Chadders wannabe called Neil picked me up at Heathrow, and here we are."

"Yes, here we are. Naomi seems to have spent a lot of time with you."

"Hardly let me out of sight. Expected her to ask for my passport, and apparently you've been closely chaperoned?" He suddenly turned on his heel and walked backward, keeping up with Pam.

"Are you looking for someone?" Since there was no answer, she continued, "Well as I said, Mrs. Murdoch clucks around like a mother hen and Major whatever—I'm sorry, they all sound the same to me—calls me. I forgot, he wanted you to call him as soon as you got back."

"And you haven't told me until now because?"

"I thought as your wife I deserved some of your time first."

"Fair enough." Apparently satisfied that there was no one following them, Steven resumed his original perambulation. "I fancy a drink before we go back."

"How far is the Victory Services Club from here?"

"It's within walking distance, but I think you have to be a resident to use the bar."

"I didn't check out." Although the nearest person was fifty feet away, she leaned and whispered in his ear, "I still have a room there."

"Good, and leave Mrs. Murdoch to worry."

"She won't worry as long as I'm back before dark."

"Back before dark? You're kidding!"

Pamela made a curiously English gesture. She raised her two fingers to her temple. "Scout's honor."

He graciously forbore to tell her, especially with the anticipation of the delights to come, that her gesture was in fact a wolf cub salute.

When they returned to the hotel, surprisingly, Mrs. Murdoch wasn't waiting on the doorstep, but after getting to their room, Steven barely had time to show Pam his present when the phone rang (so their arrival had *not* gone unobserved). "Mr. Jackson? Ashford-Bowdler here. How did you find LA?"

"LA was ... LA," Steven replied in a world-weary tone as though he'd popped over to Los Angeles just to buy some toothpaste. "Thank you, but as I've returned and am on post now, the memsahib is no longer in need of entertaining."

"Quite so old boy, *old boy*? But that's only part of my job description. I'm to hold your hand, so to speak, right through the fun and games."

"That's nice."

"So if I could just pop around, I'll bring you up to date, go through the schedule, two rehearsals, two lunches, and there'll be the fittings—"

"Only two rehearsals?"

"Oh yes, first rehearsal tomorrow, and then if that goes all right, the final dress rehearsal, but I'll explain all that when I get there—about half an hour, if that's convenient."

"Half an hour's fine. We'll put some clothes on. Major Ashford-Bowdler." He replied after he'd hung up, "Your self-appointed chaperone. I remember him now. He's the tosser who tried to get me to wear built-up shoes. Harmless, but a bit on the pompous side. Apparently he's transferred his attentions to me. He's going to, I quote, 'Hold your hand,' meaning mine, 'through the fun and games.' Won't that be nice?"

"Peachy, and I thought I'd only got Lydia to worry about."

Whatever his other attributes, Major Ashford-Bowdler was nothing if not punctual, for exactly thirty minutes later, Mrs. Murdoch summoned them downstairs, and thirty-five minutes later, fully clothed and Pam carrying Steven's present, they were greeting him.

"Major Ashford-Bowdler, good evening. I don't believe you've met the memsahib?"

"Ian, please," he replied in his no-ranks-in-the-mess voice.

"Pamela." After carefully depositing Steven's present on the sideboard, she offered her hand and her warm smile.

"Splendid, I've just ordered tea." As if on cue, Mrs. Murdoch entered bearing a tray, which earned another splendid, "Do you mind if Mrs. Murdoch joins us?"

"Not at all, it's her house." And suiting his actions to his words, Steven pulled out a chair, earning him a gracious nod from Mrs. Murdoch and yet another splendid from Ian.

"So, as I said before, but I'll just run through it for the benefit of the ladies, there'll be two rehearsals. If everything goes well, two briefings and the actual ceremony, plus, of course, there'll be the rehearsal lunch and the wedding breakfast. All right so far?"

Steven nodded together with the others, wondering if it would be justifiable homicide. "'I'm sorry, your worship, I ODed on splendid." *At least it wasn't "brilliant."*

Meanwhile, Ian had continued. "And of course there'll be fittings for the morning suit, hire of course," he added with heavy humor. "I don't suppose there's much use for them in Arizona."

"I don't know, I thought it would be just the job to clean the swimming pool. Do I get a top hat?"

"Quite." He gave a wintry smile to show that it was taken in good part. "About the fittings, we were rather hoping you'd reconsider. Yes?"

Steven held up his hand as though stopping traffic. "Major— Ian. I have given this problem much thought, and I think I've solved your problem, or at least one of them. Pamela, if you would. Thank you." Pamela had handed him the box from the sideboard. "I'm sure HMG will recompense me." He slid a receipt across the table with his forefinger.

"I don't know if HMG ..." Ian looked at Mrs. Murdoch for support, but her allegiance seemed to be shifting. "Are they leather?"

"Of course. Personally I tended toward the alligator, but probably too much of a thing." And there the matter ended, as Ian, with as much grace as he could muster, carefully folded the receipt. "So, first things first, the first rehearsal will be tomorrow. Can you be ready by seven?"

"0700 hours. Got it."

"And we've got you down for a fitting at ten on Friday, all right?"

"We're all yours."

"So the transport should be here at—"

"I think if you just give us the address we can manage."

"You sure? So there'll be a further fitting on Thursday next, again, no problem? Then the dress rehearsal at a date to be announced, with the full band."

"So we don't get a full band tomorrow?"

"No, it is I believe called canned music. The band will be rehearsing elsewhere—all a question of logistics. After the dress rehearsal, there'll be a rehearsal lunch given by Her Majesty, and if that goes well, the rehearsal, not the lunch," he gave himself another smile, "there'll be nothing else until the ceremony on the twenty-seventh after which—"

"Can I ask a question?" Perhaps emboldened by Mrs. Murdoch's endorsement of Steven's present, Pamela saw no reason why the council should go on without her.

"Of course, my dear."

"Well, we only knew of Judith's existence a couple of months ago and now—*is she pregnant?"*

The silence went on and on until finally, possibly as she was hostess, Mrs. Murdoch saw fit to break it. "I personally don't know, and I wouldn't think Ian does, but I do know that they were engaged before it was made public, and I don't think it affects anyone here."

"You're quite right." Pam was apparently unfazed by the consternation around her. "I just wanted to know how soon I'd be sleeping with a grandfather," she said, and equanimity was restored.

"And after that you can go home or stay in London if you have made other arrangements," continued Ian, as though no interruption had occurred. "I say home. I suppose you do consider Arizona your home."

"I most certainly do not. Arizona is just where the bills are sent. I suppose home is where Pamela is."

"Yes, I see, no offense meant."

But Steven was already warming to his theme. "I like Arizona, but I am still an Englishman, and England is still presumably home, although I will say that every time I come here something else is changed. God save fish and chips and national hunt racing, say I, especially Ludlow, but you know the last time I went there, the bookies actually had digitalized chalkboards, none of this, 'I can't give you seven to one on that—me chalk broke,' and what about the poor bookie's clerks? I suppose they've gone by way of the ..." He seemed at a loss to choose something else that had gone, but he rallied with, "Do you know they had a woman bookie?"

After that there were mutual good wishes all around, with Steven promising to be ready on the dot at seven "best boots and beret," and Major Ian Ashford-Bowdler took his leave thanking providence that there were no further difficulties, except perhaps presenting accounts with the receipt for two hundred pounds for of a pair of hand-tooled leather cowboy boots.

13~Not Quite Saint Paul's

"THAT REMINDS ME, MRS. MURDOCH," said Steven as though they'd spoken of little else, "where's the nearest fish and chip shop?"

There was *not*, he was assured, a fish and chip shop in *this* area, but their hostess did know how to make fish and chips. (She called it a fish supper, which confirmed Steven's suspicions that she was Scottish.) "Would seven o'clock be convenient? It would." And after Pam's offer to help with the clearing up was smilingly declined, they made their way to their room, where all that was on television appeared to be Hillary Clinton crying her mail-order tears.

"She's going to cry her way into the White House." Steven dropped the remote control on the bed beside him. "After all, Tom Connely whined his way into a knighthood on *60 Minutes*. Do you think we're expected to dress for dinner?"

"Well I don't suppose you've packed your tuxedo, but I think we should put some clothes on, and a shirt and tie would be nice."

"I've got some clothes on."

"I meant after our shower. I'm going to have one, and I assume you wanted one with me. It might put you in a better mood," and Pam began to undress.(which did)

They dined in solitary splendor, as they were obviously the only guests, in a room decorated with old hunting prints. With the walk in the park, and his wife's tender attentions, Steven had worked up quite an appetite and his empty plate was met with approval from Mrs. Murdoch, so much so that he half-expected to be awarded a pudding. The pudding was not forthcoming, but they were invited to a drink in the private lounge, after which they were invited to take a turn in the garden. "Pam knows how to get there." The garden turned out to be a long, narrow, meticulously manicured lawn with a high wall at the end, which obviously separated it from the mews behind. It was illuminated by a solitary street lamp, which bathed it in a sodium glow, giving the appearance of a sickly sunset. It reminded Steven of a well-tended prison yard.

"Be hard to climb that," he said, nodding at the wall.

"Why would you want to?"

He shrugged, dismissing the subject. "Have you met this Captain? Or is he just a figment of Mrs. Murdoch's imagination?"

"Oh, he's real enough." She linked her arm in his. "A sort of general handyman, a bit shy, but nice. I think Mrs. Murdoch's the boss."

"Of that I have no doubt. The Captain and Mrs. Murdoch, got quite a ring to it," they both laughed.

"Are you going to see Lydia?"

"I suppose, as the bride's mother, she'll be involved in the rehearsals, so I'm sure we'll run into each other."

"I mean privately. I think Judith would want you to."

"I'll have a word with her tomorrow. Nice garden, this. Have you spent much time here?"

"Yes, I used to do a lot of reading here while I was waiting for you. Mrs. Murdoch introduced me to the works of Robert Browning. I think we can go in now."

In another revelation, which, in the light of experience, surprised Steven less and less, The Captain, he was introduced as nothing else, was surprisingly knowledgeable on Jazz and had in fact played trombone with Nat Gonella and his Georgians, did Steven know him? Not personally Steven had to admit but he had seen Nat Gonella and his Georgians at the Theatre Royal, Bilston.

"Oh yes the old Theatre Royal, played there, I suppose it's been knocked down now or used to play bingo."

"No," Steven assured him, "it still exists, although not as the Theatre Royal. It does have live musical acts there. I read recently that Bill Wyman's band appeared there." He hoped an ex-member of the Rolling Stones would be more acceptable than bingo.

"And Wolverhampton Hippodrome? No, alas, that was burned down sometime in the '60s and was rebuilt as a Times Furnishing." And no, Steven hadn't seen Harry Roy there. "But we did used to go there," he recalled. "There was a street that ran between the side of the Hippodrome and the old indoor market, and there was an entrance that you could get in to the cheap seats called 'the gods' so high up it almost made your nose bleed. You know, the street was actually called Cheapside."

He gave a sad smile. "All gone now, the indoor market, the old wholesale market. They actually built an administrative building on the site, which was supposed to have a nuclear-proof cellar for the archives so in the event of a nuclear holocaust, you could be vaporized but your tax bills would be safe." He roused himself from his melancholy. "Sorry about that, I do remember there was a pub next to the entrance to the back of the theater called the Queens Arms, which hosted the March Hares Jazz Club, every Friday night. I used to attend there regularly. My sister said it was because I could get rejected by a better class of girl. She was going to grammar school at the time. The Grammar School has got a lot to answer for. Anyway, there was a March Hares Jazz Club Friday night, and they actually had another club on Tuesday nights that played modern jazz. They used to have some good guest musicians there, Ronnie Ross,

Joe Harriet, but I don't suppose you'd be familiar with these names, being modern jazz."

"Jazz is jazz." The Captain showed unexpected muscle. "I've played with Ronnie Ross at the Marquee." Then another thought seemed to strike him. "Wolverhampton, didn't they used to have a good football team?"

"They still have," he was assured shortly. "They're just going through a bad period, which unfortunately has lasted thirty years."

After that, the conversation resumed to safer channels as The Captain regaled them with stories of other bands he had played with, and Geraldo's navy so called, he courteously explained to Pam because Geraldo's orchestra used to play on the Cunard line as they plied between England and America and if you're lucky or good enough to be part of the ship's orchestra, you could play with the American jazz musicians on 52nd Street while the liners were berthed in New York, an opportunity not usually available to British musicians because of the American musicians union. "But I make no judgment."

He had led such a full life that Steven wondered when he found the time to earn his commission. He probably earned it in the Salvation Army while he was learning to play the trombone.

****

Steven woke early as usual and had time for a morning walk before returning to rouse Pam in time for the early breakfast they'd arranged with Mrs. Murdoch, or rather she'd arranged with them. "Eat well, you've a hard day in front of you, and don't forget your footwear."

With his customary punctuality, Ian collected them at seven o'clock, and after accepting a cup of tea from Mrs. Murdoch, he ushered them to the waiting car with Neil behind the wheel. Obviously he had not been invited in for tea. After making them comfortable in the rear seat, Ian occupied the front passenger seat. "On our way, I'll just go over the order of the day, if I may."

"Do you want to go via Trafalgar Square?" said Neil.

"Why not, if you can manage it."

"So I suppose that puts Piccadilly Circus out of the question," Pam murmured in Steven's ear. "Pity, I rather fancied some harmless fun circling Eros."

"I'm afraid we won't have time," said Ian, giving Neil a sharp look. Steven had the impression they were a pair of queens that had a tiff.

"Right," said Ian, bringing the meeting to order. "We will be going to …" he mentioned an obscure army barracks, "where the gymnasium is the same length as the aisle of St. Paul's."

"So we're not actually going to St. Paul's?"

"Question of logistics. The feeling is that the interruption to the day-to-day operation of St. Paul's should be kept to a minimum. We don't all get together until the dress rehearsal. Today is just about you accompanying your daughter down the aisle—"

"The nave."

"What?"

"It's called the nave. The central passageway is called the nave. It's the two side ones that are called the aisles. It's a common mistake," Steven added generously.

"Yes, everything will be explained when we get there, but I'll just run through the program, okay?"

"Sure, forewarned is forearmed, as they say."

"So, you will form up with the honor guard of the Parachute Regiment."

"Which battalion?"

"Battalion? I rather think they'll be drawn from all battalions, not that I suppose it matters."

"But if they're not from the same battalion, they'll have different-colored lanyards. Just thought I'd mention it."

"Good point. I'll make sure your concern is passed to the appropriate authority. So when the music starts, the leading soldier will give the order to slow march, and you wait until the first and second pair have passed you before you step off and you'll maintain your position between the second and third pair, with your hand in the bride's. All right so far?"

"Got it, but she won't be a bride at this point, will she? Not until I've given her away. But she'll always be my daughter, so why don't you call her that?"

"As you wish," replied Ian, showing remarkable restraint. "You don't have to keep in step as long as you maintain your position in the center of the phalanx." He paused, as though expecting an interruption, and when one was not forthcoming continued, "Until you come to be level with HRH[15], where you will come to a halt, release your daughter's hand, and that's you until the officiant, that's the person who's performing the ceremony, says, 'Who gives this woman.' Then you take her hand, put it in his, and say, 'I do' nice and clear voice, and that's you until they are pronounced man and wife. Then the bridal couple leave together with the bridesmaids, and then the best man and the maid of honor, and then you with the Princess Royal. All right so far?"

"Walk in the park, old son," said Steven, gazing at the buds that were just about to open on the passing trees.

"Then we reach the portico, and this is where we have to box clever. You do not get into the coach with the Princess Royal, okay?"

"I don't mind if she doesn't. Who do I get in the coach with?"

"You are to ride with the—the bride's mother."

"Fine, I'm sure we'll have plenty to talk about."

"The point is, and as I say here's where we have to box clever, you will be in the third coach. You position yourself near the bride's mother, but you don't start walking down the steps until the previous coach has departed. Any sooner and there'll be congestion at the bottom of the steps, and any later and your coach will be kept waiting. We want you both to arrive at the bottom of the steps together."

"Obviously a lot of thought has gone into this."

"Well it's not the first time we've done it—yes, my dear?" Pamela had just raised her hand to make a point.

"Who will be in the second coach?"

"That will be the Prince of Wales and the Duchess of Cornwall."

"And what do I do? I thought I'd be riding with Prince Charles. After all, I am the bride's stepmother."

"It's a question of protocol."

"I'm sure there'd be room for me, so couldn't protocol be stretched a little?"

A little pompous he may, be but Ian Ashford-Bowdler was no fool,

"My dear," he said, "we've already arranged for someone to come from Los Angeles to keep your husband's ex-girlfriend occupied and we've got Steven here, er," he allowed himself a thin smile, "poncing up the aisle, sorry the nave, in cowboy boots. I think protocol has already been stretched a bit thin."

He was obviously expecting further trouble, but help arrived from an unexpected quarter. "You have to take his point, Pamela," Steven said, all light and reason. "I mean, it's a matter of form. There are guidelines."

But Pamela was obviously not to be easily mollified, "So what *do I do*, whistle up a taxi?"

"I don't suppose you'd get a taxi there, my dear," Ian gave as good as he got, "but at the appropriate time, you will be escorted by an usher to the steps, where you will ride with the two pages and Miss Biderman's companion, a Mister Chaddersly-Corbet, who I believe you know."

"You have to understand, Ian," Steven explained, "Pamela has a soft spot for HRH. I think it's the parachute wings. What were you in?"

"Irish guards actually."

"Well done. Did you serve with Chadders?"

"Ah here we are." They had just pulled up outside a neo-Victorian barracks, which reminded Steven of the worst school he had ever attended, and which forestalled any further inquiry into Major Ashford-Bowdler's military service. Once inside, Ian handed them over to a character who was obviously in charge of the rehearsal. "He's to be addressed as simply H," and belying his words, "Sir, Mr. and Mrs. Jackson. Well, I'll be off. Give us a call when you're finished." Ian pressed a card into Steven's hand and left with Neil.

"They're probably going to measure their flat for curtains," muttered Steven as they entered through the forbidding doors.

"Steven, it's a lovely day, and for the next few weeks, we're going to stay in London at someone else's expense. We'll probably get to see David and spend some time with your daughter, plus you're probably going to meet the Queen, so could we take the chip off your shoulder and leave it in Coseley, if not for your daughter's sake, for mine, okay?"

Duly chastened and rebuked, Steven allowed himself to be acknowledged, "Yes, welcome to hell, Mr. Jackson and Mrs., may I call you Pamela? Splendid, I'm the Major Factotum, call me H. I'm afraid it's going to be rather boring for you, my dear, as you'll be guided by pages on the actual day, but if we get cracking, we should be finished before too long and have your husband back to you, so if you can make yourself comfortable over there with the rest of the wallflowers, we'll be ready to start in about ten minutes." The wallflowers appeared to include a dozen soldiers in No. 2 dress uniform whose maroon lanyard indicated that they were all from 1 Para.

"Poppi, how are you?" As the dutiful daughter she had become, Judith took his face in her hands and kissed him continental style. "And Pamela, you cannot trust Poppi with all these aristocratic ladies." Pamela was similarly greeted. "I have been here since six doing the, what is it? Responses, and now I have to go and get this invention for the gown and the train. Forgive me but see me again before you leave, and Mr. Chaddersly-something is here, so charming, don't you think?"

"Taught him everything I know," Steven agreed.

"Right, I'm going to join the ladies. Behave yourself." And with a wifely peck on the cheek, Pamela was gone.

"Right, if everyone's ready, let's get cracking." H's handclaps echoed around the empty walls. "Let's have the Guard of Honour five pairs, the leading soldier here, Mr. Jackson here just inside, good. Now leave space for Miss Biderman and her finery, best man, bridegroom's party in place. Ah, Miss Biderman, here if you please." He created an arc with the papers he was holding. Judith's "invention" appeared to be a curtain wrapped around her waist and what seemed to be an elaborate tablecloth attached to her shoulders.

"Mr. Jackson, you'll hold your arm thus and Miss Biderman thus, not too rigid, and Miss Biderman—no, my dear, don't grab hold of him. He's not going to run away. Like so." He actually placed his hand on Steven's arm, much to the amusement of the Honour Guard. "The opening line of the pomp and circumstances will be your cue," he addressed the Honour Guard Commander, who looked about sixteen, "give it a couple of beats and then the order to slow march, and bride, wait until the second pair has passed you, and bridesmaids, when the music starts, you pick up the train. Yes, Mr. Jackson?"

"There doesn't appear to be a band."

"We will be rehearsing to, I believe the term is, canned music. The band are rehearsing elsewhere where the acoustics are as near as possible to St. Paul's."

"Good idea," Steven said, impressed.

"Thank you. We *have* done this sort of thing before, and while questions and comments are welcome, please leave them until the break." H was obviously made of sterner stuff than Ian. "And honour guard, you halt when the leading pair have reached the front pew. Now any questions?" There were none. "Right! Music!"

As the sound of pomp and circumstance, if not exactly filling the room, at least reached them, it started. The bridesmaids picked up the "train," the Honour Guard Commander gave the command in a sort of hoarse whisper, and Judith had obviously been briefed, because they both stepped off simultaneously exactly between the second and third pair. As they progressed, Steven found he was actually enjoying it, and for the first time, he could actually imagine himself walking his daughter down the nave of St. Paul's. He'd show this lot that a chap from Coseley could put it on. The walk seemed exceptionally long (at Pam's reminding he had changed into the cowboy boots), but they finally halted abreast of someone who Steven was not really surprised to discern was not Prince William.

"Good. Now at this point, Honour Guard stay exactly as you are. Miss Biderman, you take your hand from your father's and hold your bouquet, and Mr. Jackson, lower your arm and arrange your hands thus." H discreetly covered his genitals. "And now we've already done the responses, so I will officiate, 'Dearly beloved, we are gathered together' waffle waffle, and then we come to, 'who giveth this woman.'" Although Steven was prepared for this, the "I do" came out as a strangled croak.

"Good, well done. Just a few minor points." H looked down at his notes, but no one could remember him adding anything to them. "Mr. Jackson, a little more power on the 'I do.'"

"I know, sorry about that."

"My dear chap it's perfectly understandable. If we were perfect, there'd be no need for us to be here, and I'd be playing golf. Just remember to swallow a few times during the responses, and don't forget to keep breathing. bridesmaids, just remember at the dress rehearsal and the ceremony there'll be handles on the train, so you don't have to look down, just keep looking ahead. When the Honour Guard step off, you don't follow them, irresistible though you may find them to be. You wait until the bride moves off, and Honour Guard, congratulations, you showed remarkable restraint, apart from that, everything was fine let's do it once more to this point," and they did. Steven kept his larynx suitably lubricated, the bridesmaids stepped off at the right time, and the "I do" was delivered as near perfect as to warrant H proceeding.

"Then, Mr. Jackson, for the next few seconds, you will be the only one moving. It's your moment of fame, enjoy it. You take the bride's right hand with your right hand and place it in the groom's left hand and return to your position, momentarily. Then you move at least five paces to your daughter's right and resume your 'at ease' position. Now this will be the longest time when you all have to just stand still, so *no* fidgeting or I will tear off your arm and beat you to death with the soggy end. Just a little light relief, people. So we'll go from 'who giveth this woman' in my best Archbishop of Canterbury voice. 'Who giveth this woman?'"

"I do." Steven took Judith's hand and placed it in that of her substitute fiancee's.

"Good. 'Do you, William?' And remember, no fidgeting until, 'I now pronounce you man and wife.' Now bridesmaids, your moment in the sun. At this you pick up the train, and as they turn to face each other, you swing to the right, narrowly missing Mr. Jackson if he's moved enough. Mr. Jackson, at least five paces or you could be knocked over by your daughter's train. Not quite the impression we're looking for. Then, 'you may kiss the bride' at this point. *You* don't get to kiss her, you randy sod. Prince William will lift her veil, kiss the bride, and then, 'Whom God has put together let no man put asunder.' You make a further sweep as they turn inward again to turn down the aisle, and that's it until the bridal pair take their cue from the music and you take your cue from them. You step off. Honour Guard, any time during Prince William's post-nuptial snog, you give the order to about turn. Remember the left-hand file do their about turn to the left as you both turn outward from the bridal couple. Is that clear?"

"Perfectly, thank you," came the assured reply, which Steven supposed was because the maneuver was quite familiar to them. "Good, then when the bridal pair set off, this time you take your cue from them. When they reach the second pair, you give the order to 'slow march.' After the last bridesmaid reaches the first pew, they will be followed by the best man and Maid of Honour. When the best man steps off, Mr. Jackson, you will take his place, where you will be joined by the Princess Royal. At this point, you may smile at the PR."

Steven was about to comment but was stilled by a quelling glance from H. "Then when the bridal couple reach the first pew, the giver away and matron of honor will follow, followed by the best man. When the phalanx," he seemed to enjoy this, as he paused before continuing, "reach the portico, they will remain there, to be joined by you, and the bride will be detrained—bloody awful word that. At the given moment, they will continue straight down the steps to the waiting coach. The remainder wait in the portico, but that's enough for now. Let's do a run through, and then we can break for lunch. So from the," again there was a totally unnecessary glance at his notes, "'Who giveth this woman.' Mr. Jackson, could you manage another 'I do'? Splendid," and on it went.

Steven was amazed that the time had passed so quickly, but he was feeling ravenous. Escorting your daughter down the center of a barrack's gymnasium while she was wearing a curtain and a tablecloth must be very beneficial to the appetite. So he said, "I do" and handed his daughter's hand to someone who was not her intended husband and moved five paces to safety. Then he took the place of someone he hoped was not the best man, to be joined by someone who was definitely not the Princess Royal. He exercised his option not to smile and at the appropriate time walked down what was not the nave of Saint Paul's and fervently hoped that lunch was more substantial.

"Poppi, can you believe this?" Judith had divested herself of her ersatz cape and wedding dress. "All this fuss. I hope it doesn't make you regret finding your daughter."

"Wouldn't miss it for the world," Steven assured her. "Actually, I'm quite impressed. We seem to be getting it together." At H's direction, they had broken for lunch, and the protagonists and supporting acts had drifted apart and reassembled on more familiar lines. The Guard of Honour were waiting to be invited to join the repast, dividing their attention between the buffet and the bridesmaids, who were dividing their attention between Judith and the guard of honor, while the principals were slumped on chairs against the walls. It occurred to Steven that it had been as tiring for them as it was for him, and they wanted to make a success of it as much as he did. He was actually about to go looking for Pam when Judith accosted him.

"Good, er, Poppi." She took his arm in her hands. "My mother isn't here today."

"I see." Steven waited for the other part of the news, and when it wasn't forthcoming, ventured, "Anything wrong? Not ill, is she?"

"No, not ill. You understand, things have not been easy for her, and she does not want an atmosphere. She wanted to be sure it was all right with Pamela."

"Speaking of Pamela, have you seen her?" Steven was at a loss to understand Judith's fixation with an "atmosphere," and it would be a while before he would be enlightened.

"No, that's why I wanted to have a quick word. She wants to see you soon. Would that be all right?"

"I take it you mean your mother. That would be fine. I'll clear my desk, not that there's a lot on it, and Pam will be fine with it. I can guarantee no atmosphere. Are you reassured?"

"I will telephone you and arrange, yes? The same place as we met, and this time you can walk up the river. You can have an assignation with my mother and pass by Boadicea. You can even see if your other girlfriend has turned up in Trafalgar Square."

"I will look forward to it—well speak of the devil, Chadders," for it was none other. "How are you? Makes a change from the Olde King's Head, doesn't it? You've met my daughter?"

"Indeed I have. Yes, quite a change. I'm sure England gets colder every time I come home."

"That's because every time you come home you're older, Chadders old son."

14~"So, here we are."

STEVEN WAS WAITING AT EXACTLY the same place where he had waited for Judith. He had explained the situation to Pamela, who, as expected, betrayed very little concern. "She probably just wants to go over old times so that when we meet it won't be so strained. Besides, I'm sure Charles has done his best to massage her ego."

So here he waited, only this time he planned to proceed up river, having ascertained that there were enough statues for diversion if the conversation became too heavy. There was General Gordon to get them past the first awkward moments after crossing Northumberland Avenue. Lydia would like the stories about him rescuing young boys from the London slums. Couldn't do it now. The gutter press would have a field day, and then the story about the night he was about to embark for the Sudan and arrived at Waterloo—*was* it Waterloo?—without any money and Lord Somebody or Other had to take a collection round the gentleman's clubs, (a very different meaning in those days) of Pall Mall. for his expenses.

"I say, old bean, we're about to send Chinese Gordon to give this Mahdi chappie a thing or two to think about, only thing is, Old Gordon arrived without a bean. Apparently dined at old Southerby's place and spent some time playing with the kids," again, we're talking about a more innocent world, "and didn't have time to go to the bank. Whatever you can spare, old chap. Frightfully generous. See if old Caneford's in the billiard room. Weren't they at school together?'

Then on the other side there would be the Royal Air Force Monument and conveniently close, the Battle of Britain Memorial. The Chindit Statue—that would be worth a look—and then there would be New Scotland Yard. He might not even have to go so far as Boadicea near Westminster pier. So in response to very specific instructions from Judith, he had stationed himself leaning against the embankment wall just up river from the pier.

When the taxi arrived, he knew it was her. It stopped too short of the pier for anyone embarking, and anything else was on the other side of the road. Still it stopped a good twenty yards from him, and he surmised this was to generate the maximum drama out of the situation. This notion appeared to be confirmed, as she did not look in his direction as she paid off the taxi, and he could have sworn she straightened her shoulders before she turned and walked unhurriedly toward him. She stopped about six feet away, and they both contemplated each other as though looking for something that the intervening years had left. Her eyes were still the same light blue, her skin still had that translucent look, and only the faintest lines at the side of her mouth attested to the intervening years.

"So," he said finally, "here we are."

"Steven, yes, here we are."

"You look well."

"Thank you, you also."

"Shall we?"

"So English—all this time and not even an embrace?"

He finally pushed himself away from the wall and crossed the distance between them, which he suspected was the reason for the embrace, and held her lightly in his arms.

"Good, I was beginning to think—now we walk." She released his face and clasped his arm in both hands, as Judith had done. "You seem to have captivated my daughter. She said you are the expert on London, especially the statues."

"I was sorry to hear about Ali."

"What can I tell you? I survived."

They traversed Northumberland Avenue in silence before she spoke again. "Everybody leaves me—Ali, you, and soon Judith."

"You raised Judith by yourself? It must have been hard."

She shrugged in answer. "You do what you do."

"She is a credit to you. She's very—she's delightful, and William is obviously devoted to her."

She shook her head as though her daughter's future happiness irritated her. "Tell me about yourself. What have you been doing all these years?"

"Growing older," he dismissed the question and stopped, forcing her to do the same. "Why didn't you tell me about Judith?"

"I telephoned and the American girl answered, so ..." She shrugged. "And the last time we met you were, I have to say, not sympathetic."

"I'm from Coseley. We're not big on sympathy, giving it, seeking it, or accepting it, but I do take your point. I could have—but why?"

"Steven, you already were involved with somebody else. What would you have done? What *could* you have done?"

They must have started walking again, because he halted as though the effort of both moving and answering the question was too much. He looked at the oily swell of the Thames, but apparently the answer was not there. "I don't know," he finally admitted. "I just don't know."

It was not until they reached Horse Guards Avenue that he spoke. "Did Ali think she was his?"

The question did not seem to surprise her. "As I said before, Steven, 'You do what you do.' Basta." This last expression was, if his memory was true, an Italian word that meant, 'The end, no more discussion,' and her next words confirmed this. "Do you see much of Adam?"

"No, he ran off to his mother in Texas, and the good people of the Lone Star State are welcome to them both. "

"So he was living with you and the American girl. I do not understand."

"It's—a bit involved."

"So? We have time, unless you would prefer not talk about it."

"After you—we parted, about a year later I met Pam—that's her name, by the way, Pam, if you can get your tongue 'round it."

"Ah" she said softly, and her next words showed that she did not need statues as a diversion. "I remember when I was trying to teach you the word L'Chaim, and you said, 'I don't know if I can get my Anglo-Saxon tongue 'round that,' and I said—do you know what? 'It's the only thing you are likely to get your Anglo- Saxon tongue 'round.' You were so, so ... I thought that was the most attractive thing about you, and later—but I should not talk of such things, yes? After you met Pamela?"

"We moved in together. Two years later we bought a house and got married. At this time Kathy wanted to move to Texas, and at the time she was not proving to be a very good mother and I didn't think it was a good idea for Adam, so we applied for custody. I hate that term. I convinced the judge that she was as bad a mother as she was a wife. It wasn't very difficult. By the way, that's New Scotland Yard." He indicated the red-bricked edifice that had graced the prologue of many a detective B movie. "Actually, it's not so new anymore because they moved to a new, New Scotland Yard nearer to the House of Commons."

"What happened with Adam?" Apparently Steven's family life held more allure than the former headquarters of the Metropolitan Police.

"Well about two years later, she rang up out of the blue and suggested we got back together 'for Adam's sake and be a family again,' waffle waffle. I think this is about the time that her boyfriend had dumped her, which probably, if not completely, was not unrelated to her sudden concern for Adam to live with both his parents. I probably should have hung up there and then but—"

"You were too much of a gentleman," she said in a rare interruption.

"No, nothing so noble," he countered. "More morbid curiosity. I wanted to see what she really wanted."

"And did you?"

"Oh yes, she'd been prattling on for so long that I almost missed it. She said, 'With the money you could get for that house, we'd be set up for life.' After that I just let her run out of steam. I actually put the telephone down and went to the bathroom to wash my hands and she didn't realize I had gone. When she finally paused to draw breath, I told her no, but she said think about it, and when it was time for Adam's next visit I could go down to visit with her to see what it was like. I said that after living with her for eleven years I had a fair idea of what it was like. So less than two months after, I, or rather Pam, got a telephone call while I was at work. He called to say that he was with his mother and that he was staying there. So I rang back and asked to speak to Adam. She answered and said that the only way I could see Adam again was to move down there, presumably with my share of the proceeds from the sale of the house. Anyway, I spoke to him and gave him my two sisters' telephone numbers and told him that if he was ever in need, I would help him if I could without putting Pam at risk. He asked me if I was staying in America or moving back to England, and I told him that it was nothing to do with him anymore, and that, as they say, was that. Oh, there was a little postscript. I telephoned his mother the last time I spoke to her and said I'd send her his passport and green card if she would change her name from Jackson. She didn't, so perhaps I'll persuade her if I ever get the time, and *that* is that." He suddenly smiled. "Basta. Pleasant walk this, isn't it? Neville Chamberlain's favorite. He must have walked along here while deciding whether his bit of paper would mean peace in our time. He was a good man. He just thought everyone was as honorable as him, or is it as he?"

"So you went back. You were married at the time?"

"As I said, had been for at least two years."

"She must have been crazy."

He nodded. "Or very close."

"That poor boy, and he hasn't got in touch with you?"

"No, he only had my sisters' telephone numbers, and they've both moved since. The younger one doesn't even live in England anymore. The last I heard of him was when one of my nephews saw him in the local pub when I got warned off going to Luke's—Kathy's dad's—funeral. The last time I saw Luke, he told me not to forget to look him up the next time I was in England, and I did indeed telephone and was told by one of the hangers on that there was to be no contact between the families, I can understand why. When I declined to take over the payments on Kathy, there would be another drain on Luke's purse and less for the other hangers on, and they thought that it was my responsibility, as I was indirectly the cause of her boyfriend dumping her. There is one thing I regret, though. I discovered that Luke actually knew my father when they were both young men, and I was looking forward to having a chat with him about that. It was like losing my father twice."

She noticed a look of infinite sadness sweep across his face before he continued. "I did get to speak to him once. I called his house on the off chance of contacting him and was lucky enough. He must have been passing the phone at the time. I asked him if we could go for a drink, but he was too sick by then. In fact, a month later he was dead." He gave a bitter smile. "My younger sister called me. We were living in Somerset at the time. I asked her to give me the details of the funeral so that I could pay my last respects, and I had the feeling she wouldn't call me back, so I called my other sister and got the details from her. Sure enough, the younger one called me back, and after waffling on a bit, she told me that Matt, her son had—are you following this?"

"It's fascinating, go on."

"Well, her son Matt had met Adam and some of Kathy's family in the local pub and was told there would be dire consequences if I attended the funeral. I went anyway." He remembered standing at the back of the Saint Thomas of Canterbury Roman Catholic Church while Kathy and her siblings closely followed Luke's coffin, reluctant to relinquish the last of their father's reflected prestige. "So that's the last time I heard of Adam. Would you like to see Boadicea?"

"No thank you. Whatever it is, you were more concerned about not seeing Kathy's father than not seeing your son."

"It's not an it, it's a she. The queen of the Iceni fought the Romans to a standstill until her tactics let her down."

"You don't seem very concerned about Adam. You don't know if he's … I find it very strange and very sad."

"I'm sorry, but I've shed all the tears that are to be shed on that subject. Anyway, the bitterest tears are the ones left unshed—a long time ago, about the time I sent his passport to his mother. Now let's talk about you."

"Just two questions, if you don't mind. I'm interested."

"You always were a good listener."

"Only that?"

He deliberately avoided her eyes. "Don't underestimate listening. It's a very useful quality and quite rare."

"So, did Kathy's boyfriend leave her because Adam went to stay with her?"

"No, he'd already upped stakes by then."

"Ah yes, you said that her family thought that you," she squinted in to space as though she was reading her thoughts, in a way that was vaguely familiar, "were indirectly responsible for her boyfriend dumping her. Were you?"

"Yes, I think so."

"How?"

"Pamela," he answered simply, and after they had crossed Derby Gate, he continued. "Part of his attraction for Kathy, the biggest part, was the thought that I still harbored an attraction for her, an illusion she took great efforts to foster—making it necessary for me to telephone her about picking Adam up, always managing to be at the club when she knew I'd be there—until I turned up with Pam and they sank beneath the horizon all the way to Texas."

"Is that the reason you took up with Pamela?"

"Reason had nothing to do with it my 'taking up' with Pam, although I always promised myself that if I did 'take up' with someone else, she would have to be … attractive."

"But of course, she would be attractive to you."

He shook his head. "You don't understand, not just to me. Generally, she had to be attractive."

"Steven," she said reproachfully, "that sounds very shallow."

"It probably does, my dear, but," he took a deep breath as though he was steeling himself, "at least you know that she is with you because she wants to be and not because no one else wants her, except for sex, when they can't get anyone else."

"Is that what's happened to you?"

"You've heard about the Englishman who came home and found his wife in bed with another guy? He apologized for disturbing them, took his golf clubs, and left. It's a joke, but like a lot of jokes, it's based on something real. In this case, he probably regretted marrying her, probably about the same time as sex became a bargaining chip. Then it was because of the kids, and then it was because it was too late, or," he jutted his chin, "'I gave my word.' So when he finds the old ball and chain *in flagrante,* so to speak, it's one last sweep of the area and leaving somebody else to take over the payments."

"Is that what happened to you?"

"More or less."

"I always thought it was me. So you had already left your wife when we met."

"I can't really remember which came first." He turned to face her. "Truly, I don't. Tell me, what are you doing now? Still in the jewelry business?"

"When time permits. I am working as an interpreter for the same organization as Judith. We do a lot of work for the European Union."

"Lawyers and politicians—that must be very trying. Your daughter excluded, of course."

"Our daughter," she corrected him sharply. "Yes it can be. Do you remember what you asked me when I told you that I could be, er, exact, how is it?"

"Fluent."

"Thank you, fluent, yes, fluent in five languages."

"Yes I can. I asked you what language you thought in."

"Very good, and my answer?"

It was his turn to squint in to space. "Italian when you are thinking of wine or singing, French when it's food or lying, and German when you're thinking of invading Poland."

"Steven, such a thing to say."

"German is for calling an Englishman a Nazi if he disagrees with you about *Chariots of Fire.*"

"German is for business."

"I thought you said English was for business."

"English was for making love."

"And are you seeing anyone now?" he asked, trying to keep his voice level.

"There is a friend of William's who is interested, and he is quite pleasant and so charming. I think he is hopelessly in love with me. Like all Englishmen, they only love when it is hopeless."

"Lost causes," he agreed, realizing she was talking about Chadders.

"Yes, he is very attentive, but I think he still has feelings for his ex-wife."

"Ah yes that can be a problem." He was about to repeat the homily about where children are concerned, never being able to get rid of the bag they came in, but decided that under the present circumstances, that would be less than gallant.

"So," she said, reverting to a former theme, if she had ever left it, "she used her father to punish you and her son to blackmail you. I often wonder why you ever married her."

"You seem preoccupied with my former wife, yet you've hardly mentioned Pamela."

"I was afraid, no concerned," she corrected herself, "that you had gone back to her, which would be such a waste."

"Yes," the idea seemed to amuse him, "I did, three times, and you're right, she did use Adam."

"Has she tried to since?"

"Not since I gave him my sisters' telephone numbers. She must realize he is dead to me now." They had by now reached the bridge over the lake in St. James Park, and he paused and stared bleakly in the direction of Horse Guards Parade. "I still have fond memories of him, but they are all in the past now, as he is." He suddenly seemed to become aware of his surroundings. "We must have walked miles, and we didn't see Boadicea. Have you got time for lunch, if you're not too tired?" He couldn't remember showing her the Chindit Memorial.

"But of course." She squeezed his arm, not asking who Boadicea was. "I'm not letting you go again."

"We could go to the Sherlock Holmes in Northumberland Avenue."

"The detective?"

"Yes, that's right, but don't expect to see him. More likely the flunkeys from the government having a rest from giving England away."

"But he used to live there, no?"

"No! Baker Street the other side of Hyde Park." He waved vaguely in the direction of Park Lane. "It's called the Sherlock Holmes because it's opposite the Northumberland Hotel where Sir Henry Baskerville stayed when he got his boot stolen in *The Hound of the Baskervilles*. It's one of the most identifiable locations in the Sherlock Holmes stories, although I think the Charing Cross is mentioned in the *Bruce Partington Plans.*"

"Sherlock Holmes *is* fictional, yes?" she ventured cautiously.

"Yes, but he was based on Doctor Bell, who was Conan-Doyle's tutor when he was a student in Edinburgh. There's a statue of him somewhere."

"Again with the statues?" She became totally French. "I shall have a statue of myself made and you can put it on your mantle shelf and drive Pamela crazy."

It occurred to Steven that she had interrogated Judith after their walk, which shouldn't have surprised him.

****

"So you like living in Arizona, in the desert?" Lydia asked.

After a drink at the Sherlock Holmes, she had voiced a preference to eat somewhere else, as the dog's head in the glass case, obviously a reference to the hound of the Baskervilles, had upset her sensibilities in spite of Steven's reassurances that although Sherlock Holmes had put five bullets in it, there was no allusion to it being stuffed and mounted. So it had taken the tranquility of the Villiers, complete with pianist and the sustenance of a club sandwich, before she could broach the subject of Steven's domestic circumstances.

"I'd like living anywhere," he finally answered, "as long as Pam is happy and I can write."

"You must love her."

"Ah love," he said, as though he had forgotten part of a story. "Yes," he admitted, "I must do."

She considered this as she performed another act that stirred Steven's memory. She opened the sandwich, and using a fork, studied every piece before putting it in her mouth. "So you don't mind staying in London because Pam is here with you, although I think you don't belong here."

"I'm at that stage," he began carefully, "where, while I pay my dues, I don't belong there, but every time I come here, while I enjoy it, something else has changed so it makes it easier to live somewhere else. When we visit here, I never seem to have enough time to see everything I want to see in England, so the present situation is ideal, and HMG is footing the bill."

"HMG?"

"Well, someone else."

"And what has changed this time?"

"Well, I took Pam to Ludlow races the last time we were this side of the pond. We had a great time, but the bookies actually had digital chalkboards where they used to chalk the odds up, and there was actually a woman bookie. There'll be female queens next, speaking of which." But neither this nor his reference to "this side of the pond" got the attention it deserved, as Lydia had grabbed his sleeve and pulled closer to him so that she was speaking directly in to his face.

"We are joined by Judith now, and she thinks of you as her father. Don't abandon her. You don't have to see me again, but now Judith knows you, you cannot disappear again."

I didn't disappear last time, lady, you did, he thought, and then, from "my daughter" to "our daughter" to "don't abandon her." He wondered what language she thought in when she was changing her conception of things past, probably Hebrew.

"Lydia," he said, "you were very kind to me at a time in my life when I … you will always be dear to me, and I would love to see you again. Perhaps next time I could show you Westminster Abbey and Boadicea—that is if the person who you are with doesn't mind."

He realized that he was talking about Chadders and remembered Lydia's propensity for baring her soul as their relationship was coming to an end and Ali had been upgraded from ex-boyfriend to boyfriend. She had shared her misgivings about whether she could keep "our adventure" from him. As Ali had been dismissed from a martial arts course for being too violent, Lydia's revelation had caused Steven to sleep with a loaded shotgun under his bed for weeks afterward, and if this quality had been inherited by Judith … Not for the first time, Steven cursed Pam's matchmaking.

15~American Hamburger and Then—Back in the Fifties

AS STEVEN CLIMBED THE STAIRS to their room, his annoyance felt toward his wife was somewhat mollified, as he was already thinking about his tea, the effects of the sandwich at the Villiers having long worn off. He wondered whether to impose on Pam to impose on Mrs. Murdoch or whether to take Pam out to dinner. This proved impossible, however, for when he entered their room, there was no Pam. He was considering whether to telephone Mrs. Murdoch when he happened to glance out the window, and there was Pam, fetchingly filling a halter top and shorts, ensconced in the garden (she always had that look about her after they'd been apart) with what looked remarkably like a bottle of lager at her side.

She looked up as he approached, carefully placing her bookmark in her place. "Well hello, and how did our meeting with Lydia go? Fully up to date on old times, are we?"

It would have taken a fool, which Steven was not, to miss the taut politeness in her manner. He flopped down on the grass beside her. "Do you think she's serious about Chadders?"

"You hate anyone doing that, yet you're guilty of it yourself, answering a question with a question."

"That's because the answer to your question depends on the answer to mine. How Lydia is depends on the attentions of Mr. Chaddersly-Corbett."

"Are you hungry yet?" Pamela asked in a tone that said she had no time for his cleverness. "I rather fancy trying to find a decent hamburger, but perhaps your tastes are more exotic?"

"A hamburger sounds fine. I wonder if Mrs. Murdoch could make one or do you mean going out?"

"Lydia wore you out, has she? I'll have to ask her to go easy on you next time, *if* there is going to be a next time." She opened her book, which was obviously a dismissal, and Steven was aware enough to accept it and clambered to his feet. Obviously it was not the time to mention Boadicea and Westminster Abbey.

"By the way," she didn't raise her eyes from the book, although he would have bet she wasn't reading, "could you check the telephone? I think there's something wrong with it."

Steven had grown up with a mother, two sisters, and a succession of bull terrier bitches, and so knew when women got into moods there was no talking to them, although on entering their room, he did check the telephone. It was while he was doing this that he again glanced out of the window at his wife decorating Mrs. Murdoch's lawn. To be fair, when Pam's wifely affection went off the boil, there was usually a good reason, and being *with* an old girlfriend, *without* a telephone call for—he looked at the clock: 5:30. Stroll on, six hours? After the Sherlock Holmes, there was a pub that actually consisted of two halves, and he remembered, for some reason, having a drink in each, and then various others, including one at the Big Ben end of Whitehall. It actually backed onto the old New Scotland Yard.

Mentally squaring his shoulders and pulling his stomach in, he presented himself once more at the wifely side.

"Pamela."

She carefully placed her bookmark at the page before closing her book and giving him her full attention. "Yes."

"You seem a little out of sorts, and I realize that I might be not a little responsible due to my lack of consideration. I accept this, and I also realize that it has hurt your feelings. My acceptance of the responsibility notwithstanding, I realize that it will take some time for your feelings to heal. When they do so, however, perhaps I will be given the opportunity to attempt to make amends. Thank you." He turned to walk away until her voice stopped him.

"Steven."

He turned, "Yes?"

"Were you apologizing?"

"Abjectly."

"You, tosser."

"And was that an acceptance?"

"You're not quite off the hook yet, sunshine. It'll take a hamburger, a proper hamburger, *and* you take me dancing afterward."

The dancing was not that big a problem. If all else failed, there was always the Villiers with the pianist, if it *was* the Villiers, but the hamburger would be more difficult. He would have to throw himself on what was left of Mrs. Murdoch's mercy. With a last look at his wife reclining on her chaise lounge to fortify him, he presented himself at the reception desk and rang the bell, louder than he intended, and was relieved to see that it produced The Captain. "Ah yes, you got back all right."

"Yes, thank you, but there are a couple of things you or your—Mrs. Murdoch might help me with."

"Of course, what we're here for."

"Good, first is, I'd like to take my wife dancing and wondered if you could, if you knew or ..." This was beginning to seem like not such a good idea, but The Captain rallied to his aid, "A disco something like that?"

"Oh no, something a bit quieter, a bit softer, you know, swing." Steven encircled the waist of an imaginary partner and did a graceful dip, which garnered a polite patter of applause. He turned to see that Mrs. Murdoch had joined her partner at the desk. "Bravo, quite elegant, but I'm afraid we're not licensed for dancing."

"Wants to take his wife dancing, thought we'd know somewhere. I thought—"

"Good idea. It's about time we had a night out. We could leave about nine, give you time for a nap, all right? Anything else?"

"Actually, there is." Steven was not sure who was supposed to leave at nine. "My wife would like a hamburger."

"Well I don't think that will stretch my culinary skills too much."

"But she's very specific, the onions—sweet onions—have to be minced in with the beef, plus some Worcestershire sauce is added and a slice of—"

"And who assembles this masterpiece?"

"Well usually, I do," he modestly assured her.

"I see." She turned to The Captain. "Dances *and* cooks." Then she returned her attention to Steven. "And I take it you want me to—or do you want to use my kitchen?"

"Whatever is less inconvenient to you," Steven said, knowing she would decide anyway but wanting to preserve the illusion that it was his idea.

"I suppose it will be all right if I'm there to keep an eye on you. Right, how much have you had to drink?"

"I think I'm sober enough to make a hamburger," said Steven, bridling at the inferred stricture.

Mrs. Murdoch fixed him with a look that would have quelled many a rebellious sixth former. "I was thinking that whoever collects the ingredients will need to be sober enough to drive. Can you imagine what the *Guardian* would make of it? 'The future king using his influence to bail his future father-in-law out of the pokey.' You'd better make a list and give it to The

Captain, all right?" The last remark was addressed to her fellow proprietor, who was quietly enjoying the exchange.

"Delighted, but about the Worcestershire sauce."

"Yes, don't bother I think we can rustle one up from somewhere and"—she had the disconcerting habit of changing the object of her conversation without addressing them, although Steven noticed that her tone was considerably warmer when she spoke to The Captain—"you'd better have a lie down so that you can be up to party later on. Don't forget, we're going dancing."

"We?"

"Yes, we," she said deliberately. "The three persons in this room plus Pamela, your wife."

"I was rather hoping Pam and I would spend some time alone."

"I see," she said glacially. "It is unfortunate that this concern for your wife didn't manifest itself until *after* you had spent the afternoon too busy getting refreshed, with an old girlfriend, to telephone her. I'm sorry," she said before Steven had a chance to reply, "that was unfair. It must be difficult—" The telephone rang, rescuing her from her uncharacteristic hesitancy. "Go on, don't forget to give The Captain the list."

Deciding to leave well enough alone, Steven turned to The Captain. "I'll leave the list on the desk, all right?" He was halfway up the stairs before he was summoned from behind. "Steven."

He turned to see The Captain wordlessly holding the kitchen door open. He entered to find Mrs. Murdoch on the telephone. "In the kitchen, he's going to teach me how to make an American hamburger. Yes, hidden talents. Besides, I've always believed in stretching my horizons. He's here now, thank you, sir."

Apparently Steven's hidden talents didn't stretch to lip reading, as he could not decipher Mrs. Murdoch's elaborate mime as she handed him the telephone. It sounded, or looked, like "him," which narrowed it down to roughly half the world's population.

He took the telephone. "Hello?"

"Mr. Jackson," the voice was vaguely familiar, "William."

"William?"

"William Windsor."

"Windsor? Oh yes." Steven had to stop himself from standing to attention. "How are you?" He paused. How do you address your future king while you're compiling an ingredient list for hamburgers? He took a leaf out of Mrs. Murdoch's book. She should know, "Sir, and how's my daughter?"

"We're both fine. She's just debriefing her mother on this afternoon. I gather everything went all right?"

Him as well?

"It went as one would expect a meeting with someone you haven't seen for twenty-odd years to go. It was—amicable. She hasn't changed much, essentially."

"Yes. Quite a pretty woman. By the way, is Mrs. Murdoch within earshot?"

"Yes she's—no, she must have left." Mrs. Murdoch had indeed decamped, taking The Captain with her.

"Well, it's 'William,' no rank in the kitchen, but if Mrs. Murdoch's near, believe me it would make life simpler."

"Point taken, and you can call me Steven."

"Yes, well the reason I called, Steven, is we're having a little get together on Tuesday night to say good-bye to my bachelor days, and I'd like you to come, all right?"

"Of course, glad to—suit and tie?"

"Yes that'll be fine. about ten. Any plans for the morning after?"

"No, I've got a fitting for the suit in the afternoon, but I should be recovered by then.

"Splendid." Strangely enough, it didn't sound so bad coming from him. "I'll give you the address, or would you like us to send a car?"

"No thanks, I'll get there." Steven reached for a pencil, and risking the wrath of Mrs. Murdoch, he took a calendar from the wall, and on second thought, he flipped over the page to reveal the previous month. While risking the wrath of Mrs. Murdoch, he wasn't going to seek it.

"Just one thing, William," said Steven after he had transcribed the address of a restaurant on the roguish side of Mayfair. "Is anything laid on for the ladies?"

"I don't know—you mean a sort of spinster night? Is it done?"

"It is in America. They call them bachelorettes. Must be thinking about hamburgers that made me think of it. Besides, my wife will probably ask me."

"Well, Judith is still in touch with her friends from college and then there's ... I'll speak to Judith and get her to telephone your wife. I think it's a great idea."

"They'll probably have more fun than we do."

"That wouldn't surprise me. I'll see you Tuesday night."

****

"So you dice onion up with the ground beef *and* you serve it with a raw slice on top, obviously not a prelude to a romantic evening." Having taken the required nap to bring himself up to par and with Pam watching Pot Black with The Captain, Steven was sharing the secrets of American cuisine to a wary Mrs. Murdoch. "It's why we specify *sweet* onion. There's less aftertaste, and besides"—Steven wiped his hands on a brilliantly striped apron and started shredding the lettuce, which The Captain had assured him was still growing that very morning—"as Pam and I both eat it at the same time and Pam's the only one I'll be kissing in the following twenty-four hours, *and* vice versa, the question doesn't arise, and not wishing to pry into your domestic arrangements, but if the same situation exists between The Captain and yourself, I hope you'll join us. There is enough for four."

"Wouldn't miss it for the world. I've never tasted American food."

"It's like English food in a way, very underrated because, I think, it's so easy to do badly."

The telephone rang, suspending any further discussion, and was answered by a neutral, "Yes." She frowned at the receiver before continuing, "He's rather busy at the moment. Can I take a message? I *am* security cleared. Yes, I will convey that to him. At the moment he's up to his elbows in ground beef. Yes, it's all the rage. I'll get him to ring you back, probably tomorrow. He's going to show us what he can do on the dance floor tonight. Bromfield," she announced as she replaced the receiver. "Nice enough chap, but gets a bit carried away with himself. "

"Most of them do," Steven agreed. "What did he want?"

"Wanted to discuss what sort of honour would be appropriate."

"Honour? Honour what?"

"Not 'what' but 'whom.' They want to confer some kind of honour upon you. While that," she indicated the mixture, "is cooking, do you fancy a cup of tea?"

****

He was back in the fifties. The band was in evening dress, white damask-covered tables surrounded the dance floor, there was even a revolving crystal ball, and when the female vocalist was introduced, Vera Lynn would not have looked out of place. Steven was grateful that Pam had prevailed upon him to wear his one good suit, miraculously sponged and pressed by Mrs. Murdoch, as most of the men present wore lounge suits and there was even a scattering of dinner jackets.

"Well, what will we have, ladies?"

"I think you'll find it's waitress service, and you'd better let The Captain order so you won't have to put in a separate chitty for the expenses, is that all right?" Mrs. Murdoch cocked an inquiring eye at Steven. "You look a little out of sorts."

"As you mention it, my wife professed a wish to go dancing, and as I had been away all afternoon, I thought that it would be nice to accommodate her so I inquired of, I forget who now, and ..." Steven seemed to lose his way.

"And we seem to have taken over things, usurped your position as Pamela's guide and comforter, so much so that you don't even get to buy her a drink?"

"I think that just about sums it up," said Steven tightly, but apparently Mrs. Murdoch hadn't finished.

"And worst of all, Pam might enjoy herself without having just you to thank, but that's the way it's going to be, sunshine. We're here to keep you from falling by the wayside, so enjoy it. There is one thing you can do."

"Yes?"

"They're playing our song," The band had just broken in to, "A Nightingale Sang in Berkeley Square." "You could ask me to dance."

"Mrs. Murdoch," Steven stood and offered his hand, "could I have the pleasure of the next dance? I'll watch my P's and Q's."

"I thought you'd never ask. Pamela, my dear, look after The Captain. will you? Right, lead on, young man, and never mind your P's and Q's. Just watch where you put your hands."

16~The Bachelor Night and the Fitting

"SO YOU'RE THIS CHAP FROM Arizona?" Steven had taken a taxi to the venue of William's bachelor party, which he'd had second thoughts about attending, and he had been considering when it would be polite to leave when he had looked up from his glass to be regarded by two pouchy eyes set in a pasty face. He had either been told to entertain Steven, or anyone else who looked as though they needed company, or he was one of life's leeches who fastened on to anyone who was unfortunate enough to take his fancy.

"No, I'm this chap from Coseley, or one of them."

"Coseley. I don't think I know …" He had this irritating habit of brushing his floppy hair back from his forehead.

"I am currently living in Arizona, if that's any help."

"Yes, quite, and you're the bride-to-be's father."

"I am, as science can attest to, blood tests, DNA, the lot. So you've never heard of Coseley? Coseley Tunnel? Engineering marvel in its day. Later it was to become famous for other reasons, but—"

"Do you think David Beckham will succeed over there?" To show how in touch he was with the people, he had moved on to more popular subjects, or so he thought.

"David Beckham—he could have come to Wolves, you know, but we couldn't promise him first team football." As this didn't get the reaction it deserved, Steven went on, "It's not a question of his success." He raised a glass that had found its way to his hand. "It's more if his wife can bump start her career, what there is of it, I mean. The Spice Girls? What is a quarter of nothing? Even in the Beatles, George Harrison was the only one who did something musically on his own after they split up. Pete Best's running a cover band, and good luck to him, John Lennon discovered peace and love and Yoko Ono, Paul McCartney married a rich man's daughter and started to look like Angela Lansbury, which is fine if you like *Murder She Wrote*, and Ringo grew a beard."

And there, just when whoever he was was content to let the conversation flow, posing, chin in hand and giving the occasional thoughtful nod, events took an unhelpful turn.

"Another thing about John was, he got killed, didn't he? Always a good career move. I mean, look at the Kennedys and," he nodded as though he was indicating someone on the far side of the room before lowering his voice to a confiding murmur, "you-know-who. I mean after Dodi realized he wasn't going to get the kids, he'd have lost interest, or rather his father would. She'd have ended up as the fifth Spice Girl, and then *she'd* have had a chance of marrying David Beckham and dragging him over to America. As I said, poor bugger. Chadders, old son," for none other had just materialized at his elbow, "how are you? You're looking well. And how's ... I'm sorry, this is—I didn't catch your name. The sod's gone. You must have scared him off. "And indeed, his erstwhile inquisitor appeared to have disappeared. "Not that I'm complaining ... bloody creep. That's the trouble with being a loner. The bores think you're bad off for company, even theirs. I thought he was trying to cadge a lift."

"I wouldn't have thought you two would have had much to talk about. Here." Chadders released two glasses from a passing tray and handed one to Steven.

"We hadn't—your good health, young man. Never heard of Coseley Tunnel, so we had to stick to the common subjects— David Beckham, the Spice Girls. Even suggested that had she survived to run her course with Dodi, the PP could have become the fifth Spice Girl and she could have had a shot at Becks."

"Oh, dear." Charles studied his glass regretfully. "I hope your book sells, Steven, because you are not, I fear, cut out for a career in the diplomatic service." He raised his face so that his smile would show he was joking. "Talking about the People's Princess, that"—he nodded to where he assumed Steven's erstwhile listener had disappeared to—"was her brother."

"Well there goes the knighthood. Anyway, how are you? How's Lydia?"

"I am very fit, thank you, enjoying the rarified atmosphere, and Lydia is well, although she can't stop asking about you— and Pam. I've told her all I know, which is very little, except that you seem to be besotted with your wife and vice versa. Didn't go too far, did I, old son? Tales out of school."

"No harm done. In fact, I think that puts it rather well."

"Only she seems to think that there's something unfinished with you two."

"Oh it's finished, and she finished it. There's nothing that makes you so attractive to a woman than you being happy with someone else after she's dumped you for pastures new, especially if the grass isn't as green as it looks from the other side of the fence."

"I think we're taking liberties with the metaphors, old son, but I take your point. So speaking of the delightful Pamela, how is she enjoying town? Bit of a change from Mohave Valley."

"Oh I think she's managing rather well. There's this old— well not old exactly—but there's this couple who we're staying with. I think your lot fixed it so they could keep an eye on us, and they seem to have taken to Pam. Nice couple, bit on the crusty side but good company. He's known only as The Captain, and she's Mrs. Murdoch."

"Iris Murdoch."

"I never caught her first name. You're a bit of a dark horse with the ladies, Charles."

"I wouldn't say that, but there is one thing—the memsahib will be in town on Friday, and we're having dinner. Care to join us, you and Pam?"

"Great, we've got nothing on until ... I think our evenings are clear. So I take it it's all right with Lydia giving you a night off to entertain the ex-Mrs.?"

"No, Lydia. We only see each other on formal occasions. Besides, Lydia will be going to her daughter's do, and it's not the ex. We're still more or less between the shafts. Never got 'round to getting a divorce. It's good security for her, and it always helps to have a wife in the background if you feel the waters get a bit deep." A thought suddenly seemed to take hold of him. "Of course, Pam will be going to the ladies do, but we'll get together some time. The memsahib's in town all week, and we can always do another pub lunch. You'll like Cynthia; she's great company."

Steven's thoughts were far from what good company Charles' not-quite ex-wife was or the fact that she had acquired a first name (or dare he say it, a *Christian* name).

So, Pam's not invited to their little cake and arse party. She probably wouldn't want to go anyway but still ... Bloody Lydia, if I hadn't promised Judith, I'd get Pam and sod off, and they could stick their honour where the fairy stuck the Christmas tree.

A discreet cough at his elbow interrupted his plans for the Christmas tree. "Steven, I don't believe you've met my Father." Steven abandoned his sorry train of thought to shake hands with Charles, Prince of Wales, Duke of Cornwall, butt of the yellow press, and Colonel Commandant of the Parachute Regiment.

"Sir." The handshake was firm without being gripped, which, given the practice it had had, was not surprising. "How's married life?"

"Thank you, we're fine and your wife, Pamela—she's coping with all this? Not too bored being on her own while you're doing all the rehearsals and what have you?"

"No, I think she manages rather well. She gets on quite well with our hosts, and besides, Pam makes the most of wherever she finds herself. She'd have made a good soldier's wife, pity." The thought seemed to sadden him, but he rallied. "Besides, we get enough time together, so it works out rather well."

"Good, I'm looking forward to meeting her."

"Speaking of which, where are my manners? I don't believe you've met Chadders." Steven turned to find only a space. Chadders, ever the diplomat, had effaced himself. "Now where's the man gone?"

"Probably gone to get a good view of the stripper, so if you gentlemen will excuse me, I'll withdraw before it's 'embarrass the guest of honour' time." William also made his exit.

"We didn't have all this trouble." Steven nodded after the departing William. "It was a trip to Vegas, visit city hall in the morning, and Circus Circus in the afternoon and—"

"Circus Circus?"

"Yes, it's a casino on the Strip in Las Vegas, and like most casinos, they provide a wedding chapel, among the other facilities for indulging your fancies, so we got married there at twelve noon and caught the one-thirty flight home. We were living in Long Beach at the time. We were at the British and Dominion Club by four ready for the party Pam had arranged." With his innate tact, he didn't think it worth mentioning to Prince Charles that the club was where his future daughter-in-law had been conceived in the parking lot.

"I see, sounds like quite a woman. If you don't mind me asking, where did you meet?"

"Not at all. I'd just got rid of—well, I'd just divorced my first wife. I hadn't quite got rid of her because she kept popping up wherever I was, usually wrapped around her boyfriend as close to me as possible. It was all very tacky, and this one Sunday evening I thought I wouldn't go to the club after the game, so instead I went to this night club and Pam was dancing there."

"So she was with someone else?"

"No, it was more performing. She was an exotic dancer."

"I see, well done, and what happened to your ex?"

"Took one look at Pam and did a bunk. Left town, got transferred to Texas where she is now enriching the lives of the good people of the Lone Star State, just outside Fort Worth. Took her boyfriend with her, but that didn't last long. Got a call from her about six months later that suggested we give it one more try, trip down the primrose path together. I think it's rude to hang up, so I just put the phone down and let her go on talking, and that's the last I heard from her."

"And does your wife have any difficulties with the circumstances of you being here?"

Steven smiled inwardly, thinking, *Him as well.* "No, Pamela tends to save her worrying for the important things. The circumstances, seem to bother other people more than us. In which case I think they underestimate Pam, a situation not unlike your own, sir. And how are things going with you in that respect?"

"Well said, and thank you, we seem to have weathered the storm. Did I hear you served in the paras?" The prince had apparently decided to move to firmer ground.

"I did indeed, nine years, best years of my life. Actually, I think we may have met at the fiftieth anniversary of Airborne Forces."

"We did?" The Windsor calm appeared to be momentarily ruffled.

"Well, it was Pam really. We decided to visit the fiftieth anniversary celebrations while we were in England, and I had met some people I had not seen for at least seventeen years, so during the interval, the beer tent was well patronized. One of the results was that Pam wanted to visit the ladies, which was along this perimeter track, and on the way back, you'd apparently seen enough and were making your way back to your helicopter, accompanied by all these officers and people. Anyway, as it happened, your helicopter was on the other side of the track, and a way had been cleared for you, unfortunately coming between Pam and the beer tent and various old soldiers, two of her favorite indulgences. As well as this, Pam had read somewhere about you and your family being an asset of the nation, and being of a literal mind she took this to mean you actually belonged to the nation and were available to be photographed."

"Like horse guards parade?"

"Exactly. So she marches right through your minders, grabs you by the arm, and wouldn't let go until I'd taken a photograph/ I thought she was going to get shot."

"I don't think there'd be much danger of that." Charles seemed to be momentarily lost in thought. "Er, your wife has hair down to her waist?"

"Actually it's longer now, but then it would have been waist-length, yes."

"Good figure and wearing a white dress with black roses on it?"

"Still has, and although I can't remember what she was wearing, she certainly does have, or had, such a dress."

"Yes, I do remember, not every day. Look after her. Look here, as my son has made a judicious exit before the entertainment, I will be the ... People will look to me to see my reaction, so I will follow his example, and er—"

"Scarper?"

"Yes quite. Very interesting talking to you, Steven, my regards to your wife and I'm looking forward to renewing our acquaintance. Did the photographs come out?"

"Unfortunately not. A pig ate the camera with the film still inside. I'm glad your marriage is working, sir. Don't worry, you'll be all right, as long as the love's there," and with that, Steven took his leave.

****

"Mister Jackson sir? Swinbourne, welcome. Jeremy"—he indicated a slightly built young man who appeared to have taken a vow of silence—"and I will be fitting you." It was the following Friday, and Steven, accompanied by Pam in a rather fetching miniskirt, had presented themselves at the venerable premises of Moss Brothers, Outfitters to the Gentry.

"And this would be Mrs. Jackson *and* the, er, cowboy boots. They are rather splendid, aren't they?" Steven wasn't sure if he was referring to the boots or Pam's legs. "If madam, thank you, if you would take a seat, we'll fit the trousers."

"Do you follow football?"

"Indeed I do sir, West Ham."

"That's all right. I didn't fancy having a Chelsea supporter take my inside leg measurement."

"Yes sir, quite so. Very amusing, I shall remember that, although it won't be necessary. What do we normally do for an inside leg, sir?"

"Usually thirty, but I can manage thirty one on a good day."

"So we'll allow two for the footwear. Let's see what a thirty-three medium does. A thirty-three medium please, Jeremy." And with Jeremy dispatched, he unhooked the tape from round his neck. "And the chest, sir, about a forty? We'll just check, if you don't mind. The trousers are adjustable, but the morning coat is very unforgiving. If you'll just raise the arms, sir, splendid. Forty will do nicely. You can lower the arms now, sir. Now we need from the point of the shoulder to the waist."

"I'm almost scared to ask, but why?"

"The waistcoat, sir."

"Of course."

"And the neck, sir, sixteen and ... best make it sixteen and a half so that it lies beneath the adam's apple. Saving your presence, Mrs. Jackson, yes, we don't want you choking up at the response to 'who giveth this woman' or the whole thing comes to a shuddering halt, doesn't it? Thank you, Jeremy, just slip these on, sir, over the boots, of course, and we'll see how they hang just lying on the instep with a single break."

In spite of his misgivings, Steven was prepared to go along with things for Pam's sake, and Mister Swinbourne did seem to know what he was doing, which appealed to Steven's Black Country philosophy of making a good job of it, and so it was with, if not enthusiasm, good grace he consented to, "Walk with your wife as though she was the bride-to-be. Do you mind, Mrs. Jackson? Very well, thank you. Nicely does it. Take your time, look straight ahead. Excellent, and once more see how you look from behind. Indeed, sir, as you and your daughter will be the focus of attention most of the time, you will have your back to the congregation. You take my point? Thank you."

By the time they had satisfied Mister Swinbourne from all angles, Jeremy, unbidden as far as Steven could discern, had arrived, with a morning coat on a hanger, which he flourished for Mister Swinbourne's attention as though he'd never seen one before.

"Yes, if you could slip this on, sir, I think—" He stopped in midsentence, as Steven was already holding his arms out behind him to receive the sleeves of the morning coat. "Why don't we do the Full Monty?" As though he was suggesting rounding off the evening with champagne, "Do you have time? Then you needn't see us again until the dress rehearsal."

"I think that's an excellent idea." Pam obviously thought it was time to show a little presence. "We've got nothing on for the rest of the day—nothing that could compare with seeing Steven in his go-to-meeting suit before anyone else."

"Quite, well put." It didn't appear necessary to get Steven's confirmation. "The arm, sir, horizontal to the side, and the elbow crooked at just over ninety degrees. That will give us half an inch of cuff, a nice contrast but nothing too showy. Sound about right, sir?"

"I prefer three-quarters, but I will be guided by you, Mister Swinbourne," Steven conceded graciously.

"Thank you. We could go a *little* more. Jeremy, we'll have a thirty-two sixteen and a half plain white and also a *light* blue with a contrast collar. Any thoughts on the tie, sir? We thought a conservative stripe just enough—goodness me, where *are* my manners? Mrs. Jackson, could I get you tea or coffee perhaps?"

"Tea will be fine, thank you."

"Right!" Mister Swinbourne turned on the hapless Jeremy. "We'll have tea for three please, young sir, and see if they can organize a few digestives before we go any further."

It appeared that someone had the foresight to arrange for suitable refreshment, as it arrived in the midst of Jeremy's further instructions. "Ah tea, splendid. Would you like to be mother, Mrs. Jackson? Two sugars for me, please." Mister Swinbourne ushered Pam to a side table. "We were discussing the necktie I believe?"

"Actually, I was hoping to wear my regimental tie." Steven had to stop himself from turning to Pam for support.

"I see, sir, and what color would that be?"

"Maroon with sky blue Pegasuses on it, or would it be Pegasi?"

"Yes, that would work, especially with the blue contrast."

"Unfortunately, I don't have one with me."

"If it is a recognized military formation, we *will* have one, sir. Did you get that, Jeremy? Good man." Apparently Jeremy had been forgiven for his remission concerning the tea. "And a thirty, thirty-two waistcoat. I think a dove grey *in case* we go with the maroon necktie. Any decorations during your service, Mister Jackson?"

"General service medal, with clasp for Southern Arabia and Northern Ireland."

"Well done, and when did you serve in Southern Arabia, sir, if I may?"

"Sixty-seven."

"Yes I'm sure you would have preferred wearing your own medal. Those flunkies at the foreign office forgot to tell you. We will have to verify your entitlement, sir, I'm sure you understand."

"No problem. It would be if I wasn't entitled to it." Steven suddenly rattled off an eight-digit number.

"Is that?"

"My regimental number. You'll need that."

"Quite." He wrote the number on a scratch pad. "Jeremy, a '62 GSM with clasps for South Arabia and Northern Ireland. That should do it." While they were awaiting the return of Jeremy and after it was established that Pam was enjoying her stay in London, the conversation naturally enough turned to football.

"Prince William is an Aston Villa supporter," Steven confided airily. "It came up in the conversation while we were having a chat about a few things. I don't know if Prince Charles follows football. I forgot to ask him. I wonder if the Duke of Edinburgh is a follower of the beautiful game. What do you think, Mister Swinbourne, could you see him as a Chelsea supporter or perhaps Arsenal? Boring but predictable—or maybe West Ham. Could you see him supporting 'the Hammers'?"

"Couldn't see him supporting anyone really," Mister Swinbourne retorted sniffily. "The Queen's family's been supporting him for years."

"And so they should." Pam, a voracious reader, had, during Steven's absences and with the help of Mrs. Murdoch, put this quality to good use by devouring four books on the monarchy and the Windsors in particular for just such a moment as this. "Phillip Mountbatten was a first-class naval officer, and if he hadn't happened to fall in love with Princess Elizabeth, and the other way 'round, it was generally accepted that he would have become at least an admiral, instead of spending his days walking six paces behind the Queen. So if he has to relinquish his chosen career to be married to the Queen, he should be compensated." She suddenly turned a beaming smile on Steven, as though he'd said something quite profound. "Rather like you, honey."

"Pamela, I'm sure we don't want to bore Mister Swinbourne with our domestic arrangements," Steven said in a tone that suggested he would prefer she shut up.

"Well, I think that puts Swinbourne in his place," said the gentleman placatingly. "And what is your team of preference, Mister Jackson? I won't hazard a guess in case I get it wrong, you being from the Midlands. I wouldn't want to cause offense."

"The Wolves, Wolverhampton Wanderers."

"Oh dear, well they *are* still in business and where there's life, yes? You have a very charming and erudite, and if I may say so, attractive wife, Mister Jackson."

"I do, thank you, and so?"

"I'm sure she's a great consolation to you."

When Jeremy duly returned with the remainder of Steven's ensemble, Mister Swinbourne didn't seem inclined to move. "Yes, number three fitting room please, Jeremy, and after you have favored us with your opinion, you can take your break. Mister Jackson, if you will get changed, Jeremy will show you where, and then we will see how it looks. Meanwhile, I will try to entertain your good lady. We might even have a second cup, if you will do the honors, my dear."

Thus dismissed, Steven followed Jeremy to a curtained alcove where he proceeded to undress. He was relieved that Jeremy didn't stay to assist him and started to dress. The shirt presented no difficulty—they had even provided cufflinks—and there *was* a Pegasus tie. The waistcoat appeared to be missing the back, consisting of a front with two pairs of tapes, one at the shoulders and one at the waist. He was loath to interrupt the ad hoc tea party and felt even less inclined to seek out the taciturn Jeremy, so Steven attempted to solve the intricacies of the waistcoat unaided. It wasn't as complicated as it looked. The two top tapes were fastened at the back of the neck and the lower ones at the waist. There was a minor difficulty with reaching behind to fasten the lower two, but he solved this by loosening the neck, tying the waist, and then readjusting the neck. Then it was simply a matter of sliding the morning coat over his shoulders, adjusting the sleeves so that three quarters of an inch of cuff was showing, and that was it. He used the three mirrors, conveniently placed so that you could view the back without craning your neck, to make sure that the tape was not showing at the neck *and* to view himself (after all, he had never worn a morning suit before, and he doubted if anyone from Coseley had).

His moment of quiet narcissism was interrupted by a discreet cough from behind the curtain. "Mister Jackson?"

"Correct."

"Are you all right?"

"Yes, why shouldn't I be?"

"Yes, only I'm supposed to take you back to Mister Swinbourne, when you're ready." So Jeremy *could* speak.

After a last lingering look at himself, he drew the curtain aside. "All right, sunshine, let's see if we pass muster. Lead on."

Apparently they did pass muster, as Steven was subjected to a cursory inspection by Mister Swinbourne on their return. "Yes sir, could have been made for you, and if we could see the back. Remember, that's the view that's most on display. Yes I think that will do very well. Well set up, a fine pair of shoulders, if I may say so, and very good carriage. Yes, I can see the military influence. It's surprising how many young people I have to remind to straighten their shoulders. What do you think, Mrs. Jackson, turned out well, would you say?"

"Good enough to eat," Pam agreed softly.

"Well not quite the effect—but I take your point, and Jeremy, young sir, a young pair of eyes, anything we've missed?"

Thus emboldened, Jeremy cleared his throat before answering, "Just one observation, sir." Steven wasn't sure which sir he was addressing. "The right shoulder does seem to ride a shade lower than the left. If perhaps something could be done?"

"He's right. A parachuting accident way back. We got the knee fixed, but the back …" Steven shrugged.

"I see." It appeared that it might have ruined Mr. Swinbourne's whole morning, but he rallied manfully. "Mrs. Jackson, would you mind?" And again Pam took Steven's arm, and they began a slow promenade of the room, "Yes I do see, but it doesn't spoil the line. Besides, injured in the service of his country, adds a bit of a swagger—but you were perfectly correct to mention it Jeremy," he added magnanimously. "Now, Mister Jackson." He clapped his hands in a gesture of conclusion. "I do recommend you having a few dry runs with the cowboy boots. The nave of Saint Paul's is quite long, and we don't want to sag just at the most important time, do we? Just a walk in the park with your wife, I'm sure there are worse ways of spending a few minutes on a pleasant afternoon. Now you change back into your street clothes, and you arrive at the venue no later than ten o'clock on the day of the dress rehearsal. Yes?" Steven had held up an admonishing finger.

"I take it I will be relieved of it after the rehearsal until the actual wedding and then relieved of it shortly afterward?"

"Correct."

"Quite right, like going to Sunday school—straight home and get your Sunday best off. No playing football in your Sunday best or fighting."

"Yes, we call them accidents, and if I may make a further suggestion?"

"As many as you want, old son."

"When you arrive to be fitted on the day of the dress rehearsal, it would save time if you came in suitable attire. What you're wearing now will be fine so that when you return the morning suit you will be suitably dressed to go immediately to the rehearsal lunch. I take it you are going?"

"Personal invite from you-know-who."

"I see, splendid. I'm sure you'll enjoy the occasion. After the actual ceremony, of course you will remain in morning dress until after you've attended the wedding breakfast. Then I suggest you don't employ the same routine, as you will probably want to have a nap before the actual reception."

"Sounds like a good idea. Just one more thing. I didn't get fitted for hat and gloves. Don't I …?"

"Only if you're going racing, sir, are you?"

"No, I only do national hunt, and the first meeting at Ludlow's not 'til October."

"I was thinking more of Ascot or Goodwood, sir, with the royal party."

"Oh no, I prefer over the sticks, but if invited, I mean it would be ill-mannered to refuse."

"If that happens, sir, I would be honored to fit you, and may I say it is a privilege to have you wearing one of our suits and I look forward to seeing you and your good lady again. Don't forget about breaking in the boots."

17~Of Thespis

A FTER TAKING THEIR LEAVE OF Mister Swinbourne, and even eliciting best wishes from Jeremy, Steven seemed strangely subdued. In fact, it was left to Pam to hail a taxi and direct it to "the Park," which, as a Londoner of all of three weeks, she knew that was how the locals referred to Hyde Park. She had even learned from who knew where the exact length of the nave of Saint Paul's and duly had him escort her along one of the paths adjacent to Rotten Row. He complied with a rather sluggish acquiescence, which would have satisfied someone less perceptive than Pam. "The shoes hurting a bit?"

"No, they're fine."

"Right!" She shepherded him to a bench facing Park Lane and sat facing him. "It isn't the boots, the fitting went well, you looked like a million dollars, you've just discovered you've got a daughter who any man would be proud of, you're getting a four-month holiday in London paid for by *them,* and"—she paused, contemplating the facade of the Dorchester in the distance—"you're married to *me.* All that being said, I want to know what's wrong, and we're not going to move from here until you tell me, and you'll get hungry, sunshine."

She was relieved to see a wry grin spread across his face. "Don't hold back, Pam, tell me how you really feel."

She turned to face him. "Seriously, I'll put it right, but you've got to tell me."

"It's—well Chadders and Mrs. Murdoch and now Mister whatsit Swinbourne. They've all got a job to do, a function, and they're good at it. They're professionals and we're, as you say, having a pleasant visit to London. We've even had time to visit David. It has been great, hasn't it?"

She nodded.

"Now just after I got fitted for the whistle[16], it hit me—time to pay the piper. Do you realize how a good part of the world will be watching us, and some will be waiting for someone to fall on their arse? I know I tend to be flippant but ..." She took his hands in hers and forced him to look at her, "I want a yes or no answer: are you scared?"

Despite her intensity and insistence on a single-syllable answer, she had to be satisfied with, "Petrified"

"I see." She considered this gravely. "Thank you for telling me. As I see it, we have two options. One, we've both got our passports, you've got your green card, so we could get a plane tomorrow and be back in Arizona before they know we've gone. You could even sell your story to one of the scandal sheets. I don't know if Judith would ever forgive you, I know you'd never forgive yourself, but at least you wouldn't risk being embarrassed—"

"Are you serious?"

"Two," she glared at him for interrupting her, "you can make up to Judith for all the years you weren't there, although it was not of your doing, and get on with it."

"I don't have much of a choice, do I?"

"No. The main difficulty, as I see it, is that you are understandably a little apprehensive. The trouble is, if you dwell on it too much, you'll be so wound up that you'll be a nervous wreck on the day, so I'll help keep your mind off it until the rehearsal and the actual wedding, walk in the park, right?"

He nodded. "Right."

"So," Pamela, stood dusting down her dress, "what about a picnic."

"Sounds great. We can get some sandwiches and—"

"I said a *picnic*—cold chicken, pork pies chilled Spumante," she grinned at his bewildered look. "I mean at home, more private. I asked Mrs. Murdoch to lay it on. I think she's beginning to warm to you."

"Will she be joining us? I hoped we'd be alone."

"She's taken The Captain shopping and then dinner. They won't be back 'til about nine." She gently bit his neck. "Your public gets you for two afternoons, but the rest of today, you're mine, sunshine."

"Lead on. Just remind me when we get back I need to call Solly."

"I thought you'd finished with that?"

"Circumstances alter cases. It won't take long."

****

"You're inviting me to the wedding reception of Prince William and your daughter?" David raised his eyebrows, transferring his attention from Hampstead High Street. "Is this something to do with the plot of your next book?"

Their impromptu picnic had been interrupted by Solly returning Steven's call, during which Pam had been intrigued to hear phrases like "nonnegotiable" and "a monopoly sets its own price," the actual day of the wedding "passwords," and again was surprised at her husband's lack of innocence. After the details had apparently been settled to Steven's satisfaction, Pamela, in the spirit of helping Steven forget the forthcoming calls on his resilience, had insisted on them traveling northward and had been again surprised at Steven insisting on taking a taxi *and* asking for a receipt. They had found David, as expected, holding court in the William of Orange in his favorite position, the window seat, overlooking the High Street where he could bestow greetings on a select few of the good people of Hampstead.

"No, perfectly serious. I couldn't make this up. If I could make something up like this, I wouldn't offer you a copy for free. You'd have to pay the trade price, although I'd autograph it buckshee[17]."

David, still not convinced, appealed to Pam.

"Dead serious. That's where we've been this afternoon, getting him fitted for his morning suit. Poor lamb was quite exhausted." Pam ruffled Steven's hair. "Had to take him on a picnic to recover his strength, didn't I, love?"

"Right, we tried to get you a seat in Saint Paul's, but you'd get a better view on the telly. Well, are you on?"

David and Steven had been born, David in Wolverhampton and Steven in Coseley, within three miles of each other, and when this had been mentioned, it usually caused a comment on the disparity of their accents. While David, through no fault of his own, articulated his thoughts in the plummy tones of the BBC, Steven's tone was more the earthy timbre of the Black Country. This was due to their different means of escape. With David it was the theatre while Steven had joined the army. They had met while they were in their twenties. David was just about to start his final year at drama school, and Steven had just returned from Aden. It was at a party of which neither could remember a good reason for being there. Apart from meeting David, the only thing Steven could remember about it was a young woman who, completely drunk, was trying to dance or find someone to dance with her. On hearing that David was an actor, she ceased her gyrations and tried to entice him to perform, not for the last time. This second rejection was a little too much for her, and on hearing the word exhibitionist, she rounded on Steven. "What gives you the right to call me an exhibitionist? You don't know me."

"Let's be grateful for small mercies," and with that Steven thanked his hosts and left.

The next time they were to meet was just as auspicious an occasion.

Steven had called in to the Public Bar of the Giffard Arms to wash down a curry he had just consoled himself with after traveling to Coventry to see Wolves lose three to one. He had no plans for the remainder of the evening, content to let fate take him where it would. Fate in this case was in the shape of a flighty schoolteacher who tried to pick him up. "Did you enjoy your meal?"

"Which one?"

His pale eyebrows rose in a sad parody of a clown. "Why the last one, of course."

"Why, am I condemned?"

"Condemned?"

"Yes, are you inquiring if I ate a hearty breakfast?"

"Oh I see, you are a wit. We're going to have some fun with you."

Dream on snowflake.

His hands fluttered to his necktie, and after satisfying themselves that it was still in place, they went to his pocket, where presumably he kept his cigarettes. Steven noticed that his two V fingers were stained almost to the shade of his faded ginger hair. They apparently needed more sustenance, however, as they finally descended on a pint glass at his elbow, which was met halfway by his pursed lips. He reminded Steven of a large, bony bird. "No, I mean your Chinese meal, over the road."

"It served its purpose." Steven remembered him now discussing the bill with the waiter, hands flying all over the place, every word followed by an exaggerated facial expression. It still gave him a creepy feeling that he, in turn, had been noticed.

Meanwhile, his inquisitor had decided that a cigarette wouldn't do any arm, and the hands fluttered back to the pockets and opened the packet with a flourish. *"Do* have a cigarette."

"I don't."

"I hope you don't mind." He sucked the first mouthful down greedily, which probably tasted more of the match, which he extinguished with a wide swinging motion. "Well, what are your plans for the evening?"

He was, Steven thought, a very lonely man, but as Steven had come to terms with his solitude, this pathetic presumption of friendship was beginning to wear thin, which caused him to answer more sharply than he otherwise would have.

"Private."

"Oh very sharp. Now what is so private, women? *Men?*"

Part of Steven's brain was completely detached from the conversation as he considered his situation. The Giffard was a good pub. There was a diversity of characters, which made it entertaining, although there were better places for picking up a woman. Steven, while he had all his hormones in a row, was never good at the small talk involved in sexual pursuits, and he just didn't think it was worth it. While not anti-social, he took an almost voyeuristic pleasure in being on the edge of a conversation and observing the reactions of people, especially when they're trying to impress each other. So rudeness didn't work. The other option was simply to walk out of the pub, but that would defeat the object of him being here so …

"You know what I think?"

"Do I get three guesses?"

"I think you don't have any plans for the evening. I think you're basically quite shy and you try to disguise it."

Oh my giddy aunt.

When help did come, it was from a banal but nevertheless unexpected quarter. "I must go to the little boy's room." *Bad choice of words or possibly Freudian.* "You'll be here when I come back?"

"I wouldn't think so."

And after that, it was just a case of waiting for the bladder to exert enough pressure to come to Steven's rescue. As soon as the toilet door had shut, Steven left, purposely not finishing his drink so that it would appear as though he was coming back. There was a passage outside the public bar, and instead of turning right to exit into the street, Steven turned left, which led to the lounge bar, where there would be less cloying company.

The first thing he noticed was a group of girls to the right of the door. He was to learn later that they were a coven of grass widows. Their boyfriends were in a band currently trying to find fame touring the military clubs in Germany. It was rumored that one of them might have known Robert Plant pre–Led Zeppelin. Of more immediate concern to Steven was the fact that one of them was the "exhibitionist." He was about to brush past them, assuming she wouldn't recognize him, but fate had obviously decreed that tonight he was not going to enjoy his hard-won solitude. "Are you in a better mood?"

He tried to bluster his way through. "I'm sorry, a better mood than who?"

She turned to one of her cohorts. "He called me an exhibitionist. Known me all of five minutes and called me a fucking exhibitionist."

He wondered if she'd been sober since the party. "I'm sorry, I was just thinking aloud. Any woman who wears a miniskirt or laughs a lot I think is an exhibitionist and you were doing both—the former, if I may say so, to great effect."

"You may, but it's not going to get you anywhere. I'm with the drummer."

"The drummer?" If they were going to have a band in here, it would be preferable in the bar, predatory schoolteacher included.

"With the band—the Band of Joy. You must have heard of them. Have you met David?" At the time, David was trying to sidle unnoticed past the group, but with a dipsomaniac shrewdness and without taking her eyes off Steven, she reached behind and caught David's arm, "David's an actor," she said. "What do you do?"

"Actually, I'm not. I'm in the final year at drama school. Hello." David gently disengaged his arm and offered his hand to Steven.

"You didn't tell me what you do." She reoccupied David's arm.

"No, I don't think I did."

"Do you want me to guess?"

"If you like, but you don't have to."

"I think you're in the services. The short hair is a dead giveaway."

"Actually, I'm a model."

"But you're not—"

"I model wigs. That's why I have to keep my hair short. I also do hand jewelry and watches. You might not have noticed, but I have very sexy wrists."

Steven could not have wished for a better introduction to one of the pseudo-liberal cliques that abounded at the time and passed as a circle of friends. Under the guise of being a male model (at least that's what he says he is), he was passed 'round the circle, first the coven, Linda, Cindy, Jenny and Sandra, and then there were two Indians, not together. In fact, they studiously ignored each other. There was the token queer, Barry, who was in the wine business, Paul the artist, Mavis, whose occupation appeared to be Paul's girlfriend and telling everyone who cared to listen, and some who didn't, that Enoch Powell, a local politician, was a racist. Steven took great delight in telling her that his mother had voted for Mr. Powell because he had got her a flat nearer to the shops when no one else had answered her letter. During all this, his guide remembered to introduce herself as Chris. Her boyfriend was the drummer in the band, and she was in market research. There was an extremely fetching schoolteacher with long red hair and soulful eyes. "I was just talking to one of your colleagues in the bar." Steven motioned towards the front of the house. "He's got red hair as well." "That'll be Mike Godleigh or Ungoodly, as

we call him. He usually does his talent spotting in the bar."
Apparently Steven was not to be allowed to linger long, so
with a last look at Sheila (she was later to marry one of the
Indians, who had cut a swath through the unattached females of
Wolverhampton before "settling" on Sheila), he allowed himself
to be towed round the rest of the circle. Sylvia was the yiddisher
Momma. She had quite good legs, but they didn't match the rest
of her. There was a West Indian, Bertie, who kept his distance
from both of the Indians. He wasn't granted Bertie's calling,
but when, a year later, Steven returned from Libya, Bertie
was a guest of Her Majesty, for living off the earnings of his
wife, his defense being that it did not count if it was your wife.
Coincidentally, the next character he offered his hand to, Ray,
was later to be entertained by Her Majesty but not for pimping.
The Wolverhampton CID were less than sympathetic when
the third of his businesses that had failed to show a profit had
mysteriously combusted. There was even a single parent, they
called them unmarried mothers then, whose sole occupation
seemed to be being an unmarried mother. And lastly there was
Bob, who was an ex-schoolteacher and didn't seem to have a
current occupation apart from disparaging the Black Country
and all its denizens (Wolverhampton at the time eschewed all
connections with the Black Country). Years later Steven was
to read a book authored by Bob in which he had seemed to
reconcile himself with the Black Country by cavorting round the
canals in the company with a theater manager from Bridgnorth
and write a book about their adventures, finding time to revile
Enoch Powell (three years after Mister Powell's death).

After that, they seemed to have come full circle. "David,
this is Steven. He's a model, or says he is. David's an actor."
(He must have graduated drama school between the pimp and
the unmarried mother).

"Why do you accept that he's an actor yet you have a
problem with me as a model? Oh my God." Steven stretched
his eyebrows in mock horror. "It's not that he talks nice is it?"

231

At that point, Chris apparently decided that Steven could be left on his own and rejoined the coven.

"Red fourteen."

Steven turned to find that it was David who had spoken, "Pardon?"

"Red fourteen, you were playing social roulette. Well, you weren't actually playing, you were the ball. I don't know who was playing, but you landed on me. I'm sorry, that started out very smart, but I think I've had too much."

"Or not enough. Let me get you one."

"Thank you. Chris isn't as bad as she seems."

"She couldn't be."

"That's a bit harsh. Actually, as you know, her boyfriend's the drummer with the band, and when they return from Germany, she's going to break it off and she's not looking forward to it. She doesn't want to be just Steve Jones's girlfriend, but she doesn't quite know what the alternative is."

"You first met her at that party, right—a week ago—and she's telling you all this?"

"She obviously sees me as her father confessor."

"You being so worldly and you talk nice."

"That's Beatties, and by the way, your chip's showing "

"Beatties?"

Dave nodded toward the wall in the direction of Beatties, the large department store that adjoined the Giffard Arms. "We all used to work at Beatties, and would come in here at the end of the day. Then there were boyfriends and girlfriends and there you are."

"And there you are. Any of them still work at Beatties?"

"I don't think so. You usually get them on a Saturday lunch time or early evening. You can tell, the ones that are over made up and reek of perfume."

"Even the girls?"

David laughed. "Even the girls."

They talked, sometimes alone and sometimes with one or more of the others, in that quiet, undemanding atmosphere that has made the English Pub much copied, or parodied, all over the civilized world. And although he was entertained by the others, sometime during the evening he realized what drew him to David. Although he was the only one of the company that was in the acting profession, he was the only one who wasn't acting.

And from such a beginning sprang a friendship that had prevailed through Steven's two marriages and one divorce and David's "coming out" (although he was understandably miffed when Steven asked if he was going to be presented to Prince Charles). When Steven had a weekend free from his military duties, he would take the train up and ring David from Waterloo, and they would meet. If David had arranged anything, Steven would be included in it. In David's words, "The cosmic tumblers never aligned but on one noteworthy occasion." After seeing *Hair* courtesy of one of David's fellow graduates, they *did* fall asleep in each other's arms in Trafalgar Square. After the performance (of *Hair*) they had been to a party with Sheila (the provider of the 'comps'), the only thing memorable part of which was the statuesque presence of Sheila, an African American (they were called black then). Unfortunately, Steven's presence was required elsewhere, which necessitated him catching the six o'clock from Waterloo, which prevented him from doing his bit for race relations. David, for some reason, offered to accompany him, "In case you get lost." In fact, in their state, it was a question of who was guiding whom. So with regretful best wishes from Sheila, they set off in very roughly the direction of Waterloo. Not surprisingly, by the time they reached Trafalgar Square and congratulated each other on being almost at their destination, it seemed a better idea to wait there than among the lost night creatures who inhabited Waterloo. And so like Hansel and Gretel, they made themselves comfortable on a bench facing the national gallery and fell asleep. This idyll was interrupted by a young policeman, who with careful politeness asked them what they were doing, to which David replied with equal equanimity that they were waiting for a train. And to where, if he may ask?

"Aldershot." Steven, in case the conversation took an unhelpful turn, produced his leave pass and return ticket. And were the gentlemen, as they had belatedly become, aware that the train to Aldershot departed from Waterloo, on the other side of the river? They preferred waiting here. The company was much preferable, he was impishly informed, and Steven would leave at five thirty in time to catch his train. Apparently this was approved by the law with the admonition, "You're not going to do anything else?"

He was assured that they were not, and he departed, even promising to call back in time to give them an early call at the end of his beat. "Don't want you to miss your train, do we, sir?"

Innocent days.

Steven's relationship with Chris Davis improved to the point of driving her and her boyfriend home on the night that he became her ex-boyfriend, an experience he could have survived without, as he could when she introduced him to his first wife.

So here they were. After taking a nap to recover from Pamela's wifely attentions, they had foregone the delights of the London underground to travel north and were now ensconced in the public bar of the William of Orange, the only decent pub left in Hampstead, gay-friendly or otherwise, and had just brought David up to date on their current situation, to the point of inviting him to the wedding reception as their guest. David acknowledged the greeting of a passerby before again appealing to Pam. "Let him go to Arizona and he comes back with an earring, a daughter, and a prince for a son-in-law."

"Actually, I got the earring in California and the daughter in—"

"Please," David lifted his hands to his chest, palms outward, fingers splayed, "spare me the gory details."

"At the risk of sounding pedantic," Pamela loved that word, "You actually got the second earring in Arizona. He changed ears," she whispered to David.

"Yes, he always did swing with the wind. Why did you get an earring?"

Although he addressed the question to Steven, Pam was in full spate. "It depends who you ask. He takes it out when he is about to meet his army buddies and when we go to the club, but last year the club arranged a trip to the races at Del Mar and he forgot to take it out, and I must admit I didn't remind him because it was a pain to get back in. So, as you can imagine, when we got to the club, it caused a quite a stir, and everyone who asked him why he was wearing an earring got a different reply." As was her usual habit, she paused to make sure she was being listened to out of more than politeness. "At first it was that he was so pretty, and working at Media Partners, he wanted everyone to know which side his bread was buttered. He actually asked the guy who was inserting it to make sure it was in the heterosexual side. 'People don't bother about that these days, sir,' he was told. Anyway, Mister Smartmouth said, 'They would if you worked where I worked, and I'm not going to walk backward for obvious reasons." Her smile encompassed the couple at the next table, who appeared to have abandoned their own conversation. "Another one was—and I think this one was good especially, as it was completely off the cuff—'I had a titanium implant in my left knee,' which is true, 'and I had to have something titanium as opposite as possible to balance it electronically. A bracelet might have done, but an earring was farther away from the knee, making the magnetic field stronger.' Another one I liked, probably because it was accredited to me, was that on his sixtieth birthday, he promised himself something he'd never done before, and by the time my opinion was asked he'd narrowed it down to three, which were"—she made a show of trying to remember while she checked her audience's attention—"a girlfriend, a motorbike or an earring. I suggested—no, I *decided* on the earring, because as I said, with a motorbike you could kill yourself, with a girlfriend *I* would kill you, and so, the earring." This garnered an overt show of approval from the next table, whose interest had waned at the suggestion of a girlfriend.

Having exhausted the subject of Steven's jewelry, the conversation drifted to the other subjects, David, from time to time acknowledging a wave of recognition from outside the window.

"The Willie is the only decent pub left now," he declared with a look at Steven, which dared him to make a bad joke. "So how formal is this do? I take it I don't have to go to Moss Brothers?"

"I'll get Mrs. Murdoch to telephone you. She's a bit of a gorgon but knows everything."

"She sounds grim."

"She is, but she'll put you right as long as you're a friend of Pam's. What?"

David had flung out his arm. "You've let me forget about Pam."

"She's been right here."

"But we've been talking about your earring and princesses. I haven't had a kiss, not you, you randy sod—Pam, my dear." And ignoring both Steven and the window, he stood and bestowed a kiss on Pam, Russian style, right cheek, left cheek, right cheek.

18~"Get us to the church on time."

BEFORE THAT WEEK, STEVEN HAD seen Prince Charles twice, once at the fiftieth anniversary of the Airborne Forces and once at the D-Day celebrations in Portsmouth. He had seen the Duke of Edinburgh once at a dress rehearsal of the trooping of the colors. He had caught a glimpse of Princess Margaret as she was driven past a pub in Hampstead (probably the Spaniard), but as he said, it was so full of queens, a mere princess went unnoticed, which earned him a pained look from David. He had never, however, seen the Queen, and as the dress rehearsal was to be followed by the rehearsal lunch given by Her Majesty, he was looking forward to it, as well as wearing his morning suit. His socialist dad would be turning in his grave, not for the first time. "This would never have happened if he'd gone to the Steelworks." Nevertheless, he duly presented himself at Moss Brothers, in his best rehearsal lunch suit and carrying the cowboy boots, to be greeted by looks of shocked disbelief. "Mister Swinbourne, he's at the venue, sir."

"The venue?"

"Yes sir, that's where the event is taking place."

"I know where the event is taking place, but as it is a dress rehearsal, I assumed I would have to be dressed."

"Quite correct, sir, but you will be fitted," he eschewed the vulgar word dressed, "*at* the venue, which is why our Mister Swinbourne is there. Obviously we can't have our suit traveling." He shuddered at the thought.

"Of course." *You fucking idiot, Jackson, of course he said to meet at Saint Paul's. You were too busy preening yourself you weren't even listening, and Pam had just gone to the ladies so she couldn't listen for you. Oh my God, what are we going to doooo?*

"So no harm done, I'm sure you get a lot of this. Obviously it's our first time, and our last, unless he sires another princess, which I doubt very highly. What do you think, honey? Are you all right?"

"What?" During his self-flagellation, he had failed to notice that Pam had been in conversation with the sales associate.

"Mister—I'm sorry I haven't got your name—Mister Wilshaw is going to call us a taxi. We'll make it, just, but I hope you've got the fare. You can't expect the Queen to pay. Just a joke, Mister Wilshaw, I find it helps at times like these."

If the cab fare had come out of the royal purse, Her Majesty, being of a frugal nature, would have baulked at the lavish tip Pam had promised to, "Get them to the church on time—yes I did say that."

"You gettin' married then, dahlin'? Doin' the right thing by you is he?"

"Actually," Pam decided to appeal to the Londoner's protective feeling for the Royal Family in case the tip wasn't enough, "we're attending the dress rehearsal for Prince William's wedding, and we're running a bit late, he," she indicated Steven, who was being held in her arms, "didn't realize that the guy from Moss Brothers was to meet him at Saint Paul's."

"Wasn't very smart, was it? Stands to reason, don't travel in a cab in your best soup and fish[18]. Don't know what tosser's been in before you, do you? He doing something at the wedding? Whistle and flute from Moss Bros? Sounds important."

He was speaking across Steven to Pam, as most people did, and while Pam could understand only about half of what was being said, it didn't sound very complimentary.

"I don't know if you would call it important, but he's actually giving the bride away," she said crisply, and when that had sunk in she added, "He's her father."

"Straight up? Stone the crows, I thought he looked familiar. 'ere and don't worry, I'll get you there." And performing one of those maneuvers that rightly caused some misgivings to anyone who has ridden in a London cab, he drove one-handed through an intersection while fishing under his seat to unearth that days copy of the *Evening Standard,* which he passed over his shoulder through the partition, talking all the time. "Must be more to him than meets the eye. They say it's the quiet ones. If Judy gets her looks from her mother, well—and *you're* quite tasty, if you don't mind me saying so—second page. Yes, quite tasty, and a bit of the other, on the dark side, in Los Angeles. Oh dear, oh dear, still waters, eh, still waters."

Pam had been stroking Steven's hair while with a dexterity almost equaling that of the cabby's. She opened the paper and what she saw caused her to cease her wifely ministrations. There under the heading, **"Future Queen's Father Talks Film Deal or Something—in Hollywood"** was a picture of Steven and Naomi in a sports car, which showed enough of Steven to identify him and enough of Naomi to jeopardize the *Standard's* status as a family newspaper.

"You didn't tell me she looked like this." Pamela offered Steven the newspaper.

Steven looked at the photograph. "Black? I didn't think that would mean anything to you. We're all God's children, after all."

"You know what I mean, she's gorgeous."

"Yes, she speaks very highly of you. Careful!"

Pam had folded the paper and delivered a far from gentle backhanded swipe on Steven's head.

"Yeah, careful love, I haven't read it yet." The cab driver discreetly closed the sliding partitions and gave his full attention to London's byways.

They rode for minutes in silence until Pam said, while gazing at the passing traffic, "Have I got anything to worry about, Steven?"

"No. But thank you for the compliment."

She gently stroked his head. "Sorry about that. Did it hurt much?"

He took her hand, brushing his lips across the knuckles before gently rubbing it over his head. "All better. I think we're here." And they had indeed drawn up under the giant dome of Saint Paul's.

"Here we are then. Now *tout suit*, don't keep the Queen waiting." The cabby reached through and opened the door.

"Thank you, and five minutes early." Pam started to count out the fare.

"Each man to his trade, love, that's what I do. Good luck and hey," Pam had already started to climb the steps, but she stopped and turned, offering him a better view than Saint Paul's, "keep him away from the Princess Royal."

They were stopped at the top of the steps by a man who, in a raincoat and trilby, looked much out of keeping with the grandeur of Saint Paul's. In fact, if it wasn't for the microphone clipped to his lapel, he would be a stereotype English copper of the fifties' black-and-white 'B' movies, "Good morning, sir, madam, can I ask you why you're here?"

"The dress rehearsal, what else?" Steven said with the arrogance of one who has done something stupid and got away with it.

"There is a church service due to start, sir. As well as a national landmark, it is foremost a house of worship."

"I see, my apologies, and you are?"

"Special branch, sir." As if by magic, an identity card, complete with photograph, appeared in his hand in such a way that it was only visible to Steven. He even removed his trilby.

"Thanks. Steven Jackson, here for the dress rehearsal, my wife Pamela. I haven't got my passport. Will an Arizona driving license do?"

"That won't be necessary, sir, thank you. You are already identified." He modestly indicated a closed-circuit television camera in the angle of the archway. "And is your good lady part of the ceremony?"

"No, but she is invited to the rehearsal lunch. I believe she is expected."

"Very nice too, sir, that's fine, excuse me." He turned his head slightly to speak in to the microphone. "Steven Jackson with the party, accompanied by wife, long hair, well dressed, quite attractive—*her,* that is. If you'll forgive me, sir, a little flatfoot humor. If you'll go straight through to the main doors, there will be a representative of Moss Brothers to meet you, and if your good lady will stay with me, there'll be someone along to conduct her to the spectator's gallery. If you encounter any difficulty, just ask somebody with a red carnation."

"A red carnation?"

"Yes sir, Windsor red to be precise."

"What else."

"Instead of having name tags?" Pam smiled to show it was meant in good part.

A wintry smile passed beneath the trilby. "Are you perchance American, madam?"

"California born and raised."

"And very charming too, as was Winston Churchill's mother, I believe. But we do things a little different here ma'am."

"That's what makes you so ... British."

Don't try to get the last word in with her, sunshine, it's been tried by experts.

Pam put her arms round Steven's neck. "Go and escort your beautiful daughter down the aisle and show her what a classy father she's got. Make me proud." Her voice dropped, and with uncharacteristic meanness, she whispered, "And show Lydia what she let get away." She released him. "Go! I'll be all right with special branch to look after me."

Trilby and rain coat, who by now was looking for other latecomers, acknowledged this with a barely perceptible turn of the head as Steven made his way inside Saint Paul's.

He was met by the representative of Moss Brothers in the shape of the taciturn Jeremy. "Mister Jackson, Mister Swinbourne sends his regards and I am to escort you to the robing area, where he will be with us in time for the final fitting."

"Something I've said, Jeremy?"

"Sir?"

"Personal attention last time, now I'm stuck with you. Is it because Pam's not with me?"

"Oh no sir." Jeremy was duly alarmed. "Mister Swinbourne has fourteen people to fit, but he will be with us before the rehearsal starts."

"Just a joke, Jeremy old son, helps lessen the tension. Lead on."

"Yes sir, this way." He was led past the Guard of Honour, noticing that the oldest looked about twenty-one, but they all wore campaign medals, to a stone-flagged corridor with a line of coat hooks on one wall. They walked on until they came to the end. The coat hooks were all festooned with men's clothing, except the last one, which held a complete suit of morning attire, including a maroon and blue Pegasus tie. He noticed Jeremy had stopped, so Steven hooked his finger through the coat hanger. "Right, where to now?"

"It's here sir."

"Here?" At first Steven thought that Jeremy was returning the joke, but no, this must be it, "A bit sparse, isn't it?"

"Yes, sir, but we are on site."

"Right, so we are. Well, let's get to it." He replaced the coat hanger and took off his jacket.

"I'll be outside the door, sir, when you're ready, and if I may, we are running a bit behind. There's a mirror over there in the corner."

Now that he had something to do, his apprehension dropped from him. He quickly undressed and began to don his formal finery. He realized that the clothes were on the hanger in reverse order from how they were put on. The shirt was on the outside, and then the braces holding the trousers, the waistcoat, and finally the morning coat. He assumed it was Jeremy's work and mentally patted the pomaded head. He was always a quick dresser, so he had time to retie the tie so that the knot was completely maroon and no Pegasuses (or should it be Pegasi?) faced the wrong way. The cowboy boots presented a bit of a problem, as there was no chair and he couldn't bend down. The morning coat *was* unforgiving, so he had to take it off first. He should have put them on before the waist coat. He chastised himself but still had time for a few deep breaths before presenting himself to Jeremy barely five minutes after they had parted.

"How do I look?"

"I'm to take you to Mister Swinbourne." Jeremy eschewed an opinion. Obviously he had to wait until asked by his superior. "This way, sir, if you don't mind."

"Not at all, old son, lead on."

While he was being led, or rather escorted, by Jeremy toward the main door, he became more aware of his surroundings. On his way in, he was too occupied with dealing with the Trilby and Raincoat and taking his leave of Pam, but now the full aura of the building surrounded him. They had just passed the entrance to the whispering gallery, and the dome soared two hundred feet above them. Even the floor was impressive with its inlaid mosaics. The smell, a curious mixture of incense and very old stone, assailed his nostrils, and it was a while before he remembered what the smell reminded him of—the Alamo when they had paused in San Antonio on their way to New Orleans. As a lifelong Methodist, apart from a brief flirtation with Judaism and an even briefer one with Catholicism and a longer dalliance with agnosticism, the very scale of the building filled him with awe. The figures that walked purposely past were reduced to the stature of ants until one of them spoke to him. "Mister Jackson, I see Jeremy found you, splendid. Sorry I couldn't get to you earlier. So let's have a look at you." Mister Swinbourne cast a practiced eye over him. "Yes, I think you'll do rather well. Jeremy?"

"As perfect as I can tell, Mister Swinbourne. You asked me to remind you about the hat."

"And so I did, thank you. Mister Jackson, being an old soldier, could you give us your beret size?"

"Seven and three-eighths," Steven replied automatically.

"And your hands?"

"I didn't know there was a size."

"I'm sorry, I want to see your hands. May I?" He took Steven's wrist and held it, palm upward. "I think a medium should suffice. Jeremy?"

"A medium should do fine. He'll only need to raise his hat to acknowledge the public."

This had gone far enough. It wasn't as though Pam was there. "What," he said carefully, "are you gentlemen talking about?"

"You don't need the hat and gloves here, as by this time you will have left them in the vestibule. You will collect them on the way out, before you leave to be driven to the wedding breakfast in the second coach, after the bridal couple, and during the drive to Buckingham Palace, you will, as Jeremy pointed out," he inclined his head graciously, "have to acknowledge the cheers of the crowd. Have you read the papers much since you've been in town?"

"Been giving them a miss," Steven replied carefully. "Although," he added, "we did get a glimpse of today's *Standard* in the taxi."

"Yes, I thought that bit about 'or something,' was a bit racy for the *Standard*. By the by, is the better half with us this morning?"

"She's in the spectator gallery."

"Of course, give her my regards."

"I will. And what was all that old madam about, 'hat and gloves only if I'm going racing.'"

"Really, Mister Jackson, you will let an old man have his little joke."

"Fair enough, so how do I get here?"

"My instructions are to be present at the Royal Mews on the morning of the event, so you will be fitted there, ride in the coach, together with Ms. Biderman, the bride to be, and on the return, you will share the second carriage with the bride's mother, and won't that be a dish to set before the Queen, as the saying goes. Now when you get into the coach, both on the way here and on the return journey, I must impress on you to part the tails of the morning coat so that it is not creased. If we could find a chair, would you have a little practice?"

"No I bloody well would not, but don't worry, I can do it."

Mister Swinbourne was not convinced. "But you've never sat in a morning coat."

"I know, but don't worry, I used to watch Liberace sit at the piano on the telly."

The confrontation might have gone further, and Steven was about to call an usher to mediate. He was already forming a bad joke about buttonholing a buttonhole, but as if on cue, one of them arrived at his elbow, "Mister Jackson, Mister Swinbourne, H's compliments. We are about to start. Is there a hold up?"

"No, we are ready." Was there a slight emphasis on the we? Mister Swinbourne, ever the professional, held out his hand in grudging forgiveness. "Good luck, Mister Jackson, I'm sure you will do well."

Steven took the olive branch. "Thanks for your help, Mister Swinbourne. I'll look after the suit." Then turning to the buttonhole, "Right! Let's get to it. Lead on, old flower."

As soon as they were out of earshot of Mister Swinbourne and Jeremy, the usher laid his hand on Steven's upper arm with his fingers round the biceps, gently, but his fingers felt like steel. "Not carrying any electronic devices, are we, sir? Cell phones, anything like that?"

"Hardly ever use them. The only thing I've got on me that I brought from outside is my wallet, and you're quite welcome to have a look at that. In fact, you can search me."

"That won't be necessary, sir. At the next archway, a colleague of mine will pass a device over you that will detect any device and then you will have to take them back, so if you tell me now, it will save any embarrassment."

"I've got a titanium implant in my knee, parachuting accident, but nothing electronic, unless the morning suit's been bugged."

"No sir, the morning suit has already been checked."

"You're serious?"

"Quite, sir—the times in which we live, unfortunately. Thank you for your cooperation."

"Sure, there's just one thing." Steven nodded to the hand that was still on his sleeve. "If you can loosen the grip a bit, I'm sure Mister Swinbourne would appreciate it. Mister Swinbourne of Moss Brothers, he'll have kittens if the sleeve's creased."

"Of course, sir, no offense meant."

"None taken." They walked on. The only sound was the tattoo of the cowboy boots echoing against the walls, until his guide turned his face toward his buttonhole. "Twenty and closing."

They've actually got microphones in their carnations.

Although Steven was expecting it, his next contact still appeared, seemingly out of nowhere, and was greeted by Steven's escort. "Mister Jackson, father of the bride—the cowboy boots."

"Right, sir, no naughties, I gather. f you'll just stand still, nice suit, and those *are* the cowboy boots, very snappy." The device was about the size and shape of a bar of soap, and apart from a slight buzz as it passed over his medal, it traversed him without incident. "And if you could stand at ease, sir, let's see if you're carrying any weapons, apart from the old laughing tackle that is. Pardon me, sir, just my little joke."

"No bother." Steven stood with his legs apart. "You can check that as well. It's done all the damage it's going to do."

"Yes sir, quite. You're all finished, good luck, and if I may say so, you have a beautiful daughter—a credit to you."

"Thank you." *Just a tumble in a pickup truck, old son, everything else is due to her.*

As they approached, H was in conversation with the commander of the Guard of Honour, a young Captain with two campaign medals on his chest and what looked like a military cross. The Guard of Honour were in the relaxed position soldiers have when they have been out of their beds at five, just to get somewhere where they wait for two hours.

"Ah, Mister Jackson." H turned from the young Captain,. "You've arrived, and looking very much the part. Thank you." He dismissed the red buttonhole before introducing Steven. "Mister Jackson, Captain L'Shaw, Captain L'Shaw will be commanding the Honour Guard, at your request, so I hear. So we are to take it from the bride's arrival, she will be coming from behind that curtain, whereas on the day, she will be coming through the main doors. At her entrance, while her Maids of Honour are fixing her train, you, Captain L' Shaw, will form up your Guard of Honour level with the screen, and you, Mister Jackson, will take your daughter's hand, and when the train is affixed, you will be told by the senior maid, *What a title, that'll be something to brag about at the tennis club.* Then you will advance to be level with the front rank, and there you will wait until you hear the music. Then you will give the order to slow march, and you, Mister Jackson, will step off after the second pair have passed you and go at a pace that will keep you between the second and third pair. Do you remember what happens next?"

"I will halt abreast of Prince William, let go my daughter's hand, and stand in a dignified position with my hands over the old laughing tackle, thus." Steven demurely folded his hands over the offending area. "During the responses, I will keep the old throat lubricated until I hear 'who giveth this woman.' On that I will say in a loud, clear voice, 'I do.' I will take my daughter's hand in mine and place it in his, saying, 'King or no king, if you don't look after her I'll geld you'—bit of a joke there, but I will. Then I will move about five paces to my right and keep myself there, taking care not to be swept off my feet by the bridal train when they turn to face each other, and that's it until 'who God has put together' I attend, if that's the right word, the Princess Royal and follow the best man and Maid of Honour to the vestibule and that's it, until I get in the carriage and wave to the crowds on my way to Buck House for the nosh."

"First class, really good, except for the admonition to His Royal Highness. There is one little thing—before you go down the steps to your carriage, there'll be plenty of time. Stand where Captain L'Shaw can see you, because he has to approach you as part of the bridal party to ask permission to stand down the Honour Guard, all right?"

"I see, great and do I get to inspect the Honour Guard first?"

"I think we can safely leave that to the Guard Commander," H answered crisply, and Steven realized that he was under some pressure and regretted his levity.

"Yes, of course, sorry. But one question. At what point do I put on my hat?"

"Good point. The vestibule is considered outside, so you replace your top hat as soon as you have taken leave of the Princess Royal. A page will bring your hat and gloves to you. Don't tip him; it will be considered bad form." He smiled to show that they were all friends again. "And when the Guard Commander compliments you, you will raise your hat in response. After you have given permission to dismount the guard, you will be told when to start walking down the steps so that your carriage and you, together with the Princess Royal and the bride's mother, will arrive at the bottom of the steps at the same time. You don't want to look as if you're waiting for a number eleven bus, do you? Well I think that's it. Any questions, Captain L' Shaw?"

"No, I think we are ready."

"I have just one, if I may."

"Yes." H was ready to take his leave, and now he turned toward Steven as if prepared for some bad news or an even worse joke.

"Where will my wife figure in all this? Has *she* got to wait for a number eleven bus?"

"According to protocol, the parents of the bride are in the second coach and the parent of the groom is in the third coach with the Duchess of Cornwall. Your wife will follow with Mister Chaddersly-Corbett. I am led to believe that Her Majesty will make her own arrangements so as to get to Buckingham Palace, where she will appear with you on the balcony, together with your wife and the Duchess of Cornwall together with your—Miss Biderman's escort."

So Chadders made the second eleven. Wonder where Mrs. Chadders figures in the selection. "After the newlyweds have shared their joy with the nation, you will be escorted to the wedding breakfast, after which Moss Brothers will reclaim their apparel and you will be free to go to your residence and prepare yourself for the reception. So if there are no more questions, we start when your daughter comes through that archway. We take it as though she's just arrived with you. This is your day—enjoy it and don't forget to breathe. Now if there's nothing else." Apparently there wasn't.

"Don't shoot the messenger, old son." Steven turned to see that he was being addressed by the Guard Commander. "I could tell he was uncomfortable about something. That's why we weren't properly introduced—Brian L' Shaw." He saluted and held out his hand.

"Steven Jackson, your lads are looking well."

"Thank you, pick of the best. You noticed the bit about the Guard of Honour being at your request."

"Yes, I did pick that up. We *do* make them nervous, don't we?"

"Lock up the best teaspoons." He studied Steven's campaign medal. "Did I hear you served in Aden?"

"That's right, that and Northern Ireland were the only two pieces of mischief that they could find for me." Steven noticed it *was* the Military Cross. "I was in Aden in sixty-seven, a bit before your time. You probably weren't even born."

"No, but I think you served with my father."

"L'Shaw?" It wasn't a common name. "Not Mike L'Shaw?"

"None other. He got his MBE after that he—oh my God." Something had happened behind Steven's shoulder that had caused Brian L'Shaw to forget his military bearing, enough for his jaw to sag and his guard to forget their two hours of waiting and straighten their shoulders.

Steven turned to see what had caused the frisson and saw his daughter standing in the archway. In reality, she only stood there until her eyes became adjusted to her new surroundings, but it seemed that she did not move until every eye was upon her. The dress couldn't have been more simple—a sheath of cream brocade fell from her shoulders to within inches of the floor. Above her veil her blue-black hair fell in waves to her shoulders. The veil emphasized the paleness of her skin, and her eyes gleamed through it. It was Brian L'Shaw who found his voice first. "Well let's to business. Good luck, old son." And raising his voice just enough to carry to his detail, he said, "Right, gentlemen let's do it. Guard of Honour----, fall in."

Steven had a faint impression of the ten figures lining up in pairs as he made his way, cowboy boots beating a tattoo on the flagged floor, across to his daughter and held out his hand.

"Well, Poppi, here we are. You look so handsome." He must have said something, because she smiled at him, and they moved away from the archway so that the Maids of Honour could fix her train. They all must have been feeling nervous as, when the train was arranged to their satisfaction, the leading attendant patted him on the shoulder. "When we prepare a bride, she's prepared. What do you think?"

"Words fail me. But I'm thinking of withdrawing my permission. I think she's too good for him."

There was a moment of shocked silence, and then a wave of giggles swept the phalanx before there was a general settling down as they all concentrated on the next hour.

"Right." The same Maid of Honour touched his shoulder. "We're all ready. Off you go."

They moved deliberately in between the Guard of Honour, and when Steven and Judith were level with the front pair, Brian L'Shaw brought them quietly to attention, each man looking just above the man's head in front and straining not to look sideways at Judith.

He felt her give a quiet tremor and gently patted her hand.

"Poppi, you are so calm. It's like you do this every day. You are not nervous?"

"Just a little but not much. After all, we've got the Paras to look after us." He nodded toward the Guard of Honour.

"They are so beautiful," she whispered, "and so young."

Someone hissed, "Shush," just in time, as the first strains of "Pomp and Circumstance" were heard. Brian L'Shaw gave the order to slow march. The first pair passed forward and then, after an age, the second pair, and then Judith, possibly emboldened by Steven's reassurance said, "Right girls, let's go," and they were away.

It was breathtaking, not literally, but it was certainly hard to remember H's instruction to breathe as they stepped forward. Elgar's masterpiece cascaded through the gothic arches, and with Judith outshining the radiance of the stained glass window, there was no need for him to remember to hold his head back and square his shoulders. He afterward became aware of a dark shadow that flitted down the side aisle, which turned out to be H as he appeared genie-like ahead of them when they reached the altar rail. Steven remembered to release Judith's arm as she transferred her bouquet into her right hand, and there was a moment's pause before someone who looked like the Archbishop of Canterbury began, "Dearly beloved we are gathered here in the sight of Almighty God and the presence of this congregation to unite Judith and William in holy wedlock. Marriage is an institution ..." He had remembered to fold his hands in front of him and look solemnly to his front, but there was not a lot to look at. He daren't look up, as he would risk being assailed by vertigo. It must be the same for the Maids and the Guards of Honour, but presumably they had more comfortable footwear than cowboy boots, not designed for standing on four hundred–year-old flagstones.

"If anyone knows any just cause why William and Judith should not be joined in holy wedlock, let him speak now," *And get my cowboy boot up his arse,* "or forever hold his peace."

"Who giveth this woman?" This was it, an extra swallow for luck. "I do." And what was it? Yes. He took Judith's hand, and after giving it an encouraging squeeze, placed it in Prince William's. Now five paces to the right so as not to be knocked over. He just made it and refolded his hands. That was it until,

"I now pronounce you man and wife. You may kiss the bride. Those who God has put together let no man put asunder." Then the bridal couple turned away from the altar, causing the train bearers to do another ninety-degree shuffle. They *were* good. They must have practiced, plus there was no one to get out of the way this time. They stepped off just as the hidden band began to play "Jerusalem," which seemed appropriate. As they reached the second pew, the best man, Prince Harry, together with someone who was unfamiliar to Steven, stepped off. *I wonder how much he'll miss his brother now that he's married.*

As Steven had to make up the extra five steps to get to the nave, Princess Anne was waiting for him. "You must be the Princess Royal."

"Unless you're in the habit of picking up women in Saint Paul's?"

Seems a nice girl. Pity about the mouth.

As Harry and his partner reached the second pew, they stepped off, and Princess Anne leaned toward him and whispered, "Sorry about that, it's the first time I've ever stood for so long, and my shoes are bloody killing me."

"Your shoes? I'm wearing cowboy boots."

"Why?"

"It's a long story."

Apparently too long, as they had now reached the vestibule, and H was giving his verdict, "Absolutely perfect. Do the same on Tuesday next and you will look back on the day with pride for the rest of your lives. The Guard of Honour, you did the transition perfectly, and the Maids of Honour, that last turn always a danger, but you acquitted yourselves perfectly. Again, do that on the day and you will earn the gratitude of your future queen, never a bad thing, especially if you manage the first turn without knocking her father over. "Miss Biderman, you looked so radiant, one could forgive you for anything. Fortunately, there was nothing to forgive. You were perfection." *What an old woffler.* "Mister Jackson, very good carriage. The 'I do' was just right. As you and the Princess Royal converge, a nod of acknowledgment, even a small smile, is permissible, and I'm sure that on the day, you will save your tete-a-tete until after you have reached the vestibule. Before you leave for the lunch, make sure you get your final instructions from one of the ushers, and thank you. And one more thing, we're not quite finished yet. Cars are available to take you to the lunch, and they will arrive in the same sequence as the carriages will on the day. The only difference being, this time you will change out of your finery first. So off you go, and back here as soon as you can, as there are people who don't need to change. Mister Jackson, a moment please."

As the rest of the party dispersed, Steven took his leave of the Princess Royal and made his way over to H. "Anything wrong, old son?"

"No indeed, but," he beckoned to Brian L'Shaw, "you have to give permission to dismount the guard."

"Sir," with a flourish, Brian L'Shaw brought his sword up in front of his face, "have I your permission to dismount the guard?"

"Yes, and thank you. They did very well, don't you think so, H?"

"Thank you, sir," apparently H's approval wasn't necessary, as Brian saluted, turned smartly, and made his way over to the guard, who were still at attention.

"Well, if that's all?"

"You will remember on the day, you will be wearing a top hat and you will raise it to compliment the Guard Commander."

"I'll have no trouble doing that. Just have to remember to put the bloody thing back on. Now if you could direct me to where I've left me clobber, we don't want to keep Her Majesty waiting, do we?"

In variance to his getting dressed in his morning apparel in splendid isolation, he now found himself divesting his finery in an atmosphere that resembled a rugby team dressing room after a hard-fought win. There were about a dozen men of varying ages and sizes in various stages of undress all talking at once. So exuberant was the atmosphere that it produced a wizened figure who seemed to materialize out of the very stonework, his austere cassock making him even more impressive. "Gentlemen, gentlemen, this simply will not do. You are understandably pleased at the prosecution of your duties, but kindly remember this *is* a house of worship and save your celebration for the vestibule."

William took it upon himself to apologize for them all, and the hubbub subsided to an acceptable level. It was also fundamentally democratic. As Steven attempted to get his cowboy boots off, Prince William was next to him struggling to remove his waistcoat, "Mister Jackson—Steven, would you mind helping me with this bloody thing?"

"Language, young man, you're in church. You've got one of the tie-ups twisted. Hold still."

"You'll hear a lot worse if I don't get out of this corset soon."

"There you are." Steven unraveled the tapes. "Now just take it off from the front. I hope you'll have someone to help you on the day or you'll strangle yourself, and that would ruin my daughter's whole day."

"Thanks." William pitched the waist coat onto the nearest hook. "Don't worry, on the day we'll be leaving from the big house and there'll be someone to help."

Did he sound a bit embarrassed?

"I'm surprised." Steven nodded toward where Jeremy and Mr. Swinbourne were watching over the proceedings like anxious parents on their child's first day at school. "They didn't help? Some sort of reverse snobbery?"

"Question of economics. They're only concerned with the clothes in their charge. Me and this tosser," he indicated Prince Harry, who was having equal difficulty getting undressed, "own our own morning suits. With the functions we attend, it works out cheaper." He seemed anxious to dispel any notion of royal extravagance. Then he turned to his brother. "Get a move on, we'll be here all day."

Three things occurred to Steven simultaneously. First, big brothers are always big brothers, no matter where they are born. Second, that was the reason for the concern about cell phones. Most modern cell phones are equipped to take pictures, and what would the gutter press pay for photos of William and Harry with their trousers round their ankles? And finally, Diana's son or not, William certainly wasn't behind the door when the brains were given out. He was, however, less than fair to Jeremy, for when Steven was wondering what to do with his cowboy boots—after all, you can't go to lunch with the Queen carrying a pair of cowboy boots—Jeremy came to his rescue and promised to take personal charge of them and have them to hand on "the occasion."

The atmosphere in the vestibule was a mixture of celebration and relief. It had obviously been a trial for all of them. Judith went to each of her Maids of Honour in turn, kissing each of them on both cheeks. William, content to cede the spotlight to his wife-to-be, talked quietly with his brother and Princess Anne, occasionally glancing across at Judith. The Guard of Honour were stood down, as on "the day" Steven assumed that the steps would be lined with an Honour Guard from the Blues and Royals, and stood unnoticed in a corner, sussing out[19] the Maids of Honour or perhaps, thought Steven, it was something different. His daughter broke away from her attendants to walk over to where he was talking to Brian L'Shaw, and their eyes followed her. "Poppi, wasn't it amazing? Such beautiful music, and this place—are you looking forward to it?"

"I wouldn't call it that exactly, but it was, impressive."

"Poppi, it was—you are not going to be *too* English."

"You can't be too English," Steven replied sternly. "I'm sorry, you haven't met Brian L'Shaw. He's the Commander of your Guard of Honour. Brian, my daughter Judith."

"Delighted." Brian L' Shaw saluted, and taking Judith's hand, gently brushed it with his lips.

They didn't teach you that at Sandhurst.

"Ooh la la, so gallant and your soldiers so ..."

The compliment was left unsaid as a discreet cough announced the presence of one of the buttonholes at her elbow. "If you'll pardon me, ma'am, your carriage is approaching, and would you make your way to the top of the steps?"

"And just when I was getting to know my bodyguard, but such is life. Au revoir, mon brave---Poppi." After bestowing each a light kiss on the cheek, the latter to the amusement of his troops, she drifted over to where William was waiting.

"Steven." It was Chadders with Pam on his arm. "Well done, old son, went off splendidly. I thought your wife was going to burst into applause." Pam just smiled.

"Thank you, it was pretty awe-inspiring, but everyone seems happy. Brian, I don't believe you've met my wife—"

"Mrs. Jackson, a pleasure."

"Pam." Pam held out her hand.

"And Charles Chaddersley-Corbett. Charles was in the Irish guards."

"Good show in Iraq." Brian returned his attention to Pam. "You're enjoying the occasion, Pam?"

"It's breathtaking. Is it your first time on one of these?"

"Yes we're only allowed one, and it's quite an honour. It's quite magnificent, isn't it? The lads are thrilled."

"And it does help having someone like Judith. Isn't she gorgeous?"

"She certainly is. We were wondering if she had any sisters." The last was directed at Steven.

"I'll ask her mother."

"Speaking of which," Charles said, "don't you think you should be seeking her out, her mother? You're supposed to escort her down the steps. You're in the second car, and the first pair have already left."

"Bloody hell! Yes, you're right."

"Language in a church," Pam admonished him. "I'll be all right with Charles *and* the Parachute Regiment. Go and find Lydia, and remember what the cabby said: keep your hands off the Princess Royal."

"Yes, duty calls." There was a congratulatory kiss from his wife. "Chadders, always a pleasure. Brian, see you in the guardroom." Steven reluctantly went in search of Judith's mother.

He tried not to make it too obvious. The last time he saw her was probably when she was speaking to Judith while she was getting disrobed. She could have joined them after Judith had left, although Pam was there. Brian L'Shaw and Chadders should have been enough to tip the scales. He walked slowly past the Maids of Honour who were waiting their turn to leave now that Judith had gone, smiling at the one who had spoken to him. The vestibule was not all that big. From where he was, he could see Prince Harry talking to his father. That must be Camilla with them. Pamela was still being attended to by Brian and Chadders. One or two of the bolder of the Honour Guard, their prime charge now out of sight, were talking to the Maids of Honour. So where was Lydia, and where was Princess Anne? Enough of this; he'd go without her. Having made his decision, he walked over to the top of the steps and sought out the nearest buttonhole. "Steven Jackson, father of the bride. I believe you're expecting me, or if you're not you soon will be."

"Yes sir, you appear to be missing the bride's mother."

"For a month or two, but you know how it is. Time heals all, and then I met Pam and I hardly ever think of her or didn't until this lot."

"You should be accompanied by the bride's mother, sir," the buttonhole answered with leaden patience. "She is to ride with you."

"And she's quite welcome to if she gets here in time, and as it appears to have escaped your notice, I am sans the Princess Royal."

"There has been a change of plan regarding the Princess Royal, sir."

Thanks for telling me. "So there's only one left to worry about, isn't there?"

"Look," Steven said in a more conciliatory tone, "we finished the rehearsal, I had a chat with the Guard Commander and stood the Guard down and as soon as my daughter was called, I knew we were next so I started looking for her mother. *Stretching the truth a bit but he looks as though he'd like to practice his karate on me.* I mean it's not that big a place is it, the vestibule, it shouldn't take too long. It's my daughter's wedding and obviously I don't want any mishaps, look, find her this once and come the day, I'll hogtie her, I'll do whatever it takes to get her here on time," he added as an afterthought, "except getting her pregnant again."

"Right!" he addressed the carnation, "we are missing the bride's mother - about thirty seconds. Description!" he barked at Steven.

"Think of the bride and add thirty years," Steven closed his eyes in concentration, "Early fifties - good figure - black hair not quite shoulder length light blue eyes."

"Could this be her sir?" and Steven opened his eyes to see Lydia walking towards them. Then closed them again, "Yes."

"Abort." again he addressed the long suffering carnation, "We have a visual--car in forty, right? Out."

Lydia was obviously unaware of the time schedule, her concerns lying elsewhere, "Steven would you believe the bathrooms here?"

"I don't know they've never told me anything."

She obviously missed the irony, "And they expect you to get changed in a corridor."

"Nobody complained, things like this tend to bring us together, it's a church not a theatre."

"It must be a British thing all those cold showers. So primitive."

He chose not to remind her that, of the eight Maids of Honour, two were American and three were from Belgium. "Well it certainly did no harm to your daughter's appearance. I was trying to think how she looked, but all the adjectives seemed to have been used already. I think 'breathtaking' comes closest."

"*Our* daughter."

"Pardon?"

"You said your daughter and it's our daughter."

"Well we were discussing her looks, and she certainly didn't get them from me."

"Still with the charming. I wonder that the American girl can let you out of her sight."

I was hoping that the Princess Royal would act as chaperone.

"Excuse me, madam, sir," the buttonhole intervened, "your car is approaching. If you will take the gentleman's arm, madam, nice and easy sir, don't forget that on the day you'll have to pause to acknowledge the cheers—not at all sir, good luck. And if she trips up, I hope you let her go. With a bit of luck, the snotty cow will break her neck," he muttered, bridling at the criticism of the facilities, before turning his attention to his carnation. "Bride's mother and father are away. The next one should be Prince Charles and the duchess. Got a visual?"

"Yes, having a chat with Prince Harry. They'll be all right, they know the form."

"Good, have you had contact with the father's wife?"

"Yes she's the one talking to the Guard Commander and the foreign office wallah."

"Yes got her, very tasty. What's the foreign office bod's function?"

"He's supposed to be squiring the mother, keep her motor running in case there's any green-eyed monster, as you say. The father's wife—seriously tasty."

"Yes, good-looking piece, but attitude. What's the father's wife like?"

"She's a darling, American, but a real lady. Prince Charles and the duchess have started to move."

"Well, good luck to him. Good morning, Your Highness, went well I thought. Your car will be here directly."

As instructed, they took their time going down the steps, or rather Steven did. Lydia, he suspected, was looking for something else to complain about. He had another concern no one else seemed to have considered: walking down the steps of Saint Paul's, acknowledging the cheers of a crowd who'd be ready to cheer at anything after seeing Judith on the arm of her handsome prince, *but in cowboy boots?*

They must have got the pace just right, as they reached the bottom of the steps just as the taxi was approaching. They even had a buttonhole to open the door for them. "Good morning, sir, madam. Went well, I hear. Enjoy your lunch."

"Thank you."

Steven had to restrain himself from reaching in to his pocket for a tip.

19~*I Was a Soldier Once*

AS THEY PULLED AWAY, STEVEN and Lydia stared out of opposite windows, rather like the later pictures of Charles and Diana. In fact, Steven missed the caustic presence of Princess Anne. He reached forward and rapped on the dividing glass partition. The cab driver reached back and wordlessly slid it open.

"Are we going the same route as the carriages will take on the day?"

"Nah." He never took his eyes of the road. "Wouldn't be any point. We couldn't go at the same speed, take us ages. Your fish and chips would be getting cold."

"Yes, good point. Can't stand greasy fish and chips. So we go the most direct route?"

"Well, the fastest."

"Thanks."

"No bother, squire, good luck on the day."

This friendly exchange seemed to enrage Lydia even more. Her lips were set in a grim line, and her china-blue eyes stared out of the window even more fixedly.

As they were approaching the embankment on the tide of the midweek traffic, Steven would wave to absolute strangers, and some would wave back. With the morning sun taking the chill off the city streets and the salty tang wafting up from the river, it was that sort of morning.

The charms of the day seemed lost on Lydia, however. "What are you doing?"

"I'm practicing acknowledging the greeting of the crowd. Why don't you practice smiling graciously?"

"You are being, I think, a little childish."

Steven remembered the last conversation he had with his ex-wife. *You seem to forget, we are no longer together, and one of the benefits of that happy state is the rest of my life being free from your bullshit.* "I thought Judith looked radiant."

She seemed unaware that he had mentioned this before, but even so, the strength of her answer shocked him. "She's about to marry a very rich man. Why shouldn't she be radiant?"

My God! She's jealous of her own daughter.

"Is that why you abandoned me, because I wasn't rich? I always thought it was because I wasn't Jewish."

He had the satisfaction of seeing her eyes open wide, so at least she wasn't obsessing about some imagined deprivation. "You!" The word came out like a hiss, as the cabdriver quietly but firmly closed the sliding partition.

"If that is your definition of success or fulfillment, then get one for yourself. You're definitely attractive enough, you've still got your figure, your complexion's good, obviously you quit smoking, and you've still got eyes like a Siamese cat. So go for it. In the meantime, forget Saint Paul's Cathedral, future Queen of England, and all that, madam. The thing is, Judith has grown into a beautiful, smart young woman, and you can take a lot of credit for that. She is about to marry a chap who thinks the world of her, and she's smart enough to know this. If he doesn't treat her well, king or not, he'll have me to reckon with. I owe her that much, and if that is not enough to make you happy, then get out the cab now and I'll make do with Princess Anne."

He fell back on the seat as though the harangue had exhausted him. A beautiful smile illuminated Lydia's face.

"Your eyes become on fire when you are so animated. I can still do it. And you will still take me to see Boadicea, yes?"

He realized that he had been "wound up." So that was it—light the fuse and see if you can still get a bang. Well, he'd play along with it. He owed Judith *that* much, but Pam didn't. "Yes," he said. "I will take you to see Boadicea, if Charles doesn't mind."

"Oh no, there is nothing definite between me and Charles. In fact, after the wedding, I probably won't see him again."

I'm sure Mrs. Chadders will appreciate that.

Lydia's apparent change of mood was further enhanced as they passed under Waterloo bridge. "General Gordon, is it not where we walked?"

"It is."

"So again," the cab turned right in to Northumberland Avenue, "ah yes, this is the pub with the dead dog in the case, and what do we have, Trafalgar Square where you lost a girlfriend?"

"Yes very forgetful of me." Steven was content to go with the flow, or at least not interrupt it.

In keeping with her more conciliatory attitude, Lydia found nothing wrong with the mall, and when they rounded the Queen Victoria Memorial, she was captivated by the sentries outside Buckingham Palace. "So sweet in those big black hats. Did you ever do that, Steven?"

"No. Our brigade did do ceremonial duty once, but we didn't get Buck House[20], we got the Bank of England."

"Really and did you steal anything?"

"Well, they didn't actually let us into the vaults, but I did manage to walk out with a bar of soap with EIIR stamped on it. You'd have liked the bathrooms there. Looks like we're here."

The taxi had gone through the gates of Buckingham Palace, continued through an archway at the side of the main building, and pulled up beneath a portico. The driver slid aside the glass partition. "Don't get out yet, it'll make the funny boys nervous, and a tip is unnecessary, in case you were wondering."

A softer-looking version of the buttonholes approached the car. "Miss Biderman and Mister Jackson, follow me please." He held out his hand to Lydia, leaving Steven to fend for himself. As he crouched to get through the door, he had a parting word with the driver. "I know you don't expect tips but I'll give you one: Wolves for the Premiership."

"In your dreams, sunshine. Be good, we'll be watching you on the telly."

They passed through a courtyard and into a corridor that stretched the whole length of the building. The daylight that filtered through the high windows to the left was augmented by concealed lighting, which subtly illuminated the pictures hanging on the inner wall. "This must be the picture gallery. Now if you're thinking of stealing," Steven whispered, "This is the place to do it. That one, I *think* is a Rubens. Only joking, old son."

Apparently he hadn't lowered his voice enough, as their guide had turned to transfix him with a startled look. "You are quite right, sir, it *is* a Rubens. There are I believe five of them on this wall together with works by Van Dyke, Rembrandt, and Vermeer."

They passed through a much-smaller gallery, which was decorated in an oriental style with miniature pagodas and lacquered screens decorating the walls. "They went to China for these?" Lydia whispered in awe.

"Probably got them from the royal pavilion in Brighton." Pam wasn't the only one who did her homework. Steven had gone so far as to borrow Mrs. Murdoch's laptop, after assuring her that it was to swot up[21] on Buck House. "After all, we don't want to show ourselves up, do we?"

He became aware that their guide was speaking. "Quite correct, sir. Blore brought them up from Brighton when he was redesigning this wing in the 1840s." They stopped at a set of double doors. "As it is an intimate gathering, we will be lunching in the white drawing room, and if I can proffer some advice, sir, madam, during the prelunch drinks you would do well to visit the table and see where you are to be seated. It's much better than trying to find your seat with everyone else when you are called to the table. Any questions?"

"Yes, when is the Queen due to arrive?"

"She's here, sir. She lives here."

"I know but when will she be ...?"

Their guide pointed to the door.

"She's in *there*?"

"She *is* hosting the lunch, sir."

"Yes, of course. How do I look?"

"You look fine, sir. If not, I would have mentioned it. Don't worry, she's an old dear. Ready?" He rapped softly on the door, and after what seemed like an age, it was opened by a footman in full livery. Their guide handed the footman a piece of paper, and with an encouraging wink to Steven, was gone.

"Mister Steven Jackson and Ms. Lydia Biderman."

They were standing in a small group, William, Judith, Princess Anne, and *her*. Such was the intimate atmosphere that Steven was reluctant to intrude. Princess Anne, however, broke away from the group and came forward to meet them. "Miss Biderman, how do you do? Welcome. Mister Jackson, I'm glad to see you got here safely."

"Ma'am, I thought it was something I'd said."

"Something you'd said?"

"I thought we'd be traveling together."

"Yes, these things happen. Come and meet my mother, only when we're in her presence, call me Princess Anne. If you call me ma'am, Mother will think you're talking to her."

"Fair enough, lead on."

After walking over acres of carpet, Anne made the introductions. "Mother, Miss Biderman, Judith's mother."

"Miss Biderman, I'm glad we finally meet. How are you enjoying your stay in London? Your daughter tells me it isn't your first visit."

"Every time I come, something new. Steven has been showing me the statues."

"And Mister Jackson her father—Judith's."

"Mister Jackson, I understand your wife will be joining us shortly."

"She will indeed, ma'am, about four cars back."

"Good, so you married someone eventually." She turned her attention back to Lydia. "I heard somewhere that London has more statues to the square mile than any other capital, only with me it's like looking at my family tree or visiting the House of Lords."

"But there is General Gordon and the detective—Steven?"

"Sherlock Holmes." Steven was still smarting from the "married someone eventually." Like any red-blooded chap from Coseley with an eye for a well-turned ankle, he resented any suggestions of philandering.

"I didn't know we had a statue of Sherlock Homes."

"Oh yes, outside the Baker Street—how is it? Metro? Steven is going to show it to me next time, also the Boadicea."

"Ah yes, by Westminster Pier. You are obviously keeping busy Mister Jackson. That should keep you out of trouble. Any others?"

"Mustn't forget Oliver Cromwell, if he's still outside the House of Commons, We'll have to fit that in, wouldn't you agree, ma'am?"

There was another tap on the door and another piece of paper thrust into the footman's hand. ***"His Royal Highness Prince Charles and the duchess of Cornwall."***

Didn't take them long. Must know a shortcut.

The Queen moved toward the door, and Anne went with her. She didn't introduce her brother to their mother, although

Steven was half-expecting her to. He wondered where the Duke of Edinburgh was.

"You'll have to forgive Gran." He turned to see William at his elbow. "She's been married to Grandad for sixty years, and she's never wanted to be married to anyone else. I'm afraid she's not really comfortable with the modern world."

"I have a bit of trouble with it myself." Steven regretted the crack about Oliver Cromwell, but not much. "Where's Judith?"

"She's gone to the bathroom with her mother—girl talk."

"Right." Steven took two glasses from a passing tray and offered one to William. "Speaking about—the Duke of Edinburgh, isn't he going to join us?"

"A bit under the weather." For some reason, Steven expected him **to** do a pantomime of drinking but he didn't. "That's why Aunt Anne's doing the introductions." There was another interruption at the door.

"His Royal Highness Prince Harold and the" Honourable Lady Frances Bedworthy-Down."

"Have you met my brother Harry? He was at the bachelor party."

"I don't think we've been introduced." The two glimpses Steven had of Harry was when he was getting changed after the rehearsal and before that when he was helping his well refreshed maternal uncle in to a taxi after the bachelor party.

After that the room began to fill up and while waiting for Pam, Steven, as one of life's onlookers, had the opportunity to observe the various patterns forming with the people in the room, and two things became apparent to him. It was the top of the social ladder, you had the reigning monarch, the next one, *and* the next one, but there was no jockeying for position. No cliques were formed. Most of those present were just glad that there had been no almighty shambles, especially one that could be laid at their door, and the Queen moved from group to group, shepherded with surprising gentleness by Princess Anne.

Steven found time to wander round the lunch table to see where he would be seated. The room, as befitting its name, was done in white, or a pale cream and lemon stripes, made even paler by the sunlight streaming in through the huge windows, which also gave a view of the gardens. These were obviously decoration enough, as there was little ornamentation in the room, hence the striped wallpaper. He made two circuits before he found it, due to the fact that the first time he had given the top table, backing onto the windows, a mere cursory glance, preferring the view of the gardens, but the second time, it took all of his self-control not to stare. *He was to sit next to The Queen!* No making a sandwich with his chips. The Archbishop of Canterbury was to be sitting on her other side. Well that took care of the conversation. He never could talk and eat. By the time he regained his position at the pillar, he saw that the Queen had been allowed to linger longer with William and Harry. *They say you enjoy your grandkids more than your kids, and that's just what she is, a bit better preserved than most, but underneath it all, just a proud granny.*

Mrs. Pamela Ann Jackson and Mr. Charles Chaddersley-Corbett" Steven detached himself from the pillar where he had been leaning and made his way over, grabbing two glasses of wine on the way. "Hello, you two. I wondered where you'd got to."

"Better late than never. Remind me to have a private word when time permits. Are those for us? Cheers." Chadders took the glasses and graciously handed one to Pam. "Where's you-know-who?"

"The Queen? She's over there talking to Princess Anne and Harry. Nick the Greek can't make it, a bit under the weather."

"Yes, I do know what Her Majesty looks like, I was thinking about my charge."

"The last time—no, I haven't seen her since she went to the bathroom with Judith. That was just after we got here. I suppose they're quite a distance. After all, it *is* a palace."

"Mister Jackson, you mustn't monopolize your wife." Princess Anne unlocked her smile. "Mrs. Jackson, I don't believe you've met my mother."

"Pam, I'm pleased to meet you." Pam held out her hand, remembering what someone had told her that however a sign of character a firm handshake may be, yours may be the fortieth hand that has pressed the royal palm that day. "And this is our friend Charles Chaddersley-Corbett. Have you met?"

"I think not, Mr. Chaddersley-Corbett."

"Ma'am."

The royal attention was returned to Pam. "You live in Arizona. I don't think I could survive the heat. Up to one hundred and twenty, I'm told."

"We have the swimming pool. We spend most of our evenings out there, and we have a nap in the hottest part of the day."

"How very sensible, and you have the horses. I could never get used to those American saddles, like riding in an armchair. I suppose they're based on the western saddles, but don't you find them uncomfortable?"

"I don't use them. I ride bareback, just a blanket."

"You do? I'm impressed. Would you like to meet William's brother Harry? Mr. Jackson, would you excuse us?"

"Made quite a hit, your wife," Chadders said after Pam had kissed Steven, squeezed Chadders' hand, and gone to meet Harry.

"People tend to warm to her," Steven agreed. "Speaking of which, when is your wife due in town?"

"Tomorrow, which brings up the rather delicate question that I wanted to broach."

"Broach away, old son."

"The thing is, the memsahib has expressed a desire to attend the reception, not the wedding breakfast, the big one at night."

"Yes, you can both go with us. The guest list is a bit lopsided," Steven said. "I don't know if Lydia—oh I see, I don't know if she has invited anybody. Judith has her maids of honor, and at least some of them have got boyfriends, but Lydia—when I've been in her company, she's always asking me about what I've done since we parted, but she's never offered anything about herself. I think that when she lost the love of her life—Ali, not me—she seems to have gone into a decline. She didn't even get the second prize—*that* would have been me." He warmed to his theme. "And when she sees how happy Pam is, not that I can claim much credit for that, you see how she is. Or perhaps it's a Jewish thing. You know, her daughter marrying a gentile. Anyway, it doesn't do to analyze these things too much. The thing is, you keep her sweet until the reception and then your duty's done and Lydia can either be happy for her daughter or do the other thing, but I think she will be too busy trying to emulate Michael Whelps' mom and make a few bob than bother about what you and your wife get up to."

"I see," said Charles. "Well that does put it rather succinctly. I think you're being a touch modest, but thank you."

"No bother, I already thought that if she's a bit put out at not sitting next to the Queen, I'll tell her, or it might be better coming from you that she gets to sit next to the Queen at the reception, and by the time she realizes it will be a buffet and the Queen probably won't be there anyway, past the poor dear's bedtime by then, well she, Lydia, will have other things on her mind." Steven rubbed his thumb across the fingertips of his right hand.

"I've changed my mind. You'd be an asset to the diplomatic service." Charles smiled. "Of course I'll tell her, especially as she'll probably be sitting next to me."

"I think the ceiling is a bit later, probably Nash."

"The ceiling?" Charles averted his gaze in time to see Lydia approaching them.

"Steven, Charles, you have met? What a lovely room, and the gardens. Is this the first time you've been here? You must let Judith show you around after they are married."

"Actually, I don't think they will be living here," Charles said carefully.

"But when they have the children, they will bring them here to visit their grandmother."

Steven was glad to notice that he wasn't alone in confusing the generations. "Lydia, can I get you a drink-- Charles?"

"Better not—driving."

"Right." Without waiting for a reply from Lydia, Steven detached himself. He would have liked to spend some time with his wife, but she was still talking to the Queen. He stopped a passing waiter. "Are any of those drinks nonalcoholic?"

"Yes sir, the ones with the slices of lemon are sparkling water."

"Fair enough." Steven took one, and after a moment's thought, took another. He didn't know how long these things went on for, and he wanted to telephone Solly later. "Thanks." He clasped the three drinks together, to the alarm of the waiter, and made his way back to Lydia and Charles. "The ones with the lemon are blanks. Refresh but don't inebriate."

"Good man." *At least he didn't say splendid.* Charles carefully took two drinks and handed one to Lydia. "We were just saying, we'd better go find where we are sitting. Don't want to get caught in the scrum. I suppose you've already found your seat, good." And under totally unnecessary cover, they left, leaving Steven leaning against the pillar, alone until—"Jenna." The hand was cool and firm, the face, although vaguely familiar, he couldn't place, and her next words didn't help. "We spoke briefly in the church. I'm the SMOH."

"The *what*?"

"The senior Maid of Honour. I know, it sounds like the head prefect. I have to make sure, among other things, that Judy doesn't trip over her train and go arse over tiara. Went off rather well, I thought, this morning. So," she linked her arm in his, "you're the one who Judy's mother let slip through her fingers."

"Something like that. Steven, spelled with a V."

"But not before you made Judy. You have quite a daughter. She's gorgeous, generous, and she's got a mind that I'd give my virginity for, if I still had it." She gave his arm a squeeze. "You have to get used to us crass Americans. Isn't your wife American?"

"Pasadena, California, or rather Altadena."

"Yes I know it, and she's let you come here by yourself?"

"No, that's her over there."

"Not with the long hair, talking to The Queen?"

"None other."

"Wow, no wonder ..." For once, she seemed at a loss for words.

"And what do you do, when you're not losing your virginity?"

"I'm a DP for the BBC. Sounds boring, but it serves a purpose."

"It sounds something. A what for the—I think I got the last piece. *The* BBC, auntie right?"

"None other, DP, drama producer."

"Is that where you met Judith?"

"No we go back further. We were at school together in Gloucester and we hit it off. We've been friends ever since. We write, and whenever I'm in Europe, we see each other, however busy she is. I was there when she met William." Her voice softened. "She won't take any guff from him but they are *so* in love it makes me feel a thousand years old."

"I *am* a thousand years old."

"Oh." She had to recall herself, and Steven had the uncomfortable feeling that she had forgotten that she was not alone. "Don't give me that 'poor old man' stuff. What do *you* do?"

"I watch sunrises, look after my wife and the dogs, drink vodka, and write, not necessarily in that order."

"I see, and would I have read any of your stuff?"

"Only if you were looking over my shoulder while I was typing."

Her laugh pleased him. He was beginning to warm to Jenna. "I mean, what do you do for a living if you haven't had anything published? How do you get the money to feed your wife and the dogs and buy the vodka?"

"Shouldn't we be asking this of Prince William?" He waited until her laugh had run its course before continuing. "I arranged things so that I could spend as much of the rest of my life writing as possible, which is why we live so simply, almost frugally, so that I don't have to *rely* on getting anything published. That way I can write how and what I like. I don't have to be commercial. My only financial responsibility is to Pam. As long as she's happy—"

Jenna loosened her grip on his arm enough so that she could pull away far enough to look in to his face.

"You must have some cojones." She then resumed her previous position so they were both facing toward Judith, which, he suspected was not entirely unintended. "About the hen party, you have to realize Judy's position. Her mother and her, all they had was each other—let me finish, no one's blaming you." She gripped his arm with surprising strength. "And after Judy's married she'll have her prince, literally, so if seeing Pamela— your wife's name, right?—upsets her, and she would rather not, well that's the way it's got to be, sweetheart."

"It's already sorted.

"What?" In her surprise, she slackened her grip on his arm, but he continued to look ahead.

"When somebody told me about the hen party and I knew Pam hadn't been invited, I sorted it. Look, I wasn't there for Judith—it's nobody's fault I just wasn't—but now I'm here and I'll do what I can for her, and I won't do anything to cause her grief. Pam would have liked to have been asked, but she will probably be content to watch television with our hosts, and she'll probably enjoy herself more than you—"

"She probably will," said Jenna, but it was as though she had not spoken.

"—so you can have your cake and arse party and all you've got to concern yourself with is Judith not tripping over her train."

"So you're happy, no, you've accepted you're. What do you mean sorted?"

Now Steven turned to look at her. "You've heard of Duke Ellington, not the Duke of Wellington, Duke Ellington, one of America's greatest composers, musicians, bandleaders?"

"Yes," she said carefully, "I have heard of Duke Ellington."

"Well a lot of his contemporaries questioned why he didn't get more involved with the civil rights movement. He said when he thought he had been the victim of prejudice—he was black—instead of getting bent out of shape, he would just write some blues, which made him feel better, and most of the time made him quite a bit of money. So when the big band era came to an end and other bands were going to the wall, because they couldn't pay the musicians, his band still survived because he subsidized it with his royalties. He was once asked why so many of his musicians stayed so long with him, twenty, thirty years. He said, 'I give them money,' and when his band were refused rooms in a hotel, sometimes in the very hotel where they were playing, what did he do? Go crying to the white liberals? No. Send his musicians to the negro quarter to find a room? No. He bought *a train*—a whole bloody train—so that his lads could have somewhere to sleep. Now I don't suppose I could run to a Pullman, but we could probably manage a Mercedes sports car."

"I'm sure she'd like that."

"She'd probably prefer a horse, the point being she can have either *and* it won't discomfit Judith in any way."

"And are we still friends, Steven with a V?"

"Yes, we're still friends."

"And I get to meet Pam?"

"That's one of the benefits."

She breathed deep as though she had just completed a complicated task. "Good, and just for the record, I think Lydia was a fool."

"You're never a fool to follow your heart. It just sometimes doesn't work out as you would hope, so you pick yourself up and get on with it. Is there a Mister Jenna or a boyfriend—girlfriend?"

"No, I'm quite available to try my luck with the Guard of Honour, but they all look so young, and a little sad."

"'God help us, we knew the worst too young.'"

"Where did that come from?"

"Kipling. 'Done with hope and honour, and lost to love and truth and we're dropping down the ladder rung by rung, and the measure of our torment is the measure of our youth, God help us, we knew the truth too young.'"

"That is so sad, so—sad."

"It's before they come to terms with disillusionment. After that it's, 'Bear them if we can and if we can we must, shoulder the sky my lad and drink your ale.'"

"More Kipling?"

He shook his head. "A. E. Houseman."

"You were a soldier once?"

"I was a soldier once."

"And what he's really saying is, 'Pick yourself up and get on with it.' I still say Judy's mother's a fool. If that was me when she rang and Pam answered, I'd have caught the first plane and at least gone down fighting."

Steven had been watching Pam across the room. Now he turned to face Jenna, "Judith and you *are* good friends, aren't you?"

The sound of a gong curtailed any further revelations. ***"Your majesty, my lords, ladies and gentlemen, honoured guests, pray take your seats for luncheon."***

He realized apart from a few words with Chadders, he had not been with Pam since the taxi deposited them at the steps of St. Paul's four hours ago. He offered his arm. "Jenna, may I take you to your seat?"

"About halfway down on the right, thank you. I'm glad to see that chivalry is not dead."

"No, my dear, just feeling its age."

She laughed. "That's funny, but again with the old man. Here we are."

Steven was about to pull her chair out when a voice from somewhere stopped him.

"Not yet!"

He looked round at Jenna, "What?"

"I didn't say anything." If she did, she had begun to sound more Eliza Doolittle than Cheltenham Lady's College.

It then occurred to them that the voice was coming from one of the footmen who continued to stare straight ahead. This impression was confirmed when he spoke again, still staring in front of him, and hardly moving his lips. "Nobody sits before Her Majesty."

Great, she hogs my wife's company and keeps me waiting for me nosh. Well, she's paying.

"Nearly a faux pas then, my dear." Jenna looked at the setting next to her. "Do you know Captain L'Shaw?"

"The Commander of the Honour Guard, nice chap."

"Oh my God, a soldier, not too nice I hope. Steven with a V, our affair is at an end can you handle it?"

"Shoulder the sky and drink your ale, see you later."

By the time Steven had reached his appointed place everyone else, apparently better versed in royal procedure than he, was standing behind their chairs waiting for the Queen, and she, apparently was waiting for him, "So glad you could join us Mister Jackson," she said in a Royal whisper that just pierced the scraping of chairs as they all sat, before turning her attention to the Archbishop of Canterbury.

There goes my knighthood, well at least I can eat in peace.

But apparently fate had decreed otherwise, for while he was waiting for his soup, he heard a not unfamiliar voice from his other side, "Well, how are you bearing up," and turned to see the Princess Royal regarding him gravely.

"Thank you, I am just the right side of being completely overwhelmed," he answered with equal gravity, "but there is one thing that is concerning me."

"Let's hear it, perhaps we can help?"

"I was always taught that it was rude to talk at the table, for obvious reasons. You can't talk and eat at the same time and do either properly, and all the times when I have seen these dos on the telly, everybody seems to be rabbiting away ten to the dozen, and being a guest, when do I chat and when do I eat?"

"Perfectly simple. You eat while you are listening, and if there is a response called for, you can either nod politely or think it over while you are ruminating, and when they pick up their knife and fork, or spoon, it means they've finished, so then you can talk whilst they are eating."

"There's a trick to every trade. I never thought of it like that."

"We've been doing it that long it's like second nature."

By this time the soup had been served, and as the Queen had dipped her spoon, he thought it was safe to put his new found knowledge into practice. He took a mouth full of soup and looked thoughtful—after all, you can't chew soup. He continued looking thoughtful until Anne spoke again. "You seem to be acquitting yourself rather well, especially as it's your first time."

He carefully laid his spoon down and waited until Princess Anne had addressed her soup, which was, appropriately enough, brown Windsor. "And the bloody last, if you'll forgive my French, Ma'am." He took up his spoon as the remainder of the conversation followed this rhythm.

"Unless there's another daughter knocking about somewhere who Prince Harry might be interested in?"

"If there was and he was, he would have at least Brian L'Shaw to be reckoned with."

"Brian L'Shaw?"

"The Commander of the Honour Guard."

"Oh yes, a Captain?"

Careful dear, your snobbery's showing. "But a Captain in the Paras."

"Oh I see. Lucky he didn't see Judith first, or we wouldn't be here."

After this sally, the Princess Royal was content to divide her attention between her soup and the person hidden from Steven's view on her other side. Steven was content to finish his soup in relative silence. This, however, was not as fortunate as it might be supposed. Uninterrupted, he made short work of his brown windsor and placed his spoon in the empty bowl to let a server know that it could be cleared. The bowl remained where it was, however, and instead of asking for the bill, Steven was left to contemplate the congealing remains of his soup and the equally unappetizing prospect of the next few minutes. It was small consolation, on looking down the table to see Pam in conversation with Brian L'Shaw.

The tedium was relieved sooner than expected by the schoolmistress tone of his other neighbor. "You are unusually piano, Mister Jackson. Has my daughter overwhelmed you?"

He had placed his spoon in the bowl, apparently signaling not that he was finished but that he was ready to speak. They probably didn't clear until Her Majesty had finished. "No, ma'am, only the surroundings. A little out of my usual." He noticed that her bowl was still half-full (or was it half-empty?), which bespoke either of the archbishop's garrulousness or the ability of Her Majesty to pace herself. How did these people ever finish a meal?

"Yes that's why we had it in here, a little less grand. Your wife seems a most charming girl." *Girl?* "I was quite taken with her."

"Thank you." He didn't know how he was going to manage without the prop of some food, but mysteriously, the royal soup was whisked away to be replaced by a mousse of salmon. Her Majesty must have given a secret signal; obviously they wouldn't dare to … He was contemplating what would be a suitable punishment for the unauthorized removal of the royal soup when he turned to see that the same transformation had happened to his setting. Now he had something to work with. Who had spoken last? It was he. "Thank you"—that was it. He tentatively picked up his fish knife and fork—*work from the outside*—and contrary to his regular enthusiasm for food, took the slightest morsel on his fork and chewed it thoughtfully.

"You couldn't find anyone English?"

He carefully swallowed his food and took a sip of water before answering, "No one I found suitable, ma'am." He went to take up his fork and seemed to have a second thought. "Rather like yourself. The Duke of Edinburgh won't be joining us, I hear, a trifle indisposed. Nothing serious, I trust?"

"No, just a seasonal thing, and how long have you been married to this American girl?"

"Twenty years, ma'am, and counting. I *was* married to an English woman once." *Yes, I served my time,* "Obviously, before I met Pam, I met Judith's mother after I was divorced from my first wife, and we had parted before I met Pam." That seemed to be enough to be going on with.

"It is to be hoped. You seem to have a very … checkered time with the ladies, Mister Jackson." *No more than your kids, lady.* "But you seemed to have settled down with this one, a charming girl. You would do well to take care of her," and with this advice, the Queen apparently decided that a little salmon wouldn't do any harm.

The next exchange was with Princess Anne. Her Majesty was holding forth to the archbishop about the relative merits of various genuses of tea roses. "I was just saying to Mister Chaddersly-Corbett, as one gets older, the company of horses is infinitely preferable to that of men. I wondered if it was the same with men. What do you think?"

Steven deliberately lay down his fork. "I've not had a lot to do with horses, except on the racecourse, but with dogs. I remember when Pam and I kept a pub in Somerset and one of our dogs wandered into the bar from the yard and I sent him back out. One of the local wags said, 'At least someone takes some notice of 'ee when he speaks to 'em.' I said I didn't know about that, but I'd a better chance of getting an intelligent answer." There was a barely suppressed guffaw, and Princess Anne put her fork down, but Steven was not yet finished. "On another occasion I was talking to one of the regulars about keeping Squibber tidy when he was shedding his winter coat. He said, 'The regular, not Squibber.' Squibber was the dog 'next time you taking 'im for a walk, throw him into a bramble bush and he'll come out clean as a whistle, and if you're lucky, he'll fetch you a rabbit out for your supper.' I told him that that was unlikely, as I'd taken the dog for a walk the previous night and a rabbit had run across the path barely ten yards in front and Squibber hadn't summoned up the enthusiasm to chase it. 'Well,' he said 'that's because you feed the dog too well.'

"Then Pam piped up and said that she'd been with me and she hadn't seen a rabbit. 'Well' said Maurice, that was the regular's name, Maurice, 'sounds like you feed your wife too well an' all.' As for men and horses, I wouldn't hazard a guess, but I suppose they both want the same—give them their oats regular and don't work them too hard." He eschewed the temptation to add, "and don't be too heavy on the bridle." This delicacy was rewarded by a royal, "Really," and the Princess Royal turning her attention to the less-threatening presence of Charles Chaddersly-Corbett. When he reached for his fork, he found that it had disappeared, together with the remains of his salmon mousse. It wouldn't do to be invited to too many of these dos. He could well starve to death.

"Your wife is enjoying her time in London, Mister Jackson?" Apparently the matter of the tea roses being settled, Her Majesty took a morsel of lamb. He decided if he answered, he *might* be served the next course. Talk about singing for your supper.

"Very well, thank you, ma'am. We are fortunate in having very agreeable quarters," *why was he talking like this?* "and our hosts are a very personable couple."

"And time doesn't weigh too heavily in between your commitments?"

By this time he had been served with the lamb and spring vegetables, but he'd better answer first, "We do have friends in London, and there are the parks. She adores the parks." Now he was beginning to sound like Noel Coward. "We spend hours walking 'round the parks. The only thing is, she expects me to know all the names of the flowers. Thank heavens for those little plaques, say I. Then there is the Victory Services Club. She likes old soldiers, and we might even manage a couple of visits to the theatre Pam particularly would like to see *Cats,* and I must check to see if there is a National Hunt meeting on at Ludlow. She also likes horses."

"Not particularly interested in statues, then, your wife? *Game to you, dear, nice serve.* "But as to the parks, you should take her to see Kensington Gardens. She'd enjoy that, particularly the statue of Peter Pan, being married to you." She smiled. *Game set to you, new balls please.* But Her Majesty hadn't finished. The smile faded, and she looked wistful.

"Spending hours walking 'round the parks—yes, that must be very nice."

Her Majesty didn't seem inclined to speak much after that, as though Steven had reminded her of something she hadn't missed until then. For his part, Steven was content to address himself to his lamb and spring vegetables, but slowly, in case he needed them to bolster his conversation with Princess Anne, if she decided to forget the suggestion of giving someone their oats. In this manner, he was able to observe the other guests. Brian L'Shaw was laughing at something Pamela had just said. He managed to catch Jenna's eye and winked, which was answered by a rueful smile and an inclination of her head towards Brian L'Shaw before returning her attention to Prince Charles. He wondered where Camilla was. She must be somewhere on the other side of the Queen.

Using this interlude, he reviewed the morning—not bad so far. He'd held his own with the conversation, not being too abrasive but not too—well, there was never any danger of that. The meal had been surprisingly good. He had managed to eat most of the main course except for a few peas and one potato, which he carefully cut into four pieces before resuming his contemplation. The next thing was the wedding itself. Pam would have to go to St. Paul's by herself, by taxi, to be deposited at the guests' entrance, while he would be taken to the royal mews, to be fitted in his best bib and tucker together with the cowboy boots *and* the top hat and gloves. Then there would be the ride to St. Paul's with his daughter. That wouldn't be too bad. Just a wave to the crowds or should he raise his hat? Mister Swinbourne would know. After that, there would be escorting Judith up the steps and then, dear God, the eyes of the world. Before the phrase had meant little to him, but now the enormity of it seemed to settle on his shoulders and squeeze all the joy of the afternoon out of him.

"So you're a gentleman of the turf, Mister Jackson."

He roused himself gratefully from the prospect ahead to face the Queen. "I am indeed, ma'am, the best day out possible. I particularly like the small country courses. That's why I prefer the sticks, to the flat. The camaraderie of the race-goers is something that's not changed, thank goodness, but those digital bookies boards; they must have put a lot of the bookies clerks out of work. You have the occasional flutter yourself, ma'am?"

"Indeed I do, but usually only on my own horses, when we are sure they're ready, and I always bet ante-poste. You get better odds." *So even Her Majesty isn't averse to a bit of sharp money.*

He noticed that her plate was empty, so he was unhurried in his response. "Of course, and I suppose it is with a credit bookmaker, if your majesty will forgive me," he paused so that he could receive the royal forgiveness by default, "did you have a bet on Devon Loch[22], or weren't you old enough? By all accounts, you were there when it happened. Your mother, God rest her, must have been very disappointed, although she had won the national before."

The Queen took each question separately as if she realized she was going to be quoted. "Indeed I was there, we all were, and we all had a bet on. I *was* old enough, and if you are as well versed as you appear to be, you well know that I was old enough, but your memory has played you false on one item. Mummy never won the Grand National. She *was* disappointed, but she tends to take things in her stride. As she said, 'That's racing.'"

"Didn't she?" Steven cursed himself for not checking on that particular tidbit he'd read, he'd forgotten where. Still, soldier on, "Well-fancied, if memory serves, third favorite, although everyone had sympathy for the Queen Mother. I'm sure the bookies managed to console themselves on the way to the bank. A lot of sentimental money going on the Queen Mum's horse. Yes, I bet the bookies dried their tears when they reached the bank."

"A rather apt choice of words, Mister Jackson, but who would you bet with?"

"Sorry?"

"You said, 'I bet the bookies dried their tears when they reached the bank.' If you were betting on the bookies drying their tears, who would you bet with?"

"Oh I see, touché." *You can see where Princess Anne gets it from.* "You know, I've seen the tape of that incident time and time again, and I still can't understand why the jockey couldn't get him going again. I mean he wasn't unseated, was he? And other jockeys got them going again under similar circumstances. There was one Irish horse that just recently went on his belly after, what was it? The one where they do a sharp left turn straight after, the Canal Turn, that's it. Anyway, he went on to win."

"But he had time to recover. On the run in, once you've lost the momentum, especially as in this case, there were other horses in contention being hard ridden. Well ..."

"Ah yes, the run in at Aintree: 'four hundred and ninety four yards of merciless eternity.'"

"What a good phrase, Mister Jackson. You should be a writer."

"I am, your majesty, but I can't lay claim to that. It was Lydia Hislop, the racing correspondent of the *Times*. It always struck me as ironic that the jockey, who didn't stay in racing long after that, was involved in one of the biggest mysteries in racing history should choose as a second career writing racing mysteries."

"What a censorious mind you have Mister Jackson why do you think that is?"

"I'd have to look that one up Ma'am but I think it's probably because I come from Coseley."

"And what sort of books do you write?"

He was tempted to say 'unpublished' but erred on the side of sociability, "I write mostly based on my experiences in the

Army, and elsewhere." Steven took the hint that the Devon Loch incident was closed, "I don't think they would be suitable for your Majesty --- the language."

"I don't like bad language just for the sake of it it's true, but on the other hand I have been a sailor's wife for a good many years and I have been on the gallops at the crack of dawn so my ears are not unsullied by salty language."

Steven managed the rest of the lamb before his plate was whisked away, and a fresh fruit sherbet was served before Princess Anne decided that she had neglected him for too long. "And what are your plans for the afternoon, Mister Jackson? I hope time doesn't hang too heavy on your hands." *Mister Jackson? I wonder if she calls her father "Your Royal Highness" when she talks to him.*

"Indeed not. I was just saying to your mother, I'm hoping to take my wife racing if there is a meeting on at Ludlow while we're here, and we hope to see *Cats* if it's still on, but this afternoon I'm taking her to see Kensington Gardens. Her Majesty thinks Pam would enjoy the statue of Peter Pan."

"That sounds delightful. Do you know the history of that statue?"

"I know it was commissioned by J. M. Barrie and all the royalties from his books go to support Great Ormond Street Children's Hospital."

"Well, that's more than most."

"Actually, I was in a movie called *Hook*, which was based on Peter Pan, and we were told that the royalties paid to the estate of the author went directly to the upkeep of the hospital."

"How interesting, but getting back to the statue of Peter Pan, the statue is on the very spot where Peter Pan landed when he first learned to fly. When it was finished, Mister Barrie had it erected at midnight and wrote an announcement in the *Times* to ask the children to prevail on their mommies, or nannies to take them to see it. He didn't bother with planning permission but what could the authorities do. There would have been a revolution. There were questions asked in the house about Mister Barrie using a public park to promote his work, but as you say, all the proceeds go to benefit children, so their fastidiousness was unfounded—politicians." After touching on the possibilities of revolution, she turned to more practical matters. "You can get one of the footmen to telephone for a taxi."

"Thank you, and I concur on the politicians, but we prefer to walk."

"But your wife can't walk that far in heels. She *is* wearing heels?"

"Oh yes, she's properly dressed." They had both been summarily inspected by Mrs. Murdoch before they left that morning. "But we thought if we could walk through Green Park parallel to Constitution Hill, cross in to Hyde Park, and then walk parallel to Knightsbridge, we could do it most of the way on grass, and Pam could walk most of the way barefoot. Living in Arizona, she relishes every chance to walk barefoot on grass."

"How romantic. I'm sorry I won't get to know your wife better, but tell me about the film, didn't Steven Spielberg direct it?"

"He did. I'm still waiting for his call to do a sequel." Further dialogue on Steven's film career (Jackson's, not Spielberg's) was curtailed by a loud interruption from the Queen's left. *"My lords, ladies, and gentlemen, pray silence for Her Majesty the Queen."*

And he got it. The Queen made a short speech thanking everyone for coming and congratulating them on a successful rehearsal, and that was it. A brief chat with Brian L'Shaw, a confirmation that they would get together with Chadders and Cynthia for dinner, or at least drinks, before they went back across the pond, a brief wave to the group, which included Lydia, and then it was taking leave of Her Majesty, and less than half an hour later, Pamela was feeling the grass of Hyde Park between her toes.

20~"They don't change much, do they?"

THEY HAD ALREADY REACHED THE Albert memorial before Pam spoke. "What is that?" she pointed across Knightsbridge.

"That, my dear," said Steven, adopting an avuncular voice, "is the Royal Albert Hall, also dedicated to Prince Albert. It's where they hold, among other things, the Last Night of the Proms. The promenade concert's are a series—"

"I know about the Last Night of the Proms. I do listen sometimes."

"Good." Steven was a little irked at being interrupted. "Most Americans drop the 'royal,' 1776 and all that, and call it Albert Hall. I suppose it could lead to confusion. I mean if there was a bloke called Albert Hall, he probably gets Americans calling him and trying to book tickets. I don't suppose anybody's called Festival Hall—"

"Steven?"

He halted in midstride. "Yes?"

"How did you get on with the Queen?"

"Great, lovely woman, but I think the job's getting a bit much for her. I think that's why Princess Anne was there."

"I see, and you were your usual self?"

"I hope so. Yes, I think I can say I was."

"So we can expect an honor, by appointment Royal Pain."

They walked on, as though Steven was too surprised to stop, but soon, as with a car with the engine turned off, they had slowed before Steven found his voice. "I won't ask if I've offended you, because I obviously have so—what?"

Pam took a long, calming breath. "I am used to—I have *become* used—to the occasional anti-Catholic, anti-Irish, although that's probably the same thing, anti-black, and even anti-American tirades because, in spite of myself, I found, not them, but you, amusing, but." She looked down and matched the cadence of her words to her steps. "While being caustic, even violent, you've never been spiteful. It's the nastiness for its own sake I find boring. It's a part of you I find very … not endearing." She didn't feel moved to correct her grammar, as though daring him to. She always spoke from her being and never to provoke a reaction, so she had no expectation of an answer, but nevertheless she was moved by the simplicity of his reply.

"Yes," he said. "Sorry, not one of my finer moments." They had almost slowed to a stop. "I was just thinking, after the rehearsal lunch, that was the last thing before—there's nothing else before the … thing."

"I thought," she said, still measuring her words, "we had already covered that."

"Yes." And in his distraction, he actually apologized twice for the same thing, where once was usually cause for comment. "Sorry, it was talking about the Royal Albert Hall, Last Night of the Proms. They always finish up with 'Land of Hope and Glory' or 'Pomp and Circumstance' number-something, and that's the music Judith chose for her—our—entrance, and it just reminded me of the impending—"

"Right!" Pam brought them to a complete halt. "We need a bench."

"What for?"

"To sit on, my bundle of sunshine, over here." Without replacing her shoes, she gently but firmly marched him over Exhibition Road to where a series of benches were set back in the bushes facing the Serpentine.

"Now," she said after giving a sweet smile to a rather concerned Nanny on the next bench, "while I fully understand and can sympathize with your position, I'm not going to let it spoil what is left of our day, so we are going to sit here until you've dealt with it, even if it means going straight from here to the thing, or can we call it 'the wedding,' and I will be on hand to fetch you anything you will require in the way of food or drink. If you want to relieve, yourself you can use the bushes, which we can also use if you need to be serviced, but we'll have to wait until dark. We don't want to be arrested. Nice here, isn't it?"

Steven leaned back and closed his eyes.

Good that was, she goes off on a screaming wobbler, and then we have to wait until she gets over it so that she can be gracious enough to forgive me. Still, it wasn't one of my finer moments. That was a bit—well, just because I am having a bit of a screaming wobbler myself about the coming week, no excuse to be a pratt[23].

Having fairly accepted the blame, Steven closed his eyes and let the mild afternoon sun warm him. He would break the silence soon but let her enjoy herself for a bit more. After a decent interval, he roused himself and did a little mental shoulder squaring. "Pamela, what would you like to do? I mean for the rest of the afternoon." *Let her make a decision, always a good move,* but apparently Pam wasn't ready to relinquish her vexation yet. She withdrew herself from wherever she was. "Have you anything you need to do?"

"I need to call Solly about six, our time. Apart from that, I'm all yours."

"And how far is Peter Pan's statue?"

"About half a mile that way." He waved his hand toward where the eaves of the Serpentine Gallery were just visible. "And the hotel?"

"Which one?"

"The one where you enjoy your wife's company, *our* hotel."

"Oh, that's about a mile if we go that way, over the Serpentine Bridge or slightly less if we go back the way we've come and go round the Serpentine. Either way, we'll have to cross Park Lane."

"I'm sure you'll find a way." *She's really enjoying herself.* "So we'll leave Peter Pan until tomorrow, because I do want to see it, so it's home, James. I'm sure Mrs. Murdoch will want to know about lunch."

Under the present circumstances, he didn't think it prudent to point out that he'd only asked what she wanted to do today, but he rather injudiciously voiced another concern. "I hope we are not going to spend too much time briefing Mrs. Murdoch. We haven't spent much time together."

"That's because we were a guest of Her Majesty for most of the day, but don't worry we'll have our time together—unless you find some other old queen to dally with."

Ouch.

Pamela stood and straightened her skirt. "I was going to ask you to carry me across this street," she indicated Exhibition Road, "but you've had such a trying day." And still she wasn't finished. As they passed the next bench, a nanny was trying to soothe her fretful charge, and Pam was moved to offer solace. "Cutting a tooth, is he?"

She got a tired smile and a nod in reply.

"Have you tried oil of cloves?"

"Just given him some. He should be all right in a minute."

"Yes he'll be all right with a bit of attention. It usually works." She inclined her head toward Steven. "They don't change much, do they?"

They had reached the bridge over the Serpentine before Steven broke the silence. By an unspoken accord, they paused and leaned their arms on the parapet, enjoying the vista of the Long Water. "I know why your forbearance is wearing a bit thin."

"Do you? Because I don't."

"It's getting to you a bit, isn't it?"

"What is?"

"All the ..." If she hadn't been shading her eyes from the late afternoon sun as she looked toward Kensington Palace, she would have seen him ostensibly indicating a pair of the famous mute swans taking their afternoon constitutional in the water below. "...palaver, about the wedding. I mean, I get all the attention and you get all the—you have to take all. You have to contend, yes contend, with all my insecurities. You know, I had a girlfriend once," (he didn't think it worth mentioning that it was Lydia,)"and she told me that she was living with this guy, a businessman, and he'd come home in the evening and she'd want to make love, but first she'd have to listen to all his complaints about his lazy employees, the crippling taxes, his crooked partners and all that, and by the time he'd unloaded enough so that he was ready to make love, she had absorbed so much negativity that she didn't want to, but they did. Anyway, I understand why you're not. I don't take your succor for granted."

She slowly straightened her spine, stiffening her arms. "You're welcome. I appreciate your recognition of my succor, if that means what I think it means, but I *would* have rather it not taken the memory of an ex-girlfriend to bring it about."

"It didn't." He waited until the two swans had disappeared under the bridge before he too relinquished the support of the parapet. "It was that kid with his nanny back there. You noticed that when he was crying, Mary Poppins took care of the cause, but she didn't pick him up, where if it was his mother, because obviously if the kid was working class his mother couldn't afford a nanny, then she would have picked him up to comfort him. So the upper class don't expect to be comforted. They just get on with the job of running the world, that and the cold showers. All right?"

Not for the first time, Pam was mollified without knowing quite why. "All right." She clasped his arm, and they continued their walk. "What are we going to do tonight? Fancy getting a bottle of wine and staying in? Or we could go up to Hampstead and have a drink with David. I wonder if his ticket arrived yet."

"Ticket?"

"For the wedding. They have to have a ticket *plus* a picture ID or they don't get in, except us, we're in the bridal party. Our photos are on a database, and we're visually scanned."

By now they had reached the end of the bridge and turned a half right toward the towering Dorchester. "You seem very well informed."

"Brian told me. I'm surprised Her Majesty didn't mention it. What were you talking about?"

"You. She seemed particularly concerned that we should make a go of it and was gratified that we'd nearly reached the score. Seems strange when you considered her kids' performance in the marriage stakes." He paused to look at the Norwegian monument and hoped Pam wouldn't ask him what it was. "But on the other hand, it worked out rather well. Get married for the right, or the correct, reasons, knock a couple of grandkids out, and then get married for love while there's still a few good years left, although it looks as though she's going to make a go of it with Nick the Greek."

"Who?"

"The Duke of Edinburgh—nickname."

"It doesn't sound very polite, especially after she's just entertained you to lunch."

"I take your point, but I know two Greeks and they're both—I think very highly of both of them, and they're both called Nick. You know one of them, Athena, used to work at Media Partners. Her husband's called Nick, sound engineer at one of the studios."

"Oh yes, Nick, and the other?"

"Runs a garage in Long Beach. Met him playing football. He used to take care of our cars when we lived there. You've probably met him also."

"Always complaining about not getting enough playing time?"

"That's him."

"But I still think it's impolite to call the Duke of Edinburgh Nick the Greek, especially as his name's Phillip." She suddenly threw her head back and laughed, causing a couple lying on the grass to momentarily disentangle themselves from each other to look up and smile. It was that sort of afternoon. "That reminds me of one of the afternoons when I was watching you play soccer. The game was held up for something, and you were leaning on the goalpost with your hands behind your back. After the game, they were discussing the incident, whatever it was, and someone said, 'You were just standing there with your hands behind your back trying to look like the Duke of Edinburgh.' Do you know what you said?"

"Enlighten me."

"You said, 'On the contrary, I *am* an Englishman, and he has been trying to look like an Englishman for as long as I can remember.' I thought you were trying to show off in front of me."

"I probably was."

"You know one of the things I love about you?"

"Is this going to be embarrassing?" Steven looked round, but only the courting couple were anywhere near within earshot, and they had rediscovered each other.

"You have a very quick mind. If anyone tries to put you down, you can usually turn the tables on them, but you don't mind making fun of yourself. Anyway," she gave his arm a little shake, "besides The Queen approving of your American wife, what else did you talk about?"

"Horses, or to be more exact, horse racing. That reminds me, I haven't had a bet all week."

"The poor bookies, they must be starving."

"Another thing, remind me to call Solly when we get back."

"I will, and that's the second or third time you've asked me. I'm sure you'll tell me why when you're ready"

Steven was a great believer in only giving as much truth as can be handled, especially where his wife was concerned, but occasionally he would lapse so as to reassure himself that there were limits to her capacity for the truth. "It has come to my notice that you have *not* been invited to the Cake and Arse party."

"I wish you wouldn't use that expression."

"I'm sorry, the hen party, prenuptial, pajama party, all-girls together soiree, function—"

"I get the picture."

"—and although you would probably prefer to spend the evening with Mrs. Murdoch and The Captain, or go for a drink with David, or visit the Union Jack club, *and* it's their *loss*. Princess Anne said she's sorry she won't get to know you better, and I know you'd like the—and I'm dead serious—the senior Maid of Honour, Jenna, and she'd love to meet you, if only to get the gen on Brian L'Shaw. Be that as it may, you should have been asked, and to that end … I don't know if you realize it but I—we have garnered quite an interest from the press. In fact, part of Mrs. Murdoch's function is to keep the baying hounds of the gutter press away, not for the first time, I wouldn't doubt. So I am going to get Solly to arrange an interview of at the most a half hour, during which I will answer a series of very provocative questions, which I shall concoct, and there will be a photo opportunity of us strolling down Park Lane, cost for our time will be, I'll work it out when we get there, but it will be enough for a Mercedes sports car—"

"That's very generous, but I don't want a Mercedes."

"But you'll have the money. You could buy a horse or—the point is, you'll have it. It will redress the balance a bit."

She gently nudged him with her hip. "Pity we can't send Mrs. Murdoch and The Captain out to the movies."

They had to make a detour to cross Park Lane at Marble Arch, but Steven *was* able to point out Speaker's Corner, "Democracy at work," after they had passed the arena where two rival bus tour company representatives were staging their version of a presidential debate.

Pamela was probably of the opinion that he had planned it this way, and he was not inclined to disillusion her, especially as he was able to show her where he intended them to be photographed, or as he put it, "Do our Anna Neagle and Michael Wilding thing—you know, *Spring in Park Lane.*" He was able to explain Michael Wilding as one of Elizabeth Taylor's earlier husbands and Anna Neagle as the wife of Herbert Wilcox, who probably produced *Spring in Park Lane.* Pam wondered if they could get it on DVD, but nevertheless this unsolicited information, plus a pause to reward the busker's efforts in the Marble Arch underpass, where she was informed, "This is where they filmed the busker scene in *Mrs. Palfrey at the Claremont,*" got them home.

21~"Haven't even had time to put a bet on."

STEVEN SLEPT SURPRISINGLY WELL. IN fact, it was one of the few times in their married life when Pam was already about when he woke. He lay, as was his hard-won habit, becoming aware of his surroundings before opening his eyes, it took him longer than usual, using all his discipline, to keep his eyes shut, even though he could tell by the light that pierced his closed eyelids that the sun was well up. Still plenty of time. Since the wedding breakfast they had been left alone. Even Major Ashford-Bowdler had restricted himself to the occasional telephone call, probably because they had come to the conclusion that, after all the rehearsals and fittings, the only thing left was to walk his beautiful daughter up the aisle, so he was hardly likely to do a bunk now. As his old Sergeant Major used to say before a big parade, all the shouting's been done, this is your day. There had been one surprising telephone call, and on summoning Pam, Mrs. Murdoch had given Steven a look he couldn't decipher.

"Nothing wrong is there?"

"I'm sure I wouldn't know." She sniffed virtuously. "Now if you'll excuse me, I'll see to lunch." And the door shut behind her, but not before Steven gathered that "someone's pigeons were coming home to roost."

Completely innocent of this exchange, Pamela made herself comfortable in one of the rattan chairs before picking up the telephone. "Pamela, did I disturb you? This is Lydia."

"No we were just—is anything wrong?"

"No, contraire, it is just that, it is difficult with the phone. It would be better face to face, but there is no time."

"Lydia," said Pam carefully, "just tell me what is the matter."

"Nothing, it is ..." Pam could hear her draw her breath. "Judith, like all—most young people seem to forget that we have already experienced the affairs of the heart. She is good daughter but overprotective, and she apparently thinks there will be the strangeness with you because of Steven. She even arranged Charles for the companion. I am the old hag that I need my daughter to—how is it? *Pimp* for me? That is the correct English, pimp?"

"That is the correct term, but I hardly think that, as you say ..." Pam began to lose her way, not that she was sure of it to began with, but apparently Lydia was unaware of her perplexity.

"And her friend Jenna, a lovely girl and so, but she presumes too much."

"I don't think I've met—"

"She tells Steven that you will not be welcome to Judith's party for the eve of wedding because I will feel the strangeness, the atmosphere, yes?"

"Yes, I understand." And she was actually beginning to.

"Pamela, are you still there?"

"Still here, Lydia."

"Pamela, Steven is a sweet man, so sympathetic, and those eyes, but I don't have to tell you after so many years, yes?"

"No, but thank you."

"Steven will always be dear to me, but I have finished with men. Basta for the sex. I—but never mind. You will come to the party as my guest and we will talk about things—girl talk, yes?"

"Fine, I'd love to. We can even talk about Steven. Give me the details."

"That was Lydia," she announced after she had rejoined Steven. "I *have* been invited to the—as you so happily put it—Cake and Arse party. As Lydia's guest. It must have—" she abruptly changed tack. "Obviously I can't tell you what we talk about, not that you'd be interested, but I'll tell you one thing, you are one of the happy memories that Lydia takes off the shelf to comfort herself with on a cold night."

"Where did that come from?"

"It's a woman thing, my love, you wouldn't understand. So you'll be all on your own for an evening. Can you manage?"

"You're going?"

"It would be churlish not to. So you'll be all right? I'm sure you'll manage to look up your old haunts without dragging a wife along. Do you good."

"Sure, and—don't tell Mrs. Murdoch—I could always console myself with a Steak and Kidney pie."

****

On her return, Pam had kept quiet about the bachelorette party, as it was officially named (Jenna's influence), and he was not inclined to inquire. For his part, after taking leave of his wife and assuring her for the third time that he would be all right, he set about navigating Paddington and the less salubrious parts of Mayfair, drifting from pub to pub, and the following morning he was equally taciturn. There was one incident, however, that he didn't feel able to keep from his wife.

Toward the end of his saunter, when his thoughts turned toward home, he realized that he was, to use his own words, "a bit lost." He was on Baker Street, and he knew that if he kept going, he would reach Oxford Street, if he was heading in the right direction. If not, he was going further away. He would uncharacteristically have to ask for help. He chose a person who had just exited from a building—obviously familiar with the area—don't get too close, let him see your hands, speak up but don't shout. "Am I heading the right way for Oxford Street?"

The response was a card proffered to him—just his luck—a panhandler -now his attention was being drawn to the building that had just been vacated and the title over the door, Centre for the Hearing and Speech Impaired. He'd asked directions of a mute. Still, there might be someone in there, and his newfound friend seemed to be urging him toward it. The door opened in to a lobby with a desk to one side occupied by a uniformed security guard, who was subjected to a flurry of hand signals by Steven's companion.

"From what I gather, sir, you want to reach Oxford Street. Turn left outside and follow Baker Street until it becomes Orchard Street, and that will take you to Oxford Street."

"Right, thanks." Steven turned to thank his guide. "Where's he gone?"

"That's Jan, sir, coming along a treat on the lip-reading, but a bit on the shy side. Lucky he stopped you or you'd have ended up in St. John's Wood."

Steven made it back in time to have a nightcap with Mrs. Murdoch, who offered to wait up for Pam.

****

They had been presented to Mrs. Chaddersly-Corbett, and Cynthia lived up to the description of her by her not-quite ex-husband, a good sort who could take a joke with the best of them. She had needed to call on her reserves of humor when Chadders had to prevail on Steven to keep the meeting with Cynthia from Lydia as he thought "the lady had expectations."

It rather helped matters when Cynthia suggested they should have a pub lunch on the following day and Steven had asked for the favor to be returned, as he had more or less promised Lydia tomorrow to show her Boadicea.

"Why does she want to see Boadicea?"

Steven had shrugged. "Women." And it seemed that *that* would be the limit of his explanation but apparently it had needed some elucidation. "I'm sure the irony hasn't escaped you, Charles, of the fact that you and I are both prevailing upon each other to keep the fact that we are spending time in the company of our wives from a lady whose last attachment to either of us was a good twenty years ago." And still he hadn't finished. "I was watching a football match once, a local England-Scotland thing, and I was giving some advice to the referee, as you do. There was this guy Martin who I had played cricket with, standing within earshot, and he happened to be a friend of the referee. Anyway, after a particularly enthusiastic comment on the referee's abilities, Martin was moved to give voice. 'Steven,' he said, 'I thought you knew nothing about cricket, but you are obviously an all rounder.' And that was that until after the game, Martin, being of a conciliatory nature, came up to me in the club. 'Steven,' he said to me, 'I hope you didn't take offence at my witticism.' 'Not at all, old son,' I said, 'your point is well taken. In fact, you should see what I don't know about women. I'm a Hall-of-Famer in that.'" After the briefest of pauses to make sure he was finished, the sally got the appreciation it deserved.

The following day, he did find time to take Lydia for a walk, and she was suitably impressed with Boadicea. The Boadicea pub, however, did not fare so well in her estimation, and to be fair, her fastidiousness was not misplaced. It lived down to its review, where it was described as having all the atmosphere of a station buffet, which was, in effect, what it was. Apparently the effect of the mother of parliaments *and* Boadicea was enough for Lydia, plus the fact that she was expecting a telephone call from "you-know-who"(he didn't but didn't press the matter), so he was able to curtail their promenade after a half-hearted offer to show her the statue of Sherlock Holmes at Baker Street underground was regretfully declined.

He had moved on to musing about his sisters and regretting the fact that he had not time to see them, still plenty of time after the … Then it came to him—this *was the day*, and although he now knew what had to be faced, there was something else that was not in the natural order of things. He felt toward Pam and suddenly opened his eyes without any more preamble and there it was. He was the sole occupant of the marital bed. This had the effect of concentrating his mind. Find out where Pam was and deal with everything else later. Pulling on his trousers, without the benefit of underwear, followed by shoes—better put some socks on or old mother Murdoch will probably send him back upstairs to get dressed properly. After rinsing his face under the cold water tap and checking himself in the mirror, he pulled a sweater over his head and made his way downstairs.

"Good morning, sleeping beauty." Mrs. Murdoch turned from the range. "I thought I'd have to get The Captain to blow reveille. Are you all right?"

"Yes, it's just that, until I smelled your bacon, I'd almost convinced myself it was all a dream. Dreams are visual and audible but you can't dream smells, can you?"

"No, I don't suppose you can, but if you could, I suppose Cumberland bacon frying is the best you could get." Then her tone turned practical. "Pam's in the garden, all right?"

"Right."

"And Steven," it was the first time he could remember her using his Christian name, "it *will* be all right, especially after you've had a good breakfast. Enjoy it, because if you don't, you'll wish you could do it over again but you can't. Tell Pam, breakfast in twenty minutes."

Surprisingly, The Captain and Mrs. Murdoch joined them. Whether it was to keep Steven focused on the mission before him without getting too preoccupied or her inherent nurturing instincts, it was impossible to tell, but Steven noticed that she was there to guide the conversation in to less-threatening channels when she thought that they had dwelt enough on the morning's activities.

"The car will call for you at ten thirty, so you've got plenty of time for a walk before then, and Pamela, my dear, we'll share a taxi, if that's all right?"

"We don't get a car?"

"I'm afraid not, my dear, only those considered essential to the operation."

"Do you know where they keep their walkie-talkies? They probably call them PCDs now," Steven asked.

"PCDs?"

"Personal Communications Devices."

"Quite, and where do they keep them?"

"In their buttonholes."

"How ingenious. Wherever did they get that idea?"

"I think it was from the movie *Singing in the Rain.* It was a musical based roughly on the transition from silent movies to talkies. They actually hid the microphones in the flowers. That's all I can remember, apart from Cyd Charrise's contribution."

"Something new every day." But apparently having enough of cinema history, Mrs. Murdoch continued, "Pam can return from the palace with us, as you will be required at the wedding breakfast. Give us a call after the meal has finished and we'll come and collect you."

"So there won't be transport arranged for me to come back." Steven was rightly aggrieved. "Bit cheap that."

"Unfortunately the Monarchy and its trappings have to be cost effective these days, and once they've got you to the palace and you've performed, well, having been a soldier, my dear, I'm sure you understand. Besides, they probably thought it would be a nice walk back across the park." She smiled gravely. "Obviously they didn't know about the cowboy boots."

After that, or even before that, and no one had noticed, Mrs. Murdoch took charge. She allowed Steven one telephone call where Solly assured him that the check had been credited to his account and that he'd be watching on the cable network and the best of luck. Darlene sent her love. She fielded all the other calls, assuring everyone that Mr. Jackson was resting but would be told of their best wishes and thank you very much, from his two sisters, one of whom Mrs. Murdoch had to assure quite crisply that it certainly was *not* a joke, and a telephone number of the Lord Chamberlain's office was furnished to ensure veracity. The only hiccup was when they were about to be ushered out of the house to have a twenty-minute walk to settle the breakfast and to spend some time together as, from the time the car called for him at ten thirty until Steven returned after the wedding breakfast, in Mrs. Murdoch's word's, Steven would belong to the nation. Steven had to halt her in full flow to say that twenty minutes would not be enough—at least an hour—and no, he wasn't going to put a bet on, although there was a wager involved.

"This will have something to do with the telephone call?" The occasion notwithstanding, Mrs. Murdoch had lost none of her usual perspicacity.

It was, she was assured, and could she and Steven have a quick word? There were whispered negotiations behind the closed kitchen door before the mystified Pamela and The Captain were informed of "her" change of plans. The Major would stand by with the car, Steven would change in to his good suit, Pamela, with Mrs. Murdoch's assistance, would select a suitable dress, suitable for what she didn't feel inclined to vouchsafe, and in fifteen minutes' time, The Captain would drive them to Marble Arch, and after depositing them by the tour bus stop, would proceed to the car park on the park side of Park Lane, where he would wait for forty minutes before leaving to collect them at the same place.

With Mrs. Murdoch once more wielding her influence, they were on their way in sixteen minutes. Then Steven addressed his wife. "I suppose you would like to know what we're doing?"

"I'm sure you'll tell me in your own good time, and I'm sure, as it obviously has Mrs. Murdoch's approval, I will not have cause to regret my customary presumption that you know what the heck you're doing."

Ouch. Steven addressed The Captain, hoping for a more sympathetic ear, but was only partially assuaged. "I'm sure I'll be debriefed by the memsahib on return, old chap, but you tell me just in case, but obviously," he added with an old soldier's shrewdness, "I'll have to pretend you haven't."

After leaving The Captain at the parking facility, they were walking down Park Lane in the direction of Marble Arch. "As it was to do with your phone call from Solly, I take it the media is involved," said Pamela, unbending a little.

It was, he assured her, and told her.

****

"So you're doing this because I was slighted?"

"Exactly."

"But my darling, Cinderella *did* go to the ball. Lydia invited me to the"—she couldn't bring herself to repeat it—"C and A party."

"But it's all arranged. One has a responsibility, and we can always use the money. We only pass this way but once."

"And your last chance to stick it to the media?"

"Ah!" He conceded graciously, "There *is* that."

She hugged his arm. "Will there be many there?"

Steven waited until two joggers had passed before answering. "Three maximum. That was one of the conditions."

"Are there any more?"

"They have to answer three questions, the answers of which are only known to me."

306

"You've been reading too many spy stories. That it?"

"No, there has to be a plain van, no logos on it. I'm not having the usual morons jumping up and down and waving to Mom. This could be it, and them." And indeed, the three figures clustered by the side of a plain black van were the only people in the vicinity, apart from the joggers on Rotten Row and the tour bus operators setting up their wares.

"You looking for me?" he addressed the woman, as she was the only one of the three who was looking at them as they approached. One of the men was hoisting a camera on to his shoulder, and the other was gazing at the tour bus operators.

"Mister Jackson." She waited until he confirmed this before smiling, "And this must be Pamela." Her smile encompassed Pam. Obviously she didn't want to overstretch the makeup before the filming started, "Cindy Rapport." She didn't offer to shake hands, as Steven had his hands in his pockets, and Pam, her previous pique forgotten, had her hands linked around his arm.

"Right, as soon as Mike's ready, we'll begin right away. As you know, we are after the opinion of people who have been thrust in the spotlight and—what?" She had suddenly noticed that Steven was holding his hand flat out like a school crossing guard.

"Aren't we forgetting something? No more than three people, and you have to answer three questions."

"I have to?"

"Answer three questions."

"You're kidding? I don't have time for this bullshit."

"Called establishing your bona fides, my dear. Well?"

With Pamela watching in amusement, their interviewer yanked a cell phone and attacked it; there was no other way to describe it as she viciously punched in a series of digits. "Yes he's here, but it seems I'm to answer some stupid questions." She then suggested he did something that was physically impossible with his head so that she could be told what was going on.

Evidently the offending cranium was removed, as Cindy said "got it" three times in rapid succession before ramming the cell phone back in to her coat pocket.

"Where the—" She began before she remembered she had to smile, "Where is he?"

Pam silently pointed to where Steven had just appeared from behind one of the massive elms that lined Rotten Row.

"That's all we need. He gets arrested for taking a leak in public."

"I rather think," Pam was enjoying herself now, "that he is checking to see that you have not exceeded the personnel allowed. He's from Coseley."

"What the fuck?" She remembered to hoist her smile, which now was more a grimace, "Are we ready, Steven? We are on a tight schedule."

"Well *I'm* ready, so if you are, by all means, let's press on. I've got one or two things to do myself today. I haven't even had time to put a bet on," Steven assured her blandly. "And if you *could* watch your language, there *is* at least *one* lady present. So, here we go. What is my sister's middle name?"

"Susan."

"Good, and could you do my nickname for Pamela?"

"Crazy legs."

"I say, well done, nearly there. The first horse I ever put a bet on?"

She had to retrieve the long-suffering cell phone for this one and subject it to a further assault.

"Trelawney," she read.

"Smack on, and the jockey? Just joking," he told her as she glared from him to the cell phone. "Right, carry on. By the way, it was Scobie Breasley."

"Thanks, first the photograph. Mike, could you get a shot of them moving toward you?" She then lowered her voice almost enough, "Before I strangle the bastard."

Steven turned toward the cameraman, "Mike? Steven, this is Pam. Better not shake hands, you need both. Where do you want us?"

"Just go to the third tree," Mike carefully avoided making eye contact with them while in Cindy's presence. "When you see the orange light come on, just walk toward me slow as you can, got it?"

"No bother, third tree, wait for the orange light."

"So this is why we're here," Pam murmured as they leaned against the appropriate tree.

"Why we're here is a Mercedes C130, or the equivalent, because—I think that's us." An orange light had just winked on from the front of the camera. "Ready?"

"Walk in the park, sunshine, let's go." She leaned into him and kissed his cheek. "Just to put a smile on your face."

And indeed, it did as they slowly sauntered toward Mike. Cindy had disappeared in to the van with the third member of the trio. *Probably to get her smile fixed.*

"Right, first question." Mike, being satisfied with their efforts (which was fortunate, in that one shot was all he was going to get) and Cindy's smile back in place, the interview commenced. "Our person in the spotlight this week is someone who is something of a mystery to most of us as. Until Prince William fell for his daughter, no one had heard of Steven Jackson outside of Mohave Valley Arizona. Steven, welcome to *Spotlight*. Is that about right?"

"Until three months ago, I didn't know I had a daughter," Steven confirmed. "It has been overwhelming."

"I can imagine. Now Steven, you know how this works. We take someone who wouldn't normally be in the public eye and ask them for their opinions on various items in the news, all right?"

"I'll do my best," Steven modestly assured the viewers of *Spotlight*.

"That's great. Now first, a subject I'm sure is on everyone's mind, the economy. What do you think of it, and do you think enough is being done?"

"As to what do I think about it, not much, as to, is enough being done, time will tell, but I will say that while the Republicans have been quick to offer an alternative plan, they weren't so quick in the previous eight years, which is one of the reasons that we are where we are. I also think that not enough is being done to hold to account those that have been largely responsible for this mess. As President Obama said, this didn't happen overnight. A schoolteacher who has to do a bit of whoring to make ends meet is thrown out of a job. A guy who is so desperate he holds up a sandwich shop for fifty dollars is thrown in jail while a ponzi scheme operator who has stolen billions, and is responsible for at least one suicide, is still living in his five-million-dollar penthouse. The employees of the SEC who let him get away with it *after* they had been warned got a slap on the wrist. They should be investigated for corruption, and if found not guilty, should be fired for incompetence. That about covers it."

"Well you certainly gave this a lot of thought. Have you had time to review the current Oscar contenders?"

"I don't need time. *Milk*."

"You've seen the others?"

"I've not seen any, but I know it's *Milk*, about the homosexual mayor of San Francisco who was murdered. It's a chance for Hollywood to create a martyr and show how caring they are, particularly with the Martin Luther King connection." He actually waited for her mouth to open before he continued. What Martin Luther King connection?" Milk, not Harvey Milk but just milk and spelled in block capitals and with the I being close to the L it could be confused with MLK or Martin Luther King. I'm surprised no one else spotted that. anything else?"

Cindy vainly soldiered on. "I believe you have strong views on the Soviet invasion of Georgia?"

"I have views on the invasion of Georgia." Steven waited for his correction to take root before he continued. "The invasion of Georgia was immoral and illegal, not to mention cowardly." He paused just long enough for Cindy to draw breath. "And Sherman should have been hung as a war criminal." He paused shortly to let it sink in. "And don't get me started on slavery. Believe me, you don't want to go down that road."

22~With the Help of Special Branch

WHEN, WITH THE HELP OF The Captain, they returned from their "twenty-minute walk," Steven's shaving gear was already laid out. "Best to shave before you have a shower, and then if you cut yourself, run it cold to finish off. It will help stop the bleeding, and while you're there, I'll give the suit a sponge and press. We can't have William's future father-in-law looking like a ruffian." Mrs. Murdoch explained. "And the other thing, in the park, went all right did it?"

"Couldn't have gone better. Sin to take the money," she was informed brightly, but when Steven ventured that he would prefer to shower after he returned from the wedding breakfast, before they left for the reception, he was informed that they *did* have sufficient hot water for *two* showers should the need arise, and while he was having his second one, his suit could be given a nice sponge and press. His suit was getting almost as much attention as he was. He hoped it was up to it. After that, Steven was content to be guided by Mrs. Murdoch while he talked about racing with The Captain and no, Mrs. Murdoch informed them, there was not time to put a bet on.

There was a polite but firm tap on the door. "Your car's here," said Mrs. Murdoch in a masterpiece of redundancy. Then she did something else that was completely out of character.

She kissed him on the cheek and not moving away, murmured, "We'll look after Pam. Just enjoy yourself." Then she stepped back. "We won't come to the door with you. I'm sure Pam would like to see you off." Then there was a handshake from The Captain, "Good luck old chap," and he made his way toward the hallway.

"It's like seeing my kids off to school for the first time. How're you feeling?" Pam had a catch to her voice.

"Actually, I'm looking forward to it. It helps with somebody taking care of the details." He nodded toward the kitchen door. "Good people."

"Couldn't be better," Pam agreed.

"So all I've got to do—"

She put her hands round the back of his neck and kissed him. "Just a walk in the park."

"Well." He released her, as there was a second knock on the door, and squared his shoulders. "Let's do it." He walked into the hallway, leaving her in the dining room, as he didn't want to take leave of his wife in front of a foreign office flunkey.

There were two of them. One was tall with short-cropped blond hair and the other more muscular, whose dark hair was long enough to curl, but both of them had that well-scrubbed, wholesome look that spoke of absolute faith in their capabilities.

"I'm Sergeant Beverley, special branch. This is Sergeant Lewis," the taller one offered. "Would you be Mister Steven Jackson?"

"I would. You sound as though you've come to arrest me."

They both laughed at the joke, and then the taller one spoke. "Sorry about that, just a matter of form. Speaking of which," they both produced warrant cards, which Steven noticed bore their pictures, "and you sir?"

"Right." Steven felt in his pocket and was relieved to feel the bulk of his wallet and the slimmer form of his passport.

"I've got two, what passes for a British passport nowadays and my Arizona driving license."

"Passport please, sir. Not like the old ones, are they?" He perused Steven's European Union passport. "That's fine, sir." Without seeming to, they had insinuated themselves so that all three were standing in the hallway. It wasn't until later that he realized that it was because they didn't want to exchange credentials in view of the street.

"Do you, mind sir?" The dark-haired one pointed toward the wallet. It was the first time he had spoken, and for a moment Steven didn't know what he meant. "The driving license, sir. Thank you, first time I've seen one. That the Grand Canyon in the background? Yes, very impressive, thank you, sir. I see you've not lost your tan. Anyway," he surrendered the license, "let's get you to the church on time."

The fair one got behind the wheel while Lewis ushered Steven in to the back, and they were away. They seemed friendly enough but did not intrude, and for his part Steven was content to lapse in to a daydream as he stared out of the window. He wondered how many people he knew would be watching. There'd be the people at church, Solly definitely, at "the Hide Out" they had eight television screens. At least one would be tuned to the wedding. At the British Club they'd be making a do of it as well. They should, considering the connection between the bride and the club, or at least the parking lot. Then there were the three gentlemen living in the Dumpster near the Anaheim Stadium parking lot who he had met while he was opening negotiations with the media. The Captain was going to record the wedding in case they didn't get back in time to catch the evening edition. He'd ask for a copy and get it transposed. Thinking of The Captain, it's a pity Mrs. Murdoch had put the kibosh on placing a bet. He'd considered slipping him a bet in spite of the memsahib's injunction, but he probably wouldn't want to go against orders. Never one to cause trouble between man and wife.

"Whose man and wife, sir?"

"Sorry." He hadn't realized he'd spoken out loud. "Our host where we are staying, he puts the occasional bet on for me, and I fancied a flutter this morning but the old trouble and strife put her foot down. Lovely woman but not to be trifled with, if you get my meaning."

"Yes, I do indeed, sir."

Steven had already drifted back to his contemplation of Park Lane, having exhausted his global guest list, when Sergeant Lewis spoke. "We could find time to place a wager for you, sir, as you'll be so busy today."

Steven's head jerked round. "You would? But I haven't got a paper, IC"

Silently he was handed a copy of the day's *Daily Mail,* and he noticed that it was open at the racing page.

"Magic." He drew out a pencil from his inner jacket and had already started perusing the runners at Ludlow before he remembered his manners. "I'm sorry, do you mind?"

"You carry on, sir," he was assured blandly. "I never get tired of watching the ever-changing panoply of London." Apparently satisfied with this sally, he settled himself comfortably in his seat.

Steven had studied the runners at the two meetings scheduled for the day and wrote down his four selections when he realized they had only just reached Hyde Park corner. "Traffic's a bit thick. Where did all these people come from?"

"Come to see you, sir, or rather your daughter and ..." Sergeant Beverly had pulled up at the entrance to Hyde Park Corner and indicated the reason. A troop of the Household Cavalry clattered their way in front of them, apparently from Knightsbridge Barracks. "In the Paras, weren't you, sir?"

"Yes, nine years."

"And did your bit in Northern Ireland?"

"And Aden."

"Yes, well done."

With Steven's military service dealt with, he waited until the troop had passed before pulling out, and as they wheeled left in to Constitution Hill, he drove on to Grosvenor Place.

Apparently that was his contribution to the conversation, and they had reached Buckingham Palace Road before the silence was broken. "That your commission, sir?" Sergeant Lewis indicated the slip of paper in Steven's hand.

"Yes, thanks." Steven surrendered the paper and reached for his wallet. "Six doubles, four trebles, and a four-horse roll up. Eleven quid, right?"

"Correct, sir, a one-pound Yankee.[24]"

"Right, but we don't use that term, my wife's from the South." (He didn't mention it was Southern California, but they probably knew.)

While Steven was counting out the money, Sergeant Lewis was scowling at his selections. "Are you sure, sir? Would you like me to bring you the slip, or shall I collect your winnings, if there are any?"

"That's very accommodating of you. Are you sure you don't work for the bookies?"

"Glad to be of help, sir, and no, I'm Church of England. Here we are, sir, see you later." With a combination of Sergeant Beverley's dexterity and avoiding being held back by the Blues and Royals, they had reached the entrance to the royal mews without any more hold ups.

"Thanks." The door was opened smartly by Sergeant Beverley but not before Steven had noticed that there were no handles on the inside. "You going to pick me up? I was told that I had to make my own arrangements."

"Orders from the top, sir, we're supposed to keep you out of trouble until tonight." Sergeant Lewis smiled at some private joke. "Besides, I'll have to give you your winnings. Straight through the double doors, sir, you're expected. Good luck."

And indeed he was, complete with buttonhole. He briefly wondered if they were artificial or they had a fresh one every day.

"He's here," the long-suffering petals were addressed before the attention was transferred to Steven. "We're waiting for you, sir, if you would follow me."

We were Mister Swinbourne and Jeremy, the latter with Steven's morning suit and accouterments draped over his arm, and both contriving a smiling welcome while exuding an air of restrained impatience. It was naturally Mister Swinbourne who spoke. "Ah, there you are."

And where would I be? "As ordered, fit and rarin' to go, courtesy of Special Branch, Sorry we're a bit late. Had to stop and put a bet on."

"Quite, sir, always a little joke for me, and how are we feeling, no butterflies in the tummy?"

"Just a few, perhaps, a sort of nervous anticipation."

"Yes, a nice turn of phrase, and Mrs. Jackson, well, I trust, looking forward to the big day?"

"Yes, blooming thank you, and quite looking forward to it."

"Yes, a very classy lady. I'm sure she'll enjoy it, a once-in-a-lifetime occasion. So." He held out his hand, and Jeremy carefully draped the suit across it. "This way, sir." Steven was led down a further corridor, which opened up in to a large, wood-paneled room with curtained alcoves ranged round the walls. "Any one, sir. This one?" Without waiting for an affirmation, Mister Swinbourne swept aside the nearest curtain and hooked the suit hanger on to a rail that ran across the mirror covering the back of the alcove. "We'll just be outside when you're finished, sir."

"Right thanks and the—thank you."

After surrendering Steven's ensemble, Jeremy had apparently laid his hands on the cowboy boots, which he now produced. "I took the liberty of giving them a light polish so that the trousers would ride over them easily," he said, breaking his vow of silence.

"Good, only I hope you used the right polish. You should really use saddle soap."

Jeremy's uncharacteristic verbosity had apparently exhausted him, so he looked to Mister Swinbourne to answer.

"We *do* know how to treat riding boots, Mister Jackson, even western ones."

"Of course, probably more nervous than I thought. Sorry." Steven took the boots from Jeremy and entered the alcove, reflecting that his fastidiousness was probably misplaced, as technically they weren't *his* boots.

He was grateful for the task of donning unfamiliar clothing, as his mind, while telling his hands what to do, would not dwell on the millions of television viewers waiting for him to fall on his arse. He carefully removed his jacket and hung it on the coat hanger provided, very thoughtful, next the waistcoat, the shoes came next, and then the trousers. This is where a woman looked her sexiest and a man looked his most ridiculous. He'd read that somewhere. He should have asked Mr. Swinbourne which alcove William had used. It would be illuminating to picture his future king standing in this very spot in his shirttails, democracy at its most basic, although he probably got changed in the palace itself. Where was his mind going? Soldier on.

He undid his tie and unbuttoned his shirt. They'd provided a hanger for that too. Right, now the difficult part—first the shirt, thank God it was a soft collar or he'd have to signal the "I do" in mime, and then the trousers. He slipped the braces over his shoulders, or suspenders as Pam still insisted on calling them—the braces, not the shoulders. Better put the boots on next. He pulled them on using the straps at the side and stamped on the floor to settle his feet in them. For the first time, he chanced a look in the mirror. Not bad. When he stood tall, the hems of the trousers rested lightly on the insteps. He always liked to adjust the tie so that there was a complete Pegasus on the knot or have it completely maroon. He didn't want to have one half-arsed Pegasus. Perfect, he might just get through this.

Then disaster struck. He couldn't fold down his collar. The right side was all right, but the left arm just couldn't get enough purchase to smooth its half down. After two attempts and a nearly dislocated shoulder, he was forced to summon assistance, and notwithstanding Mister Swinbourne's assurance that they were immediately outside, they would not have been surprised if his summons had reached the sentry at Horse Guards Parade.

"Could I get some help in here?"

That being said, Mister Swinbourne answered the call and was able to smooth Steven's plumage both literally and metaphorically and the world continued to turn.

After Mister Swinbourne had made a discreet withdrawal, assuring Steven that not at all, he was sure, Steven addressed himself to the waistcoat. He remembered what to do with the tapes, so that didn't present any problem, and then the morning coat, and he was ready.

As he was smoothing down his waistcoat, and it had to be admitted, preening himself in the mirror, it suddenly came to him this was no rehearsal. After submitting to the scrutiny of his two dressers—sorry, fitters—it was not a case of changing back into his street clothes and returning his finery and then going for a walk in the park with Pam. This was *it*. Then he remembered what Mrs. Murdoch had said, "Enjoy it because it will never come again."

He had one last look in the mirror. "Right, Jackson," he murmured to his reflection. "Let's see if you've got the bottle." Then, squaring his shoulders, he swept aside the curtain.

"Oh yes, I think that will do." Mister Swinbourne swept Steven with a critical gaze and walked 'round him. "I'm going to touch you, Mister Jackson, if you don't mind?"

"Go ahead, I won't break."

Mister Swinbourne brushed a minute speck of lint from the shoulder of the morning coat. "Perfect. Now then, Jeremy, young sir, what do you think?"

Jeremy's inspection was even sharper. It seemed to take him an age to circumnavigate their charge, and even then he wasn't satisfied. "Perhaps a little walk?"

Mister Swinbourne thought this a capital idea, so who was Steven to argue? So he, hands clasped across his middle, slowly walked to the far wall and back, and as a dividend, or to make up for his remark about the boots, he sat on the bench they had vacated. He flicked the tails aside, reminding himself that when he did this, only his daughter would see, and while holding them apart as though he was going to relieve himself, he hitched up the trousers before he sat. Mister Swinbourne's joy was total.

"Right, Jeremy will escort you to H. Good luck. I'm sure you'll be a credit to us." He handed Steven his hat and gloves.

"Thank you, and thanks for all your help. Right, Jeremy old flower, let's go."

It was obviously not the first time Jeremy had taken this journey, as he confidently led Steven through what seemed like a maze of corridors until they came to a room larger and more elaborate than the fitting room. "I should put your gloves on now sir," he whispered, "because when the principal arrives, it'll be all go."

"Right, thanks." Steven donned his gloves, assuming that the principal was his daughter. "What happens now?"

"I'm afraid we wait, sir."

"Not to worry, I spent nine years in the army, so I'm familiar with the 'hurry up and wait' system. Can we sit?"

"I wasn't – I don't know, sir."

"Let's live a little," and suiting his deeds to his words, Steven went through the routine with the tails and the trousers and made himself comfortable on one of the gilded chairs arranged along the back wall. It was obvious that Jeremy, naturally taciturn, was nervously waiting to discharge his duty, so Steven contented himself with his own thoughts. He'd already gone through the different groups that would be watching who might recognize him, and then it came to him. He had first thought of it while he was getting dressed, but the near disaster with the collar had driven it from his mind. Braces, Pam would call suspenders, what the British called suspenders, formed a very different image, trousers called pants, a waistcoat was called a vest. A noise outside interrupted his thoughts on what the Americans had done to the English language, and to Jeremy's alarm, he sauntered toward the double glass doors, "Not to worry, old son, just having a shufti, sounds like horses," and indeed, it was four magnificent chestnut bays pulling an open top coach. The horses gleamed with good health, and the coach and trappings had the glow only a diligent care could produce. One of the scarlet-coated coachmen had dismounted and was holding the lead horse's head, talking softly to him.

"Morning."

"Morning, sir." The coachman nodded at Steven's finery. "I take it we'll be taking you to church?"

"That's the idea. I'm the bride's father."

"Yes sir, lovely girl. Don't worry, we'll get you there, won't we, my 'andsome." He fondled the horse's ear. "Us and the big fellers," he nodded toward six outriders from the Household Cavalry that had formed up on each side of the landau. "Big" was the word used, with each of them being over seven feet tall with their plumed helmets, and being mounted, they almost blocked out the sun. Despite himself, Steven felt awe-struck.

He turned once more to the coachman and nodded toward his charges. "Did you prepare them yourself? Must have been quite a job."

"Up since five, sir, but worth it."

"They're a credit to you. Do you mind?"

"No, sir, loves a bit of attention. Only come from the front where he can see you."

Steven patted the glossy neck. "All right, beauty. Nothing like the sheen on the coat of a healthy horse, is there?"

"Right, know a lot about horses do you, sir?"

"Enough to keep the bookies in cigars."

They both had a laugh at that, but their merriment was curtailed by the appearance of an overwrought Jeremy. "Mister Jackson, *please!*"

"Well duty calls. Nice talking to you Mister?"

"Price sir, Ernie Price, and you?"

"Steven." He shook the white-gloved hand.

"And good luck to you, sir, it's going to be a lovely day."

As Steven re-entered through the glass doors, the reason for Jeremy's disquiet became obvious. "Good morning Mister Jackson," said H with heavy patience. "It *would* help, especially at this stage in the proceedings, if you didn't go wandering off."

"Good morning, H, yes, quite. Sorry about that. Just went to check on the transport, they *are* turned out well. Don't blame Jeremy for my restiveness. He couldn't very well rugby tackle me, could he?"

"Yes quite." He said to Jeremy, "Thank you, we'll take it from here."

"Yes, Jeremy," Steven held out his hand as Jeremy was about to escape, "thanks for all your help. Hope I wasn't too much trouble."

And with the briefest acknowledgment, Jeremy left.

"And how are you, Mister Jackson? Feeling all right, no butterflies?"

"If there were, they're all fluttered out by now."

"Excellent, and very well turned out if I may say so. Roy has done you proud."

"Roy?"

"Roy Swinbourne, Moss Brothers. Just one more detail. When you are mounting the steps, you will have your hands linked across the front and your daughter will have her hand tucked into your arm, but just before then, it would be well to acknowledge the crowds opposite. Happy?"

"As a lark, old son."

"You seem," said H carefully, "remarkably confident."

"Why shouldn't I be? We've got the Parachute Regiment to look after us when we get to the church, and Ernie promised to get us there."

"Ernie?"

"Ernie Price, the coachman."

"Ah yes, touché," H conceded graciously. "I think I hear the lady of the hour approaching."

23~"Walk in the park—see you in the guardroom."

JUDITH HAD JUST ENTERED THE room, and it was a while before Steven realized what was different in her. It seemed so long ago that he had seen her without any attendants. She was quite alone.

"Good morning, Horatio." *Horatio? No wonder.* "Could I have a few words with my father first? Thank you," presuming his acquiescence, she led Steven to one side, and after giving a warning glance to one of Jenna's cohort's who had followed her, she spoke with a funereal gravity, "Steven—Poppi—you are no doubt aware that Pamela was not originally invited to my pre nuptial soiree, and no doubt you were a little put out, yes?"

"Yes."

"But what you must understand is that every time my mother sees Pam and her joie de vive, it makes her realize what she missed. I make no reproach, and I love Pam for making you happy, but my mother has not had a happy life. I personally think she was a bloody fool, but she is my mother, so if Pamela's—let me think—nose was put out, I am truly sorry, but that's the way it has to be, you understand?"

"Completely. Thank you for telling me. But I think," and here he was unconsciously echoing Lydia, "you underestimate your mother's power of resilience. She has seen a lot, and I'm really sorry that it was not all happy, but it has made her strong. Nevertheless, I will convey your concern to Pam."

"And she will be consoled?"

"She will." *With a little help from a Mercedes C130 or the equivalent.*

"Poppi, you are so wise."

"It's called age, my dear, and now, madam, your public awaits. Shall we?" He indicated the waiting landau. "Before Horatio has a heart attack."

While Judith was being settled in to her seat, Steven, as instructed, made his way to the opposite door, where H appeared at his elbow. "Good luck, old son, I'm sure you'll do us proud. One word—when you arrive at the church, you will follow your daughter out of the nearside door. We don't want you stepping into the traffic, do we? And one more thing, the crowds are twenty deep all the way to the church, and the biggest congregation is just outside those doors. They want something to be proud of, and they are looking to your daughter, especially after the Di thing, so try not to look too surprised, right? Enjoy it." And with that, Steven climbed aboard the coach, seating himself a la Liberace. Then with a wave from H, and an over-the-shoulder wink from Ernie Price, they were away.

"I want to ask you something, Poppi," Judith whispered.

Steven inwardly sighed and prepared himself for another of the joys of fatherhood. "Ask away, but it's a bit late now."

"Mon braves, the Guards of my Honour?"

"Yes?"

"They are not to be invited to the party tonight. I learned about this too late to change it. Could you?" She delved in to her purse and thrust a bundle of bank notes in to Steven's hand. "It is one hundred pounds each for them to drink my health and show my appreciation. They would not be offended?"

"I think that is very gracious, and they would be far from offended, but I wouldn't think many of the notes will see a bar counter. Don't forget it is a day for them and—Jesus Christ!" The gates had swung open, and a wall of sound engulfed them as the waiting crowd caught the first glimpse of, as one newspaper put it with its customary hyperbole, "The Girl Who Saved the Monarchy."

It even shook Judith from her customary equanimity, so much that it was a few moments before she mildly reproached him. "Such language in front of a nice Jewish girl. Now raise your hat and acknowledge your public like a good Poppi."

She settled back in the seat, acknowledging the outpouring of affection, and didn't speak again until they had passed Birdcage Walk. "You are all right?"

"Walk in the park," Steven confirmed as he waved his hat in the direction of a group of old soldiers who had parked their wheelchairs in front of the Victoria Memorial. "What a day, what a bloody day."

Someone had told him once that the secret of being focused in front of a crowd is to pick one person out and address them, and to his amazement, he found that out of the thousands of onlookers, he could actually distinguish individual faces. Going up the mall, it was an elderly couple standing back from the crush in Saint James's Park, and the woman actually toasted them with the contents of her vacuum flask. Then they had passed Admiralty Arch and turned into Trafalgar Square, when he realized that his daughter was speaking to him. "Admit it."

"I'm sorry, admit what?"

"You're enjoying it."

"Wouldn't miss it for the world. I was just wondering, surprisingly, you can pick individual faces out. They must have been here since dawn."

"I also."

"Right, so, presuming we return by the same route, we will both be on the other side, so what are the odds of us picking the same people to wave to?"

"Poppi," she said softly, "we won't be together. I will be with my husband."

"Oh," his face fell, "of course. It looks like I've lost you already."

"Poppi, such a thing you say. I have only just found you. Whoever I marry, you will be my father, and you will be charming to my friends, yes?"

"I don't know about that."

"But of course, mai oui," Judith blew a kiss in the direction of a skinhead with, *"We love you, Judy dahlin',"* emblazoned on his T-shirt. "You will have the dry humor, that is so sexy, how is it, 'Have I read your book?'" she recited "'Only if you've been looking over my shoulder while I have been typing.' Yes, you will captivate my friends. You have already started. I'm afraid one or two might try to steal you from Pamela."

"Will they indeed?" Steven raised his hat and winked to a bevy of office workers who were probably using their lunch break to wish the bride-to-be well. "I take it my little witticism was from Jenna?"

"She is quite taken with you. Not as good looking as Brian who is guarding my honor, but then he is much younger."

"Ah youth, I served with his father, you know."

"You did?" Judith forgot her public enough to turn toward him. "Where?"

"In Aden. Mike L'Shaw was my Commanding Officer." And while he had her attention, he waved to some suitably refreshed patrons of the Sherlock Holmes who were leaning out of the upper windows. "Your mother and I had a drink there. We were going to have lunch, but the dog in the glass case rather put her off."

"Why a dog in a glass case?"

"It was supposed to be the Hound of the Baskervilles. Sherlock Holmes was supposed to meet Sir Henry Baskerville at the Northumberland Hotel, which should be on your side."

"Ah, now I see, but she never told me."

"Well, us old people must be allowed our secrets, my dear."

"Oh touché' mon pere. Could you imagine what all these people would think if they knew this conversation? You should have brought a tape recorder and sold it to the newspapers. I'm afraid, my dear, you have not the nose for the business opportunities."

As I said, my dear, us old people have our secrets.

They proceeded along the embankment, and he was alarmed to see that some had climbed on to the riparian wall to get a better view. For the rest, he was quite content to succumb to the early morning sunshine, and he had to remind himself that it was his choice to be here. He could have said no and they could have got someone else, probably Chadders, but no, they'd have to upgrade him to Lydia's fiancée, and Mrs. Chadders would not have gone for that. And when he'd met Judith, did he really have a choice? *And* he'd had a good breakfast while these people had been here since dawn, so follow your own advice and choose a person or group to concentrate on and, "Shoulder the Sky." As they turned into Lancaster Place, he recognized the shape of Somerset House and was about to interrupt Judith's attention to her side of the street when his attention was caught by a group of nuns on the steps.

So, we have a group of Catholics giving their blessing to a Jewess on her way to a ceremony that will make her, one day, the defender of the Protestant faith. He made a point of half-standing and doffing his hat to them. *As the Navajos would say, "It is a good day to die."* Even the trees on the embankment gardens had looked their best.

They were halfway down Ludgate Hill when Steven discovered something else to panic about. Until now he had waved with his left hand, while doffing his hat with the right, and it wasn't until he put his right hand out to steady himself while he rose to repeat his salutation of the nuns to a half-dozen nurses (they were still in uniform, so they must have come straight from the night shift) when he realized that he still had Judith's money in his hand. Better put it away or he might forget himself and wave with his right hand, and there would go the lads' beer money. After he had acknowledged the nurses and got a series of delighted waves in return, he lifted the flap of his morning coat and realized *there were no pockets.* They must have been sewn up to prevent keeping junk in there and spoil the line, but where could he put it? The trousers were no better. When he felt through the slit at the side, all he could feel was the Jackson leg. This was no time to panic, just think the situation through as he waved and smiled, this time on autopilot. He ran through the possibilities. The hat was out of the question, as the next time he found someone to wave to, someone else would profit from his daughter's magnanimity. The waistcoat, surely there must be a watch pocket, and there was, he folded the notes carefully and patted them into the pocket. Piece of cake.

"At a time like this you are hungry?"

"No." He realized he had spoken out loud again. "It's an expression meaning it is not as traumatic as I thought it would be."

"Bon. The piece of cake is even easier than the walk in the park. This must come naturally to you, Poppi, and you have done nothing like it before?"

"Unless I was a queen in a previous life."

"So to eat a piece of cake walking the park makes you a queen. I thought I had English. You must teach me the other." Then something seemed to distract her. "This is where William and I met, at the Cheshire Cheese, yes?"

"Correct, a very famous pub."

"And those in the red coats?" She indicated some scarlet-coated figures sitting at a bench outside the Courts of Justice.

"Chelsea pensioners, they're old soldiers who live in the Royal Hospital in Chelsea. It was founded a long time ago, 1700, I think."

"They are splendid, oh that is so …" She had waved to them, and to a man they stood and saluted. This simple gesture of respect affected her so much that they were at Ludgate Hill before her natural buoyancy returned, "Could you be a Chelsea Pensioner with the red coat?"

"I suppose I could be, yes, but then you have to have no relatives, I think, so no, unless Pam kicks me out."

"Then I shall tell her about you walking that park eating the cake and she will kick you out for being the Queen and you will be an old soldier in the red coat."

Then they were there. There was no change in the density or the intensity of the crowd. They simply came to a halt, and the majesty of Wren's masterpiece soared above them. The outrider on Steven's side drew level with the door and brought his sword up to his face in a salute, garnering a nod from Steven.

What's the matter, sunshine, think I'm going to make a bolt for it?

They actually heard the attendant approaching when Judith turned to him and with harrowing simplicity said, "I love you, Poppi."

"I love you, Judith."

"And you will be kind to my mother?"

The attendant opened the door and placed the step, but her eyes didn't leave him. "I will," he said.

"Right." She turned a dazzling smile on to the attendant as she took his hand. "Why, thank you." She stood there waving to the crowd as she waited for her father to join her. He remembered to give one last wave to the crowds opposite before addressing the driver, "Thank you, Mister Price."

Ernie turned in his seat and saluted with his whip. "Go on, my son, enjoy it, best day of your life."

With the proprieties performed, Steven took his daughter's arm. Afterward he remembered that this was the part he had dreaded most, climbing the steps of Saint Paul's in cowboy boots, which he had insisted, in a fit of vanity, on wearing, but it went without a stutter, mainly because by now he had surrendered to the atmosphere and was enjoying every moment of it.

At the top, they entered the vestibule, and the noise of the crowd subsided to a distant murmur, as there was a general relaxing of the atmosphere. Steven released his daughter's arm and at the direction of one of the buttonholes placed his hat, with his gloves inside on a bench that ran along the south wall.

"I thought you two would never get here. Did you stop for a drink?"

"We thought of stopping in the Sherlock Holmes in Northumberland Avenue, but it was full of bloody trippers. There must be something on."

Jenna kissed Judith. "You look gorgeous. Makes me regret being straight, and look at you." She turned to Steven. "You look good enough to eat."

"You're looking seriously tasty yourself, Jenna, but I think you would find me a bit tough. We from the Black Country tend to be a bit on the dry side."

Jenna's reply, and Steven was sure there was one, was postponed by her future queen, "Oh mon braves so beautiful, my Maids of Honour will."

"Come on, let's get you entrained and safely married before you spoil it for the rest of us." Jenna winked at Steven. It was that sort of day. "And don't you go getting my maids all hot and bothered. They are enough distractions." She nodded towards the cause of Judith's excitement.

The detachment from the Parachute Regiment were being briefed by Brian L'Shaw, but it was their uniform, obviously designed for the occasion, that caught the eye. Instead of the normal No. 2s, which always reminded Steven of a drab bus driver's uniform, the Guard of Honour were attired in a chocolate-colored battledress with the trousers tucked in to American-style jump boots, and at the throat of the blouse type tunic was wrapped a white ascot type cravat. The medals gleamed proudly above the left breast pocket. The only survivor of the original uniform was the maroon beret with the silver parachute wing cap badge shining in the filtered sunlight.

While Judith was being fussed over by Jenna, Steven, never able to be still for very long, wandered over to where Brian L'Shaw was still talking to his men. As he drew nearer, he realized that it was not exactly a briefing but closer to a good old-fashioned rollocking[25] that was being administered,

"So all you have to be concerned with, *gentlemen,* is not letting yourselves or the regiment down and being a credit to the lady who is in your charge. Anything else is irrelevant. Now fall out and hold yourself in readiness!"

He turned and saw Steven. "Mr. Jackson, everything going well?"

"I *thought* so," Steven nodded to the troops standing in an at ease position along the wall.

"No just a bit of regimental pride might have got a bit out of hand." He nodded toward the opposite wall where about eight very old but ramrod-straight men stood, resplendent in boots and scarlet be-medaled tunics and topped with plumed hats. "The Knights of The Garter. The lads had their noses put a little out of joint when they were referred to as the Ceremonial Guard of Honour."

"Well I think that I could help there." Steven was feeling in his waistcoat pocket for the guard's gratuity when he was startled by Brian L'Shaw coming to attention, "Guard of Honour, 'shun." He threw up a salute. Steven, having divested himself of his hat, wasn't sure how to respond but was saved from further confusion by a slight pressure on his arm. "Good morning, Brian, you look so dignified and mon braves so—I'm sure my honour will be safe." She smiled at them before turning back to Brian. "Would you excuse us for a bit and ask them to relax? They look so uncomfortable like that." She gently led Steven out of earshot. "Poppi, you still have the money for mon braves?"

"Actually I put it on a horse—of course I've still got it."

For once, Judith was not seduced by the vagaries of the English language. "Give it to me. I have time to do it myself. You do not mind?"

"No, I think it's a splendid idea, very gracious." Steven handed over the roll of notes, saying a silent prayer of thanks for its safe delivery.

"I'm glad." She turned and walked the few steps to Brian L'Shaw, who had been watching the preceding exchange with interest, "Brian, would you mind if I spoke to your men a bit?"

"Please do. Right, listen in." It was an unnecessary admonishment, as every eye was upon her.

"Mon braves, I am sorry you were not invited to the party afterward. I think the old tossers are frightened of you stealing the women's hearts, and I'm sure they are right. But I hope you will accept this"—for once she seemed to lose her way until Steven leaned forward and murmured in her ear—"token of my esteem, and you can drink my health." And in a moment of pure show business, she made a show of counting the notes. "There should be one each, unless my father has slipped one out. You know what the civvies are like."

Then, to the accompaniment of some good-natured smirks in Steven's direction, and a cursory, "With your permission," to Brian L'Shaw, she proceeded to go down the line handing a hundred-pound note to each man, and a kind providence decreed that the first in line was Corporal Lofty Pringle. No one remembered where, or from whom, the sobriquet came from (Lofty standing a good five feet eight in his stockinged feet), but Lofty Pringle was the most experienced soldier there, and Lofty was known to never "flap." On one occasion, a young Lieutenant was trying to make a name for himself (he did, but not in the way that he intended) saw fit to remove an imaginary piece of lint from Lofty's shoulder during muster parade with the traditional admonishment, "I am going to touch you, Corporal."

"Be gentle with me sir," said Lofty, not moving a muscle, "it's my first time."

This unflappability came to the rescue of the occasion now, as Judith came to him. He came to attention, and looking straight into her eyes said, "Thank you, ma'am, and my best wishes," and still with his eyes locked on hers, took a check pace and slipped the note in to his battledress pocket (the right one, so as not to disturb the lanyard on his left shoulder, but in the words of Private Frank Trousedale, who was of a more romantic disposition, "Just as close to my heart"). As Lofty seemed to have got away with it, the next soldier in line did the same and so it went on down the line and the ritual was repeated exactly, except for Lance Corporal Alan Fellows. Lance Corporal Fellows came from Portobello in the Black Country, which was near Willenhall, which, since the dog track had gone, nobody had heard of either. Notwithstanding his iron self-discipline, this gave him a certain attitude, and when it was his turn to receive the token, he followed Lofty's lead to the letter but couldn't resist adding, "And I think His Royal Highness is a very lucky man, ma'am."

Put that on the fire and see how the smoke goes up the chimney.

"Right, when you've quite finished captivating the talent, let's get you married." Jenna whisked Judith off, leaving Brian and Steven.

"I say, that was well put," Brian said sotto voce. "You have quite a daughter there."

"I can't take any credit for, that old son," *except a spot of how's your father in a pickup truck more than twenty years ago,* "Lydia raised her by herself."

"Yes, well said, liked that bit about old tossers frightened of stealing the women's hearts. I detect your influence there."

"Yes, well, makes a change from hiding the silverware."

"Quite, well soon I'll be asking your permission to mount the guard so with your permission?"

"Sure, carry on, and Brian?"

"Yes?"

"It's going to be a great day, isn't it?"

"Indeed it is."

For the next few minutes, Steven had nothing to do except, in H's words, keep "out of trouble and don't trip over anyone." Brian L'Shaw, with his troops, was obviously waiting for the word from H. The Maids of Honour were rolling out the train behind Judith, and the Knights of the Garter were arranging themselves in double rows and ignoring everyone else with a demeanor that only years of self-induced superiority can give.

At a similar stage in the rehearsal he had occupied himself with the smells and first impressions of Saint Paul's Cathedral, but now with those distractions denied him, the enormity of the next hour engulfed him. The eyes of the English-speaking world would be upon him, a goodly portion expecting him to fall on his arse as he walked his daughter to the altar. *In cowboy boots?* Which he had insisted on out of sheer bloody-mindedness. He had never felt so alone.

"Mister Jackson, having second thoughts?"

Steven turned to confront the Princess Royal.

"No, ma'am just enjoying the occasion, and yourself? I thought you'd be up front by now."

"No, I'm Matron of Honour, I'm supposed to oversee the preparation of the bride. A bit insulting, really. I mean, the senior maid, she looks very capable, doesn't she?"

"Yes, ma'am, very capable."

"I take it you are coming to the reception?"

"Oh yes, trousers pressed and best boots."

"You won't be wearing those, will you?" She nudged his cowboy boots peeping from beneath the edge of his morning dress trousers.

"I wouldn't think so."

"Good, because as Mummy's paying for this, I'll expect a dance at least."

"It will be an honour ma'am."

"Of course, you dance with your daughter first."

"Quite." *Generous of you. I wonder if Pam gets in the frame.* "Now if you'll forgive me, I think I need to mount the guard."

"Of course. But don't do it too often, you might get to like it.

At that moment, a rhythm resounded 'round the vestibule. It was a series of dull thuds interspersed with sharp clicks. The Knights of the Garter had started to move (was it just the imagination or were there a few wary glances at the Paras?). The thuds were their heavy boots, and the clicks were the long lances they carried and tapped against the marble floor in unison as they marched.

At that time, Brian L' Shaw fortuitously arrived. He brought his sword up to his face in salute, "Sir, my compliments. Have I your permission for the guard to be mounted?"

This was it. Steven squared his shoulders and looked Brian L' Shaw in the eye, soldier to soldier. "My compliments to you, Captain L'Shaw, and indeed you do have my permission. Please carry on."

"Thank you, sir." As Brian turned away to address his men, there was another call on Steven's attention. "We're ready," Jenna murmured in his ear. "Will she do?"

"As I said before," Steven said quietly, "she might be too good for him. But if that's what she wants ..."

"Well, she's all yours—for the next half hour."

Steven walked over, and they stood looking at each other. "Well, Poppi, here we are."

"Yes, here we are." He leaned forward, and holding her hands, kissed her on the cheek. "You look beautiful. Your mother must be very proud."

"And you, Poppi?"

"Yes, I am very proud also."

She threw her head back and laughed. "Oh, Poppi, I meant that you are beautiful too."

There was a discreet cough, which intruded on this tender moment, "Ma'am," said Brian L'Shaw, The Guard of Honour is ready and waiting. Would you and your escort care to join us?"

As though they were going for a stroll in the park, Judith linked her arm in her father's. "Lead on, mon brave."

With her Maids of Honour trailing behind, they positioned themselves between the two files of the Guard of Honour. The silence was so intense, it seemed that even the old walls were listening as Brian L'Shaw spoke quietly. "Right, lads, the next sound you will here is the fanfare, after that will be the music, 'Pomp and Circumstance,' the 'Regimental Slow March.' You're all familiar with it, but just listen for my voice. The left file lead off with the left foot, the right file with the right, shoulders back. Look just above the man's head in front. This is your day as much as anybody's, enjoy it. And let's show these toffee-nosed bastards how it's done, saving your presence, ladies." He glanced briefly at Steven. "All right?"

He was answered with a wink. "A walk in the park. See you in the guardroom."

"A piece of cake is better in the guardroom than—" Judith got no farther, as she was silenced by a furious "shush" from Jenna.

They waited what seemed like an age, where in reality it must have been no more than a few seconds, as Brian L'Shaw nodded his head slowly, in what Steven afterward realized was to get in to the rhythm. Then great doors swung open, and he raised his voice just enough to be heard, "Guard of Honour, by the right, slow march."

As soon as the second pair had passed, Steven gently squeezed Judith's hand, and they were away.

Someone had told him during the preparations that the back view was the most important, as they would only be observed after they had passed. Whoever it was, they were probably correct in everything else, but in this they were misinformed, for as soon as they passed through, the door every eye was upon them.

24~"Just an old soldier and a granny."

THE WEDDING WAS BEAMED AROUND a world hungry for something besides global warming and crooked politicians, but nowhere was it viewed more intensely than in a bar near Anaheim Stadium in California, a doctor's house in Henderson, a suburb of Las Vegas, and in the office of Patrick Cairns the director in charge of the production payroll department of Media Partners in Burbank, California, where they had, ostensibly volunteered to work early in response to the government's "early to work" program, designed to reduce the output of greenhouse gases on LA's notoriously congested freeways. The fact that there was a large screen TV in the office was never mentioned, but Cindy Seabock brought in some fruitcake, Linda Sanchez brought in those special things she did with ham and corn tortillas, Moses, the janitor, had seen fit to start the coffee machine early, and soon Media Partners was indulging its well-earned reputation for making a party out of anything. Totally "dry"of course. Lindy Henry, the managing director, extremely liberal in most things, was adamant on this, and only the least charitable would observe that she never reached noon without being suitably refreshed herself.

339

By the time it came for the bride-to-be to enter the church on the arm of her father, there were no less than seven people in Patrick's office with urgent queries. "She's twenty-one. I didn't know he'd been married that long," Dier Carlson, the vanguard of Media's gay front, offered.

"I believe she was the product of a previous relationship," Patrick countered. "He does carry it off well, doesn't he?"

"A wife *and* a girlfriend," Dier said with a tragic air. "He really *is* straight."

"It's not all about you, Dier."

The speaker was silenced by Patrick, who wanted to hear what the commentator was saying, and after all, it *was* his office.

"You will notice the Guard of Honour, instead of the usual detachment from the household cavalry, resplendent in their plumed helmets. We have the stocky, slightly menacing figures of The Parachute Regiment, as a direct request from the bride to be, out of respect for her father, who served in the Paras" , and in an adjunct that was later to cost him dear, "---or to be more exact, the First Battalion. The Parachute Regiment just returned from Iraq and are the only major unit of the 16 Independent Parachute Brigade who are not currently serving overseas."

"I didn't know he was in the Airborne." Patrick, an old navy man himself, seemed embarrassed by the omission.

"I did." The speaker was Hiromi Crouder, an exquisite Japanese girl who rarely spoke to anyone.

"Did you now?" Dier declared huffily. "I wouldn't have thought you had anything to talk about other than the Beatles."

"Oh no," she demurred softly, "we spoke of many things." She seemed about to list some of their topics of conversation and then merely contented herself with saying, "It came up when we were talking about *Fawlty Towers*[26]. When he went on vacation last year, he went to an airborne reunion and met people there that he had served with thirty years ago. It seemed to make him a little sad."

"Well *Fawlty Towers* has a lot to answer for." Dier was rightly incensed. "Then, you can never tell with you people." And Dier left, taking his outrage with him but fortunately leaving the cream cheese and spinach manicotti and Hiromi to resume her silent contemplations.

Doctor Alicia Brennan, the brown-haired, long-legged head of the VA clinic in Henderson, was, by her own admission, a neat freak. Although she owned a house in Henderson, she spent most of her time at her boyfriend's. In fact, she had more closet space there than he had. In spite of this, however, once a week she left her boyfriend's bed at five AM to clean her house, in case a speck of dust had dared to invade its pristine virginity, before she reported to the Veteran's Administration where she worked. She was thus engaged when she had a telephone call from Pamela, the receptionist at the VA clinic and one of her few friends. "Have you got the television on?"

"Of course not. I didn't get up at five in the morning to watch television, although I am taping Prince William's wedding." (Doctor Brennan, like many Americans and despite her republican, leanings had a fixation with the monarchy).

"That's it, turn it on now."

"Why, are you going to ask me questions about it?"

"As a matter of fact, I am."

Doctor Brennan switched on the television with the remote in time to join millions of viewers in watching the future wife of Prince William being escorted by her father, who looked vaguely familiar. "Oh my, is that?"

"It is, isn't it? That's what I wanted to ask *you*. You didn't know?"

"Let me think." Doctor Brennan sat, her house temporarily neglected. "Our first appointment, he said that his wife had two sons from a previous marriage, who he called his sons, an Old Testament thing. There was a son by *his* previous marriage who he'd disowned and whose parentage, what did he say? 'I beg leave to doubt,' and he'd got a third of a Jewish daughter. I know you can't, but he said that she, the mother, had a boyfriend at the time they were involved and she also danced the tango in San Francisco with a baseball player while on a business trip, and the daughter was born shortly after she went back to Europe. And so he was a third, the father. I thought I would have to explain the facts of life to him, but obviously he was—"

"Have you got his file there?"

"Of course not!"

"Only you seem to know and remember a heck of a lot."

"I make no apology for taking an interest in my patients."

"Chill out, girlfriend, just showing an interest. He obviously was what?"

"The father. You remember I told you about that British guy who called when you were on that course, and your replacement put him through? What was her name you know, the last of the flower people."

"Lavinia."

"That's right, Lavinia. She must have been impressed with the British accent and she put him through. Just what I needed with Doctor Lee sick. Anyway, he wanted me to turn over Steven's medical files to him, cheeky bastard." She paused, as if trying to remember something else. "The last time I saw him, Steven, I'd been telling him about my vacation and he asked if I was going to London and I said no, Italy. I'd done Britain last year. He said it was a pity, I could go to his daughter's wedding, but I never thought—I never connected the two. There's one thing that, what was his name? Bryant, that was it, he did get one piece of information from me."

"I'm afraid to ask."

"I was able to state that, as a result of my examination, I can confirm that Mister Jackson sunbathed in the nude."

"Doctor Brennan, you're a wicked girl, and I think you'll lead this country girl in to a life of sin."

"Sure, it's my turn for the doughnuts today, right? Now get off the line, I need to clean my house, it's filthy."

But for once Doctor Brennan's house stayed, if not filthy, certainly neglected, as she watched the ceremony to the end and was nearly late for the clinic.

As Doctor Brennan's house was uncharacteristically neglected, the opposite could be said of the three characters who presented themselves to the Dugout Bar and Grill near Anaheim Stadium. For one thing, they were newly showered and shaved, courtesy of the Salvation Army, and for another, they wore clean clothes from head to foot including underwear (the Full Monty) again, thanks to that august organization. It took a while for the bartender to recognize them, although they were not unknown to him. In fact, as they kept mostly to themselves and did not try to panhandle the customers, he would occasionally let them clean out the back area for a few of yesterday's hamburgers. He knew only one of them by name, Lonny, who had appointed himself spokesman, probably because he used to work for NBS. He approached now with more than his usual confidence and indicated the television behind the bar. "Could you change the channel? We want to see the wedding."

"You know that the television's only for the customers, and what would you want to see the wedding for?"

Lonny placed two twenties reverently on the bar. "And three Michelobs, please. We want to watch the wedding because the bride is the daughter of a friend of ours. In fact, we promised to drink her health. Perhaps you'd like to join us?"

After tending bar for thirty years, nothing surprised Tony Young, but this came close. They looked all right and they didn't smell. "It's a bit early for me, I've only just come on shift, but I'll have a club soda, all right? And maybe you should get a pitcher, it'll be cheaper. So that's a pitcher of Michelob and three glasses?"

At the Hideout (where the locals go) in Laughlin, Nevada, Brian, the bar manager, was more terse than usual, as he always said, "If you want your ass kissed, go to one of the casinos. You won't get it here." The Hideout was officially designated a sports bar, which explained the seven television screens arranged against the far wall each tuned to a different NFL game, all except one, which was showing, after much manipulation of the remote, the wedding of Prince William of England. "Her father is a regular here," was the answer to anyone who questioned this departure from the normal practice. "He usually comes in after church on Sunday with his wife, and sometimes in the week, and specials like New Year's Eve and Halloween. He came in as Willie Nelson last year. Now what is it, same again?"

While mentioning these groups as having a special, almost proprietary interest in the bride's father, it would be remiss to overlook two others, The United Methodist Church of Mohave Valley, Arizona, together with its affiliate the United Methodist Fellowship of Needles, California, for weren't Steven and Pam regular worshipers *and* members of the choir? (Pam more regular and less disruptive than Steven.)

Lastly, there were the members of the British and Dominion Social club near Long Beach, California, although some of the newer members (less than twenty years) were a little dubious about his relationship to the bride, as they had seen him with no one else but Pam. Some of the older hands could, however, well remember Steven's younger days and especially a dark-haired bird who looked like a young Elizabeth Taylor, Elizabeth Taylor, they explained patiently, the one who took one of the greatest actors in the English-speaking world and used him as a fashion accessory. Some even remembered a blonde who he nearly married and his first wife, who was not considered worthy of much discussion. These senior members had no trouble with the authenticity of the story of the bride's conception. "Oh yes, if that parking lot could talk, it could tell some stories."

The focus of the attention of these good people had just steadied himself in to a rhythm. While keeping pace with the second pair of the Honour Guard, he was also able to match his steps to his daughter's. He was past nervousness now, everything was going as it should, just remember the, "who giveth this woman – I do," and then four paces to the right so that Jenna's cohorts wouldn't knock him on his arse when the bridal couple turned to face each other. As they passed through the portals, the music pouring forth, the congregation turned to them as flowers to the sun, there was a frisson, an audible gasp, at the sight of them, or rather, her. His face set in a suitable expression, proud but not arrogant, with the hint of a smirk. He even affected a slight swagger, only just preventing himself from winking to his sister in one of the rear pews, for in the words of Brian L'Shaw, "Let's show these toffee nosed[27] bastards how it's done." Sadly, the class war was still prevailing, for without it England would still be ... But he was impressed, with Elgar's masterpiece cascading through the ancient arches, the morning sun streaming through the stained-glass windows, and reflecting off the cap badges and medals of the Guard of Honour, and with his daughter on his arm, outshining them all, he could almost hear his heart beating from beneath the Moss Brothers waistcoat. All too soon they were at the altar rail, and Judith handed her bouquet to Jenna before reclaiming his arm. The Guard of Honour dispersed outward and as a man, turned to stare at the congregation, as though any threat to their charge would come from there. They must have rehearsed it many times. The archbishop of Canterbury cleared his throat. "Dearly beloved ..."

Steven felt a slight pressure as Judith squeezed his arm, whether in reassurance or gratitude, he had no way of knowing, and as he had nothing to do now until, "Who giveth this woman?" Which came shortly after, "If anyone knows of any just cause------" he amused himself by covertly studying the architecture. *I wonder if Rudyard Kipling's buried here or in*

Westminster Abbey. I can never remember which. I know David Livingstone is buried in Westminster Abbey, except his heart, which was buried in Africa. Nice touch that.

"If anyone knows just cause why this man and this woman should not be joined in holy matrimony, let him speak now," *and I'll personally kick you out of here,* "or forever hold his peace." After a suitably dramatic pause, "Who giveth this woman?" *And what do you think I'm here for, with me Sunday best and me cowboy boots?* Steven paused, swallowed twice, and said, "I do." He transferred Judith's hand to Prince William's and slowly walked the four paces to his right. It was almost too slowly, as, when Judith and William turned to face each other, the last Maid of Honour actually brushed his arm before he came to rest, and resumed his contemplation of Wren's masterpiece.

"You may kiss the bride. He who God has put together let no man put asunder," and that was it. He distinctly heard the bells ringing and outside the swelling murmur that he later realized was the cheering of the crowd. He linked arms with the Princess Royal, and they slowly followed the bridal couple down the nave. He did not have to match his pace to that of the Guard of Honour as they were in front of them escorting Judith and her husband. The return navigation of the nave was not as perilous as the entrance,. There were nods and smiles, instead of the awestruck contemplation of his daughter. He even decided that a wink to his sister wouldn't cause too much bother. He had somehow expected the bridal couple to carry on straight through the vestibule to the waiting carriage, but when they passed through the portals, he saw that Judith was being hugged by Jenna while she was being de-trained, and her groom was apparently being congratulated by his father. Of Brian L'Shaw and his men there was no sign, and Steven was moved to ask Princess Anne about this omission.

"The Honour Guard's duties don't end until the couple actually move off, so they will be formed up outside now. You did very well, but if you don't mind," she looked over her shoulder, "I'll attend to my mother now. She gets tired. So I'll leave you to the tender care of the bride's mother."

"Of course, give her my respects, *your* mother I mean." And Princess Anne left, leaving Steven thinking that, for all her well-documented shortcomings, both real and invented, the Princess Royal was a caring daughter.

Steven was roused from his reflections on the yellow press by a tug on his sleeve. "Poppi, I need your advice."

"Yes, my dear." *If it's the facts of life, it's a bit late for that, love.*

"I should throw my bouquet into the crowd, yes? And who catches it will have good luck?"

"Or a husband, yes."

"So, there are so many people out there and the route is so long, which would be the best place?"

"I see." Steven affected to think about this, but he knew the answer. "Traditionally it's as soon as you leave the church, so anybody who is serious about catching it should have been there early. The onus is not on you."

"What is onus?"

"Responsibility. If someone wants your bouquet, it's up to them to get up early enough to get in position. I should wait until you're in the carriage. The higher you are, the better chance of your bouquet reaching the crowd."

"My father, the Solomon, you will dance with me at the reception?"

"Father's privilege."

"And will I get a dance?" They both turned to confront Lydia, who'd quietly joined them.

"Of course. I'd better leave my cowboy boots at home. Went well, I thought?"

"It was beautiful. You looked very well together, It's a pity you were so long away."

"I am painfully aware of that, but the situation was not of my choosing."

"Both of you," Judith's voice had a knife edge quality, "stop it now or I will—when I am queen, I will have you both locked up in the stuping tower."

"I think you mean the Bloody Tower," Steven demurred.

"All right, the stuping Bloody Tower, right?"

"Right. Jackson well and truly put in his place. Are you going to make us shake hands?"

"I'm sorry," said Lydia graciously, "that *was* unfair."

"I probably bring out the worst in you, I always did."

"Oh contraire," Lydia lowered her eyes demurely, and strangely she could still carry it off. "But I *did* miss you."

"It always works out that way," said Steven sagely. "The one who ends the relationship always feels a little regret, and the other one, they ..." He seemed to lose his way. "Look, I think we are getting in deep waters here. You look absolutely stunning, Lydia, the hat, pure Marlene Dietrich."

"Oh this? I look like a schoolteacher next to your wife."

Steven was wondering whether to give voice to his thought that women who spend the most time trying to look glamorous always disavow the effect or merely to remark that he had met a few very fetching schoolteachers. He was relieved from this quandary by the approach of a buttonhole. "Mrs. Windsor," and in a moment of pure farce, they all looked 'round before Judith gave a delighted chuckle,

"Oh *me*, what is it, mon petite?"

He bent forward in that curious, tight-kneed curtsy that always amuses or puzzles non-Londoners. "I am informed that your carriage approaches."

"Ah, to business." Judith turned to go but checked herself and looked over her shoulder from one to the other. "Can I leave you two alone?"

"Suitably chastened and rebuked, my dear." Steven watched her walk toward her husband before he turned and offered his arm to Lydia. "Shall we watch them on their way? And if we stay there, they won't have to come looking for us."

She graciously accepted the proffered support, and they made their way to the shadows of the main door, where the reason for the Guard of Honour's absence from the vestibule was revealed. As though reluctant to relinquish their charge, they had formed up on the steps facing inward with their rifles shouldered, and as the bridal pair passed, Brian L'Shaw again brought his sword to his face in salute, and as if this was a cue, there was a crashing, present arms from his men. Judith blew a kiss to Brian L'Shaw and turned to wave to her parents before being handed in to the Landau, and what happened next was a piece of pure theater that outdid any of Princess Diana's contrived performances. Before taking her seat, she leaned forward, and placing a hand on Ernie Price's shoulder, she whispered something to him, and after a moment's thought, he nodded. She appeared to ask him if he was sure, and after getting a more definite assent, she sat down, to the obvious relief of her husband. When the carriage moved off, it became obvious what the hasty conference had been about. Instead of moving off in a direct line, Ernie skillfully turned the lead horses so that they led the team slantwise across the road until they were within six feet of the crowds opposite Saint Paul's. Forsaking her husband of thirty minutes, once more she squeezed Ernie Price's shoulder, and leaving her hand there for extra purchase, she drew her arm back and hurled her bouquet up to the sixth rank of the crowd with a throw that would have done credit to any outfielder.

"Good you're here." The buttonhole ushered them through the doorway without the benefit of a curtsey. "Quick as you like, madam, sir, only we don't want them to go off the boil, the crowd, I mean. After the bride and groom, they might start to drift away."

"Well we cannot have that, come." Lydia reclaimed Steven's arm. "Let's keep them on the boil." They descended the steps between the ranks of the Honour Guard (sans the present arms), and the second landau glided to a stop with impeccable timing.

Steven paused as Lydia was being handed in to the coach by attendant and waved in the general direction of where Judith's bouquet had disappeared. He was about to follow her when he was stopped. "Sir."

He turned to confront Brian L'Shaw, who brought his sword up to his face in salute.

Careful, my son, you'll cut your nose off.

"Have I your permission to stand down the Honour Guard?"

"Have you finished now?"

"Yes, we are foot soldiers. Our responsibility ends, reluctantly, when our charge alights the carriage. After that she is the responsibility of the Household Cavalry."

"I see, and what about the rest?" Steven gestured back toward the cathedral.

"Just the bridal party, after Prince Charles and the Duchess of Cornwall, the rest can look after themselves."

"I see. Their duty is well done, they may rest with honour. Please carry on, Captain L'Shaw."

"Thank you, sir."

"See you in the guardroom." and Steven climbed into the landau to sit beside a fretful Lydia.

The return from the cathedral was for Steven, although the hat was doffed gallantly, spent largely in the afterglow of the ceremony, while Lydia was content to receive the adulation that was left over from her daughter, although most of the attention stemmed from curiosity, and more than one spectator was heard to voice aloud their grievance that they were not to see "the wife,"and if Steven had heard, he would have sympathized, although what could be seen of Lydia under her wide-brimmed hat was enough to garner speculation, which was why she wore it. When they arrived at the Royal Mews through the still-exuberant crowds, they were met by the ever-present buttonholes and escorted to a waiting room that was on scale with the rest of the rooms, the only difference being that the whole outer wall being taken up by huge glass doors, which presumably opened on to the balcony. Sherry was served, and everyone seemed to be waiting for something to happen, as for once H was not directing events. Prince Charles and Camilla were next to arrive, and then came Pam and Chadders.

"Well done, love, you carried it off splendidly." Pam gave him a kiss on the cheek and pointedly looked at Lydia's hand tucked under his arm.

Chadders, ever the diplomat, relieved the situation by offering his hand to Steven, "Yes indeed, well done, old son."

This had the effect of Steven gently disengaging his arm from Lydia's grasp to take the proffered hand. "Thanks, but with Judith looking like she did, I think I could have done cartwheels and nobody would have noticed."

Just then Brian L'Shaw entered the room, and as if this was a signal, the bridal couple made their way toward the doors and there was a general putting down of glasses and adjusting of hats and ties. They were obviously about to follow the newlyweds onto the balcony and Steven, bereft of H's guidance, didn't know if he should escort Pamela or Lydia. Although preferring his wife's company, he *did* arrive with Lydia, and he didn't want to drop a bollock at this stage of the proceedings. Help arrived as swift as it was unexpected. "Your arm, Mister Jackson, if you would be so kind," came a quiet but firm voice from behind him, and Steven turned to see himself being regarded by Queen Elizabeth the Second.

"Delighted, ma'am." Steven held out his arm, and as the Queen took it, he whispered, "I don't know when we are supposed to proceed."

"Everyone will be too concerned with Judith and William to notice an old soldier and the groom's granny, and don't worry about the ladies, they'll sort it out."

As if to support the first part of her sentence, there was a mighty roar as William and Judith stepped out on to the balcony.

"Your thoughts, Mr. Jackson."

Steven dragged his eyes away from the crowd below, which engulfed the Victoria Memorial. "We're standing on the very spot where your family and Winston Churchill stood on VE night."

"We are indeed—when we were both much younger."

****

They were a lot smaller group at the wedding breakfast than Steven had supposed. In fact, there were just five of them, the bridal couple, Prince Charles, Lydia, and himself. He had been congratulated by Mister Swinbourne, while the worthy gentlemen surreptitiously surveyed the suit for any damage that could be charged for, "A most thrilling occasion, Mister Jackson, and you carried it off splendidly. Was that not my reaction, young Jeremy?"

"Your very words, Mister Swinbourne," came the dutiful reply.

"Yes indeed, well your street clothes are in here, so if you'll just leave the morning suit on the rail outside, someone will come to escort you to the wedding breakfast, as we won't be seeing you again. We have to pick up the other suits, so I'll say good-bye, and once again, well done indeed."

Steven took his time dressing, as he sensed that the whole thing was drawing to a close. He carefully hung his clothes, including the shirt and tie, on the rail outside the alcove and regretfully arranged the cowboy boots under them. As usual, he didn't like to stay still for long, so he sauntered outside. The manure left by the horses was carefully shoveled into buckets before the driveway was hosed down. *Probably goes to Charles's estate. He's very big on organic farming.* The horses and carriages were being hosed down, and he thought of seeking out Ernie Price but decided against it. *Better not, he probably wants to get home and watch the wedding on the telly, and I'd better get back so that I can be collected. Don't want to blot my copy book now.* When he returned inside, he saw that his clothes had been collected but surprisingly, the cowboy boots had been left in splendid isolation. He picked them up and was regarding them thoughtfully when there was the obligatory cough at his elbow. "Mister Jackson sir?"

"Indeed I am," and he confidently tucked the boots under his arm.

"And why the, er ..." The buttonhole indicated the boots.

"These?" *I needed a pair and the Duke of Edinburgh lent me these, and as I'm having a bit of a nosh with his son and grandson, I thought I'd take them along and they could return them.* "I needed to elevate my status, as my daughter's quite tall, and Moss Brothers don't supply them. I don't suppose you'd take charge of them for me? Better not, I'll just leave them outside the door. I mean, if you can't trust people in the palace, who can you trust? So lead on."

He had heard that it was mostly symbolic, the pair's first meal as man and wife, but he expected at least Camilla to make a show. He voiced his concern to Prince Charles over pre meal sherry. "The duchess not joining us, sir?"

"Ah, Mister Jackson, no we thought it would be best if the guests were limited to the, er, original parents. Wouldn't like to look as though Camilla's trying to take William's mother's place, do you see? And Harry, of course. Of course, had it been deemed proper for Camilla to attend, your wife would have been asked. Besides, it was thought that, with the reception tonight, the simpler the better."

"Of course. Very wise, and Her Majesty?"

"Anno Domini, Mister Jackson, she's over eighty, and with the reception tonight, it would be too much."

"She's coming to the reception?"

"Indeed she is, but don't expect a dance. You'll have to make do with my sister, but yes she'll put in an appearance, if only to see the couple off. She's quite fond of William and Harry." He suddenly looked sad.

"Never mind, you'll soon have grandkids to spoil. It's always easier with grandkids. There's not the discipline."

"No, I suppose not. You have grandchildren, Mister Jackson?"

"Not yet, it depends on your eldest."

"Yes, I see, well said. Ah Miss Biderman," he turned to meet Lydia, who had just joined them, "we were just discussing your grandchildren."

"I go to the bathroom and all ready you make me a grandmother?" Lydia looked from one to the other. "That is the boy's talk I think, yes? Where is Judith?"

"I think she's changing out of her wedding dress," Steven offered. *And if William's helping her, they're probably making you a grandmother.*

The conversation was curtailed by the arrival of the host and hostess. "Are you two behaving yourselves?" Judith eyed them severely.

"Of course, your father-in-law's been keeping an eye on us, and in the carriage on the way here, your mother captivated everyone with that Marlene Dietrich hat."

William waited until Lydia's protests had subsided before he made his presence felt, "Does anybody mind if we eat now? I'm starving, hard work getting married."

Without the expected comment from Lydia, they arranged themselves round the circular table. Judith and William sat with their back to the windows, Lydia surprisingly left Judith to Prince Charles, while she arranged herself next to William, leaving Steven to sit between them facing the married couple.

"Are you all right down there, Poppi?"

"Thank you," Steven replied gravely, "after my moment in the spotlight, I am well content to return to my well-deserved obscurity." The meal was light, and so was the conversation. Those present seemed to be in a hiatus between the events of the morning and a pre reception nap. After Charles had proposed the pair's health, and Lydia had made a speech that was remarkable in its modesty and its brevity, Steven thought it was time to catch the eye of one of the serving footmen. "Do you think it possible to call me a taxi? I'll be going to Knightsbridge." He gave the address of Mrs. Murdoch's domain. "And we could drop the bride's mother off, I'm sure she doesn't live far away."

"My instructions are that there will be transport arranged for you, sir, and Miss Biderman, separately. ---Not at all, sir, I'm sure."

There were two more instances of note before Steven was to see his wife again. After he had taken his leave of the bridal couple, he found himself sharing the southern portico with Lydia and Prince Charles. After his joke about the buses being on strike had received its due response and Lydia had been ushered in to the first staff car, Steven found himself alone with Charles. There wasn't even a buttonhole to be seen. "I didn't get to tell you before, Mister Jackson, but you acquitted yourself admirably. Well done."

"Thank you, sir, and if I don't get to see your mother at the reception, sir, would you give her my regards and tell her, that when the barbarians are at the gates of Buckingham Palace, at least one Englishman will put his body where his duty lies?"

The second occurrence was after Prince Charles had insisted he took the next car, and he found that he was once again in the presence of Sergeants Beverley and Lewis. One of them was driving and the other was ... not. He'd forgotten which was which. It soon became obvious that it was not the only thing that had evaded his memory. "Went very well this morning, sir, well done, magic."

"Thank you." *I could take this up for a living.*

"Saw your wife in the cathedral sir, lovely lady. You can certainly pick them, don't you think?"

"He certainly can," the driver agreed and they shared a private joke.

"There you are, sport." The nondriver held out an envelope. "One four eight five, your winnings."

"My … oh, I forgot."

"Only natural, you had a lot on your mind."

"So," Steven accepted the proffered envelope, "how many?"

"Three, Comanche Moon at ten to one, Teddie's Son at seven to one, and," he screwed up his face in effort, "I believe Moon Dancer obliged at fives. Tara's Pride was a nonrunner, so there you are. One thousand four hundred and eighty-five pictures of Her Majesty. Better count it."

"There's no need."

"I'd rather you did, sir."

"Very well." Steven carefully counted the fourteen hundred-pound notes and peeled off three of the twenties. "Would you …?"

He was transfixed by the flat-eyed stare. "You wouldn't be attempting to bribe two police officers, sir?"

"Bribe?"

"We don't accept tips, sir."

"I wasn't offering you one." Steven regained his balance. "I was hoping you'd drink my daughter's health."

"Of course." The notes were graciously accepted. "Very proper, thank you, sir. Be honoured to, and if you'll excuse me, sir, looks like our other passenger." He swiftly took his leave in time to open the rear door for Pam, who'd just joined them.

Since Steven had "retired," he had become a devotee of the midday nap—not long enough so that he would not be able to sleep at night, but just enough to top up his batteries, especially if he had to be fully charged to keep up with his youthful wife in the evening. The premature twilight had already fallen over North Audley Street when they were delivered by Sergeants Lewis and Beverly, and Steven was looking forward to his siesta, but it was not to be. No sooner had they opened the door after taking leave of their driver and turf accountant, and promising to be ready at six sharp, when the door to the resident's lounge opened to reveal a positively gushing, well at least smiling, Mrs. Murdoch. "Quick, you're on the television, simply marvelous."

If it was difficult to deny Mrs. Murdoch. It was impossible to deny his wife, especially after their enforced separation and their tender reconciliation in the rear seat of the special branch rover, so Steven allowed himself to be ushered in to the lounge.

"Did you arrange for anyone to videotape the occasion for you in America?"

"No," Steven confessed, "it never occurred to me, what with everything. I don't know if it was televised in the States. Perhaps we could purchase a recording off the BBC." *Why do I feel the need to excuse myself, not once but three times? Probably Mrs. Murdoch had that effect.*

"Never mind, I've taped it for you. Perhaps you could get it transformed when you get back."

"Transposed."

"Pardon?"

"When you change it to the American system, it's called transposed."

"Very well, I suppose you'd like some tea. This is the part I like best."

Obviously the suggestion of tea was taken as being accepted, as two things happened simultaneously. The Captain appeared with the tea tray while, on the television screen, Steven followed William and Judith on to the balcony with the Queen on his arm.

"You cut quite a figure coming down the aisle." Mrs. Murdoch turned to look at him. "I suppose that's why they let you escort Her Majesty on to the balcony."

"*They* had nothing to do with it." Steven bridled at the suggestion that he had been offered a lump of sugar for performing a trick, and spoke sharper than the suggestion warranted. Then he seemed to relent. "Actually, it was Her Majesty's idea. We were not given any order. It seemed that William and Judith were to go on to the balcony and the rest of us were supposed to trickle out after them, and I was just wondering whether my tour of duty with Lydia had ended or if I was supposed to be reclaimed by the Princess Royal or heaven forbid, my wife, but the Queen made up her mind for me. She asked for my arm and," he shrugged, "there you are."

"You took it very well, having quite a chat."

"Yes I asked her where we were supposed to stand, and she said everyone would be looking at the bridal pair, who'd be interested in an old soldier and the groom's granny. You know, considering her job, she's very unassuming."

"I know why she chose you." Pamela didn't take her eyes off the screen. "Women feel safe with you. It's an instinct, because deep down you're quite chivalrous."

Steven carefully drained his tea and stood. "Ladies, sir, I'm feeling a little tired. If you'll excuse me, I think I'll go and take a nap. Perhaps I'll find my manners. Would someone wake me about five?"

"Of course, and I'll get Pamela to bring your suit down and give it a quick sponge and press. Will you require something to eat? I know there'll be a buffet at the reception but ..." Mrs. Murdoch uncharacteristically left her sentence hanging.

"I would like something. I'm afraid buffets and I don't mix very well."

"Very wise. You don't know who's been breathing over them, egg bacon, and sausage, all right, or I've got some nice lamb chops or—anything take your fancy?"

"A fry up will be fine—magic! I'll see you all later."

****

"Hello, sweet prince." Steven felt the bed move as Pam knelt on it. "Are you awake?"

He had been awake for a few minutes, becoming aware of his circumstances before opening his eyes. While lying there, he had immersed himself in the feeling of euphoria before he tried to remember what caused it in case it didn't bear closer scrutiny. His concern was needless. What caused his feeling of well being was that the testing time was over. He hadn't fallen on his arse, he had kept his soldierly bearing, he had said "I do," not shouted it but said it purposely, and he had seen his beautiful daughter married and later, captivate the crowds lining the streets with her natural and uncontrived joie de vivre. He'd also been on the balcony of Buck House with the Queen on his arm *and* his gorgeous wife was waking him.

"Yes I'm awake. Is it—" He sniffed the air. "Bacon, yes, must be time to get up,"

Pam pushed herself off the bed. "You're not going back to sleep, are you? Just put some jeans and slippers on. We're not dressing for dinner."

"*Back* to sleep, you mean, this is real." He reached around her waist, pulling her on top of him, stroking his hands over her buttocks. "No, this is real."

"I should let you lie in more often." Steven opened his eyes to see the smiling face of his wife illuminated by the sun streaming in the window.

The SUN?

"What time is it?"

"Ten thirty."

"I must have got drunk last night. Did I blot my copy book?"

"No, you were your usual self."

"I can't remember, did I dance with Princess Anne?"

"The Queen's daughter? No, you didn't dance with anybody."

For the first time, he became aware of his surroundings not the floral patterned room of Mrs. Murdoch's best room in North Audley Street but the more spartan beige walls of their bedroom in Mohave Valley Arizona. "Oh my—how long have we been back?"

"From where?"

"England."

"We haven't. The last time we were in England was two years ago. We went to the Parachute Logistic Regiment reunion, among other things."

"Not since then?"

"No, honey, unless you went with someone else, and I'm sure I would have noticed."

"Oh sweet Jesus."

Pam's concern was such that she did not, for once, castigate him for his profanity. "Look, I've brought you a cup of coffee, which I fortunately put on the bedside table before you attacked me. Also, I've got some bacon frying." She handed him the cup. "Have a drink and I'll bring you up to speed. You are Steven Jackson, you are officially retired, but really you are working on your great novel and taking care of your wife, me—who, by the way, you are crazy about. Last night you were working on the said novel when the said wife—did I mention you were crazy about me?—came to bed. I don't know how long you worked on it, but you've never slept this late, so I made you a cup of coffee and was debating whether to get in bed with you when you grabbed hold of me and began gabbling something about just coming back from England where you danced, or didn't, with Princess Anne, cowboy boots, and there goes your knighthood."

Steven sipped the coffee thoughtfully, "So it was all a dream?"

"Hopefully."

"And what time did you say it was?"

"Ten thirty. The mail's already arrived. In fact, you've got a letter from the British Embassy."

"Oh sweet Jesus."

This time, having been relieved of her wifely concern, she *did* remonstrate with him for taking the Lord's name in vain.

The End (probably)

Author's Note

The glossary will explain words or phrases that are not readily known on the other side of "the pond" or in some cases outside of the Black Country. There are, however, two items that call for a more detailed description, as they go some way to explaining our "hero's" attitude, and the attitude of the hero provides the thread that runs through the story. The two items are the Black Country and Wolverhampton Wanderers (the Wolves).

If there is one joke that sums up the attitude of people of the Black Country, it is this, as far as I can remember: A group of colliers (coal miners), having just finished their shift, were having a rest and a chat before making their way home. A tinker's cart was passing, and the roads were so rough that a huge, newly repaired kettle was jolted off the cart. After unsuccessfully trying to attract the tinker's attention, they wondered what to do with the kettle and decided that whoever could tell the biggest lie could take the kettle home. And so it went. "I've never touched a drop of drink in my life." "I'm rich I only work down the pit as a hobby," and so on, the lies getting more outrageous with each turn, when a pony and trap pulled up and out stepped the local Member of Parliament. "What are you doing my good fellows?" he asked. (Apparently they really did speak like that.) The colliers explained the situation and sportingly asked if he would like to try to win the kettle.

"My dear fellows" he said, "I have been your representative for twenty years. My life is dedicated to public service, and my honesty is paramount. I don't think I could tell a lie if I tried."

They gave him the kettle.

There is a more detailed description of the Black Country to follow. I placed it at the end of the book because if it was at the front, you probably wouldn't read the book.

There I go again, with the attitude.

Glossary

1. Tosser: a semi-affectionate term of derision
2. Pan's People: A group of comely lady dancers who appeared on *Top of the Pops*, a weekly TV show.
3. Ten quid: ten pounds. Today, about sixteen dollars
4. BBC: British Broadcasting Corporation, known to its intimates as "Auntie."
5. Ta, very much our kid: Brummiespeak for, "Thank you very much, homeboy."
6. Smethwick: Area of Birmingham (England)
7. Wolverhampton: A blue-collar city with white-collar pretensions
8. Shirty: troublesome, unhelpful
9. Bottle: originally rhyming slang for class (bottle and glass, therefore bottle), but in this case it has been used sarcastically to mean nerve or audacity.
10. The Highwayman Steven's knowledge of this beautiful poem is imperfect as my own. The fact that the writer Alfred Noyes was born in Wolverhampton is coincidental, but it's funny how we keep coming back to Wolverhampton. SEC

11.Enoch Powell: politician who courted unpopularity
by making uncomfortable references to uncontrolled
immigration

12 Marks and Spencer's: British department store noted for
good quality inexpensive clothing (there's also the British
Home Stores).

13 Dinner jackets: tuxedos.

14 Twit: like a tosser, only with a more refined accent (after
all, he *did* work for the BBC)

15 HRH: Her or His Royal Highness, in this case, Prince
William.

16 Whistle: whistle and flute, suit.

17 Buckshee: An expression the army brought back from
India meaning free or gratis.

18 Soup and Fish: suit, or whistle and flute, to be worn at
formal dinner that would include, at least, five courses,
hence, soup and fish. Are we getting the hang of it yet

19 Sussing out: an army expression meaning to observe or
study (I don't know *where* this came from).

20 Buck House: soldiers slang for Buckingham Palace

21 Swot up: study, obtain preemptive knowledge of

22 Devon Loch: A racehorse owned by the Queen Mother
that inexplicably fell when leading about two hundred
yards from the finish of the Grand National, the premier
steeplechase (some say the greatest horse race in the
world,) run at Aintree, Liverpool.

23 Pratt I'm sure you've got a pretty good idea

24 A Yankee: a bet on four horses with the maximum number
of combinations (eleven).

25 Rollocking: berating, chewing out.

26 *Fawlty Towers*: a British sitcom about a hotel that's so
badly run it's funny. (It's a British thing.)

27 Toffee-nosed: snooty, snobbish.

The Black Country is an area of England that is bordered (but not necessarily inclusive of) Birmingham to the south, Walsall to the east, Stourbridge to the west, and Wolverhampton to the north. How the area came to be known as the Black Country was, with three inventions that revolutionized the production of iron and steel, simultaneously large deposits of iron ore and limestone were discovered to lie just beneath the surface together, with the "Staffordshire Thirty-Foot Coal Seam." It was this that gave the Black Country its name—either the depiction of it on the map or the result of it spewing from the steelworks and foundry chimneys. "The Black Country, black by day, red by night," (Elihu Burrit, "Walks in the Black Country").

Limestone was found under the estates of rich people, which made them even richer and the working people even more exploited. A prime example of this is the limestone workings of the earl of Dudley where, the percentage of Black Country miners killed who worked in the Earl of Dudley's pits varied from 10 percent in the 1850s and '60s to more than 20 percent in the 1890s. The obtaining of the coal to fire the furnaces was a little more democratic. While there were massive coal mines, the Staffordshire Thirty-Foot Coal Seam lay so near to the surface that smaller coal mines even in the backyards were profitable. Unfortunately, this led to the abandonment of some quite large coal mines when they had been worked out. To this day there is a pumping station that is still working raising water from a flooded mine to replenish the main Wolverhampton to Birmingham canal (where the author learned to swim—and now I bother about a bit of algae in the swimming pool?). This produced two results, the first being subsidence, where in some cases one side of a street can be two feet higher than the other, but the best example of this is a pub called the Himley House Hotel, known locally as the crooked house. where, it is so out of alignment that if you come out of it sober, you stagger, but if you exit suitably refreshed, you walk straight. This phenomenon might also explain the reputation of natives of the area as having a balanced outlook on life, "Because they've got a chip on both shoulders."

There was also the problem of toxic wastes formed when chemical by-products are dumped without regard for the aftereffects and a gas called fire damp, a result of ill-ventilated mining. There is an area of the Black Country called the Fiery Holes where an underground fire is still smouldering. If the toxic waste didn't cause underground fires, they were left to seep in to the water supply, with obvious results. The area was reputed to have the highest infant mortality rate in Europe. I have not been able to verify this, but I do know that as late as the sixties when I was serving in the army we occasionally would stay for the weekend in each other's homes, and when it would be my turn to be the host, it was always remarked how many deformed people there were to be seen in the area.

Two well-known people would share my guests' views of the Black Country.

John Wesley, the founder of Methodism, together with his brother Charles, preached in the Black Country, and their message, that living a good life in fellowship with one's fellow man was more important than the acquisition of wealth, found ready listeners with the working people of the area but obviously not with the landed gentry. The established church thought his sermons a little anemic, with no mention of hellfire and damnation. His answer was that with all his powers of description he could not describe hell so unattractive as to match the everyday life of the working people of the Black Country.

When Queen Victoria took the train to Balmoral, she would order the blinds to be drawn as the royal train approached the Black Country. Apparently the industrial wasteland was so ugly that it put Her Majesty off her marmalade.

Then there are Wolverhampton Wanderers. They are of the Black Country but apart, as is Wolverhampton. Two towns in England were always good for a cheap laugh. Their name only had to be mentioned by a music hall comedian to garner a chuckle or two. One was Wigan in Lancashire and the other was Wolverhampton. I don't know how the good people of Wigan dealt with this distinction, but the burghers of Wolverhampton discovered the "Yam Yams" of the Black Country. I'm sure there is a psychological term for this attitude.

I was born in Coseley, in the Black Country, and can remember going with my father on the bus to watch the Wolves. On crossing the Parkfield Road, which was effectively the boundary between Coseley and Wolverhampton, we were confronted with a huge floral display of the Wolverhampton Coat of Arms, complete with the motto. The motto of Wolverhampton is, "Out of Darkness Cometh Light," and it is generally supposed that the darkness was the Black Country and the light was Wolverhampton. Also, the Wolves' colors illuminate the social apartheid that prevails, (although some of their greatest players come from the Black Country) Gold and Black. (This explains why one displaced son of the Black

Country pledged his allegiance to the Pittsburgh Steelers, plus the fact that his father worked at the steelworks.) The gold represents the shining beacon that is Wolverhampton and the black—you get the picture.

Any football team, or any sports team, for that matter, are judged by how good they were at their best, and by that criteria, the Wolves had to be judged among the greatest in the world. From 1949 until 1960, they were top of the league (judged by a points system over the season when two points were awarded for a win and one for a tie) three times and won the cup (the FA Challenge cup, a knockout competition that starts in November and lasts until the final played in May) twice. In between these domestic triumphs, they found time to play and beat the cream of foreign opposition, including Real Madrid and Honved of Hungary, the latter including seven of the Hungarian national team, who had humiliated England six to three and seven to one. There was a suggestion that Wolves should represent England instead of the national team. Unfortunately, although ten of the regular first team were English, the right full back was South African, which probably explains why Stan Cullis, the manager, didn't get a knighthood, but that is another story.

Acknowledgments, Apologies, and Anything Else that Prevents Me Getting Sued

I HAVE BEEN INSIDE SAINT PAUL'S Cathedral (once), but my depictions of the domestic arrangements inside Buckingham Palace rely solely on my imagination. There *is* a British and Dominion Social club in Garden Grove, California, and I have spent many interesting times there, and continue to do so. There is a very personable barmaid called Barbara and there *is* a *feisty* Scot by the name of Joe Donnelly who has served as president. Everything else was subject to interpretation.

There *is* a very pleasant racecourse at Ludlow, but most of the bookies have gone digital, and the last time I attended, one of the bookies who took my money *was* a woman.

There is a company called Moss Brothers who hire out the appropriate ensembles for royal garden parties and the like, but I have never had dealings with that august institution, and after my remarks about my future king's mother, probably I never shall (unless this book sells really well and I'm inclined to buy a racehorse and run it at Ascot). And speaking of the PP …

Reflections on the People's Princess and MA 26

O N AUGUST 31, WHEN THE world was plunged in to mourning over the death of the People's Princess, a prostitute in Wolverhampton, England, was reported missing by her sister, Irene. After the requisite twenty-four hours, reports were filed and assurances were given and there the matter rested. By the 6th of September, the sister, Irene, was beginning to make a nuisance of herself, but the desk sergeant at Bilston road police station did drag himself away from watching the state funeral on the television to assure her that everything possible was being done. What particularly irked Irene was that her sister wasn't referred to by name, just the file name, MA 26.

On the 10th of September, when the floral tributes had reached the height of four feet outside the residence of the People's Princess, Irene and a few of her sister's colleagues found her body less than thirty yards from where she was reported last seen on a patch of wasteland behind the Royal Hospital and within shouting distance of one of the busiest roads in Wolverhampton. She had been covered by a mattress that was as rotten as the lower layer of wreaths that had been left outside Clarence House, which had decomposed due to the weight of the grief above them.

There were strange parallels between the People's Princess and MA 26. They both had two sons of roughly the same age, and they were both divorced from the boy's father. The People's Princess was awarded two palaces after the divorce, whereas MA 26 came away with the council flat. There was speculation about both of their deaths (although I have to say a lot more about the one than the other). They both had a date on the last day of their lives that they were rewarded for. The People's Princess acquired a ring that was valued at a half million pounds (about $800,000). MA 26 was compensated enough for her labors to make up the rent on the council flat. MA 26's body was released to her sister without much fuss, and she was laid to rest, attended by the sister her two sons, and a few of her colleagues under her own name.

She was named Diana too.

About the Author

S. E. Clarkson was born and educated in England, in the Black Country, the industrial heart of England (when it had one), although he likes to claim he finished his education at Oxford or rather eight hundred feet above the dreaming spires. After a varied career (eleven separate occupations, including betting office manager, truck driver, ditch digger, sheet metal worker, and archivist), nine years in the army, two marriages, and one divorce, he spends most of his time in Arizona with his wife, Pamela.